DEAD IN THE FAMILY

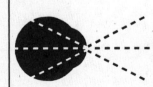

DEAD IN THE FAMILY

CHARLAINE HARRIS

WHEELER PUBLISHING
A part of Gale, Cengage Learning

Detroit • New York • San Francisco • New Haven, Conn • Waterville, Maine • London

GALE
CENGAGE Learning™

LIBRARY OF CONGRESS CATALOGING-IN-PUBLICATION DATA

Harris, Charlaine.
  Dead in the family / by Charlaine Harris.
    p. cm.
  ISBN-13: 978-1-4104-2650-5
  ISBN-10: 1-4104-2650-5
    1. Vampires—Fiction. 2. Werewolves—Fiction. 3. Louisiana—Fiction. 4. Large type books. I. Title.
  PS3558.A6427D4257 2010b
  813'.54—dc22   2010009045

Published in 2010 by arrangement with The Berkley Publishing Group, a member of Penguin Group (USA) Inc.

Printed in the United States of America
1 2 3 4 5 6 7 14 13 12 11 10

This book is dedicated to our son
Patrick,
who has not only met our hopes,
dreams, and expectations for him,
but exceeded them.

ACKNOWLEDGMENTS

I am only the first step in the creation of this book. Many other people helped in different capacities along the way: Anastasia Luettecke, who taught me about Roman names; Dr. Ed Uthman, who helps me with medical stuff; Victoria and Debi, my continuity mavens; Toni L. P. Kelner and Dana Cameron, whose gentle comments after their first reading keep me from committing many an error; Paula Woldan, whose help and friendship keep me going; Lisa Desimini, the cover artist; Jodi Rosoff, my wonderful publicist; Ginjer Buchanan, my long-suffering editor; and my Mod Squad: Michele, Victoria, Kerri, MariCarmen, and Lindsay (current), and Debi, Beverly, and Katie (retired).

MARCH

THE FIRST WEEK

"I feel bad that I'm leaving you like this," Amelia said. Her eyes were puffy and red. They'd been that way, off and on, ever since Tray Dawson's funeral.

"You have to do what you have to do," I said, giving her a very bright smile. I could read the guilt and shame and ever-present grief roiling around Amelia's mind in a ball of darkness. "I'm lots better," I reassured her. I could hear myself babbling cheerfully along, but I couldn't seem to stop. "I'm walking okay, and the holes are all filled in. See how much better?" I pulled down my jeans waistband to show her a spot that had been bitten out. The teeth marks were hardly perceptible, though the skin wasn't quite smooth and was visibly paler than the surrounding flesh. If I hadn't had a huge dose of vampire blood, the scar would've looked like a shark had bitten me.

Amelia glanced down and hastily away, as if she couldn't bear to see the evidence of the attack. "It's just that Octavia keeps e-mailing me and telling me I need to come home and accept my judgment from the witches' council, or what's left of it," she said in a rush. "And I need to check all the repairs to my house. And since there are a few tourists again, and people returning and rebuilding, the magic store's reopened. I can work there part-time. Plus, as much as I love you and I love living here, since Tray died . . ."

"Believe me, I understand." We'd gone over this a few times.

"It's not that I blame you," Amelia said, trying to catch my eyes.

She really didn't blame me. Since I could read her mind, I knew she was telling me the truth.

Even *I* didn't totally blame myself, somewhat to my surprise.

It was true that Tray Dawson, Amelia's lover and a Were, had been killed while he'd been acting as my bodyguard. It was true that I'd requested a bodyguard from the Were pack nearest me because they owed me a favor and my life needed guarding. However, I'd been present at the death of Tray Dawson at the hands of a sword-wielding fairy, and I knew who was responsible.

So I didn't feel guilty, exactly. But I felt heartsick about losing Tray, on top of all the other horrors. My cousin Claudine, a full-blooded fairy, had also died in the Fae War, and since she'd been my real, true fairy godmother, I missed her in a lot of ways. And she'd been pregnant.

I had a lot of pain and regret of all kinds, physical and mental. While Amelia carried an armful of clothes downstairs, I stood in her bedroom, gathering myself. Then I braced my shoulders and lifted a box of bathroom odds and ends. I descended the stairs carefully and slowly, and I made my way out to her car. She turned from depositing the clothes across the boxes already stowed in her trunk. "You shouldn't be doing that!" she said, all anxious concern. "You're not healed yet."

"I'm fine."

"Not hardly. You always jump when someone comes into the room and surprises you, and I can tell your wrists hurt," she said. She grabbed the box and slid it into the backseat. "You still favor that left leg, and you still ache when it rains. Despite all that vamp blood."

"The jumpiness'll get better. As time

11

passes, it won't be so fresh and at the front of my mind," I told Amelia. (If telepathy had taught me anything, it was that people could bury the most serious and painful of memories, if you gave them enough time and distraction.) "The blood is not just any vampire's. It's Eric's blood. It's strong stuff. And my wrists are a lot better." I didn't mention that the nerves were jumping around in them like hot snakes just at this moment, a result of their having been tied together tightly for several hours. Dr. Ludwig, physician to the supernatural, had told me the nerves — and the wrists — would be back to normal, eventually.

"Yeah, speaking of the blood . . ." Amelia took a deep breath and steeled herself to say something she knew I wouldn't like. Since I heard it before she actually voiced it, I was able to brace myself. "Had you thought about . . . Sookie, you didn't ask me, but I think you better not have any more of Eric's blood. I mean, I know he's your man, but you got to think about the consequences. Sometimes people get flipped by accident. It's not like it's a math equation."

Though I appreciated Amelia's concern, she'd trespassed into private territory. "We don't swap," I said. *Much.* "He just has a sip

from me at, you know . . . the happy moment." These days Eric was having a lot
more happy moments than I was, sadly. I
kept hoping the bedroom magic would
return; if any male could perform sexual
healing, that male would be Eric.

Amelia smiled, which was what I'd been
aiming for. "At least . . ." She turned away
without finishing the sentence, but she was
thinking, *At least you feel like having sex.*

I didn't so much feel like having sex as I
felt like I ought to keep trying to enjoy it,
but I definitely didn't want to discuss that.
My ability to cast aside control, which is
the key to good sex, had been pinched out
of existence during the torture. I'd been
absolutely helpless. I could only hope that
I'd recover in that area, too. I knew Eric
could feel my lack of completion. He'd
asked me several times if I was sure I
wanted to engage in sex. Nearly every time,
I said yes, operating on the bicycle theory.
Yes, I'd fallen off. But I was always willing
to try to ride it again.

"So, how's the relationship doing?" she
said. "Aside from the whoopee." Every last
thing was in Amelia's car. She was stalling,
dreading the moment when she actually got
into her car and drove away.

It was only pride that was keeping me

from bawling all over her.

"I think we're getting along pretty well," I said with a great effort at sounding cheerful. "I'm still not sure what I feel as opposed to what the bond is making me feel." It was kind of nice to be able to talk about my supernatural connection to Eric, as well as my regular old man-woman attraction. Even before my injuries during the Fae War, Eric and I had established what the vampires called a blood bond, since we'd exchanged blood several times. I could sense Eric's general location and his mood, and he could feel the same things about me. He was always faintly present in the back of my mind — sort of like turning on a fan or an air filter to provide a little buzz of noise that would help you get to sleep. (It was good for me that Eric slept all day, because I could be by myself at least part of the time. Maybe he felt the same way after I went to bed at night?) It wasn't like I heard voices in my head or anything — at least no more than usual. But if I felt happy, I had to check to make sure it was me and not Eric who felt happy. Likewise for anger; Eric was big on anger, controlled and carefully banked anger, especially lately. Maybe he was getting that from me. I was pretty full of anger myself these days.

I'd forgotten all about Amelia. I'd stepped right into my own trough of depression.

She snapped me out of it. "That's just a big fat excuse," she said tartly. "Come on, Sookie. You love him, or you don't. Don't keep putting off thinking about it by blaming everything on your bond. Wah, wah, wah. If you hate the bond so much, why haven't you explored how you can get free of it?" She took in the expression on my face, and the irritation faded out of her own. "Do you want me to ask Octavia?" she asked in a milder voice. "If anyone would know, she would."

"Yes, I'd like to find out," I said, after a moment. I took a deep breath. "You're right, I guess. I've been so depressed I've put off making any decisions, or acting on the ones I've already made. Eric's one of a kind. But I find him . . . a little overwhelming." He was a strong personality, and he was used to being the big fish in the pond. He also knew he had infinite time ahead of him.

I did not.

He hadn't brought that up yet, but sooner or later, he would.

"Overwhelming or not, I love him," I continued. I'd never said it out loud. "And I guess that's the bottom line."

15

"I guess it is." Amelia tried to smile at me, but it was a woeful attempt. "Listen, you keep that up, the self-knowledge thing." She stood for a moment, her expression frozen into the half smile. "Well, Sook, I better get on the road. My dad's expecting me. He'll be all up in my business the minute I get back to New Orleans."

Amelia's dad was rich, powerful, and had no belief in Amelia's power at all. He was very wrong not to respect her witchcraft. Amelia had been born with the potential for the power in her, as every true witch is. Once Amelia had some more training and discipline, she was going to be really scary — scary on purpose, rather than because of the drastic nature of her mistakes. I hoped her mentor, Octavia, had a program in place to develop and train Amelia's talent.

After I waved Amelia down the driveway, the broad smile dropped from my face. I sat on the porch steps and cried. It didn't take much for me to be in tears these days, and my friend's departure was just the trigger now. There was so much to weep about.

My sister-in-law, Crystal, had been murdered. My brother's friend Mel had been executed. Tray and Claudine and Clancy the vampire had been killed in the line of duty. Since both Crystal and Claudine had been pregnant, that added two more deaths to the list.

Probably that should have made me long for peace above all else. But instead of turning into the Bon Temps Gandhi, in my heart I held the knowledge that there were plenty of people I wanted dead. I wasn't directly responsible for most of the deaths that were scattered in my wake, but I was haunted by the feeling that none of them would have happened if it weren't for me. In my darkest moments — and this was one of them — I wondered if my life was worth the price that had been paid for it.

March

THE END OF THE FIRST WEEK

My cousin Claude was sitting on the front porch when I got up on a cloudy, brisk morning a few days after Amelia's departure. Claude wasn't as skilled at masking his presence as my great-grandfather Niall was. Because Claude was fae, I couldn't read his mind — but I could tell his mind was there, if that isn't too obscure a way to put it. I carried my coffee out to the porch, though the air was nippy, because drinking that first cup on the porch had been one of my favorite things to do before I . . . before the Fae War.

I hadn't seen my cousin in weeks. I hadn't seen him during the Fae War, and he hadn't contacted me since the death of Claudine.

I'd brought an extra mug for Claude, and I handed it to him. He accepted it silently. I'd considered the possibility he might throw it in my face. His unexpected presence had knocked me off course. I had no

18

idea what to expect. The breeze lifted his long black hair, tossed it around like rippling ebony ribbons. His caramel eyes were red-rimmed.

"How did she die?" he said.

I sat on the top step. "I didn't see it," I said, hunching over my knees. "We were in that old building Dr. Ludwig was using as a hospital. I think Claudine was trying to stop the other fairies from coming down the corridor to get into the room where I was holed up with Bill and Eric and Tray." I looked over at Claude to make sure he knew the place, and he nodded. "I'm pretty sure that it was Breandan who killed her, because one of her knitting needles was stuck in his shoulder when he busted into our room."

Breandan, my great-grandfather's enemy, had also been a prince of the fae. Breandan had believed that humans and the fae should not consort. He'd believed that to the point of fanaticism. He'd wanted the fae to completely abstain from their forays into the human world, despite the fae's large financial stake in mundane commerce and the products it had produced . . . products that helped them blend into the modern world. Breandan had especially hated the occasional taking of human lovers, a fae indulgence, and he'd hated the children

19

born as a result of such liaisons. He'd wanted the fae separate, walled away into their own world, consorting only with their own kind.

Oddly enough, that's what my great-grandfather had decided to do after defeating the fairy who believed in this apartheid policy. After all the bloodshed, Niall concluded that peace among the fae and safety for humans could be reached only if the fae blocked themselves into their world. Breandan had achieved his ends by his own death. In my worst moments, I thought that Niall's final decision had made the whole war unnecessary.

"She was defending you," Claude said, pulling me back into the moment. There was nothing in his voice. Not blame, not anger, not a question.

"Yeah." That had been part of her job, defending me, by Niall's orders.

I took a long sip of coffee. Claude's sat untouched on the arm of the porch swing. Maybe Claude was wondering if he should kill me. Claudine had been his last surviving sibling.

"You knew about the pregnancy," he said finally.

"She told me right before she was killed." I put down my mug and wrapped my arms around my knees. I waited for the blow to fall. At first I didn't mind all that much, which was even more horrible.

Claude said, "I understand Neave and Lochlan had hold of you. Is that why you're limping?" The change of subject caught me off guard.

"Yeah," I said. "They had me for a couple of hours. Niall and Bill Compton killed them. Just so you know — it was Bill who killed Breandan, with my grandmother's iron trowel." Though the trowel had been in my family's toolshed for decades, I associated it with Gran.

Claude sat, beautiful and unreadable, for a long time. He never looked at me directly nor drank his coffee. When he'd reached some inner conclusion, he rose and left, walking down the driveway toward Hummingbird Road. I don't know where his car was parked. For all I knew, he'd walked all the way from Monroe, or flown over on a magic carpet. I went into the house, sank to my knees right inside the door, and cried. My hands were shaking. My wrists ached.

The whole time we'd been talking, I'd been waiting for him to make his move.

I realized I wanted to live.

March

THE SECOND WEEK

JB said, "Raise your arm all the way up, Sookie!" His handsome face was creased with concentration. Holding the five-pound weight, I slowly lifted my left arm. Geez Louise, it hurt. Same with the right.

"Okay, now the legs," JB said, when my arms were shaking with strain. JB wasn't a licensed physical therapist, but he was a personal trainer, so he'd had practical experience helping people get over various injuries. Maybe he'd never faced an assortment like mine, since I'd been bitten, cut, and tortured. But I hadn't had to explain the details to JB, and he wouldn't notice that my injuries were far from typical of those incurred in a car accident. I didn't want any speculation going around Bon Temps about my physical problems — so I made the occasional visits to Dr. Amy Ludwig, who looked suspiciously like a hobbit, and I enlisted the help of JB du Rone, who was a good trainer but dumb as a box of rocks.

JB's wife, my friend Tara, was sitting on one of the weight benches. She was reading *What to Expect When You're Expecting.* Tara, almost five months pregnant, was determined to be the best mother she could possibly be. Since JB was willing but not bright, Tara was assuming the role of Most Responsible Parent. She'd earned her high school spending money as a babysitter, which gave her some experience in child care. She was frowning as she turned the pages, a look familiar to me from our school years.

"Have you picked a doctor yet?" I said, after I'd finished my leg lifts. My quads were screaming, particularly the damaged one in my left leg. We were in the gym where JB worked, and it was after hours, because I wasn't a member. JB's boss had okayed the temporary arrangement to keep JB happy. JB was a huge asset to the gym; since he'd started working, new female clients had increased by a noticeable percentage.

"I think so," said Tara. "There were four choices in this area, and we interviewed all of them. I've had my first appointment with Dr. Dinwiddie, here in Clarice. I know it's a little hospital, but I'm not high risk, and it's so close."

Clarice was just a few miles from Bon Temps, where we all lived. You could get from my house to the gym in less than twenty minutes.

"I hear good things about him," I said, the pain in my quads making stuff start to slide around inside my head. My forehead broke out in a clammy sweat. I was used to thinking of myself as a fit woman, and mostly I'd been a happy one. There were days now when it was all I could do to get out of bed and get in to work.

"Sook," JB said, "look at the weight on here." He was grinning at me.

For the first time, I registered that I'd done ten extensions with ten more pounds than I'd been using.

I smiled back at him. It didn't last long, but I knew I'd done something good.

"Maybe you'll babysit for us sometime," Tara said. "We'll teach the baby to call you Aunt Sookie."

I'd be a courtesy aunt. I'd get to take care of a baby. They trusted me. I found myself planning on a future.

MARCH
THE SAME WEEK

I spent the next night with Eric. As I did at least three or four times a week, I woke up panting, filled with terror, completely at sea. I held on to him as if the storm would sweep me away unless he was my anchor. I was already crying when I woke. It wasn't the first time this had happened, but this time he wept with me, bloody tears that streaked the whiteness of his face in a startling way.

"Don't," I begged him. I had been trying so hard to act like my old self when I was with him. Of course, he knew differently. Tonight I could feel his resolve. Eric had something to say to me, and he was going to tell me whether I wanted to listen or not.

"I could feel your fear and your pain that night," he said, in a choked voice. "But I couldn't come to you."

Finally, he was telling me something I had been waiting to learn.

"Why not?" I said, trying very hard to

keep my voice level. This may seem incredible, but I had been in such shaky condition I hadn't dared to ask him.

"Victor wouldn't let me leave," he said. Victor Madden was Eric's boss; he'd been appointed by Felipe de Castro, King of Nevada, to oversee the conquered kingdom of Louisiana.

My initial reaction to Eric's explanation was bitter disappointment. I'd heard this story before. *A vampire more powerful than me made me do it:* Bill's excuse for going back to his maker, Lorena, revisited. "Sure," I said. I turned over and lay with my back to him. I felt the cold, creeping misery of disillusionment. I decided to pull my clothes on, to drive back to Bon Temps, as soon as I gathered the energy. The tension, the frustration, the rage in Eric was sapping me.

"Victor's people chained me with silver," Eric said behind me. "It burned me everywhere."

"Literally." I tried not to sound as skeptical as I felt.

"Yes, literally. I knew something was happening with you. Victor was at Fangtasia that night, as if he knew ahead of time he should be there. When Bill called to tell me you'd been taken, I managed to call Niall before three of Victor's people chained me

26

to the wall. When I — protested — Victor said he couldn't *allow* me to take sides in the Fae War. He said that no matter what happened to you, I couldn't get involved."

Rage made Eric fall silent for a long moment. It poured through me like a burning, icy stream. He resumed his story in a choked voice.

"Pam was also seized and isolated by Victor's people, though they didn't chain her." Pam was Eric's second-in-command. "Since Bill was in Bon Temps, he was able to ignore Victor's phone messages. Niall met Bill at your house to track you. Bill had heard of Lochlan and Neave. We all had. We knew time would run out for you." I still had my back to Eric, but I was listening to more than his voice. Grief, anger, desperation.

"How did you get out of the chains?" I asked the dark.

"I reminded Victor that Felipe had promised you protection, promised it to you *personally.* Victor pretended not to believe me." I could feel the bed move as Eric threw himself back against the pillows. "Some of the vampires were strong and honorable enough to remember they were pledged to Felipe, not Victor. Though they wouldn't defy Victor to his face, behind his back they let Pam call our new king. When she had Felipe on the line, she explained to him that you and I had married. Then she demanded Victor take the telephone and talk to Felipe. Victor didn't dare to refuse. Felipe ordered Victor to let me go." A few months ago, Felipe de Castro had become the king of Nevada, Louisiana, *and* Arkansas. He was powerful, old, and very crafty. And he owed me big-time.

"Did Felipe punish Victor?" Hope springs eternal.

"There's the rub," Eric said. Somewhere along the line, my Viking honey had read Shakespeare. "Victor claimed he'd temporarily forgotten our marriage." Even if I sometimes tried to forget it myself, that made me angry. Victor had been sitting right there in Eric's office when I'd handed the ceremonial knife to Eric — in complete ignorance that my action constituted a marriage, vampire-style. I might have been ignorant, but Victor certainly wasn't. "Victor told our king that I was lying in an attempt to save my human lover from the fae. He said vampire lives must not be lost in the rescue of a human. He told Felipe that he hadn't believed Pam and me when we'd told him Felipe had promised you protection after you saved him from Sigebert."

I rolled over to face Eric, and the bit of moonlight coming in the window painted him in shades of dark and silver. In my brief experience of the powerful vampire who'd maneuvered himself into a position of great power, Felipe was absolutely no fool. "Incredible. Why didn't Felipe kill Victor?" I asked.

"I've given that a lot of thought, of course. I think Felipe has to pretend he believes Victor. I think Felipe realizes that in making Victor his lieutenant in charge of the whole state of Louisiana, he has inflated Victor's ambitions to the point of indecency."

It was possible to look at Eric objectively, I discovered, while I was thinking over what he'd said. My trust had gotten me burned in the past, and I wasn't going to get too close to the fire this time without careful consideration. It was one thing to enjoy laughing with Eric or to look forward to the times when we twined together in the dark. It was another thing to trust him with more fragile emotions. I was really not into trust right now.

"You were upset when you came to the hospital," I said indirectly. When I'd wakened in the old factory Dr. Ludwig was using as a field hospital, my injuries had been so painful I'd thought dying might prove easier than living. Bill, who had saved me, had been poisoned with a bite from Neave's silver teeth. His survival had been up in the air. The mortally wounded Tray Dawson, Amelia's werewolf lover, had hung on long enough to die by the sword when Breandan's forces stormed the hospital.

"While you were with Neave and Lochlan, I suffered with you," he said, meeting my eyes directly. "I hurt with you. I bled with you — not only because we're bonded, but because of the love I have for you."

I raised a skeptical eyebrow. I couldn't help it, though I could feel that he meant what he was saying. I was just willing to believe that Eric would have come to my help much faster, if he could have. I was willing to believe that he'd heard the echo of the horror of my time with the fae torturers.

But my pain and blood and terror had been my own. He might have felt them, but from a separate place. "I believe you would have been there if you could have," I said, knowing my voice was too calm. "I really do believe that. I know you would have killed them." Eric leaned over on one elbow, and his big hand pressed my face to his chest.

I couldn't deny that I felt better since he'd

brought himself to tell me. Yet I didn't feel as much better as I'd hoped, though now I knew why he hadn't come when I'd been screaming for him. I could even understand why it had taken so long for him to tell me. Helplessness was a state Eric didn't often encounter. Eric was supernatural, and he was incredibly strong, and he was a great fighter. But he was not a superhero, and he couldn't overcome several determined members of his own race. And I realized he'd given me a lot of blood when he himself was healing from the silver chains.

Finally, something inside me relaxed at the logic of his story. I believed him in my heart, not just in my head.

A red tear fell on my bare shoulder and coursed down. I swept it up on my finger, putting my finger to his lips — offering his pain back to him. I had plenty of my own.

"I think we need to kill Victor," I said, and his eyes met mine.

I'd finally succeeded in surprising Eric.

MARCH
THE THIRD WEEK

"So," my brother said. "As you can tell, me and Michele are still seeing each other." He was standing with his back to me, turning the steaks on the grill. I was sitting in a folding chair, looking out over the large pond and its dock. It was a beautiful evening, cool and brisk. I was actually content to sit there and watch him work; I was enjoying being with Jason. Michele was in the house making a salad. I could hear her singing Travis Tritt.

"I'm glad," I said, and I was sincere. It was the first time I'd been in a private setting with my brother in months. Jason had been through his own bad time. His estranged wife and their unborn child had died horribly. He'd discovered his best male friend had been in love with him, sick in love. But as I watched him grilling, listened to his girlfriend singing inside the house, I understood that Jason was a great survivor.

Here my brother was, dating again, pleased at the prospect of eating steak and the mashed potato casserole I'd brought and the salad Michele was making. I had to admire Jason's determination to find pleasure in his life. My brother was not a very good role model in a lot of ways, but I could hardly point fingers.

"Michele is a good woman," I said out loud.

She was, too — though maybe not in the way our gran would have used the term. Michele Schubert was absolutely out-front about everything. You couldn't shame her, because she wouldn't do something she wouldn't own up to. Operating on the same principle of full disclosure, if Michele had a grievance with you, you knew about it. She worked in the Ford dealership's repair shop as a scheduler and clerk. It was a tribute to her efficiency that she still worked for her former father-in-law. (In fact, he'd been known to say he liked her a tad better than he liked his son, some days.)

Michele came out on the deck. She was wearing the jeans and Ford-logo polo shirt she wore to work, and her dark hair was twisted in a knot on her head. Michele liked heavy eye makeup, big purses, and high heels. She was barefoot now. "Hey, Sookie, you like ranch dressing?" she asked. "Or we got some honey mustard."

"Ranch will be fine," I said. "You need any help?"

"Nope, I'm good." Michele's cell phone went off. "Dammit, it's Pop Schubert again. That man can't find his ass with both hands."

She went back in the house, the phone to her ear.

"I worry, though, about putting her in danger," Jason said in the diffident voice he used when he was asking my opinion about something supernatural. "I mean . . . that fairy, Dermot, the one that looks like me. Do you know if he's still around?"

He'd turned to face me. He was leaning against the railing of the deck he'd added to the house my mom and dad had built when they were expecting Jason. Mom and Dad hadn't gotten to enjoy it for much more than a decade. They'd died when I was seven, and when Jason had gotten old enough to live on his own (in his estimation), he'd moved out of Gran's and into this house. It had seen many a wild party for two or three years, but he'd become steadier. Tonight it was very clear to me that his recent losses had sobered him further.

I took a swallow from my bottle. I wasn't much of a drinker — I saw too much overindulgence at work — but it had been impossible to turn down a cold beer on this bright evening. "I wish I knew where Dermot was, too," I said. Dermot was the fraternal twin of our half-fairy grandfather Fintan. "Niall sealed himself into Faery with all the other fairies who wanted to join him, and I'm keeping my fingers crossed that Dermot's in Faery with him. Claude stayed here. I saw him a couple of weeks ago." Niall was our great-grandfather. Claude was his grandson from Niall's marriage to another full fae.

"Claude, the male stripper."

"The owner of a strip club, who strips himself on ladies' night," I corrected. "Our cousin models for romance covers, too."

"Yeah, I bet the girls faint when he walks by. Michele's got a book with him on the cover in some genie costume. He must love every minute of it." Jason definitely sounded envious.

"I bet he does. You know, he's a pain in the butt," I said, and laughed, surprising myself.

"You see him much?"

"Just the once, since I got hurt. But when I picked up the mail yesterday, he'd sent me some free coupons for ladies' night at Hooligans."

"You think you'll ever take him up on it?"

"Not yet. Maybe when I'm . . . in a better mood."

"You think Eric would mind you seeing another guy naked?" Jason was trying to show me how much he'd changed by his casual reference to my relationship with a vampire. Well, give my brother points for "willing."

"I'm not sure," I said. "But I wouldn't watch other guys take off their clothes without letting Eric know about it ahead of time. Give him a chance to put in his two cents. Would you tell Michele you were going to a club to watch women strip?"

Jason laughed. "I'd at least mention it, just to hear what she'd say." He put the steaks on a platter and gestured to the sliding glass doors. "We're ready," he said, and I pulled the door open for him. I'd set the table earlier, and now I poured the tea. Michele had put the salad and the hot potato casserole on the table, and she got some A-1 steak sauce from the pantry. Jason loved his A-1. With the big barbecuing fork, Jason put one steak on each plate. In a couple of minutes, we were all eating. It was kind of homey, the three of us.

"Calvin came into the dealership today," Michele said. "He's thinking of trading in his old pickup." Calvin Norris was a good man with a good job. He was in his forties, and he carried a lot of responsibility on his shoulders. He was my brother's leader, the dominant male in the werepanther community centered in the little settlement of Hotshot.

"He still dating Tanya?" I asked. Tanya Grissom worked at Norcross, same as Calvin, but she sometimes filled in at Merlotte's when one of the other waitresses couldn't work.

"Yeah, she's living with him," Jason said. "They fight pretty often, but I think she's staying."

Calvin Norris, leader of the werepanthers, did his best not to get involved in vampire affairs. He'd had a lot on his plate since the Weres had come out. He'd declared that he was two-natured the next day in the break room at work. Now that the word had gotten around, it had only earned Calvin more respect. He had a good reputation in the Bon Temps area, even if most of the people who lived out in Hotshot were regarded with some suspicion since the community was so isolated and peculiar.

"How come you didn't come out when

Calvin did?" I asked. That was a thought I'd never heard in Jason's head.

My brother looked thoughtful, an expression that sat a little oddly on him. "I guess I just ain't ready to answer a lot of questions," he said. "It's a personal thing, the change. Michele knows, and that's all that's important."

Michele smiled at him. "I'm real proud of Jason," she said, and that was enough. "He manned up when he turned panther. Wasn't like he could help it. He's making the best of it. No whining. He'll tell people about it when he's ready."

Jason and Michele were just startling me all over the place. "I haven't ever said anything to anyone," I assured him.

"I never thought you would. Calvin says Eric is like a chief vampire," Jason said, hopping into a different topic.

I don't talk about vampire politics at any length with nonvamps. Just not a good idea. But Jason and Michele had shared with me, and I wanted to share a little back. "Eric's got some power. But he's got a new boss, and things are touchy."

"You want to talk about that?" I could tell Jason was uncertain about hearing whatever I chose to tell them, but he was trying hard to be a good brother.

"I better not," I said, and saw his relief. Even Michele was glad to turn back to her steak. "But apart from dealing with other vampires, Eric and I are doing okay. There's always some give and take in relationships, right?" Though Jason had had scores of relationships over the years, he'd learned about give and take only recently.

"I been talking to Hoyt again," Jason said, and I understood the pertinence. Hoyt, Jason's shadow for years, had dropped off my brother's radar for a while. Hoyt's fiancée, Holly, who worked at Merlotte's with me, wasn't a big Jason fan. I was surprised Jason had his best buddy back, and I was even more surprised Holly had consented to this renewal.

"I've changed a lot, Sookie," my brother said, as if (for once) he'd been reading *my* mind. "I want to be a good friend to Hoyt. I want to be a good boyfriend to Michele." He looked at Michele seriously, putting his hand over hers. "And I want to be a better brother. We're all we got left. Except for the fairy relations, and I'd just as soon forget about them." He looked down at his plate, embarrassed. "I can't hardly believe that Gran cheated on Grandpa."

"I had an idea about that," I said. I'd been struggling with the same disbelief. "Gran really wanted children, and that wasn't going to happen for her and Grandpa. I was thinking maybe she was enchanted by Fintan. Fairies can mess with your mind, like the vamps can. And you know how beautiful they are."

"Claudine sure was. And I guess if you're a woman, Claude looks pretty good."

"Claudine really toned it down since she was passing for human." Claudine, Claude's triplet, had been a stunning six-foot-tall beauty.

Jason said, "Grandpa wasn't any picture in the looks department."

"Yeah, I know." We looked at each other, silently acknowledging the power of physical attraction. Then we said, simultaneously, "But *Gran?*" And we couldn't help but laugh. Michele tried hard to keep a straight face, but finally she couldn't help grinning at us. It was hard enough thinking about your parents having sex, but your grandparents? Totally wrong.

"Now that I'm thinking about Gran, I've been meaning to ask you if I could have that table she put up in the attic," Jason said. "The pie-crust table that used to sit by the armchair in the living room?"

"Sure, swing by and pick it up sometime," I said. "It's probably sitting right where you

40

put it the day she asked you to take it up to the attic."

I left soon after with my almost-empty casserole dish, some leftover steak, and a cheerful heart.

I certainly hadn't thought having dinner with my brother and his girlfriend was any big deal, but when I got home that night I slept all the way through until morning, for the first time in weeks.

MARCH

"There," said Sam. I had to strain to hear him. Someone had put Jace Everett's "Bad Things" on, and just about everyone in the bar was singing along. "You've smiled three times tonight."

"You counting my facial expressions?" I put down my tray and gave him a look. Sam, my boss and friend, is a true shape-shifter; he can change into anything warm-blooded, I guess. I haven't asked him about lizards and snakes and bugs.

"Well, it's good to see that smile again," he said. He rearranged some bottles on the shelf, just to look busy. "I missed it."

"It's good to feel like smiling," I told him. "I like the haircut, by the way."

Sam ran a self-conscious hand across his head. His hair was short, and it hugged his scalp like a red gold cap. "Summer's coming up. I thought it might feel good."

"Probably will."

"You already started sunbathing?" My tan was famous.

"Oh, yeah." In fact, I'd started extra early this spring. The first day I'd put on my swimsuit, all hell had broken loose. I'd killed a fairy. But that was *past.* I'd lain out yesterday, and not a thing had happened. Though I confess I hadn't taken the radio outside, because I'd wanted to be sure I could hear if something was sneaking up on me. But nothing had. In fact, I'd had a remarkably peaceful hour lying in the sun, watching a butterfly waft by every now and then. One of my great-great-grandmother's rosebushes was blooming, and the scent had healed something inside me. "The sun just makes me feel real good," I said. I suddenly remembered that the fae had told me that I came from sky fairies, instead of water fairies. I didn't know anything about that, but I wondered if my love of the sun was a genetic thing.

Antoine called, "Order up!" and I hurried over to fetch the plates.

Antoine had settled in at Merlotte's, and we all hoped he'd stick with the cooking job. Tonight he was moving around the small kitchen like he had eight arms. Merlotte's menu was the most basic — hamburgers, chicken strips, a salad with chicken strips cut up on it, chili fries, French-fried pickles — but Antoine had mastered it with amazing speed. Now in his fifties, Antoine had gotten out of New Orleans after staying in the Superdome during Katrina. I respected Antoine for his positive attitude and his determination to start over after losing everything. He was also good to D'Eriq, who helped him with food prep and bused the tables. D'Eriq was sweet but slow.

Holly was working that night, and in between hustling drinks and plates she stood by Hoyt Fortenberry, her fiancé, who was perched on a barstool. Hoyt's mom had proven to be only too glad to keep Holly's little boy on the evenings Hoyt wanted to spend time with Holly. It was hard to look at Holly and recognize her as the sullen Goth Wiccan she'd been in one phase of her life. Her hair was its natural dark brown and had grown to nearly shoulder length, her makeup was light, and she smiled all the time. Hoyt, my brother's best friend again since they'd mended their differences, seemed like a stronger man now that he had Holly to brace him up.

I glanced over at Sam, who'd just answered his cell phone. Sam was spending a lot of time on that phone these days, and I suspected he was seeing someone, too. I could find out if I looked in his head long enough (though the two-natured are harder to read than simple basic humans), but I tried hard to stay out of Sam's thoughts. It's just rude to rummage around inside the ideas of people you care about. Sam was smiling while he talked, and it was good to see him looking — at least temporarily — carefree.

"You see Vampire Bill much?" Sam asked when I was helping him close up an hour later.

"No. I haven't seen him in a long time," I said. "I wonder if Bill's dodging me. I went by his house a couple of times and left him a six-pack of TrueBlood and a thank-you note for all he did when he came to rescue me, but he never called me or came over."

"He was in a couple of nights ago when you were off. I think you ought to pay him a visit," Sam said. "I'm not saying any more."

MARCH

On a beautiful night later that week, I was rummaging in my closet for my biggest flashlight. Sam's suggestion that I needed to see Bill had been nagging at me, so after I got home from work, I resolved to take a walk across the cemetery to Bill's house.

Sweet Home Cemetery is the oldest cemetery in Renard Parish. There isn't much room left for the dead, so there's one of those new "burial parks" with flat headstones on the south side of town. I hate it. Even if the ground is uneven and the trees are all grown up and some of the fences around the plots are falling down, to say nothing of the earliest headstones, I love Sweet Home. Jason and I had played there as kids, whenever we could escape Gran's attention.

The route through the memorials and trees to Bill's house was second nature, from the time he'd been my very first boyfriend. The frogs and bugs were just starting up their summer singing. The racket would only build with the hotter weather. I remembered D'Eriq asking me wasn't I scared, living by a graveyard, and I smiled to myself. I wasn't afraid of the dead lying in the ground. The walking and talking dead were *much* more dangerous. I'd cut a rose to lay on my grandmother's grave. I felt sure she knew I was there and thinking of her.

There was a dim light on at the old Compton house, which had been built about the same time my house had been. I rang the doorbell. Unless Bill was out in the woods roaming around, I was sure he was home since his car was there. But I had to wait some time until the creaking door swung open.

He switched on the porch light, and I tried not to gasp. He looked awful.

Bill had gotten infected with silver poisoning during the Fae War, thanks to the silver teeth of Neave. He'd had massive amounts of blood then — and since — from his fellow vampires, but I observed with some unease that his skin was still gray instead of white. His step was faltering, and his head hung a little forward like an old man's.

"Sookie, come in," he said. Even his voice didn't seem as strong as it had been.

Though his words were polite, I couldn't tell how he really felt about my visit. I can't read vampire minds, one of the reasons I'd initially been so attracted to Bill. You can imagine how intoxicating silence is after nonstop unwanted sharing.

"Bill," I said, trying to sound less shocked than I felt. "Are you feeling better? This poison in your system . . . Is it going away?"

I could swear he sighed. He gestured me to precede him into the living room. The lamps were off. Bill had lit candles. I counted eight. I wondered what he'd been doing, sitting alone in the flickering light. Listening to music? He loved his CDs, particularly Bach. Feeling distinctly worried, I sat on the couch, while Bill took his favorite chair across the low coffee table. He was as handsome as ever, but his face lacked animation. He was clearly suffering. Now I knew why Sam had wanted me to visit.

"You are well?" he asked.

"I'm much better," I said carefully. He'd seen the worst they'd done to me.

"The scars, the . . . mutilation?"

"The scars are there, but they're much fainter than I ever expected they'd be. The missing bits have filled in. I kind of have a dimple in this thigh," I said, tapping my left

48

knee. "But I had plenty of thigh to spare." I tried to smile, but truthfully, I was too concerned to manage it. "Are you getting better?" I asked again, hesitantly.

"I'm not worse," he said. He shrugged, a minimal lift of the shoulders.

"What's with the apathy?" I said.

"I don't seem to want anything any longer," Bill told me, after a lengthy pause. "I'm not interested in my computer anymore. I'm not inclined to work on the incoming additions and subtractions to my database. Eric sends Felicia over to package up the orders and send them out. She gives me some blood while she's here." Felicia was the bartender at Fangtasia. She hadn't been a vampire that long.

Could vampires suffer from depression? Or was the silver poisoning responsible?

"Isn't there anyone who can help you? I mean, help you heal?"

He smiled in a sardonic sort of way. "My creator," he said. "If I could drink from Lorena, I would have healed completely by now."

"Well, that sucks." I couldn't let him know that bothered me, but *ouch*. I'd killed Lorena. I shook the feeling off. She'd needed killing, and it was over and done with. "Did she make any other vampires?"

Bill looked slightly less apathetic. "Yes, she did. She has another living child."

"Well, would that help? Getting blood from that vamp?"

"I don't know. It might. But I won't . . . I can't reach out to her."

"You don't know if it would help or not? You-all need a Handy Hints rule book or something."

"Yes," he said, as if he'd never heard of such an idea. "Yes, we do indeed."

I wasn't going to ask Bill why he was reluctant to contact someone who could help him. Bill was a stubborn and persistent man, and I wasn't going to be able to persuade him otherwise since he'd made up his mind. We sat in silence for a moment.

"Do you love Eric?" Bill said, all of a sudden. His deep brown eyes were fixed on me with the total attention that had played a large part in attracting me to him when we'd met.

Was everyone I knew fixated on my relationship with the sheriff of Area Five? "Yes," I said steadily. "I do love him."

"Does he say he loves you?"

"Yes." I didn't look away.

"I wish he would die, some nights," Bill said.

We were being really honest tonight.

"There's a lot of that going around. There are a couple of people I wouldn't miss myself," I admitted. "I think about that when I'm grieving over the people I've cared about who've passed, like Claudine and Gran and Tray." And they were just at the top of the list. "So I guess I know how you feel. But I — please don't wish bad stuff on Eric." I'd lost about as much as I could stand to lose in the way of important people in my life.

"Who do you want dead, Sookie?" There was a spark of curiosity in his eyes.

"I'm not about to tell you." I gave him a weak smile. "You might try to make it happen for me. Like you did with Uncle Bartlett." When I'd discovered Bill had killed my grandmother's brother, who'd molested me — that's when I should have cut and run. Wouldn't my life have been different? But it was too late now.

"You've changed," he said.

"Sure, I have. I thought I was going to die for a couple of hours. I hurt like I've never hurt before. And Neave and Lochlan enjoyed it so much. That snapped something inside me. When you and Niall killed them, it was like an answer to the biggest prayer I'd ever prayed. I'm supposed to be a Christian, but most days I don't feel like I can even presume to say that about myself any longer. I have a lot of mad left over. When I can't sleep, I think about the other people who didn't care how much pain and trouble they caused me. And I think about how good I'd feel if they died."

That I could tell Bill about this awful secret part of me was a measure of how close I'd been to him.

"I love you," he said. "Nothing you do or say will change that. If you asked me to bury a body for you — or to make a body — I would do it without a qualm."

"We've got some bad history between us, Bill, but you'll always have a special place in my heart." I cringed inside when I heard the hackneyed phrase coming from my own mouth. But sometimes clichés are true; this was the truth. "I hardly feel worthy of being cared about that strongly," I admitted.

He managed a smile. "As to your being worthy, I don't think falling in love has much to do with the worth of the object of love. But I'd dispute your assessment. I think you're a fine woman, and I think you always try to be the best person you can be. No one could be . . . carefree and sunny . . . after coming as close to death as you did."

I rose to leave. Sam had wanted me to see Bill, to understand his situation, and I'd done that. When Bill got up to see me to the door, I noticed he didn't have the lightning speed he'd once had. "You're going to live, right?" I asked him, suddenly frightened.

"I think so," he said, as if it didn't make any difference one way or another. "But just in case, give me a kiss."

I put one arm around his neck, the arm that wasn't burdened with the flashlight, and I let him put his lips against mine. The feeling of him, the smell of him, triggered a lot of memories. For what seemed like a very long time, we stood pressed together, but instead of growing excited, I grew calmer. I was oddly conscious of my breathing — slow and steady, almost like the respiration of someone sleeping.

I could see that Bill looked better when I stepped away. My eyebrows flew up.

"Your fairy blood helps me," he said.

"I'm just an eighth fairy. And you didn't take any."

"Proximity," he said briefly. "The touch of skin on skin." His lips quirked up in a smile. "If we made love, I would be much closer to being healed."

Bullshit, I thought. But I can't say that cool voice didn't make something leap south of my navel, in a momentary twinge of lust.

"Bill, that's not gonna happen," I said. "But you should think about tracking down that other vampire child of Lorena's."

"Yes," he said. "Maybe." His dark eyes were curiously luminous; that might have been an effect of the poisoning, or it might have been the candlelight. I knew he wouldn't make an effort to reach out to Lorena's other get. Whatever spark my visit had raised in him was already dying out.

Feeling sad, concerned, and also just a tiny smidge pleased — you can't tell me it's not flattering to be loved so much, because it is — I went home through the graveyard. I patted Bill's tombstone by habit. As I walked carefully over the uneven ground, I thought about Bill, naturally enough. He'd been a Confederate soldier. He'd survived the war only to succumb to a vampire after his return home to his wife and children, a tragic end to a hard life.

I was glad all over again that I'd killed Lorena.

Here's something I didn't like about myself: I realized I didn't feel bad when I killed a vampire. Something inside me kept insisting they were dead already, and that the first death had been the one that was most important. When I'd killed a human I'd loathed, my reaction had been much

54

more intense.

Then I thought, *You'd think I'd be glad that I was avoiding some pain instead of thinking I should feel worse about taking out Lorena.* I hated trying to figure out what was best morally, because so often that didn't jibe with my gut reaction.

The bottom line of all this self-examination was that I'd killed Lorena, who could have cured Bill. Bill had gotten wounded when he came to my rescue. Clearly, I had a responsibility. I'd try to figure out what to do.

By the time I realized I'd been alone in the dark and should have been mortally afraid (at least according to D'Eriq), I was walking into my well-lit backyard. Maybe worrying about my spiritual life was a welcome distraction from reliving physical torture. Or maybe I felt better because I'd done someone a good turn; I'd hugged Bill, and that had made him feel better. When I went to bed that night, I was able to lie on my side in my favorite position instead of tossing and turning, and I slept with no dreams — at least, none that I could remember in the morning.

For the next week, I enjoyed untroubled sleep, and as a result I began to feel much more like my former self. It was gradual, but perceptible. I hadn't thought of a way to help Bill, but I bought him a new CD (Beethoven) and put it where he'd find it when he got out of his daytime hiding place. Another day I sent him an e-card. Just so he knew I was thinking about him.

Each time I saw Eric, I felt a little more cheerful. And finally, I had my very own orgasm, a moment so explosive it was like I'd been saving up for a holiday.

"You . . . Are you all right?" Eric asked. His blue eyes looked down at me, and he was half-smiling, as if he weren't sure whether he should be clapping or calling an ambulance.

"I am very, very all right," I whispered. Grammar be damned. "I'm so all right I might slide off the bed and lie in a puddle on the floor."

His smile became more secure. "So that was good for you? Better than it's been?"

"You knew that . . . ?"

He cocked an eyebrow.

"Well, of course you knew. I just . . . had some issues that had to work themselves out."

"I knew it couldn't be my lovemaking, wife of mine," Eric said, and though the words were cocky, his expression was definitely on the relieved side.

"Don't call me your wife. You know our so-called marriage is just strategy. To get back to your previous statement. *A-one* love-making, Eric." I had to give credit where credit was due. "The no-orgasm problem was in my head. Now I've self-corrected."

"You are bullshitting me, Sookie," he murmured. "But I'll show you some A-one lovemaking. Because I think you can come again."

As it turned out, I could.

CHAPTER 1
APRIL

I love spring for all the obvious reasons. I love the flowers blooming (which happens early here in Louisiana); I love the birds twittering; I love the squirrels scampering across my yard.

I love the sound of werewolves howling in the distance.

No, just kidding. But the late, lamented Tray Dawson had once told me that spring is the favorite season of werewolves. There's more prey, so the hunt is over quickly, leaving more time to eat and play. Since I'd been thinking about Weres, it wasn't such a surprise to hear from one.

On that sunny morning in the middle of April, I was sitting on my front porch with my second cup of coffee and a magazine, still wearing my sleep pants and my Superwoman T-shirt, when the Shreveport pack-leader called me on my cell phone.

"Huh," I said, when I recognized the

number. I flipped the phone open. "Hello," I said cautiously.

"Sookie," said Alcide Herveaux. I hadn't seen Alcide in months. Alcide had ascended to the position of packleader the year before in a single evening of mayhem. "How are you?"

"Right as rain," I said, nearly meaning it. "Happy as a clam. Fit as a fiddle." I watched a rabbit hop across the clover and grass twenty feet away. Spring.

"You're still dating Eric? He the reason for the good mood?"

Everyone wanted to know. "I'm still dating Eric. That sure helps keep me happy." Actually, as Eric kept telling me, "dating" was a misleading term. Though I didn't think of myself as married since I'd simply handed him a ceremonial knife (Eric had used my ignorance as part of his master strategy), the vampires did. A vampire-human marriage isn't exactly like a "love, honor, and obey" human pairing, but Eric had expected the marriage would earn me some perks in the vampire world. Since then, things had gone pretty well, vampire-wise. Aside from the huge glitch of Victor not letting Eric come to my aid when I was dying, that is — Victor, who really needed to die.

I turned my thoughts away from this dark direction with the determination of long practice. See? That was better. Now I was hopping out of bed every day with (almost) my old vigor. I'd even gone to church the past Sunday. Positive! "What's happening, Alcide?" I asked.

"I got a favor to ask," Alcide said, not entirely to my surprise.

"What can I do for you?"

"Can we use your land for our full-moon run tomorrow night?"

I made myself pause to think about his request rather than automatically saying yes. I'm learning through experience. I had the open land the Weres needed; that wasn't the issue. I still own twenty-odd acres around my house, though my grandmother had sold off most of the original farm when she was faced with the financial burden of raising my brother and me. Though Sweet Home Cemetery took a chunk out of the land between my place and Bill's, there'd be enough room — especially if Bill didn't mind allowing access to his land as well. I remembered the pack had been here once before.

I turned the idea around to look at it from all angles. I couldn't see any obvious downside. "You're welcome to come," I said. "I think you should check with Bill Compton, too." Bill hadn't responded to any of my little gestures of concern.

Vampires and werewolves are not inclined to be buddies, but Alcide is a practical man. "I'll call Bill tonight, then," he said. "You got his number?"

I gave it to him. "Why are you-all not going to your place, Alcide?" I asked, out of sheer curiosity. He'd told me in casual conversation that the Long Tooth pack celebrated the full moon at the Herveaux farm south of Shreveport. Most of the Herveaux land was left in timber for the pack hunts.

"Ham called today to tell me there's a small party of oneys camping by the stream." "Oneys," the one-natured, is what the two-natured Weres call regular humans. I knew Hamilton Bond by sight. His farm was adjacent to the Herveaux place, and Ham farmed a few acres for Alcide. The Bond family had belonged to the Long Tooth pack as long as the Herveauxes.

"Did they have your permission to camp there?" I asked.

"They told Ham my dad always gave them permission to fish there in the spring, so they didn't think to ask me. It might be true. I don't remember them, though."

"Even if they're telling the truth, that's pretty rude. They should have called you," I said. "They should have asked you if it was convenient for you. You want me to talk to them? I can find out if they're lying." Jackson Herveaux, Alcide's late dad, hadn't seemed like the kind of man who'd casually allow people to use his land on a regular basis.

"No thanks, Sookie. I hate to ask you for another favor. You're a friend of the pack. We're supposed to watch out for you, not you for us."

"Don't worry about it. Y'all can come out here. And if you want me to shake hands with these supposed buddies of your dad's, I can do that." I was curious about their appearance on the Herveaux farm so close to the full moon. Curious and suspicious.

Alcide told me he'd think about the fishermen situation, and thanked me about six times for saying yes.

"No big deal," I said, and hoped I was telling the truth. Eventually, Alcide felt he'd thanked me enough, and we hung up.

I went inside with my coffee cup. I didn't know I was smiling until I looked in the living room mirror. I admitted to myself I was looking forward to the wolves' arrival. It would be pleasant to feel I wasn't alone in the middle of the woods. Pathetic, huh?

Though our few evenings together were good, Eric was still spending a *lot* of time on vampire business. I was getting a little tired of it. Well, not a little. If you're the boss, you should be able to get some time off, right? That's one of the perks of being a boss.

But something was up with the vampires; I was unhappily familiar with the signs. By now, the new regime should have been firmly in place, and Eric should have thoroughly established his new role in the scheme of things. Victor Madden should have been fully occupied down in New Orleans with the running of the kingdom, since he was Felipe's representative in Louisiana. Eric should have been left to run Area Five in his own efficient way.

But Eric's blue eyes got all glittery and steely when Victor's name came up. Mine probably did, too. As things stood now, Victor had power over Eric, and there wasn't much we could do about that.

I'd asked Eric if he thought Victor might claim dissatisfaction with Eric's performance in Area Five, a terrifying possibility.

"I'm keeping paperwork to prove differently," Eric said. "And I'm keeping it in several places." The lives of all Eric's people, and maybe my life, depended on Eric planting his feet firmly in the new regime. I knew so much rested on Eric's making his position impregnable, and I knew I shouldn't whine. It's not always easy to make yourself feel the way you ought to feel.

All in all, some howling around the house would be a nice change. At least it would be something new and different.

When I went to work that day, I told Sam about Alcide's phone call. True shapeshifters are rare. Since there aren't any others in this area, Sam occasionally spends time with others who have two forms. "Hey, why don't you come out to the house, too?" I suggested. "You could turn into a wolf, right, since you're a pure shifter? And then you'd blend right in."

Sam leaned back in his old swivel chair, glad to have an excuse to stop filling in forms. Sam, who is thirty, is three years older than me.

"I've been dating someone in the pack, so it might be fun," he said, considering the idea. But he shook his head after a moment. "That would be like going to an NAACP meeting in blackface. Being an imitation in front of the real thing. That's why I've never gone out with the panthers, though Calvin's told me I'd be welcome."

"Oh," I said, feeling embarrassed. "I didn't think of that. I'm sorry." I did wonder who he was dating, but there again, not my business.

"Ah, don't worry about it."

"I've known you for years, and I should know more about you," I said. "Your culture, that is."

"My own *family* is still learning. You know more than they do."

Sam had come out when the Weres had. His mother had come out the same night. His family had had a rough time handling the revelation. In fact, Sam's stepfather had shot Sam's mother, and now they were getting divorced — no big surprise there.

"Is your brother's wedding back on?" I said.

"Craig and Deidra are going to counseling. Her parents were pretty upset that she was marrying into a family with people like me and Mom in it. They don't understand that any kids Craig and Deidra have simply can't turn into animals. It's only the first-born of a pure shifter couple." He shrugged. "I think they'll pull through, though. I'm just waiting for them to set a new date. You still willing to go with me?"

"Sure," I said, though I had an uneasy twitch when I pictured myself telling Eric I was going out of state with another man. At the time I'd promised Sam I'd go, the situation between Eric and me hadn't gelled into a relationship. "You're assuming taking a Were as your date would be offensive to Deidra's family?"

"Truth be told," Sam said, "the Great Reveal in Wright didn't go over as well for the two-natured as it did in Bon Temps."

I knew from the local news that Bon Temps had been lucky. Its citizens had simply blinked when the Weres and the other two-natured announced their existence, taking a page from the vampire book. "Just let me know what happens," I said. "And come out to my place tomorrow if you change your mind about having a run with the pack."

"Packmaster didn't invite me," Sam said, smiling.

"Landowner did."

We didn't talk about it any more the rest of my shift, so I figured Sam would find something else to do for his moon time. The monthly change actually runs for three nights — three nights when all the two-natured, if they can, take to the woods (or the streets) in their animal form. Most of the twoeys — those born with their condition — can change at other times, but the

67

moon time . . . that's special to all of them, including those who'd come to their extra nature by being bitten. There's a drug you can take, I hear, that can suppress your change; Weres in the military, among others, have to use it. But they all hate to do that, and I understand they're really no fun to be around on those nights.

Fortunately for me, the next day was one of my days off that week. If I'd had to come home from the bar late at night, the short distance from the car into the house might have been a little nerve-racking with the wolves on the loose. I'm not sure how much of their human consciousness remains when the Weres change, and not all of Alcide's pack members are personal friends of mine. Since I'd be at home, the prospect of hosting the Weres was more or less carefree. When company's coming to hunt in your woods, there's no preparation to be done. You don't have to cook or clean house.

However, having outside company was good motivation to complete some yard chores. Since it was another beautiful day, I put on one of my bikinis, pulled on sneakers and gloves, and set to work. Sticks and leaves and pinecones all went in the burn barrel, along with some hedge clippings. I made sure all the yard tools were put away in the shed, which I locked. I wound up the hose I'd used to water the potted plants I'd arranged around the back steps. I checked the clamp on the lid on the big garbage can. I'd bought the can specifically to keep the raccoons out of the trash, but a wolf might get interested, too.

I passed a pleasant afternoon, puttering around in the sun, singing off-key whenever the spirit moved me.

Right at dusk, the cars started arriving. I went to the window. I noticed the Weres had been considerate enough to carpool; there were several people in each vehicle. Even so, my driveway would be blocked until morning. *Lucky I planned to stay at home,* I thought. I knew some of the pack members, and I recognized a few of the others by sight. Hamilton Bond, who'd grown up with Alcide, pulled up and sat in his truck, talking on his cell phone. My eyes were drawn to a skinny, vivid young woman who favored flashy fashions, the kind I thought of as MTV clothes. I'd first noticed her in the Hair of the Dog bar in Shreveport, and she'd been assigned the task of executing injured enemies after Alcide's pack had won the Were war; I thought her name was Jannalynn. I also recognized two women who'd been members of the attacking pack; they'd surrendered at the end of the fight. Now they'd joined their former enemies. A young man had surrendered, too, but he could have been any one of a dozen moving restlessly around my yard.

Finally, Alcide arrived in his familiar truck. There were two other people sitting in the cab.

Alcide himself is tall and husky, as Weres tend to be. He's an attractive man. He's got black hair and green eyes, and of course, he's very strong. Alcide is usually well mannered and considerate — but he has his tough side, for sure. I'd heard rumors through Sam and Jason that since he'd ascended to packleader, that tough side had been getting a workout. I noticed that Jannalynn made a special effort to be at the truck door when Alcide emerged.

The woman who slid out after him was in her late twenties, and she had some good solid hips on her. She wore her brown hair slicked back into a little knob, and her camo tank top let me know she was muscular and fit. At the moment, Camo was looking around the front yard like she was the tax assessor. The man who got out the other door was a little older and a lot harder.

Sometimes, even if you're not telepathic, you can tell by looking at a man that he's had a rough life. This man had. The way he moved told me he was on the alert for trouble. Interesting.

I watched him, because he needed watching. He had shoulder-length dark brown hair that flared around his head in a cloud of corkscrews. I found myself eyeing it enviously. I'd always wished I could get my hair to do that.

After I'd gotten over my hair envy, I noticed that his skin was the brown of mocha ice cream. Though he wasn't as tall as Alcide, he had thick shoulders on an aggressively muscled body.

If I'd had a "Bad to the Bone" alert on the brick path up to the front porch, it would have gone off just after Corkscrew set his foot on it. "Danger, Will Robinson," I said out loud. I'd never seen Camo or Corkscrew before. Hamilton Bond got out of his truck and came over to join the little group, but he didn't come up the porch steps to stand beside Alcide, Corkscrew, and Camo. Ham held back. Jannalynn joined him. The Long Tooth pack appeared to be both expanding its ranks and rearranging its pecking order.

When I answered the knock on the door, I had my hostess smile in place. The bikini would have been sending the wrong message (*Yum, yum, available!*), so I'd pulled on some cutoff jeans and a Fangtasia T-shirt. I pushed open the screen door. "Alcide!" I said, truly glad to see him. We gave each other a brief hug. He felt awfully warm, since all my recent hugging experiences had been with the less-than-room-temperature Eric. I felt a sort of emotional ripple and realized that though Camo was smiling at me, our embrace hadn't been a welcome sight to her. "Hamilton!" I said. I nodded at him since he wasn't within hugging distance.

"Sookie," Alcide said, "some new members for you to meet. This is Annabelle Bannister."

I'd never met anyone who looked less like an "Annabelle" than this woman. I shook hands with her, of course, and told her I was pleased to meet her.

"You know Ham, and you've met Jannalynn, too, I think?" Alcide said, inclining his head back.

I nodded at the two at the foot of the steps.

"And this is Basim al Saud, my new second," Alcide said. It was pronounced "bah-SEEM," and Alcide trotted the name out like he introduced Arabic people to me all the time. Okeydokey. "Hi-dee-do, Basim," I said. I held out my hand. One of the meanings of "second," I knew, was the

72

person who scares the shit out of everyone, and Basim seemed well qualified for the job. Somewhat reluctantly, he extended his own hand to mine. I shook it, wondering what I'd get from him. Weres are often very hard to read because of their dual nature. Sure enough, I didn't get specific thoughts: only a confused blur of mistrust and aggression and lust.

Funny, that was pretty much what I was getting from the misnamed Annabelle. "How long have you been in Shreveport?" I asked politely. I glanced from Annabelle to Basim to include them both in the question.

"Six months," Annabelle said. "I transferred from the Elk Killer pack in South Dakota." So she was in the Air Force. She'd been stationed in South Dakota and then reassigned to Barksdale Air Force Base in Bossier City, adjacent to Shreveport.

"I've been here two months," Basim said. "I'm learning to like it." Though he looked exotic, he had only the faintest trace of an accent, and his English was much more precise than mine. Going strictly by the haircut, he was definitely not in the armed services.

"Basim left his old pack in Houston," Alcide said easily, "and we're glad he's become

73

one of us." "We" didn't include Ham Bond. I might not be able to read Ham's mind as clearly as if he were human, but he was no big Basim fan. Neither was Jannalynn, who seemed to regard Basim with both lust and resentment. There was lots of lust going around the pack this evening. Looking at Basim and Alcide, that wasn't too hard to understand.

"You have a good time here tonight, Basim, Annabelle," I said, before turning to Alcide. "Alcide, my property extends maybe an acre beyond the stream to the east, about five acres south to the dirt track that leads to the oil well, and north around the back of the cemetery."

The packleader nodded. "I called Bill last night, and he's okay with us spilling over into his woods. He's not going to be at home until dawn, so we won't be bothering him. What about you, Sookie? Are you going into Shreveport tonight, or staying home?"

"I'll be here. If you need me for anything, just come to the door." I smiled at all of them.

Annabelle thought, *Not effing likely, Blondie.*

"But you might need the phone," I said to her, and she jumped. "Or some first aid.

After all, Annabelle, you never know what you're going to meet up with." Though I'd started out smiling, there was no smile on my face by the time I finished.

People should make an effort to be polite.

"Thanks again for the use of your land. We'll be heading into the woods," Alcide said quickly. The dark was falling steadily, and I could see the other Weres drifting into the cover of the trees. One of the women threw back her head and yipped. Basim's eyes were rounder and more golden already.

"Have a good night," I said, as I stepped back and latched the screen door. The three Weres started down the front steps. Alcide's voice drifted back. He was saying, "I *told* you she was telepathic," to Annabelle as they went across the driveway into the woods, trailed by Ham. Jannalynn suddenly started running for the tree line, she was so anxious to change. But it was Basim who glanced back at me as I pushed the wooden door shut. It was the kind of look you get from the animals in the zoo.

And then it was full dark.

The Weres were a bit of a disappointment. They didn't make as much noise as I'd thought they would. I stayed in the house, of course, all locked up, and I pulled my curtains closed, which wasn't my normal habit. After all, I lived in the middle of the woods. I watched a little television, and I read some. Somewhat later, while I was brushing my teeth, I heard howling. I thought it came from far off, probably near the eastern edge of my property.

Early the next morning, just as dawn was breaking, I woke up because I heard car engines. The Weres were taking their departure. I almost turned over to go back to sleep, but I realized I had to get up and pay a trip to the bathroom. After I took care of that, I was a little more awake. I padded down the hall to the living room and peeked through a gap in the front curtains. Out of the tree line came Ham Bond, a bit worse for wear. He was talking to Alcide. Their trucks were the only remaining vehicles. Annabelle appeared a moment after.

As I looked at the early morning light falling across the dewy grass, the three Weres walked across the lawn slowly, clothed as they had been the night before, but carrying their shoes. They looked exhausted but happy. Their clothes weren't bloody, but their faces and arms were speckled. They'd had a successful hunt. I had a *Bambi* twinge, but I suppressed it. This was little different from going up in a blind with a rifle.

A few seconds later Basim emerged from

the woods. In the slanted light, he looked like a woodland creature, his wild hair full of bits of leaf and twig. There was something ancient about Basim al Saud. I had to wonder how he'd become a werewolf in wolfless Arabia. As I watched, Basim turned away from the other three and came to my front porch. He knocked, low and firm.

I counted to ten and opened the door. I tried not to stare at the blood. You could tell he'd washed his face in the stream, but he'd missed his neck.

"Miss Stackhouse, good morning," Basim said courteously. "Alcide says I should tell you that other creatures have been passing through your property."

I could feel the pucker between my eyes as I frowned. "What kind, Basim?"

"At least one was a fairy," he said. "Possibly more than one fairy, but one for sure."

That was incredible for about six reasons. "Are these tracks . . . or traces . . . fresh? Or a few weeks old?"

"Very fresh," he said. "And the scent of vampire is strong, too. That's a bad mixture."

"That's unpleasant news, but something I needed to know. Thanks for telling me."

"And there's a body."

I stared at him, willing my face to stillness. I have a lot of practice at not showing what I'm thinking; any telepath has to be good at that. "How old a body?" I asked, when I was sure I had my voice under control.

"Around a year and a half, maybe a little less." Basim wasn't making a big deal about finding a body. He was strictly letting me know it was there. "It's quite far back, buried very deeply."

I didn't say anything. Geez Louise, must be Debbie Pelt. Since Eric had recovered his memory of that night, that's one thing I'd never asked him: where he'd buried her body after I'd killed her.

Basim's dark eyes examined me with great attention. "Alcide wants you to call if you need help or advice," he said finally.

"Tell Alcide I appreciate the offer. And thanks again for letting me know."

He nodded, and then he was halfway back to the truck, where Annabelle sat with her head resting on Alcide's shoulder.

I raised my hand to them as Alcide started the truck, and I shut my door firmly as they left.

I had a lot to think about.

CHAPTER 2

I went back to the kitchen, looking forward to my coffee and a slice of the applesauce bread Halleigh Bellefleur had dropped off at the bar the day before. She was a nice young woman, and I was real glad she and Andy were expecting a baby. I'd heard that Andy's grandmother, ancient Mrs. Caroline Bellefleur, was beside herself with delight, and I didn't doubt it for a moment. I tried to think about good things, like Halleigh's baby, Tara's pregnancy, and the last night I'd spent with Eric; but the disturbing news Basim had told me gnawed at me all morning.

Of all the ideas I had, calling the Renard Parish's sheriff's office was the one that got almost zero brain time. There was no way I could tell them why I was worried. The Weres were out, and there was nothing illegal about letting them hunt on my land. But I couldn't picture myself telling Sheriff

Dearborn that a Were had told me fairies had been crossing my property.

Here's the thing. As far as I'd known until this moment, all the fairies except my cousin Claude had been barred from the human world. At least, all the fairies in America. I'd never wondered about those in other countries, and now I closed my eyes and winced at my own stupidity. My great-grandfather Niall had closed all the portals between the fae world and ours. At least, that was what he'd told me he was going to do. And I'd assumed they were all gone, except for Claude, who'd lived among humans as long as I'd known him. So how come there'd been a fairy tromping through my woods?

And who could I ask for advice on the situation? I couldn't just sit on my hands and do nothing. My great-grandfather had been looking for the self-loathing half-human renegade Dermot until the moment he closed the portal. I needed to face the possibility that Dermot, who was simply insane, had been left in the human world. However it had come about, I had to believe that fae proximity to my house couldn't be a good thing. I needed to talk to someone about this.

I might confide in Eric, since he was my

lover, or in Sam, because he was my friend, or even in Bill, because his land shared a boundary with mine and he would also be concerned. Or I could talk to Claude, see if he'd give me any insight into the situation. I sat at the table with my coffee and my hunk of applesauce bread, too distracted to read or turn on the radio to catch the news. I finished one cup of coffee and started another. I showered, in an automatic sort of way, and made my bed and did all my usual morning tasks.

Finally, I sat down at the computer I'd brought home from my cousin Hadley's New Orleans apartment, and I checked my e-mail. I'm not methodical about doing this. I know very few people who might send me e-mail, and I simply haven't gotten into the habit of looking at my computer every day.

I had several messages. I didn't recognize the return address on the first one. I moved the mouse to click on it.

A knock at the back door made me jump like a frog.

I pushed back my chair. After a second's hesitation, I got the shotgun from the closet in the front room. Then I went to the back door and peeked through the new peephole. "Speak of the devil," I muttered.

This day was just full of surprises, and it

81

wasn't even ten o'clock.

I put down the shotgun and opened the door. "Claude," I said. "Come in. You want a drink? I've got Coke and coffee and orange juice."

I noticed that Claude had the strap of a big tote bag slung over his shoulder. From its solid appearance, the bag was jammed with clothes. I didn't remember inviting him to a slumber party.

He came in, looking serious and somehow unhappy. Claude had been in the house before, but not often, and he looked around at my kitchen. The kitchen happened to be new because the old kitchen had burned down, so I had shiny appliances and everything still looked squared away and level.

"Sookie, I can't stay in our house by myself any longer. Can I bunk with you for a while, Cousin?"

I tried to pick my jaw up off the floor before he noticed how shocked I was — first, that Claude had confessed he needed help; second, that he confessed it to me; and third, that Claude would stay in the same house with me when he normally thought of me as about on the same level as a beetle. I'm a human and I'm a woman, so I've got two strikes against me as far as Claude's concerned. Plus, of course, there was the whole issue of Claudine dying in my defense.

"Claude," I said, trying to sound only sympathetic, "have a seat. What's wrong?" I glanced at the shotgun, unaccountably glad it was within reach.

Claude gave it only a casual glance. After a moment, he put down his bag and simply stood there, as if he couldn't figure out what to do next.

It seemed surreal to be in my kitchen alone with my fairy cousin. Though he had apparently made the choice to continue living among humans, he was far from warm and fuzzy about them. Claude, albeit physically beautiful, was an indiscriminate jerk, as far as I'd observed. But he'd gotten his ears surgically altered to look human, so he wouldn't have to expend his energy perpetuating a human appearance. And as far as I knew, Claude's sexual connections had always been with human males.

"You're still living in the house you shared with your sisters?" It was a prosaic three-bedroom ranch in Monroe.

"Yes."

Okay. I was looking for a little expansion on the theme here. "The bars aren't keeping you occupied?" Between owning and operating two strip clubs — Hooligans and a new place he'd just taken over — and performing at Hooligans at least once a week, I'd imagined Claude to be both busy and well-to-do. Since he was handsome to the nth degree, he made a lot of money in tips, and the occasional modeling job boosted his income. Claude could make even the most staid grandmother drool. Being in the same room with someone so gorgeous gave women a contact high . . . until he opened his mouth. Plus, he no longer had to share the club income with his sister.

"I'm busy. And I don't lack for money. But without the company of my own kind . . . I feel I'm starving."

"Are you *serious?*" I said without thinking, and then I could have kicked myself. But Claude needing me (or anyone, for that matter) seemed so unlikely. His request to stay with me was wholly unexpected and unwelcome.

But my gran chided me mentally. I was looking at a member of my family, one of the few still living and/or accessible to me. My relationship with my great-grandfather Niall had ended when he'd retreated into Faery and pulled the door shut behind him. Though Jason and I had mended our fences, my brother very much led his own life. My mom, my dad, and my grandmother were dead, my aunt Linda and my cousin Hadley were dead, and I rarely saw Hadley's little son.

I had depressed the hell out of myself in the space of a minute.

"Do I have enough fairy in me to be any help to you?" That was all I could think of to say.

"Yes," he said very simply. "I already feel better." This seemed a weird echo of my conversation with Bill. Claude halfway smiled. If Claude looked incredible when he was unhappy, he looked divine when he smiled. "Since you've been in the company of fairies, it's accentuated your streak of fairy essence. By the way, I have a letter for you."

"Who from?"

"Niall."

"How's that possible? I understood the fae world was shut off now."

"He has his ways," Claude said evasively. "He's the only prince now, and very powerful."

He has his ways. "Humph," I said. "Okay, let's see it."

Claude pulled an envelope out of his overnight bag. It was buff-colored and sealed with a blue blob of wax. In the wax was imprinted a bird, its wings spread in flight.

"So there's a fairy mailbox," I said. "And you can send and receive letters?"

"This letter, anyway."

Fae were very good at evasion. I huffed out a breath of exasperation.

I got a knife and slid it under the seal. The paper I extracted from the envelope had a very curious texture.

"Dearest great-granddaughter," it began. "There are things I didn't get to say to you and many things I didn't get to do for you before my plans collapsed in the war."

Okay.

"This letter is written on the skin of one of the water sprites who drowned your parents."

"Ick!" I cried, and dropped the letter on the kitchen table.

Claude was by my side in a flash. "What's wrong?" he asked, looking around the kitchen as if he expected to see a troll pop up.

"This is skin! Skin!"

"What else would Niall write on?" He looked genuinely taken aback.

"Ewww!" Even to myself, I sounded a little too girly-girly. But honestly . . . skin?

"It's clean," Claude said, clearly hoping

that would solve my problem. "It's been processed."

I gritted my teeth and reached down for my great-grandfather's letter. I took a deep, steadying breath. Actually, the . . . material hardly smelled at all. Smothering a desire to put on oven mitts, I made myself focus on reading.

"Before I left your world, I made sure one of my human agents talked to several people who can help you evade the scrutiny of the human government. When I sold the pharmaceutical company we owned, I used much of my profit to ensure your freedom."

I blinked, because my eyes were tearing up a little. He might not be a typical great-grandfather, but by golly, he'd done something wonderful for me.

"He's bribed some government officials to call off the FBI? Is that what he's done?"

"I have no idea," Claude said, shrugging. "He wrote me, too, to let me know that I had an extra three hundred thousand dollars in my bank account. Also, Claudine hadn't made a will, since she didn't . . ."

Expect to die. She had expected to raise a child with a fairy lover I'd never met. Claude shook himself and said in a cracked voice, "Niall produced a human body and a will, so I don't have to wait years to prove her death. She left me almost everything. She said this to our father, Dillon, when she appeared to him as part of her death ritual."

Fairies told their relatives they had passed, after they'd translated to spirit form. I wondered why Claudine had appeared to Dillon instead of to her brother, and I asked Claude, phrasing it as tactfully as I could.

"The next oldest receives the vision," Claude said stiffly. "Our sister, Claudette, appeared to me, since I was older than her by a minute. Claudine made her death ritual to our father, since she was older than I."

"So she told your dad she wanted you to have her share of the clubs?" It was pretty lucky for Claude that Claudine had let someone else know about her wishes. I wondered what happened if the oldest fae in the line was the one who was doing the dying. I'd save that question for later.

"Yes. Her share of the house. Her car. Though I already had one." For some reason, Claude was looking self-conscious. And guilty. Why on earth would he look guilty?

"How do you ride in it?" I asked, side-tracked. "Since fairies have such issues with iron?"

"I wear the invisible gloves over exposed skin," he said. "I put them on after every shower. And I've built up a little more tolerance with every decade of living in the human world."

I returned to the letter. "There may be more I can do for you. I will let you know. Claudine left you a gift."

"Oh, Claudine left me something, too? What?" I looked up at Claude, who didn't look exactly pleased. I think he hadn't known the contents of the letter for certain. If Niall hadn't revealed Claudine's legacy, Claude might not have. Fairies don't lie, but they don't always tell all the truth, either.

"She left you the money in her bank account," he said, resigned. "It contains her wages from the department store and her share of the income from the clubs."

"Aw . . . that was so nice of her." I blinked a couple of times. I tried not to touch my savings account, and my checking account wasn't too healthy because I'd missed a lot of work recently. Plus, my tips had suffered because I'd been so down. Smiling waitresses make more than sad waitresses.

I could sure use a few hundred dollars. Maybe I could buy some new clothes, and I really needed a new toilet in the hall bathroom. "How do you do a transfer like that?"

"You'll get a check from Mr. Cataliades.

He is handling the estate."

Mr. Cataliades — if he had a first name, I'd never heard it — was a lawyer, and he was also (mostly) a demon. He handled the human legal affairs of many supernaturals in Louisiana. I felt subtly better when Claude said his name, because I knew Mr. Cataliades had no bone to pick with me.

Well, I had to make up my mind about Claude's housemate proposal.

"Let me make a phone call," I said, and pointed to the coffeepot. "If you need some more, I can make some. Are you hungry?"

Claude shook his head.

"Then after I call Amelia, you and I need to have a little chitchat."

I went to the phone in my bedroom. Amelia was an earlier riser than me, because my job kept me up late. She answered her cell phone on the second ring. "Sookie," she said, and she didn't sound as gloomy as I'd anticipated. "What's up?"

I couldn't think of any casual way to lead into my question. "My cousin would like to stay here for a while," I said. "He could use the bedroom across from mine, but if he stays upstairs, we'd each have a little more privacy. If you're coming back anytime soon, of course he'll go on and put his stuff in the downstairs bedroom. I just didn't want you to come back to find someone sleeping in your bed."

There was a long silence. I braced myself.

"Sookie," she said, "I love you. You know that. And I loved living with you. It was a godsend to have somewhere to go after that thing with Bob. But right now I'm stuck in New Orleans for a while. I'm just . . . in the middle of a lot of stuff."

I'd expected this, but it was still a tough moment. I hadn't really expected her to come back. I'd hoped she'd heal faster in New Orleans — and it was true she hadn't mentioned Tray. It sounded like more than grieving was going on. "You're okay?"

"I am," she said. "And I've been training with Octavia some more." Octavia, her mentor in witchcraft, had returned to New Orleans with her long-lost love. "Also, I finally got . . . judged. I've got to pay a penalty for — you know — the thing with Bob."

"The thing with Bob" was Amelia's way of referring to accidentally turning her lover into a cat. Octavia had returned Bob to his human form, but naturally Bob hadn't been happy with Amelia, and neither had Octavia. Though Amelia had been training in her craft, clearly transformational magic had been beyond her skills.

91

"So, they're not going to whip you or anything, right?" I asked, trying to sound as if I were joking. "After all, it's not like he died." Just lost a big chunk of his life and missed Katrina entirely, including being able to inform his family that he'd survived.

"Some of them would whip me if they could. But that's not how we witches roll." Amelia tried to laugh, but it wasn't convincing. "As a penalty, I've got to do, like, community service."

"Like picking up litter or tutoring kids?"

"Well . . . mixing potions and making up bags of common ingredients so they're ready to hand. Working extra hours in the magic store, and killing chickens for rituals every now and then. Doing a lot of legwork. Without pay."

"*That* sucks," I said, because money is almost always a touchy subject with me. Amelia had grown up rich, but I had not. If someone deprives me of income, I get pissed off. I had a fleeting moment of wondering how much Claudine's bank account might have had in it, and I blessed her for thinking of me.

"Yeah, well, Katrina wiped the New Orleans covens out. We lost some members who'll never come back, so we don't get their contributions anymore, and I never use my dad's money for the coven."

"So, the bottom line?" I said.

"I've gotta stay down here. I don't know if I'll ever make it back to Bon Temps. And I'm really sorry about that, because I really liked living with you."

"Same here." I took a deep breath, determined not to sound forlorn. "What about your stuff? Not that there's that much here, but still."

"I'll leave it there for now. I've got everything here I need, and the rest is yours to use as you see fit till I can make arrangements to get it."

We talked a bit more, but we'd said everything important. I forgot to ask her if Octavia had found a way to dissolve Eric's blood bond with me. Possibly I wasn't very interested in an answer. I hung up, feeling both sad and glad: glad that Amelia was working off her debt to her coven and that she was happier than she'd been in Bon Temps after Tray's death, and sad because I understood she didn't expect to return. After a moment of silent farewell to her, I went to the kitchen to tell Claude that the upstairs was all his.

After I'd absorbed his gratified smile, I moved on to another issue. I didn't know how to approach my question, so finally I simply asked him. "Have you been out in my woods back of the house?"

His face went absolutely blank.

"Why would I do that?" he said.

"I didn't ask for your motivation. I asked if you had been there." I know evasion when I hear it.

"No," he said.

"That's bad news."

"Why?"

"Because the Weres tell me a fairy's been back there very recently." I kept my eyes fixed on his. "And if it's not you, who could it be?"

"There aren't many fairies left," Claude said.

Again, evasion. "If there are other fairies that didn't make it in before the portal was shut, you could hang around with them," I said. "You wouldn't need to stay with me, with my little dash of fairy blood. Yet here you are. And somewhere in my woods is yet another fairy." I eyed his expression. "I don't see you excited about tracking down whoever it is. What's the deal? Why don't you dash out there, find the fairy, do some bonding, and be happy?"

Claude looked down. "The last portal to close was in your woods," he said. "Possibly it's not completely shut. And I know Der-

94

mot, your great-uncle, was on the outside. If Dermot is the fairy the Weres sensed, he wouldn't be glad to see me."

I thought he would have more to say, but he stopped right there.

That was plenty of bad news, and another whopping dollop of dodging the issue. I was still dubious about his goals, but Claude was family, and I had precious little family left. "All right," I said, opening a kitchen drawer where I stowed odds and ends. "Here's a key. We'll see how this pans out. I have to go to work this afternoon, by the way. And we have to have a talk. You know that I've got a boyfriend, right?" I was already feeling kind of embarrassed.

"Who are you seeing?" Claude asked, with a sort of professional interest.

"Ah, well . . . Eric Northman."

Claude whistled. He looked both admiring and cautious. "Does Eric spend the night? I need to know if he's going to jump me." Claude looked as though that wouldn't be totally unwelcome. But the pertinent issue was that fairies are really intoxicating to vampires, like catnip to cats. Eric would have a hard time restraining himself from biting if Claude was close to him.

"That would probably end badly for you," I said. "But I think, with a little care, we can get around it." Eric seldom spent the night at my house because he liked to be back in Shreveport before dawn. He had so much work to get through every night that he'd found it was better for him to wake up in Shreveport. I do have a hidden place where a vampire can stay in relative safety, but it's not exactly deluxe, not like Eric's house.

I was a little more concerned about the possibility of Claude bringing strange men back to my house. I didn't want to encounter someone I didn't know when I was on my way to the kitchen in my nightie. Amelia had had a couple of overnight guests, but they'd been people I knew. I took a deep breath, hoping what I was about to say wouldn't come out homophobic. "Claude, it's not that I don't want you to have a good time," I said, wishing this conversation were over and done with. I admired Claude's unblushing acceptance of the fact that I had a sex life, and I only wished I could match that nonchalance.

"If I want to have sex with someone you don't know, I'll take him to my house in Monroe," Claude said, with a wicked little smile. He could be perceptive when he chose, I noted. "Or I'll let you know ahead of time. That okay?"

"Sure," I said, surprised at Claude's easy compliance. But he'd said all the right words. I relaxed some as I showed Claude where strategic kitchen stuff was, gave him some tips on the washer and the dryer, and told him the hall bathroom was all his. Then I led him upstairs. Amelia had worked hard on making one of the little bedrooms pretty, and she'd decorated the other one as a sitting room. She'd taken her laptop with her, but the TV was still there. I checked to make sure that the bed was made up with clean linens and the closet was mostly clear of Amelia's clothing. I pointed out the door to the walk-in attic, in case he needed to store anything. Claude pulled it open and took a step inside. He looked around at the shadowy, crowded space. Generations of Stackhouses had stored things they thought they might need someday, and I admit it was a little on the cluttered and chaotic side.

"You need to go through this," he said. "Do you even know what's up here?"

"Family debris," I said, looking in with some dismay. I'd just never worked up the heart to tackle it since Gran died.

"I'll help you," Claude declared. "That will be my payment to you for my room."

I opened my mouth to point out that Amelia had given me cash, but then I reflected, again, that he was family. "That would be great," I said. "Though I don't know if I'm up to it yet." My wrists had been aching this morning, though they were definitely better than they'd been. "And there are some other jobs around the house that are beyond me, if you wouldn't mind giving a hand."

He bowed. "I would be delighted," he said.

This was a different side of Claude from the one I'd come to know and disparage.

Grief and loneliness seemed to have woken something in the beautiful fairy; he appeared to have come to the realization that he had to show a little kindness to other people if he wanted to receive kindness in return. Claude seemed to understand that he needed others, especially now that his sisters were gone.

I was a little more at ease with our arrangement by the time I left for work. I'd listened to Claude moving around upstairs for a while, and then he'd come down with an armful of hair-care products to arrange in the bathroom. I'd already put out clean towels for him. He seemed satisfied with the bathroom, which was very old-fashioned. But then Claude had been alive in a time before indoor plumbing, so maybe he saw it from a different perspective. Truthfully, hearing someone else in the house had relaxed something deep inside me, a tension I hadn't even known I felt.

"Hey, Sam," I said. He was behind the bar when I came out of the back room, where I'd left my purse and put on an apron. Merlotte's wasn't very busy. Holly, as always, was talking to her Hoyt, who was dawdling over his supper. With her Merlotte's T-shirt, Holly was wearing pink and green plaid shorts instead of the regulation black.

"Looking good, Holly," I called, and she gave me a radiant smile. While Hoyt beamed, Holly held out her hand to show off a brand-new ring.

I let out a shriek and hugged her. "Oh, this is so great!" I said. "Holly, it's so pretty! So, have you picked a date yet?"

"It'll be in the fall, probably," Holly said. "Hoyt has to work long hours through the spring and summer. That's his busy time, so we figured maybe October or November."

"Sookie," Hoyt said, his voice dropping and his face growing solemn. "Now that Jason and I have mended our fences, I'm going to ask him to be my best man."

I glanced very quickly over to Holly, who'd never been a big Jason fan. She was still smiling, and if I could detect the reservations she had, Hoyt couldn't.

I said, "He'll be thrilled."

I had to hustle off to make the rounds of my tables, but I smiled while I worked. I wondered if they'd have the ceremony after dark. Then Eric could go with me. That would be great! That would transform me from "poor Sookie who hasn't even ever been engaged" to "Sookie who brought the gorgeous guy to the wedding." Then I thought of a contingency plan. If the wedding was a daytime wedding, I could get *Claude* to go with me! He looked exactly like a romance cover model. He'd *been* a romance cover model. (Ever read *The Lady and the Stableboy,* or *Lord Darlington's Naughty Marriage*? Woo-hoo!)

I was unhappily aware that I was thinking about the wedding strictly in terms of my own feelings . . . but there's nothing more forlorn than being an old maid at a wedding. I realize that it's silly to feel like you're on the shelf at twenty-seven. But I had missed some prime time, and I was increasingly conscious of that fact. So many of my high school friends had gotten married (some more than once), and some of them were pregnant — like Tara, who was coming through the door in an oversized T-shirt.

I gave a wave to let her know I'd come

talk to her when I could, and I got an iced tea for Dr. Linda Tonnesen and a Michelob for Jesse Wayne Cummins.

"What's up, Tara?" I bent over to give her a neck hug. She had plunked herself down at a table.

"I need some caffeine-free Diet Coke," she said. "And I need a cheeseburger. With lots of French-fried pickles." She looked ferocious.

"Sure," I said. "I'll get the Coke and put in your order right now."

When I returned, she drank the whole glass. "I'll be sorry in five minutes because I'll have to go to the bathroom," she said. "All I do is pee and eat." Tara had big rings under her eyes, and her complexion was not at its best. Where was the glow of pregnancy that I'd heard so much about?

"How much longer do you have to go?"

"Three months, a week, and three days."

"Dr. Dinwiddie gave you a due date!"

"JB just can't *believe* how big I'm getting," Tara said, with an eye roll.

"He said that? In those words?"

"Yep. Yes. He did."

"Geez Louise. That boy needs a lesson or two in rephrasing."

"I'd settle for him keeping his mouth shut entirely."

Tara had married JB knowing brains weren't his strong suit, and she was reaping the result, but I *so* wanted them to be happy. I couldn't be all, "You made your bed, now you gotta lie in it."

"He loves you," I said, trying to sound soothing. "He's just . . ."

"JB," she said. She shrugged and summoned up a smile.

Then Antoine called that my order was up, and the avid expression on Tara's face told me that she was more focused on the food than on her husband's tactlessness. She returned to Tara's Togs a happier and fuller woman.

As soon as it was dark, I called Eric on my cell while I was in the ladies' room. I hated to sneak off on Sam's time to call my boyfriend, but I needed the support. Now that I had his cell number, I didn't have to call Fangtasia, which was both bad and good. I'd never known who was going to answer the phone, and I'm not a universal favorite among Eric's vampires. On the other hand, I missed talking to Pam, Eric's second-in-command. Pam and I are actually almost friends.

"I am here, my lover," Eric said. It was hard not to shiver when I heard his voice, but the atmosphere of the ladies' room in

Merlotte's was not at all conducive to lust.

"Well, I'm here, too, obviously. Listen, I really need to talk to you," I said. "Some things have come up."

"You're worried."

"Yes. With good reason."

"I have a meeting in thirty minutes with Victor," Eric said. "You know how tense that's likely to be."

"I do know. And I'm sorry to pester you with my problems. But you're my boyfriend, and part of being a good boyfriend is listening."

"Your boyfriend," he said. "That sounds . . . strange. I am so *not* a boy."

"Foof, Eric!" I was exasperated. "I don't want to stand here in the bathroom trying to talk terminology! What's the bottom line? Are you going to have free time later or not?"

He laughed. "Yes, for you. Can you drive over here? Wait, I'll send Pam for you. She'll be at your house at one o'clock, all right?"

I might have to hurry to get home by then, but it was doable. "Okay. And warn Pam that . . . Well, tell her not to get carried away by anything, hear?"

"Oh, certainly, I'll be glad to pass that very specific message along," Eric said. He hung up. Not big on saying good-bye, like most vampires.

This was going to be a very long day.

CHAPTER 3

Luckily for me, all the customers cleared out early, and I was able to get my closing work done in record time. I called, "Good night!" over my shoulder and hared out the back door to my car. When I parked behind the house, I noticed Claude's car wasn't there. So he was probably still in Monroe, which simplified matters. I hurried to change clothes and freshen my makeup, and just as I put on some lipstick, Pam knocked at the back door.

Pam was looking especially Pammish tonight. Her blond hair was absolutely straight and shining, her pale blue suit looked like a vintage gem, and she was wearing hose with seams up the back, which she turned around to show me.

"Wow," I said, which was the only possible response. "You're looking great." She put my red skirt and red and white blouse to shame.

"Yes," she said with considerable satisfaction. "I am. Ah . . ." She became utterly still. "Do I smell fairy?"

"You do, but there's not one here now, so just rein it in. My cousin Claude was here today. He's going to be bunking with me for a while."

"Claude, the mouthwateringly beautiful asshole?"

Claude's fame preceded him. "Yes, that Claude."

"Why? Why is he staying with you?"

"He's lonely," I said.

"Do you really believe that?" Pam's pale brows were arched incredulously.

"Well . . . yes, I do." Why else would Claude want to stay at my house, which was not convenient to his job? He certainly didn't want to get in my pants, and he hadn't asked to borrow money.

"This is some fairy intrigue," Pam said. "You were a fool to be taken in."

Nobody likes being called a fool. Pam had stepped over the line, but then "tact" was not her middle name. "Pam, that's enough," I said. I must have sounded serious, because she stared at me for all of fifteen seconds.

"I've offended you," she said, though not as if the idea gave her pain.

"Yeah, you have. Claude's missing his

sisters. There aren't any fairies left for him to intrigue with since Niall closed the portal, or doors, or whatever the heck he closed. I'm the closest Claude's got to his kind — which is pretty pitiful, since I just have a dab of fairy in me."

"Let's go," Pam said. "Eric will be waiting."

Changing the subject when she had nothing left to say was another of Pam's characteristics. I had to smile and shake my head. "How'd the meeting with Victor go?" I asked.

"It would be a good thing if Victor met with an unfortunate accident."

"You really mean that?"

"No. I really wish someone would kill him."

"Me, too." Our eyes met, and she gave me a brisk nod. We were in synch on the Victor issue.

"I suspect his every statement," she said. "I question his every decision. I think he's out to take Eric's position. He doesn't want to be the king's emissary any longer. He wants to carve out his own territory."

I pictured a fur-clad Victor paddling a canoe down the Red River with an Indian maiden sitting stoically behind him. I laughed. As we got into Pam's car, she

107

looked at me darkly.

"I don't understand you," she said. "I really don't." We went out to Hummingbird Road and turned north.

"Why would being a sheriff in Louisiana be a step above being the emissary of Felipe, who has a rich kingdom?" I asked very seriously, to make up my lost ground.

" 'Better to reign in hell than serve in heaven,' " Pam said. I knew she was quoting someone, but I didn't have a clue who it was.

"Louisiana is hell? *Las Vegas* is heaven?" I could almost believe some cosmopolitan vampire would consider Louisiana as less than desirable as a permanent residence, but Las Vegas — divine? I didn't think so.

"I'm just saying." Pam shrugged. "It's time for Victor to get out from under Felipe's thumb. They've been together a long time. Victor is ambitious."

"That's true. What do you think Victor's strategy is? How do you think he plans to dislodge Eric?"

"He'll try to discredit him," Pam said, without pausing a beat. She'd really been thinking about this. "If Victor can't do that, he'll try to kill Eric — but he won't do it directly, in combat."

"He's scared of fighting Eric?"

"Yes," Pam said, smiling. "I do believe he is." We'd reached the interstate and were on our way west to Shreveport. "If he challenged Eric, it would be Eric's right to send me in first. I would so love to fight Victor." Her fangs gleamed briefly in the dashboard light.

"Does Victor have a second? Wouldn't he send that second in?"

Pam cocked her head to one side. She seemed to be thinking about it as she passed a semi. "His second is Bruno Brazell. He was with Victor the night Eric surrendered to Nevada," she said. "Short beard, an earring? If Eric allowed me to fight for him, Victor might send in Bruno. He's impressive, I grant you. But I would kill him in five minutes or less. You can put money on that."

Pam, who had been a Victorian middle-class young lady with a secret wild streak, had been liberated by becoming a vampire. I had never asked Eric why he'd chosen Pam for the change, but I was convinced it was because Eric had detected her inner ferocity.

On an impulse, I said, "Pam? Do you ever wonder what would have happened to you if you hadn't met up with Eric?"

There was a long silence, or at least it

seemed long to me. I wondered if she was angry or sad about her lost chance for a husband and children. I wondered if she was looking back with longing on her sexual relationship with her maker, Eric, which (like most vampire-vampire relationships) hadn't lasted long, but had surely been very intense.

Finally, just when I was going to apologize for asking, Pam said, "I think I was born for this." The faint light from the dashboard illuminated her perfectly symmetrical face. "I would have been a dismal wife, a terrible mother. The part of me that has taken to slashing the throats of my enemies would have surfaced if I'd remained human. I wouldn't have killed anyone, I suppose, because that wasn't on my list of things *I could do,* when I was human. But I would have made my family very miserable; you can be sure of that."

"You're a great vampire," I said, since I couldn't think of anything else to say.

She nodded. "Yes. I am."

We didn't speak again until we reached Eric's house. Oddly enough, he'd bought a place in a gated community with a strict building code. Eric liked the daytime security of the gate and the guard. And he liked the fieldstone house. There weren't too many basements in Shreveport, because the water level was too high, but Eric's house was on a slope. Originally, its downstairs was a walk-in from the back patio. Eric had had that door pulled out and the wall made solid, so he had a great place to sleep.

Until we'd become blood bonded, I'd never been to Eric's house.

Sometimes it was exciting being so closely yoked with Eric, and sometimes it made me feel trapped. Though I could scarcely believe it, the sex was even better now that I'd recovered, at least in large part, from the attack. At this moment, I felt like every molecule in my body was humming because I was near him.

Pam had a garage-door opener, and she pressed it now. The door swung up to reveal Eric's car. Other than the gleaming Corvette, the garage was spotless: no lawn chairs, no bags of grass seed or half-empty paint cans. No stepladder, or coveralls, or hunting boots. Eric didn't need any of those accoutrements. The neighborhood had lawns, pretty lawns, with rigidly planted and mulched flower beds — but a lawn-care service trimmed every blade of grass there, pruned every bush, raked every leaf.

Pam got a kick out of closing the garage

door once we were inside. The kitchen door was locked, and she used a key so we could pass from the garage into the kitchen. A kitchen is largely useless to a vampire, though a little refrigerator is necessary for the synthetic blood, and a microwave is handy to heat it to room temperature. Eric had bought a coffeemaker for me, and he kept some food in the freezer for whatever human was in the house. Lately, that human had been me.

"Eric!" I called, when we came through the door. Pam and I took off our shoes, which was one of Eric's house rules.

"Oh, go get your greeting over with!" Pam said, when I looked at her. "I've got some TrueBlood and some Life Support to put away."

I passed from the sterile kitchen into the living room. The kitchen colors were bland, but the living room echoed Eric's personality. Though it wasn't often reflected in his clothing, Eric harbored a love of deep colors. The first time I'd been to his house, the living room had surprised the hell out of me. The walls were a sapphire blue, the crown molding and baseboards a pure, gleaming white. The furniture was an eclectic collection of pieces that had appealed to him, all upholstered in jewel tones, some intricately patterned — deep red, blue, the yellow of citrine, the greens of jade and emerald, the gold of topaz. Since Eric is a big man, all the pieces were big: heavy, sturdy, and strewn with pillows.

Eric came out of the doorway to his home office. When I saw him, every hormone I had stood to attention. He's very tall, his hair is long and golden, and his eyes are so blue the color practically pops out of the whiteness of his face, a face that is bold and masculine. There's nothing epicene about Eric. He wears jeans and T-shirts, mostly, but I've seen him in a suit. *GQ* missed a good thing when Eric decided his talents lay in building a business empire rather than modeling. Tonight he was shirtless, sparse dark gold hair trailing down to the waist of his jeans and gleaming against his pallor.

"Jump," Eric said, holding out his hands and smiling. I laughed. I took a running start, and leaped. Eric caught me, his hands clamped around my waist. He lifted me up until my head touched the ceiling. Then he lowered me for a kiss. I wrapped my legs around his torso, my arms around his neck. We were lost in each other for a long moment.

Pam said, "Back to earth, monkey girl. Time is passing."

I noted that she was blaming me and not Eric. I pulled away and gave him a special smile.

"Come, sit, and tell me what's wrong," he said. "Do you want Pam to know, too?"

"Yes," I said. I figured he'd tell her anyway.

The two vampires sat at opposite ends of the dark red couch, and I sat across from them on the gold and red love seat. In front of the couch was a very large square coffee table with inlaid woodwork on the top and elaborately carved legs. The table was scattered with things Eric had been enjoying recently: the manuscript of a book about the Vikings that he'd been asked to endorse, a heavy jade cigarette lighter (though he didn't smoke), and a beautiful silver bowl with a deep blue enamel interior. I always found his selections interesting. My own house was kind of . . . cumulative. In fact, I hadn't picked out anything in it but the kitchen cabinets and appliances — but my house was the history of my family. Eric's house was the history of Eric.

I brushed a finger across the inlaid wood. "Day before yesterday," I began, "I got a call from Alcide Herveaux."

I wasn't imagining that the two vampires had a reaction to my news. It was minute (most vampires aren't given to extravagant expressions), but it was definitely there. Eric leaned forward, inviting me to continue my account. I did, telling them that I'd also met some of the new additions to the Long Tooth pack, including Basim and Annabelle.

"I've seen this Basim," Pam said. I looked at her with some surprise. "He came to Fangtasia one night with another Were, another new one . . . that Annabelle, the brown-haired woman. She's Alcide's new . . . squeeze."

Though I'd suspected as much, it was still a little astonishing to me. "She must have hidden assets," I said, before I thought.

Eric raised an eyebrow. "Not what you thought Alcide would pick, my lover?"

"I liked Maria-Star," I said. Like so many other people I'd met in the past two years, Alcide's previous girlfriend had met an awful end. I'd grieved for her.

"But before that, he had long associated with Debbie Pelt," Eric said, and I had to struggle to control my face. "You can see that Alcide's catholic in his pleasures," Eric continued. "He carried the torch for you, didn't he?" Eric's slight accent made the outmoded phrase sound exotic. "From a true bitch, to a startling talent, to a sweet photographer, to a tough girl who doesn't mind visiting a vampire bar. Alcide has very variable taste in women."

That was true. I'd never put it together before.

"He sent Annabelle and Basim to the club for a purpose. Have you been reading the newspapers lately?" Pam asked.

"No," I said. "I've been enjoying *not* reading the papers."

"Congress is thinking of passing a bill requiring all the werewolves and shifters to register. Legislation and issues regarding them would then fall under the Bureau of Vampire Affairs, as laws and lawsuits pertaining to us, the undead, do now." Pam was looking very grim.

I almost said, "But that's not *right!*" Then I understood how that would sound — as if I thought it was okay to require the vampires to register, but Weres and shifters shouldn't have to. Thank God I didn't open my mouth.

"Not too surprisingly, the Weres are furious about this. In fact, Alcide has told me himself that he thinks the government has sent people to spy on his pack, the idea being that they would then give some kind of secret report to the people in Congress who are considering this bill. He doesn't believe it's only his pack that's being singled out. Alcide has good sense." Eric sounded approving. "But he believes he's being watched."

Now I understood why Alcide had been so concerned about the people camping on his land. He'd suspected they weren't what they appeared to be.

"It would be awful to think your own government was spying on you," I said. "Especially after you'd been thinking of yourself as a regular citizen your entire life." The enormity of the impact of this piece of legislation was still sinking in. Instead of being a respected and wealthy citizen in Shreveport, Alcide (and the other members of his pack) would become like . . . illegal aliens. "Where would they have to register? Could the kids still go to school with all the other children? What about the men and women at Barksdale Air Force Base? After all these years! Do you think the bill really has a chance of passing?"

Pam said, "The Weres believe it does. Maybe it's paranoia. Maybe they've heard something through the members of Congress who are two-natured. Maybe they know something we don't know. Alcide sent this Annabelle and Basim al Saud to tell me they might be in the same boat with us soon. They wanted to know about the area representative for the BVA, what kind of woman she is, how they could deal with her."

"Who is the rep?" I asked. I felt ignorant and ill-informed. Obviously I should have known this, since I was intimately involved with a vampire.

"Katherine Boudreaux," Pam said. "She likes women somewhat more than men, like I do." Pam grinned a toothy grin. "She also loves dogs. She has a steady lover, Sallie, who shares her house. Katherine is not interested in having a side affair, and she is unbribable."

"You've tried, I take it."

"I tried to interest her sexually. Bobby Burnham tried the bribe." Bobby was Eric's daytime man. We disliked each other intensely.

I took a deep breath. "Well, I'm real glad to know all this, but my real problem came after the Weres used my land."

Eric and Pam were looking at me sharply and with great attention, all of a sudden. "You let the Weres use your property for their monthly run?"

"Well, yeah. Hamilton Bond said there were people camping out on the Herveaux land, and now that I've heard what Alcide's told you — and I'm wondering why he didn't tell me all this — I can see why he didn't want to have a run on his own land. I guess he thought the campers were government agents. What would the new agency be called?" I asked. It wouldn't be BVA, would it? If the BVA was still only "representing" vampires.

Pam shrugged. "The legislation going through Congress proposes it be called the Bureau of Vampire and Supernatural Affairs."

"Get back to your issues, my lover," Eric said.

"Okeydokey. Well, when they were leaving, Basim came to the front door and told me he'd smelled at least one fairy and some other vampire traveling through my land. And my cousin Claude says he wasn't the fairy."

There was a moment of silence.

"Interesting," Eric said.

"Very odd," Pam said.

Eric ran his fingers over the manuscript on the coffee table as if it could tell him who'd been traipsing around my property. "I don't know the credentials of this Basim, except that he was thrown out of the pack in Houston and Alcide took him in. I don't know why he was expelled. I expect it was for some disruption. We'll check on what Basim told you." He turned to Pam. "That new girl, Heidi, says she's a tracker."

"You got a new vamp?" I asked.

"This is one sent us by Victor." Eric's mouth was set in a grim line. "Even from New Orleans, supposedly, Victor is running the state with a tight hand. He sent Sandy, who was supposed to be the liaison, back to Nevada. I suspect Victor thought he didn't have enough control over her."

"How can he get New Orleans up and running if he travels around the state as much as Sandy did?"

"I'm assuming he's leaving Bruno Brazell in charge," Pam said. "I think Bruno pretends Victor is in New Orleans, even when Victor isn't. The rest of Victor's people don't know where he is half the time. Since he killed off all the New Orleans vampires he could find, we've had to rely on the information of our one spy who survived the massacre."

Of course I wanted to veer off and discuss the spy — who would be that brave and reckless, to spy for Eric in the bailiwick of his enemy? But I had to stick to the main subject, which was the sneakiness of Louisiana's new regent head honcho. "So Victor likes to be in the trenches," I said, and Eric and Pam looked at me blankly. Older vampires don't always have a complete grasp of

120

the vernacular. "He likes to see for himself and do for himself, rather than rely on the chain of command," I explained.

"Yes," Pam said. "And the chain of command can be quite heavy and literal, under Victor."

"Pam and I were talking about Victor on the drive over here. I wonder why Felipe de Castro chose Victor to be his representative in Louisiana?" Victor had actually seemed okay the two times I'd met him face-to-face, which only went to show that you can't judge a vampire by his good manners and his smile.

"There are two schools of thought about that," Eric said, stretching his long legs out in front of him. I had a flash of how those long legs looked spread wide on crumpled sheets, and I forced my mind back to the current subject of discussion.

Eric gave me a fangy smile (he knew what I was feeling) before he continued. "One is that Felipe wants Victor as far away as he can get him. I believe that Felipe feels that if he gives Victor a big chunk of red meat, he won't be tempted to try to snatch the whole steak."

"While others of us," Pam said, "think that Felipe simply appointed Victor because Victor is very efficient. That Victor's devotion to Felipe is possibly sincere."

"If the first theory is correct," Eric said, "there isn't perfect trust between Felipe and Victor."

"If the second theory is correct," Pam said, "and we act against Victor, Felipe will kill us all."

"I'm getting your drift," I said, looking from First Theory (shirtless with blue jeans) to Second Theory (cute vintage suit). "I hate to sound really selfish, but the first thought that popped into my mind is this. Since Victor wouldn't let you come to help me when I needed you — and incidentally I know that I owe you big-time, Pam — that means Victor's not honoring the promise, huh? Felipe promised me that he would extend his protection to me, which he ought to have, because I saved his life, right?"

There was a significant pause while Eric and Pam considered my question.

"I think Victor will do his best not to openly cause you harm, until and if he decides to try to become king in his own right," Pam said. "If Victor decides to make a grab for the kingship, all promises made by Felipe are so many words without meaning." Eric nodded in agreement.

"That's just great." I probably sounded petulant and selfish, because that was the way I felt.

"This is all assuming we don't find a way to kill him first," Pam said quietly. And we were all silent for a long moment. There was something that creeped me out, no matter how much I agreed that Victor should die, about the three of us talking about murdering him.

"And you think this Heidi, who's supposed to be such a great tracker, is here in Shreveport to be Victor's eyes and ears?" I said briskly, trying to throw off the chill that had fallen on me.

"Yes," said Pam. "Unless she's here to be Felipe's eyes and ears, so Felipe can keep track of what Victor is doing in Louisiana." She had that ominous look on her face, the one that said she was going to get her vampire game on. You did not want Pam to look that way when your name entered the conversation. If I were Heidi, I would take care to keep my nose clean.

"Heidi," which conjured up braids and full skirts in my imagination, seemed like a very perky name for a vampire.

"So what should I do about the Long Tooth pack's warning?" I said, to bring the discussion back to the original problem. "You're going to send Heidi to my place to try to track the fairy? I have to tell you something else. Basim scented a body, not a fresh one, buried very deep at the back of my property."

"Oh," Eric said. "Whoops." Eric turned to Pam. "Give us some alone time."

She nodded and went out through the kitchen. I heard the back door shut.

Eric said, "I'm sorry, my lover. Unless you've buried someone else on your property and kept it from me, that body is Debbie Pelt's."

That was what I'd been afraid of. "Is the car back there, too?"

"No, the car is sunk in a pond about ten miles south of your place."

That was a relief. "Well, at least it was a werewolf who found it," I said. "I guess we don't have to worry about it, unless Alcide can identify her scent. They won't go digging the body up. It's none of their doings." Debbie had been Alcide's ex-girlfriend when I'd had the misfortune to meet her. I don't want to drag out the story, but she'd tried to kill me first. It took me a while, but I'm over the angst of her death. Eric had been with me that night, but he hadn't been in his right mind. And that's yet another story.

"Come here," Eric said. His face held my very favorite expression, and I was doubly glad to see it because I didn't want to think too much about Debbie Pelt.

"Hmmm. What will you give me if I do?" I gave him a questioning eye.

"I think you know very well what I will give you. I think you love me to give it to you."

"So . . . you don't enjoy it at all?"

Before I could blink he was on his knees in front of me, pushing my legs apart, leaning in to kiss me. "I think you know how I feel," he said, in a whisper. "We are bonded. Can you believe I'm not thinking of you while I work? When my eyes open, I think of you, of every part of you." His fingers got busy, and I gasped. This was direct, even for Eric. "Do you love me?" he asked, his eyes fixing mine.

This was a little difficult to answer, especially considering what his fingers were doing. "I love being with you, whether we're having sex or not. Oh, God, do that again! I love your body. I love what we do together. You make me laugh, and I love that. I like to watch you do anything." I kissed him, long and lingeringly. "I like to watch you get dressed. I like to watch you undress. I like to watch your hands when you're doing this to me. *Oh!*" I shuddered all over with pleasure. When I'd had a moment of recovery, I murmured, "If I asked you the same question, what would your answer be?"

"I would say exactly the same thing," Eric said. "And I think that means I love you. If this is not true love, it's as close as anyone gets. Can you see what you've done to me?" He didn't really have to point. It was pretty damn obvious.

"That looks painful. Would you like me to nurse it?" I asked, in the coolest voice I could manage.

In reply, he simply growled. We switched places in an instant. I knelt in front of Eric, and his hands rested on my head, stroking. Eric was a sizable guy, and this was a part of our sex life that I'd had to work on. But I thought I was getting pretty good at it, and he seemed to agree. His hands tightened in my hair after a minute or two, and I made a little noise of protest. He let go and gripped the couch instead. He growled, deep in his throat. "Faster," he said. "Now, now!" He shut his eyes and his head fell back, his hands opening and closing spasmodically. I loved having that power over him; that was another thing I loved. Suddenly, he said something in an ancient language, and his back arched, and I moved with increased purpose, swallowing down everything he gave me.

And all this with most of our clothes on. "Was that enough love for you?" he asked, his voice slow and dreamy.

I climbed into his lap and wound my arms around his neck for an interlude of cuddling. Now that I had recovered my pleasure in sex, I felt limp as a dishrag after a session with Eric; but this was my favorite part, though it made me feel very "women's magazine" to admit it.

As we sat holding each other, Eric told me about a conversation he'd had with a fangbanger at the bar, and we laughed about it. I told him about how torn up Hummingbird Road was while the parish was patching it. I suppose this is the kind of thing you talk about with someone you love; you figure they'll care about trivial topics, since those things are important to you.

Unfortunately, I knew that Eric had more business to get through that night, so I told him I'd go back to Bon Temps with Pam. Sometimes I stayed at his place, reading while he worked. It's not easy to arrange alone time with a leader and businessman who's awake only during the hours of darkness.

He gave me a kiss to remember him by. "I'll send Heidi to you, probably night after next," he said. "She'll verify what Basim

127

says he smelled in the woods. Let me know if you hear from Alcide."

When Pam and I left Eric's house, it had started raining. The rain put a little chill in the air, and I turned the heat on low in Pam's car. It wouldn't make any difference to her. We drove for a while in silence, each lost in our own thoughts. I watched the windshield wipers fan back and forth.

Pam said, "You didn't tell Eric about the fairy staying with you."

"Oh, gosh!" I put my hand over my eyes. "No, I didn't. There was so much else to talk about, I completely forgot."

"You realize Eric won't like another man living in the same house with his woman."

"Another man who is my cousin and also gay."

"But very beautiful and a stripper." Pam glanced over at me. She was smiling. Pam's smiles are somewhat disconcerting.

"You can strip all you want to — if you don't like the person you're looking at while you're naked, it's not going to happen," I said tartly.

"I kind of understand that sentence," she said, after a moment. "But still, having such an attractive man in the same house . . . It's not good, Sookie."

"You're kidding me, right? Claude is *gay.*

Not only does he like men, he likes men with beard stubble and oil stains on their blue jeans."

"What does that mean?" Pam said.

"That means he likes blue-collar guys who work with their hands. Or their fists."

"Oh. Interesting." Pam still had an air of disapproval. She hesitated for a moment, then said, "Eric hasn't had anyone like you in a long, long time, Sookie. I think he's levelheaded enough to keep on course, but you have to consider his responsibilities. This is a perilous time for the few of us in his original crew remaining since Sophie-Anne met her final death. We Shreveport vampires doubly belong to Eric, since he's the only surviving sheriff from the old regime. If Eric goes down, we all go down. If Victor succeeds in discrediting Eric or somehow eating into his base here in Shreveport, we'll all die."

I hadn't put the situation to myself in terms that dire. Eric hadn't spelled it out to me, either. "It's that bad?" I said, feeling numb.

"He is male enough to want to look strong in front of you, Sookie. Truly, Eric's a great vampire, and very practical. But he isn't practical nowadays — not when it comes to you."

"Are you saying you don't think Eric and I should see each other anymore?" I asked her directly. Though generally I was very glad that vampire minds were closed to me, sometimes I found it frustrating. I was used to knowing more than I wanted to know about how people were thinking and feeling, rather than wondering if I was right.

"No, not exactly." Pam looked thoughtful. "I would hate to see him unhappy. And you, too," she added, as an afterthought. "But if he's worried about you, he won't react the same as he would — as he should . . ."

"If I weren't in the picture."

Pam didn't say anything for a while. Then she said, "I think the only reason Victor hasn't abducted you to hold you over Eric is because Eric married you. Victor's still trying to cover his ass by doing everything by the book. He isn't ready to rebel against Felipe openly. He'll still try to show justification for whatever he does. He's walking on thin ice with Felipe right now because he almost let you get killed."

"Maybe Felipe will do the job for us," I said.

Pam looked thoughtful. "That would be ideal," she said. "But we'll have to wait for it. Felipe's not going to do anything rash when it comes to killing a lieutenant of his.

That would make his other lieutenants uneasy and uncertain."

I shook my head. "That's too bad. I don't think it would bother Felipe very much at all to kill Victor."

"And it would bother you, Sookie?"

"Yes. It would bother me." Though not as much as it ought to.

"So if you could do it in a rush of rage when Victor was attacking you, that would be far preferable to planning a way to kill him when he couldn't fight back effectively?"

Okay, put like that my attitude didn't make much sense. I could see that if you were willing to kill someone, planning to kill someone, wishing someone would die, quibbling about the circumstances was ridiculous.

"It shouldn't make a difference," I said quietly. "But it does. Victor has to go, though."

"You've changed," Pam said, after a little silence. She didn't sound surprised or horrified or disgusted. For that matter, she didn't sound happy. It was more as though she'd realized I'd altered my hairstyle.

"Yes," I said. We watched the rain pour down some more.

Suddenly, Pam said, "Look!" There was a

131

sleek white car parked on the shoulder of the interstate. I didn't understand why Pam was so agitated until I noticed that the man leaning against the car had his arms crossed over his chest in an attitude of total nonchalance, despite the rain.

As we drew abreast of the car, a Lexus, the figure waved a languid hand at us. We were being flagged down.

"Shit," Pam said. "That's Bruno Brazell. We have to stop." She pulled over to the shoulder and stopped in front of the car. "And Corinna," she said, sounding bitter. I glanced in the side mirror to see that a woman had gotten out of the Lexus.

"They're here to kill us," Pam said quietly. "I can't kill them both. You have to help."

"They're going to try to kill us?" I was really, really scared.

"That's the only reason I can think of that Victor would send two people on a one-person errand," she said. She sounded calm. Pam was obviously thinking much faster than I was. "Showtime! If the peace can be kept, we need to keep it, at least for now. Here." She pressed something into my hand. "Take it out of the sheath. It's a silver dagger."

I remembered Bill's gray skin and the slow way he moved after silver poisoning. I shud-

132

dered, but I was angry with myself for my squeamishness. I slid the dagger from the leather sheath.

"We have to get out, huh?" I said. I tried to smile. "Okay, showtime."

"Sookie, be brave and ruthless," Pam said, and she opened her door and disappeared from sight. I sent a last waft of love toward Eric by way of good-bye while I was sticking the dagger through my skirt's waistband at the back. I got out of the car into the pelting darkness, holding my hands out to show they were empty.

I was drenched in seconds. I shoved my hair behind my ears so it wouldn't hang in my eyes. Though the Lexus's headlights were on, it was very dark. The only other light came from oncoming headlights from both sides of the interstate, and the brightly lit truck stop a mile away. Otherwise, we were nowhere, an anonymous stretch of divided interstate with woods on either side. The vampires could see a lot better than I could. But I knew where everyone was because I cast out that other sense of mine and felt for their brains. Vampires register as holes to me, almost black spots in the atmosphere. It's negative tracking.

No one spoke, and the only noise was the pelting of the rain drumming on the cars. I couldn't hear an oncoming vehicle. "Hi, Bruno," I called, and I sounded perky in a crazy way. "Who's your buddy?"

I walked over to him. Across the median, a car whizzed by going west. If the driver caught a glimpse of us, it probably looked as though two Good Samaritans had stopped to help some people with car trouble. Humans see what they want to see . . . what they expect to see.

Now that I was closer to Bruno, I could tell that his short brown hair was plastered to his head. I'd seen Bruno only once before, and he was wearing the same serious expression on his face that he'd worn the night he'd been standing in my front yard ready to move in and burn down my house with me in it. Bruno was a serious kind of guy in the same way I'm a perky kind of woman. It was a fallback position.

"Hello, Miss Stackhouse," Bruno said. He wasn't any taller than me, but he was a burly man. The vampire Pam had called Corinna loomed up on Bruno's right. Corinna was — had been — African-American, and the water was dripping off the tips of her intricately braided hair. The beads worked into the braids clicked together, a sound I could just pick up under the drumming of the rain. She was thin and tall, and she'd added to her height with three-inch heels. Though she was wearing a dress that had probably been very expensive, her whole ensemble had suffered by the drenching it had taken. She looked like a very elegant drowned rat.

Since I was almost out of my head with alarm anyway, I started laughing.

"You got a flat tire or something, Bruno?" I asked. "I can't imagine what else you'd be doing out here in the middle of nowhere in the pouring rain."

"I was waiting for you, bitch."

I wasn't sure where Pam was, and I couldn't spare the brainpower to search for her. "Language, Bruno! I don't think you know me well enough to call me that. I guess you-all have someone watching Eric's house."

"We do. When we saw you two leaving together, it seemed like a good time to take care of a few things."

Corinna hadn't spoken still, but she was looking around her warily, and I realized she didn't know where Pam had gone. I grinned. "For the life of me, I don't know why you're doing all this. It seems like Victor should be glad to have someone as smart as Eric working for him. Why can't he appreciate that?" *And leave us alone.*

Bruno took a step closer to me. The light was too poor for me to make out his eye color, but I could tell he was still looking serious. I thought it was strange when Bruno took the time to answer me, but anything that bought us more time was good. "Eric is a great vampire. But Eric will never bow to Victor, not really. And he's accumulating his own power at a pace that makes Victor anxious. He's got you, for one thing. Your great-grandfather may have sealed himself away, but who's to say he won't come back? And Eric can use your stupid ability whenever he chooses. Victor doesn't want Eric to have that advantage." And then Bruno had his hands around my neck. He'd moved so quickly I couldn't possibly react, and I knew vaguely over the pounding in my ears that there was a sudden and violent commotion going on to my left. I reached behind me to pull the knife, but we were suddenly down in the tall, wet grass at the edge of the shoulder, and I kicked my leg up and over, and pushed, trying to get on top. I kind of overdid it, because we began rolling down into the drainage ditch. That was a pity, because it was filling with water. Bruno couldn't drown, but I sure could. Wrenching my shoulder with the force of my effort, I

136

yanked the knife out of my skirt when I rotated to the top, and as we rolled yet again I saw dark spots in front of my eyes. I knew this was my last chance. I stabbed Bruno up under his ribs.

And I killed him.

CHAPTER 4

Pam yanked Bruno's body off me and rolled him all the way down into the water coursing through the ditch. She helped me up.

"Where were you?" I croaked.

"Disposing of Corinna," literal-minded Pam said. She pointed to the body lying by the white car. Fortunately, the corpse was on the side of the car concealed from the view of the rare passerby. In the poor light it was hard to be sure, but I believed Corinna was already beginning to flake away. I'd never seen a dead vampire in the rain before.

"I thought Bruno was such a great fighter. How come *you* didn't take him on?"

"I gave you the knife," Pam said, giving a good imitation of surprise. "He didn't have a knife."

"Right." I coughed and, boy, did that hurt my throat. "So what do we do now?"

"We're getting out of here," Pam said.

"We're going to hope that no one noticed my car. I think only three cars passed since we pulled over. With the rain and poor visibility, if the drivers were human, we have a very good chance that none of them will remember seeing us."

By then we were back in Pam's car. "Wouldn't it be better if we moved the Lexus?" I said, wheezing out the words.

"What a good idea," Pam said, patting me on the head. "Do you think you can drive it?"

"Where to?"

Pam thought for a moment, which was good, because I needed the recovery time. I was soaked through and shivering, and I felt awful.

"Won't Victor know what's happened?" I asked. I couldn't seem to stop asking questions.

"Maybe. He wasn't brave enough to do this himself, so he has to take the consequences. He's lost his two best people, and he has nothing to show for it." Pam was enjoying the hell out of that.

"I think we get out of here right now. Before some more of his people come to check, or whatever." I sure wasn't up for fighting again.

"It's you who keeps asking questions. I

think Eric will be here soon; I'd better call him to tell him to stay away," Pam said. She looked faintly worried.

"Why?" I would have loved to have Eric appear to take charge of this situation, frankly.

"If someone is watching his house, and he leaps into his car and drives in this direction to come rescue you, it'll be a pretty clear indication that we're responsible for what happened to Bruno and Corinna," Pam said, clearly exasperated. "Use your brain, Sookie!"

"My brain is all soggy," I said, and if I sounded a little testy, I don't think that's any big, amazing thing. But Pam was already hitting a speed-dial number on her cell. I could hear Eric yelling when he answered the phone.

Pam said, "Shut up and I'll explain. Of course, she lives." There was silence.

Pam summed up the situation in a few pithy phrases, and she concluded with, "Go somewhere it's reasonable to be going in a hurry. Back to the bar in answer to some crisis. To the all-night dry cleaners to pick up your suits. To the store to pick up some TrueBlood. Don't lead them here."

After a squawk or two, Eric apparently saw the sense in what Pam was saying. I couldn't hear his voice clearly, though he was still talking to her.

"Her throat will be bruised," Pam said impatiently. "Yes, she killed Bruno herself. All right, I'll tell her." Pam turned to me. "He's proud of you," she said with some disgust.

"Pam gave me the knife," I croaked. I knew he could hear me.

"But it was Sookie's idea to move the car," Pam said, with the air of someone who's going to be fair if it kills her. "I'm trying to think of where to put it. The truck stops will have security cameras. I think we'll leave it on the shoulder well past the Bon Temps exit."

That's what we did. Pam had some towels in her trunk, and I put them down on the seat of Bruno's car. Pam poked around in his ashes to retrieve the Lexus key, and after looking over the instrument panel, I figured I could drive it. I followed Pam for forty minutes, staring longingly at the Bon Temps sign as we sped past it. I pulled over to the shoulder right after Pam did. Following Pam's instructions, I left the key in the car, wiped off the steering wheel with the towels (which were damp from their contact with me), and then scuttled to Pam's car and climbed in. It was still raining, by the way.

Then we had to return to my house. By then I was aching in every joint and a little sick to my stomach. Finally, finally, we pulled up to my back door. To my amazement, Pam leaned over to give me a hug. "You did very well," she said. "You did what had to be done." For once, she didn't look as if she were secretly laughing at me.

"I hope this all turns out to be worth it," I said, sounding as gloomy and exhausted as I felt.

"We're still alive, so it was worth it," Pam said.

I couldn't argue with that, though something within me wanted to.

I climbed out of her car and trudged across the dripping backyard. The rain had finally stopped.

Claude opened the back door as I reached it. He had opened his mouth to say something, but when he took in my condition, he closed it again. He shut the door behind me, and I heard him lock it.

"I'm going to shower," I said, "and then I'm going to bed. Good night, Claude."

"Good night, Sookie," he said, very quietly, and then he shut up. I appreciated that more than I could say.

When I got into work the next day at eleven,

Sam was dusting all the bottles behind the bar.

"Good morning," he said, staring at me. "You look like hell warmed over."

"Thanks, Sam. Good to know I'm looking my best."

Sam turned red. "Sorry, Sookie. You always look good. I was just thinking . . ."

"About the big circles under my eyes?" I pulled down the skin of my cheeks, making a hideous face for his benefit. "I was real late getting in last night." *I had to kill someone and move his car.* "I had to go over to Shreveport to see Eric."

"Business or pleasure?" And he ducked his head, clearly not believing he'd said that, either. "I'm sorry, Sookie. My mom would say I got up on the tactless side of the bed today."

I gave him a half hug. "Don't worry. Every day is like that for me. And I have to apologize to you. I'm sorry I've been so ignorant about the legal trouble facing shifters and Weres right now." It was definitely time for me to look at the big picture.

"You had some good reasons to concentrate on yourself the past few weeks," Sam said. "I don't know that I could have recovered the way you have. I'm real proud of you."

I didn't know what to say. I looked down at the bar, reached for a cloth to polish away a ring. "If you need me to start a petition or call my state representative, you just say the word," I told him. "No one should make you register anywhere. You're an American. Born and bred."

"That's the way I look at it. It's not like I'm any different from the way I've always been. The only difference is that now people know about it. How did the pack run go?"

I'd almost forgotten about it. "They seemed to have a good time, far as I can tell," I said cautiously. "I met Annabelle and the new guy, Basim. Why is Alcide beefing up the ranks? Have you heard anything about what's been happening in the Long Tooth pack?"

"Well, I told you I'd been dating one of them," he said, looking away at the bottles behind the bar as if he were trying to spot one that was still dusty. If this conversation continued in the same vein, the whole bar would be spanking clean.

"Who would that be?" Since this was the second time he'd mentioned it, I figured it was okay for me to ask.

His fascination with the bottles was transferred to the cash register. "Ah, Jannalynn. Jannalynn Hopper."

"Oh," I said, in a neutral way. I was trying to give myself a little time to make my face bland and receptive.

"She was there the night we fought the pack that was trying to take over. She, ah . . . took care of the wounded enemies."

That was an extreme euphemism. She'd cracked their skulls with her clenched fists. Trying to prove that it wasn't National Tactless Day at *my* house, I said, "Oh, yes. The, ah, very slim girl. The young one."

"She's not as young as she looks," Sam said, bypassing the obvious fact that her age was not the first issue one could have with Jannalynn.

"Okeydokey. How old is she?"

"Twenty. One."

"Oh, well, she's quite a girl," I said solemnly. I forced a smile to my lips. "Seriously, Sam, I'm not judging your choice." Not much. "Jannalynn's really, really . . . She's dynamic."

"Thanks," he said, his face clearing. "She gave me a call after we fought in the pack war. She's into lions." Sam had changed into a lion that night, the better to fight. He'd made a magnificent king of beasts.

"So, how long have you two been dating?"

"We've been talking for a while, but we went out for the first time maybe three weeks ago."

"Well, that's great," I said. I made myself relax and smile more naturally. "You sure you don't need a note from her mom?"

Sam threw the dust cloth at me. I grabbed it and threw it back.

"Can you two quit playing? I got to talk to Sam," Tanya said. She'd come in without my hearing her.

She's never going to be my best friend, but she's a good worker and she's willing to come in two evenings a week after she gets off her day job at Norcross. "You want me to leave?" I asked.

"No, that's okay."

"Sorry, Tanya. What do you need?" Sam asked, smiling.

"I need you to change my name on my paychecks," Tanya said.

"You changed your name?" I must have been extra slow that day. But Sam would have said it if I hadn't; he looked just as blank.

"Yeah, me and Calvin went to a court-house across the state line in Arkansas and got married," she said. "I'm Tanya Norris now."

Sam and I both stared at Tanya in a moment of silent astonishment.

"Congratulations!" I said heartily. "I know

you'll be real happy." I wasn't so sure about Calvin being happy, but at least I managed to say something nice.

Sam chimed in, too, with all the right things. Tanya showed us her wedding ring, a broad gold band, and after going into the kitchen to show it to Antoine and D'Eriq, she left as abruptly as she'd arrived to drive back to work at Norcross. She'd mentioned they'd registered at Target and Wal-Mart for the few things they needed, so Sam dashed into his office and picked out a wall clock to give them from all the Merlotte's employees. He put a jar out by the bar for our contributions, and I dropped in a ten.

By that time, people were coming in for lunch, and I had to get busy. "I never did get around to asking you some questions," I said to Sam. "Maybe before I leave work?"

"Sure, Sook," he said, and began filling glasses with iced tea. It was a warm day.

After I'd served drinks and food for about an hour, I was surprised to see Claude coming through the door. Even in rumpled clothes he'd obviously picked up off the floor to pull on, he looked breathtakingly gorgeous. He'd pulled his hair back into a messy ponytail . . . and it didn't detract.

It was almost enough to make you hate him, really.

Claude slouched over to me as if he were in Merlotte's every day . . . and as if his kind and tactful moment last night had never been. "The water heater's not working," he said.

"Hi, Claude. Good to see you," I said. "Did you sleep well? I'm so glad. I slept well, too. I guess you better do something about the water heater, huh? If you want to shower and wash your clothes. Remember me asking you to help me out by handling some things I can't? You could call Hank Clearwater. He's come out to the house before."

"I can go have a look," a voice said. I turned to see Terry Bellefleur standing behind me. Terry is a Vietnam War vet, and he's got some awful scars — both the kind you can see and the kind you can't. He'd been very young when he'd gone to war. He'd been very old when he returned. His auburn hair was graying, but it was still thick, and long enough to braid. I'd always gotten along real well with Terry, who could do just about anything around the yard or in the house, by way of repairs.

"I would sure appreciate it," I said. "But I don't want to take advantage, Terry." He'd always been kind to me. He'd cleared away the debris of my burned kitchen so the builders could start working on the new one, and I'd had to insist he take a fair wage for it.

"No problem," he muttered, his eyes on his old work boots. Terry survived on a monthly government check and on several odd jobs. For example, he came into Merlotte's either very late at night or early in the morning to clean the tables and the bathrooms, and to mop the floors. He always said keeping busy kept him fit, and it was true that Terry was still built.

"I'm Claude Crane, Sookie's cousin." Claude held out his hand to Terry.

Terry muttered his own name and took Claude's hand. His eyes came up to meet Claude's. Terry's eyes were unexpectedly beautiful, a rich golden brown and heavily lashed. I'd never noticed before. I realized I'd never thought about Terry as a *man* before.

After the handshake, Terry looked startled. When he was faced with something out of his normal path, usually Terry reacted badly; the only question was of degree. But at the moment, Terry seemed more puzzled than frightened or angry.

"Ah, did you want me to come look at it now?" Terry asked. "I have a couple of hours free."

"That would be wonderful," Claude said. "I want my shower, and I want a hot one." He smiled at Terry.

"Dude, I'm not gay," Terry said, and the expression on Claude's face was priceless. I'd never seen Claude nonplussed before.

"Thanks, Terry, I'd sure appreciate it," I said briskly. "Claude's got a key, and he'll let you in. If you have to buy some parts, just give me the receipts. You know I'm good for it." I might have to transfer some money from my savings to my checking, but I still had what I thought of as my "vampire money" safely stashed at the bank. And Mr. Cataliades would be sending me poor Claudine's money, too. Something relaxed inside me every time I thought about that bit of money. I'd been balanced on the fine edge of poverty so many times that I was used to it, and the knowledge of that money I'd be able to sock in the bank was a huge relief to me.

Terry nodded and then went out the back door to get his pickup. I speared Claude with a scowl. "That man is very fragile," I said. "He had a bad war. Just remember that."

Claude's face was slightly flushed. "I'll remember," he said. "I've been in wars myself." He gave me another quick graze on

150

the cheek, to show me he'd recovered from the blow to his pride. I could feel the envy of every woman in the bar beating against me. "I'll be gone to Monroe by the time you get home, I suppose. Thanks, Cousin."

Sam came to stand beside me as Claude went out the door. "Elvis has left the building," he said dryly.

"No, I haven't seen him in a while," I said, definitely on auto-mouth. Then I shook myself. "Sorry, Sam. Claude's one of a kind, isn't he?"

"I haven't seen Claudine in a while. She's a lot of fun," Sam said. "Claude seems to be . . . more typical of the general run of fairies." There was a question in his voice.

"We won't be seeing Claudine anymore," I said. "As far as I know, we won't be seeing any fairies but Claude. The doors are shut. However that works. Though I understand there's still one or two lurking around my house."

"There's a lot you haven't told me," he said.

"We need to catch up," I agreed.

"What about this evening? After you get off? Terry's supposed to come back and do some repairs that have piled up around here, but Kennedy is scheduled to take the bar." Sam looked a little worried. "I hope

Claude doesn't make another pass at Terry. Claude's ego is as big as a barn, and Terry's so . . . You never know how he's going to take stuff."

"Terry's a grown man," I reminded Sam. Of course, I was trying to reassure myself. "They both are."

"Claude isn't a man at all," Sam said. "Though he's a *male*."

It was a huge relief when I noticed Terry'd returned an hour later. He seemed absolutely normal, not flustered, angry, or anything else.

I had always tried to keep out of Terry's head, because it could be a very frightening place. Terry did well as long as he kept his focus on one thing at a time. He thought about his dogs a lot. He'd kept one of the puppies from his bitch's last litter, and he was training the youngster. (In fact, if ever a dog was taught to read, Terry would be the man who'd done it.)

After he'd worked on a loose doorknob in Sam's office, Terry sat at one of my tables and ordered a salad and some sweet tea. After I took his order, Terry silently handed me a receipt. He'd had to get a new element for the water heater. "It's all fixed now," he said. "Your cousin was able to get his hot shower."

"Thanks, Terry," I said. "I'm going to give you something for your time and labor."

"Not a problem," Terry said. "Your cousin took care of that." He turned his attention to his magazine. He'd brought a copy of *Louisiana Hunting and Fishing* to read while he waited for his food.

I wrote Terry a check for the element and gave it to him when I brought his food. He nodded and slipped it in his pocket. Since Terry's schedule meant he wasn't always available to fill in, Sam had hired another bartender so he could have some regular evenings off. The new bartender, who'd been at work for a couple of weeks, was really pretty in a supersized way. Kennedy Keyes was five-eleven, easy; taller than Sam, for sure. She had the kind of good looks you associate with traditional beauty queens: shoulder-length chestnut hair with discreet blond highlights, wide brown eyes, a white and even smile that was an orthodontist's wet dream. Her skin was perfect, her back straight, and she'd graduated from Southern Arkansas University with a degree in psychology.

She'd also done time.

Sam had asked her if she wanted a job when she'd drifted in for lunch the day after she'd gotten out of jail. She hadn't even asked what she'd be doing before she'd said yes. He'd given her a basic bartender's guide, and she'd studied every spare moment until she'd mastered an amazing number of drinks.

"Sookie!" she said, as if we'd been best friends since childhood. That was Kennedy's way. "How you doing?"

"Good, thank you. Yourself?"

"Happy as a clam." She bent to check the number of sodas in the glass-fronted refrigerator behind the bar. "We need us some A&W," she said.

"Coming right up." I got the keys from Sam, then went back to the stockroom to find a case of root beer. I got two six-packs.

"I didn't mean you to get that. I coulda gotten them!" Kennedy smiled at me. Her smile was kind of perpetual. "I appreciate it."

"No problem."

"Do I look any smaller, Sookie?" she said hopefully. She half turned to show me her butt and looked at me over her own shoulder.

Kennedy's issue didn't seem to be that she had been in jail, but that she had put on weight in jail. The food had been crappy, she'd told me, and it had been high on the carbohydrate count. "But I'm an emotional eater," she'd said, as if that were a terrible thing. "And I was real emotional in jail." Ever since she'd gotten back to Bon Temps, she'd been anxious to return to her beauty queen measurements.

She was still beautiful. There was just more of her to look good.

"You're gorgeous, as always," I said. I looked around for Danny Prideaux. Sam had asked Danny to come in when Kennedy was working at night. This arrangement was supposed to last for a month, until Sam was sure people wouldn't take advantage of Kennedy.

"You know," she said, interpreting my glance, "I can handle myself."

Everyone in Bon Temps knew that Kennedy could handle herself, and that was the problem. Her reputation might constitute a challenge to certain men (certain men who were assholes). "I know you can," I said mildly. Danny Prideaux was insurance.

And there he came through the door. He was taller than Kennedy by a couple of inches, and he was of some racial mixture that I hadn't figured out. Danny had deep olive skin, short brown hair, and a broad face. He'd been out of the army for a month, and he hadn't yet settled into a career of any sort. He worked part-time at the home builders' supply store. He was willing enough to be a bouncer for a few nights a week, especially since he got to look at Kennedy the whole time.

Sam drifted out of his office to say good night and brief Kennedy on a customer whose check had bounced, and then he and I went out the back door together. "Let's go to Crawdad Diner," he suggested. That sounded good to me. It was an old restaurant just off the square around the courthouse. Like all the businesses in the area around the square, the oldest part of Bon Temps, the diner had a history. The original owners had been Perdita and Crawdad Jones, who'd opened the restaurant in the forties. When Perdita had retired, she'd sold the business to Charlsie Tooten's husband, Ralph, who'd quit his job at the chicken processing plant to take over. Their deal was that Perdita would give Ralph all her recipes if he'd agree to keep the name Crawdad Diner. When Ralph's arthritis had forced him to retire, he'd sold Crawdad Diner to Pinkie Arnett with the same condition. So generations of Bon Temps diners were ensured of getting the best bread pudding in the state, and the heirs of Perdita and Crawdad Jones were able to point with pride.

I told Sam this bit of local history after we'd ordered country-fried steak with green beans and rice.

"Thank God Pinkie got the bread pudding recipe, and when the green tomatoes are in season, I want to come in every other night to have 'em fried," Sam said. "How's living with your cousin?" He squeezed his lemon slice into his tea.

"I hardly know yet. He just moved in some stuff, and we haven't had a lot of overlap."

"Have you seen him strip?" Sam laughed. "I mean, professionally? I sure couldn't do that on a stage with people watching."

Physically, there sure wouldn't be anything stopping him. I'd seen Sam naked when he changed from a shifter form into human. Yum. "No, I always planned on going with Amelia, but since she went back to New Orleans I haven't been in a strip-club kind of mood. You should ask Claude for a job on your nights off," I said, grinning.

"Oh, sure," he said sarcastically, but he looked pleased.

We talked about Amelia's departure for a while, and then I asked Sam about his family in Texas. "My mom's divorce came through," he said. "Of course, my stepdad's been in jail since he shot her, so she hasn't seen him in months. At this point, I'm guessing the main difference to her is going to be financial. She's getting my dad's military pension, but she doesn't know if her job at the school will be waiting for her or not when the summer's over. They hired a substitute for the rest of the school year after she got shot, and they're waffling over having Mom back."

Before she'd gotten shot, Sam's mom had been the receptionist/secretary at an elementary school. Not everyone was calm about having a woman who turned into an animal working in the same office as them, though Sam's mom was the same woman she'd been before. I was baffled by this attitude.

The waitress brought our plates and a basket of rolls. I sighed with anticipated pleasure. This was much nicer than cooking for myself.

"Any news on Craig's wedding?" I asked, when I could yank myself away from my country-fried steak.

"They finished couples counseling," he said with a shrug. "Now her parents want them to have genetics counseling, whatever that is."

"That's nuts."

"Some people just think anything different is bad," Sam said as he buttered his second roll. "And it's not like Craig could change." As the firstborn of a pure shifter couple, only Sam felt the call of the moon.

"I'm sorry." I shook my head. "I know the situation's hard on everyone in your family."

He nodded. "My sister Mindy's gotten over it pretty well. She let me play with the kids the last time I saw them, and I'm going to try to get over to Texas for the Fourth of July. Her town has a big fireworks display, and the whole family goes. I think I'd enjoy it."

I smiled. They were lucky to have Sam in their family — that was what I thought. "Your sister must be pretty smart," I said. I took a big bite of country-fried steak with milk gravy. It was blissful.

He laughed. "Listen, while we're talking family," he said. "You ready to tell me how you're really doing? You told me about your great-grandfather and what happened. How are your injuries? I don't want to sound like I expect you to tell me everything that goes on in your life. But you know I care."

I did a little hesitating myself. But it felt right to tell Sam, so I tried to give him a nutshell account of the past week. "And JB has been helping me with some physical therapy," I added.

"You're walking like nothing happened, unless you get tired," he observed.

"There's a couple of bad patches on my left upper thigh where the flesh actually . . . Okay, not going there." I looked down at my napkin for a minute or two. "It grew back. Mostly. There's a kind of dimple. I have a few scars, but they're not terrible. Eric doesn't seem to mind." In fact, he had a scar or two from his human life, though they hardly showed against the whiteness of his skin.

"Are you, ah, coping okay with it?"

"I have nightmares sometimes," I confessed. "And I have some panic moments. But let's not talk about it anymore." I smiled at him, my brightest smile. "Look at us after all these years, Sam. I'm living with a fairy, I've got a vampire boyfriend, you're dating a werewolf who cracks skulls. Would we ever have thought we'd say this, the first day I came to work at Merlotte's?"

Sam leaned forward and briefly put his hand over mine, and just then Pinkie herself came by the table to ask us how we'd liked the food. I pointed to my nearly empty plate. "I think you can tell we did," I said, smiling at her. She grinned back. Pinkie was a big woman who clearly enjoyed her own cooking. Some new customers came in, and she went off to seat them.

Sam took his hand back and began working on his food again. "I wish . . ." Sam began, and then he closed his mouth. He ran a hand through his red gold hair. Since he'd had it trimmed so short, it had looked tamer than usual until he tousled it. He laid his fork down, and I noticed he'd managed to dispose of almost all his food, too.

"What do you wish?" I asked. Most people, I'd be scared to ask them to complete that sentence. But Sam and I had been friends for years.

"I wish that you would find happiness with someone else," he said. "I know, I know. It's none of my business. Eric does seem to really care about you, and you deserve that."

"He does," I said. "He's what I've got, and I'd be real ungrateful if I weren't happy with that. We love each other." I shrugged, in a self-deprecating way. I was uncomfortable with the turn of the conversation.

Sam nodded, though a wry twist to the corner of his mouth told me, without even hearing his thoughts, that Sam didn't think Eric was such an object of worth. I was glad I couldn't hear all his thoughts clearly. I thought Jannalynn was equally inappropriate for Sam. He didn't need a ferocious,

161

anything-for-the-packmaster kind of woman. He needed to be with someone who thought he was the greatest man around.

But I didn't say anything.

You can't say I'm not tactful.

It was dreadfully tempting to tell Sam what had happened the night before. But I just couldn't. I didn't want to involve Sam in vampire shit any more than he already was, which was very little. No one needed stuff like that. Of course, I'd worried all day about the fallout from those events.

My cell phone rang while Sam was paying his half of the bill. I glanced at it. Pam was calling. My heart leaped into my throat. I stepped outside the diner.

"What's up?" I asked, sounding just as anxious as I really was.

"Hello to you, too."

"Pam, what happened?" I wasn't in the mood for playfulness.

"Bruno and Corinna didn't show up in New Orleans for work today," Pam said solemnly. "Victor didn't call here, because, of course, there was no good reason for them to come up here."

"Did they find the car?"

"Not yet. I'm sure the highway-patrol officers have put a sticker on it today, asking the owners to come and remove it. That's what they do, I've observed."

"Yes. That's what they do."

"No bodies will appear. Especially since after the downpour of last night, there won't be a trace." Pam sounded smug about that. "No blame can attach to us."

I stood there, phone to my ear, on an empty sidewalk in my little town, the streetlight only a few feet away. I'd seldom felt more alone. "I wish it had been Victor," I said, from the bottom of my heart.

"You want to kill someone else?" Pam sounded mildly surprised.

"No, I want it to be over. I want everything to be okay. I don't want any more killing at all." Sam came out of the restaurant behind me and heard the distress in my voice. I felt his hand on my shoulder. "I have to go, Pam. Keep me posted."

I shut the phone and turned to face Sam. He was looking troubled, and the light streaming from overhead cast deep shadows on his face.

"You're in trouble," he said.

I could only keep silent.

"I know you can't talk about it, but if you ever feel like you have to, you know where I am," he said.

"You, too," I said, because I figured with

a girlfriend like Jannalynn, Sam might be in almost as bad a position as I was.

CHAPTER 5

The phone rang while I was in the shower Friday morning. Since I had an answering machine, I ignored it. As I was reaching out for my towel with my eyes shut, I felt it being thrust into my hand. With a gasp, I opened my eyes to see Claude standing there in his altogether.

"Phone's for you," he said, handing me the portable phone from the kitchen. He left.

I put it to my ear automatically. "Hello?" I said weakly. I didn't know what to think about first: me seeing Claude naked, Claude seeing me naked, or the whole fact that we were related and naked in the same room.

"Sookie? You sound funny," said a faintly familiar male voice.

"Oh, I just got a surprise," I said. "I'm so sorry. . . . Who is this?"

He laughed, and it was a warm and friendly sound. "This is Remy Savoy,

165

Hunter's dad," he said.

Remy had been married to my cousin Hadley, who was now dead. Their son, Hunter, and I had a connection, a connection that we needed to explore. I'd been meaning to call Remy to set up a playdate for me and Hunter, and I chided myself now for putting it off. "I hope you're calling to tell me that I can see Hunter this weekend?" I said. "I've got to work Sunday afternoon, but I have Saturday off. Tomorrow, that is."

"That's great! I was going to ask if I could bring him over this evening, and maybe he could spend the night."

That was a lot of time to spend with a kid I didn't know; more important, a kid who didn't know me. "Remy, do you have special plans or something?"

"Yeah. My dad's sister died yesterday, and they've set the funeral for tomorrow morning at ten. But the visitation is tonight. I hate to take Hunter to the visitation and the funeral . . . especially considering, you know, his . . . problem. It might be pretty hard on him. You know how it is. . . . I can't ever be sure what he'll say."

"I understand." And I did. A preschool telepath is tough to be around. My parents would have appreciated Remy's predicament. "How old is Hunter now?"

"Five, just had a birthday. I was worried about the party, but we got through that okay."

I took a deep breath. I'd told him I'd help out with Hunter's problem. "Okay, I can keep him overnight."

"Thanks. I mean, *really* thanks. I'll bring him over when I get off work today. That okay? We'll be there about five thirty?"

I would get off work between five and six, depending on my replacement being on time and how full my tables were. I gave Remy my cell number. "If I'm not home, call my cell, I'll be back here as soon as I can. What does he like to eat?"

We talked about Hunter's routine for a few minutes, and then I hung up. By then, I was dry, but my hair was hanging in damp rattails. After a few minutes with the blow-dryer, I set off to talk to Claude once I was securely dressed in my work clothes.

"Claude!" I yelled from the bottom of the stairs.

"Yes?" He sounded totally unconcerned.

"Come down here!"

He appeared at the head of the stairs, his hairbrush in his hand. "Yes, Cousin?"

"Claude, the answering machine would have picked up the phone call. Please don't come in my room without knocking, and especially don't come in my bathroom without knocking!" I would definitely employ the door lock from now on. I didn't think I'd ever used it before.

"Are you a prude?" He seemed genuinely curious.

"No!" But after a second, I said, "But maybe compared to you, yes! I like my privacy. I get to decide who sees me naked. Do you get my point?"

"Yes. Objectively speaking, you have beautiful points."

I thought the top of my head would pop off. "I didn't expect this when I told you that you could stay with me. You like men."

"Oh, yes, I definitely prefer men. But I can appreciate beauty. I *have* visited the other side of the fence."

"I probably wouldn't have let you stay here if I'd known that," I said.

Claude shrugged, as if to say, "Wasn't I smart to keep it from you, then?"

"Listen," I said, and then stopped, because I was rattled. No matter what the circumstances, seeing Claude naked . . . Well, your first reaction wouldn't be rage, either. "I'm going to tell you a few things, and I want you to take me seriously."

He waited, brush in hand, looking only

politely attentive.

"Number one. I have a boyfriend, and he's a vampire, and I'm not interested in cheating on him, and that includes seeing other guys naked . . . in my bathroom," I tacked on hastily, thinking of twoeys of all sorts. "If you can't respect that, you need to leave, and you'll just have to cry all the way home. Number two. I'm having company tonight, a little kid I'm babysitting, and you better act appropriate around him. You picking up what I'm laying down?"

"No nudity, be nice to the human kid."

"Right."

"Is the child yours?"

"If he were mine, I'd be raising him, you can bet your money. He's Hadley's. She was my cousin, the daughter of my aunt Linda. She was the, ah, the girlfriend of Sophie-Anne. You know, the former queen? And she became a vampire, eventually. This little boy, Hunter, is the son Hadley had before all that happened to her. His dad's bringing him by." Was Claude related to Hadley? Yes, of course, and therefore to Hunter. I pointed that out.

"I like children," Claude told me. "I'll behave. And I'm sorry to have upset you." He gave a stab at sounding contrite.

"Funny, you don't look sorry. At all."

"I'm crying inside," he said, smiling a wicked smile.

"Oh, for goodness' sake," I said, turning away to complete my bathroom routine alone and unobserved.

I'd calmed down by the time I got to work. *After all,* I thought, *Claude has probably seen a gazillion people naked in his time.* Most supes didn't think nudity was any big deal. The fact that Claude and I were distantly related — my great-grandfather was his grandfather — wouldn't make any difference to him; in fact, it wouldn't make any difference to most of the supes. *So,* I told myself stoutly, *no big deal.* When I hit a slow time at work, I called Eric's cell and left a message to tell him I was expecting to babysit a child that night. "If you can come over, great, but I wanted you to know ahead of time that someone else will be here," I told the voice mail. Hunter would make a pretty effective chaperone. Then I thought about my new upstairs roomer. "Plus, I kind of forgot to tell you something the other night, and probably you aren't going to like it much. Also, I miss you." There was a beep. My message time was up. Well . . . good. There was no telling what I would've said next.

The tracker, Heidi, was supposed to arrive in Bon Temps tonight. It seemed like a year since Eric had decided to send her over to check my land. I felt a little concerned when I thought of her arrival. Would Remy think Hunter attending the funeral was so bad, if he knew who else was dropping by my house? Was I being irresponsible? Was I putting the child at risk?

No, it was paranoid to think so. Heidi was coming to scout around in my woods.

I had thrown off my niggling worry by the time I was preparing to leave Merlotte's. Kennedy had arrived to work for Sam again because he'd made plans to take the Were girl, Jannalynn, to the casinos in Shreveport and out to dinner. I hoped she was real good to Sam, because he deserved it.

Kennedy was contorting herself in front of the mirror behind the bar, trying to discern a weight loss. I looked down at my own thighs. Jannalynn was really, really slim. In fact, I'd call her skinny. God had been generous with me in the bosom department, but Jannalynn was the possessor of little apricotlike boobs she showed off by wearing bustiers and tank tops with no bra. She gave herself some attitude (and altitude) by wearing fantastic footwear. I was wearing Keds. I sighed.

"Have a nice night!" Kennedy told me

brightly, and I straightened my shoulders, smiled, and wiggled my fingers good-bye. Most people thought Kennedy's big smile and good manners had to be put on. But I knew Kennedy was sincere. She'd been trained by her pageant-queen mom to keep a smile on her face and a good word on her lips. I had to hand it to her; Danny Prideaux didn't faze Kennedy at all, and I felt like he'd make most girls pretty nervous. Danny, who'd been brought up to expect the world to beat him down so he better throw the first punch, lifted a finger to me to second Kennedy's farewell. He had a Coke in front of him, because Danny didn't drink on duty. He seemed content to play Mario Kart on his Nintendo DS, or to simply sit at the bar and watch Kennedy work.

On the other hand, lots of men would be nervous about working with Kennedy since she'd served time for manslaughter. Some women would be, too. But I had no problem with her. I was glad Sam had stepped up for her. It's not that I approve of murder — but some people just beg to be killed, don't they? After all I'd been through, I was forced to simply admit to myself that I felt that way.

I got home about five minutes before

Remy arrived with Hunter. I'd had just enough time to pull off my work clothes, toss them in the hamper, and put on a pair of shorts and a T-shirt before Remy knocked at the front door.

I looked through the peephole before I opened the door, on the theory that it's better to be safe than sorry.

"Hey, Remy!" I said. He was in his early thirties, a quietly good-looking man with thick light brown hair. He was wearing clothes suitable for an evening visitation at a funeral home: khakis, a white-and-brown-striped broadcloth shirt, polished loafers. He'd looked more comfortable in the flannel and jeans he'd been wearing the first time I'd met him. I looked down at his son. Hunter had grown since I'd seen him last. He had dark hair and eyes like his mother, Hadley, but it was too early to say who he'd favor when he grew up.

I squatted down and said, *Hi, Hunter.* I didn't say anything out loud, but I smiled at him.

He'd almost forgotten. His face lit up. *Aunt Sookie!* he said. Pleasure ran through his head, pleasure and excitement. "I have a new truck," he said out loud, and I laughed.

"You gonna show it to me? Come on in,

173

you two, and let's get you settled."

"Thanks, Sookie," Remy said.

"Do I look like my mama, Dad?" Hunter asked.

"Why?" Remy was startled.

"That's what Aunt Sookie says."

Remy was used to little shocks like this by now, and he knew it would only get worse. "Yes, you look like your mom, and she was good-looking," Remy told him. "You're a lucky young man, Son."

"I don't want to look like a girl," Hunter said doubtfully.

You don't. "Not a bit," I said. "Hunter, your room is right here." I indicated the open doorway. "I used to sleep in this room when I was a kid," I said.

Hunter looked around, alert and cautious. But the low twin bed with its white bedspread and the old furniture and the worn rug by the bed were all homey and unthreatening. "Where will you be?" he asked.

"Right here, across the hall," I told him, opening the door to my room. "You just call out, and I'll come a-running. Or you can come climb in the bed with me, if you get scared in the night."

Remy stood, watching his son absorb all this. I didn't know how often the little boy had spent the night away from his dad; not too often, from the thoughts I was picking up from the boy's head.

"The bathroom's the next door down from your room, see?" I pointed in. He looked into the old-fashioned room with his mouth hanging open.

"I know it looks different from your bathroom at home," I said, answering his thoughts. "This is an old house, Hunter." The claw-foot tub and the black-and-white tiles were not what you saw in the rental houses and apartments Remy and Hunter had lived in since Katrina.

"What's upstairs?" Hunter asked.

"Well, a cousin of mine is staying up there. He's not home right now, and he comes in so late you may not even see him. His name is Claude."

Can I go up there and look around?

Maybe tomorrow we'll go up together. I'll show you the rooms you can go into and the rooms that Claude is using.

I glanced up to see that Remy was looking from Hunter to me, and he didn't know whether to be relieved or worried that I could talk to his son in a way he could not.

"Remy, it's okay," I said. "I grew up, and it got easier. I know this is going to be tough, but at least Hunter is a bright boy with a sound body. His little problem is

175

just . . . less straightforward than most other kids'."

"That's a good way to look at it." But Remy's worry didn't diminish.

"You want a drink?" I said, not sure what to do with Remy now. Hunter had asked me silently if he could unpack his bag, and I'd told him — the same way — that unpacking was fine with me. He'd already unloaded a little backpack full of toys onto the bedroom floor.

"No, thank you. I got to get going."

It was unpleasant to realize that I spooked Remy in the same way his son spooked other people. Remy might need my help, and I could tell he thought I was a pretty woman, but I could also see that I gave him the creeps. "Is the visitation in Red Ditch?" I asked. That was the town where Remy and Hunter lived. It was about an hour and a quarter's drive southeast from Bon Temps.

"No, in Homer. So this is kind of on the way. If you run into any problems, just call my cell and I can come pick him up on the way home. Otherwise, I'll stay the night in Homer, go to the funeral at ten tomorrow, stay for the lunch at my cousin's home afterward, and pick Hunter up later in the afternoon, if that suits you."

"We'll be fine," I said, which was sheer

bravado on my part. I hadn't taken care of kids since I'd sat with my friend Arlene's young 'uns, way back when. I didn't want to think about that; friendships that end bitterly are always sad. Those kids probably hated me now. "I've got videos we can watch, and a puzzle or two, and even some coloring books."

"Where?" Hunter asked, looking around like he expected to see a Toys "R" Us.

"You say good-bye to your daddy, and we'll go looking for them," I told him.

"Bye, Dad," Hunter said, waving a casual hand at Remy.

Remy looked nonplussed. "Want to give me a hug, champ?"

Hunter held up his arms, and Remy picked him up and swung him around.

Hunter giggled. Remy smiled over the child's shoulder. "That's my boy," he said. "Be good for your aunt Sookie. Don't forget your manners. I'll see you tomorrow." He put Hunter down.

"Okay," Hunter said, quite matter-of-factly.

Remy had been expecting a big fuss, since he'd never been away from the boy for so long. He glanced at me, then shook his head with a smile. He was laughing at himself, which I thought was a good reaction.

I wondered how long Hunter's calm acceptance would last. Hunter looked up at me. "I'll be okay," he said, and I realized he was reading my mind and interpreting my thought in his own way. Though I'd had this experience before, it had been filtered through an adult's sensibility, and we'd had the fun of experimenting with combining our telepathy to see what happened. Hunter wasn't filtering and rearranging my thoughts as someone older would.

After hugging his son again, Remy left reluctantly. Hunter and I found the coloring books. It turned out that Hunter liked to color more than anything else in the world. I settled him at the table in the kitchen and turned my attention to supper preparation. I could have cooked a meal from scratch, but I figured something that required little attention would be best the first time he stayed with me. *You like Hamburger Helper?* I asked silently. He looked up, and I showed him the box.

I like that, Hunter said, recognizing the picture. He seemed to turn all his attention back to the turtle and butterfly scene he was coloring. The turtle was green and brown, approved turtle colors, but Hunter had gone to town on the butterfly. It was magenta, yellow, blue, and emerald green . . . and he hadn't finished it yet. I noted that staying in the lines was not Hunter's main goal. Which was okay.

Kristen used to make Hamburger Helper, he told me. Kristen had been Remy's girlfriend. Remy had told me he and Kristen had broken up over her inability to accept Hunter's special gift. Not so surprisingly, Kristen had come to believe Hunter was creepy. Adults had thought I was a weird kid, too. Though I understood that now, at the time it had been painful. *She was scared of me,* Hunter said, and he looked up for a second. I could understand that look.

She just didn't understand, I said. *There aren't many people like us.*

Am I the only other one?

No. I know one other, a guy. He's a grown-up. He lives in Texas.

Is he okay?

I wasn't sure what Hunter meant by "okay" until I looked at his thoughts a little longer. The little boy was thinking of his dad and some other men he admired — men who had jobs and wives or girlfriends, men who worked. Regular men.

Yes, I answered. *He found a way to make a living with it. He works for vampires. You can't hear vampires.*

I never met one. Really?

179

The doorbell rang. "I'll be back in a minute," I told Hunter, and I walked swiftly to the front door. I used the peephole. My caller was a young vampire female — presumably Heidi, the tracker. My cell phone rang. I fished it out of my pocket.

"Heidi should be there," Pam said. "Has she come to the door?"

"Brown ponytail, blue eyes, tall?"

"Yes. You can let her in."

This was all very timely.

I had the door open in a second. "Hi. Come in," I said. "I'm Sookie Stackhouse." I stood aside. I didn't offer to shake hands; vampires don't do that.

Heidi nodded to me and stepped into the house, darting quick looks around her, as if openly examining her surroundings were rude. Hunter came running into the living room, skidding to a stop as he saw Heidi. She was tall and bony, and possibly a mute. However, now Hunter could test my words.

"Heidi, this is my friend Hunter," I said, and waited for Hunter's reaction.

He was fascinated. He was trying to read her thoughts, as hard as he could. He was delighted with the result, with her silence.

Heidi squatted. "Hunter, you're a fine boy," she said, to my relief. Her voice had an accent I associated with Minnesota. "Are you going to be staying with Sookie for long?" Her smile revealed teeth that were a little longer and sharper than the general run of humans', and I thought Hunter might be scared. But he eyed her with genuine fascination.

Did you come to eat supper with us? he asked Heidi.

Out loud, please, Hunter, I said. *She's different from humans, but she's not like us, either. Remember?*

He glanced at me as if he were afraid that I was angry. I smiled at him and nodded.

"You gonna eat supper with us, Miss Heidi?"

"No, thank you, Hunter. I'm here to go back in the woods and look for something we're missing. I won't disturb you any longer. My boss asked me to introduce myself to you, and then go about my work." Heidi stood, smiling down at the little boy.

Suddenly, I saw a pitfall right in front of me. I was an idiot. But how could I help the boy if I didn't educate him? *Don't let her know you can hear things, Hunter,* I told the child. He looked up at me, his eyes amazingly like my cousin Hadley's. He looked a little scared.

Heidi was glancing from Hunter to me, obviously feeling that something was going

181

on that she couldn't discern.

"Heidi, I hope you find something back there," I said briskly. "Let me know before you leave, please." Not only did I want to know if she found anything, but I wanted to know when she was off the property.

"This should take no more than two hours," she said.

"I'm sorry I didn't tell you, 'Welcome to Louisiana,' " I told her. "I hope you didn't mind too much, moving here from Las Vegas."

"Can I go back to color?" Hunter asked.

"Sure, honey," I said. "I'll be there in a minute."

"I gotta go potty," Hunter called, and I heard the bathroom door close.

Heidi said, "My son was his age when I was turned."

Her statement was so abrupt, her voice so flat, that it took me a moment to absorb what she'd told me.

"I'm so sorry," I said, and I meant it.

She shrugged. "It was twenty years ago. He's grown now. He's a drug addict in Reno." Her voice still sounded flat and emotionless, as if she were talking about the son of a stranger.

Very cautiously, I said, "Do you go see him?"

"Yes," she said. "I go to see him. At least I did before my former — employer — sent me here."

I didn't know what to say, but she was still standing there, so I ventured another question. "Do you let him see you?"

"Yes, sometimes. I called an ambulance one time when I saw he'd overdosed. Another night, I saved him from a vamp-blood addict who was going to kill him."

A herd of thoughts thundered through my head, and they were all unpleasant. Did he know the vampire watching him was his mother? What if he OD'd in the daytime, when she was dead to the world? How would she feel if she wasn't there the night his luck finally ran out? She couldn't always be on hand. Could it be he'd become an addict because his mother kept popping up when she should be dead?

"In the old days," I said, because I had to say something, "vampires' makers left the area with the new vamps as soon as they were turned, to keep them away from their kin, who'd recognize them." Eric and Bill and Pam had all told me that.

"I left Las Vegas for over a decade, but I returned," Heidi said. "My maker needed me there. Being part of the world isn't as great for all of us as it is for our leaders. I think Victor sent me to work for Eric in Louisiana to get me away from my son. I wasn't any use to them, they said, as long as Charlie's troubles were distracting me. But then again, my skill in tracking was only discovered when I was finding the man who sold bad drugs to Charlie."

She smiled a little, and I knew what kind of end that man had met. Heidi was spooky in the extreme.

"Now, I'll be going to the back of your property to see what I can find. I'll let you know when I'm through." Once she'd walked out the front door, she vanished into the woods so swiftly that by the time I went to the back of the house to look out, she'd melted into the trees.

I've had a lot of strange conversations, and I've had some heart-wrenching conversations — but my talk with Heidi had been both. Fortunately, I had a couple of minutes to recover while I served our plates and monitored Hunter's hand washing.

I was glad to discover that the boy expected to say a prayer before he ate, and we bowed our heads together. He enjoyed his Hamburger Helper and green beans and strawberries. While we ate, Hunter told me all about his father, by way of table conversation. I was sure Remy would be horrified if he could hear the tell-all approach Hunter took. It was all I could do not to laugh. I guess the discussion would have seemed strange to anyone else, because half of it was mind-to-mind and half of it was spoken.

Without any reminder from me, Hunter took his plate from the table to the sink. I held my breath until he slid it onto the counter carefully. "Do you have a dog?" he asked, looking around as if one might materialize. "We always give our scraps to the dog." I remembered the little black dog I'd seen running around the backyard of Remy's little house in Red Ditch.

No, I don't, I told him.

You've got a friend that turns into a dog? he said, his eyes big with astonishment.

"Yes, I do," I said. "He's a good friend." I hadn't counted on Hunter picking that up. This was very tricky.

"My dad says I'm smart," Hunter said, looking rather doubtful.

"Sure you are," I told him. "I know it's hard being different, because I'm different, too. But I grew up to be okay."

You sound kind of worried, though, Hunter said.

I agreed with Remy. Hunter was a smart little boy.

I am. It was hard for me, growing up, be-

185

cause no one understood why I was different. People won't believe you. I sat down in a chair by the table and pulled Hunter onto my lap. I was worried this was too much touching for him, but he seemed glad to sit there. *People don't want to know that someone can hear what they're thinking. They don't have any privacy when people like us are around.*

Hunter didn't exactly get "privacy," so we talked about the concept for a while. Maybe that was over the head of most five-year-olds — but Hunter wasn't the average kid.

So is the thing out in the woods giving you privacy? Hunter asked me.

What? I knew I'd reacted with too much anxiety and dismay when Hunter looked upset, too. *Don't worry about it, honey,* I said. *No, he's no problem.*

Hunter looked reassured enough for me to feel that it was time to change the subject. His attention was wandering, so I let him scramble down. He began playing with the Duplos he'd brought in his backpack, transporting them from the bedroom to the kitchen with his dump truck. I thought of getting him some Legos for a belated birthday present, but I'd check with Remy first, get his okay. I listened in to Hunter while I was doing the dishes.

I found out that he was as interested in his anatomy as most five-year-olds are, and that he thought it was funny that he got to stand up when he peed and I had to sit down, and that he hadn't liked Kristen because she didn't really like him. *She pretended to,* he told me, exactly as if he'd known when I was listening in to him.

I'd been standing at the sink with my back to Hunter, but it didn't make any difference in our conversation, which was another strange feeling.

Can you tell when I'm listening to your head? I asked, surprised.

Yeah, it tickles, Hunter told me.

Was that because he was so young? Would it have "tickled" in my head, too, if I'd met another telepath when I was that age? Or was Hunter unique among telepaths?

"Was that lady who came to the door dead?" Hunter said. He'd jumped up and run around the table to stand by my side while I dried the skillet.

"Yes," I said. "She's a vampire."

"Will she bite?"

"She won't bite you or me," I said. "I guess sometimes she bites people if they tell her that's okay." Boy, I was worried about this conversation. It was like talking about religion with a child without knowing the parents' preferences. "I think you said you'd never met a vampire before?"

"No, ma'am," he said. I started to tell Hunter he didn't have to call me "ma'am," but then I stopped. The better manners he had, the easier this world would be for him. "I never met anything like that man in the woods, either."

This time he had my undivided attention, and I tried hard not to let him read my alarm. Just as I was about to ask him careful questions, I heard the screen door to the back porch open, and then footsteps across the boards. A light knock at the back door told me that Heidi had returned from scouting in the woods, but I looked out the little window in the door to be sure. Yep, it was the vampire.

"I'm through," she said, when I opened the door. "I'll be on my way."

I noticed Hunter didn't run to the door as he had last time. He was behind me, though; I could feel his brain buzzing. He was not exactly scared, but anxious, as most children are about the unknown. But he was definitely pleased that he couldn't hear her. I'd been pleased when I found out vampire brains were silent to me, too.

"Heidi, did you learn anything?" I said hesitantly. Some of this might not be appropriate for Hunter to hear.

"The fae tracks in your woods are fresh and heavy. There are two scents. They crisscross." She inhaled, with apparent delight. "I love the smell of fae in the night. Better than gardenias."

Since I'd already assumed she'd detect the fae Basim had reported smelling, this wasn't a big revelation. But Heidi said there were definitely two fae. That was bad news. It confirmed what Hunter had said, too.

"What else did you find?" I stepped back a little, so she could see Hunter was behind me and tailor her remarks accordingly.

"Neither of them is the fairy I smell here in your house." Not good news. "Of course, I smelled many werewolves. I also smell a vampire — I think Bill Compton, though I've only met him once. There's an old c-o-r-p-s-e. And a brand-new c-o-r-p-s-e buried due east from your house, in a clearing by the stream. The clearing is in a stand of wild plums."

None of this was reassuring. The old c-o-r-p-s-e, well, I'd expected that, and I knew who it was. (I spared a moment to wish Eric hadn't buried Debbie on my property.) And if Bill was the vampire walking through the woods, that was all right . . . though it did make me worry that he was just roaming around brooding all night instead of trying to build a new life for himself.

The new corpse was a real problem. Basim hadn't said anything about that. Had someone buried a body on my property in the last two nights, or had Basim simply left it off his list for some reason? I was staring at Heidi while I thought, and she finally raised her eyebrows. "Okay, thanks," I said. "I appreciate your taking the time."

"Take care of the little one," she said, and then she was across the back porch and out the door. I didn't hear her walk around the house to her car, but I didn't expect to. Vampires can be mighty quiet. I did hear her engine start up, and she drove away.

Since I knew my thoughts might worry Hunter, I forced myself to think of other things, which was harder than it sounds. I wouldn't have to do it long; I could tell my little visitor was getting tired. He put up the expected fuss about going to bed, but he didn't protest as much when I told him he could take a long bath first in the fascinating claw-foot tub. While Hunter splashed and played and made noises, I stayed in the bathroom, looking through a magazine. I made sure he actually cleaned himself in between sinking boats and racing ducks.

I decided we'd skip washing his hair. I

figured that would be an ordeal, and Remy hadn't given me any instructions one way or another on hair washing. I pulled the plug. Hunter really enjoyed the gurgle of the water as it went down the drain. He rescued the ducks before they could drown, which made him a hero. "I am the king of the ducks, Aunt Sookie," he crowed.

"They need a king," I said. I knew how stupid ducks were. Gran had kept some for a while. I supervised Hunter's towel usage and helped him get his pajamas on. I reminded him to use the toilet again, and then he brushed his teeth, not very thoroughly.

Forty-five minutes later, after a story or two, Hunter was in bed. At his request, I left the light in the hall on, and his door was ajar an inch or two.

I found I was exhausted and in no mood to puzzle over Heidi's revelation. I wasn't used to tending to a child, though Hunter had been easy to care for, especially for a little guy who was staying with a woman he didn't know well. I hoped he'd enjoyed talking to me brain-to-brain. I also hoped Heidi hadn't spooked him too much.

I hadn't let myself focus on her macabre little biography, but now that Hunter was asleep, I found myself thinking about her story. It was an awful pity that she'd had to return to Nevada during her son's lifetime. In fact, she now probably looked the same age as her son, Charlie. What had happened to the boy's father? Why had her maker required her return? When she'd first been turned, vampires hadn't yet shown themselves to America and the rest of the world. Secrecy had been paramount. I had to agree with Heidi. Coming out of the coffin hadn't solved all the vamps' problems, and it had created quite a few new ones.

I would almost rather not have known about the sadness Heidi carried around with her. Naturally, since I was my grandmother's product, such a wish made me feel guilty. Shouldn't we always be ready to listen to the sad stories of others? If they want to tell them, aren't we obliged to listen? Now I felt I had a relationship with Heidi, based on her misery. Is that a real relationship? Was there something sympathetic about me that she liked, something that called this story forth? Or did she routinely tell new acquaintances about her son, Charlie? I could hardly believe that. I figured Hunter's presence had triggered her confidences.

I knew (though I didn't want to admit it to myself) that if Heidi remained so distracted by the issue of her junkie son, one night he'd get a visit from someone ruthless. After that, she'd be able to focus her whole attention on the wishes of her employer. I shivered.

Though I didn't think Victor would hesitate a second to do such a thing, I wondered, *Would — or* could — *Eric?*

If I could even ask myself that, I knew the answer was yes.

On the other hand, Charlie made a great hostage to ensure Heidi's good behavior. As in: "If you don't spy on Eric, we'll pay Charlie a visit." But if that ever changed . . .

All this Heidi meditation was by way of dodging the more immediate issue. Who was the fresh corpse in my woods, and who had planted it there?

If Hunter hadn't been there, I would've picked up the phone to call Eric. I would've asked him to bring a shovel and come to help me dig a body up. That was what a boyfriend should do, right? But I couldn't leave Hunter alone in the house, and I would've felt terrible if I'd asked Eric to go out in the woods by himself, even though I knew he wouldn't think anything about it. In fact, probably he'd have sent Pam. I sighed. I couldn't seem to get rid of one problem without acquiring another.

CHAPTER 6

At six in the morning, Hunter climbed onto my bed. "Aunt Sookie!" he said, in what he probably thought was a whisper. Just this once, his using our mind-to-mind communication would have been better. But naturally, he decided to talk out loud.

"Uh-huh?" This had to be a bad dream.

"I had a funny dream last night," Hunter told me.

"Uh?" Maybe a dream within a dream.

"This tall man came in my room."

"Did?"

"He had long hair like a lady."

I pushed up on my elbows and looked at Hunter, who didn't seem frightened. "Yeah?" I said, which was at least borderline coherent. "What color?"

"Yellow," Hunter said, after a little thought. I suddenly realized that most five-year-olds might be a little shaky on the identification of colors.

Uh-oh. "So what did he do?" I asked. I struggled to sit all the way up. The sky outside was just getting lighter.

"He just looked at me, and he smiled," Hunter said. "Then he went in the closet."

"Wow," I said inadequately. I couldn't be sure (until dark, that is), but it sounded very much as though Eric was in the secret hiding place in my closet and dead for the day.

"I gotta go pee," Hunter said, and slid off my bed to scamper into my bathroom. I heard him flush a minute later, and then he washed his hands — or at least, he turned on the water for a second. I collapsed back onto my pillows, thinking sadly of the hours of sleep I was doomed to lose. By sheer force of will, I got out of bed in my blue nightgown and threw on a robe. I stepped into my slippers, and after Hunter exited my bathroom, I entered it.

A couple of minutes later we were in my kitchen with the lights on. I went directly to the coffeepot, and I found a note propped on it. I recognized the handwriting immediately, and the endorphins flooded my system. Instead of being incredulous that I was up and moving so ungodly early, I felt happy that I was sharing this time with my little cousin. The note, which had been written on one of the pads I keep around for grocery lists, said, "My lover, I came in too close to dawn to wake you, though I was tempted. Your house is full of strange men. A fairy upstairs and a little child downstairs — but as long as there's not one in my lady's chamber, I can stand it. I need to talk to you when I rise." It was signed, in a large scrawl, "ERIC."

I put the note aside, trying not to worry about Eric's urgent need to talk to me. I started the coffee to perking, and then I pulled out the griddle and plugged it in. "I hope you like pancakes," I told Hunter, and his face lit up. He put his orange juice cup down on the table with a happy bang, and juice slopped over the edge. Just as I was about to give him a long look, he jumped up and fetched a paper towel. He took care of the spill with more vigor than attention to detail, but I appreciated the gesture.

"I love pancakes," he said. "You can make 'em? They don't come out of the freezer?"

I hid a smile. "Nope. I can make 'em." It took about five minutes to mix up a batch, and by then the griddle was hot. I put on some bacon first, and Hunter's expression was ecstatic. "I don't like it floppy," he said, and I promised him it would be crisp. That was the way I liked it, too.

"That smells wonderful, Cousin," said

Claude. He was standing in the doorway, his arms spread wide, looking as good as anyone can look that early in the morning. He was wearing a maroon University of Louisiana at Monroe T-shirt and some black workout shorts.

"Who are you?" Hunter asked.

"I'm Sookie's cousin Claude."

He has long hair like a lady, too, Hunter said.

He's a man, though, just like the other man. "Claude, this is another cousin of mine, Hunter," I said. "Remember, I told you he was coming to visit?"

"His mother was —" Claude began, and I shook my head at him.

Claude might have been about to say any number of things. He might have said, "the bisexual" or "the one the albino, Waldo, killed in the cemetery in New Orleans." These would both have been true, and Hunter needed to hear neither of them.

"So we're all cousins," I said. "Were you hinting around that you wanted to eat some breakfast with us, Claude?"

"Yes, I was," he said gracefully, pouring himself some coffee from the pot without asking me. "If there's enough for me, too. This young man looks like he could eat a lot of pancakes."

Hunter was delighted with this idea, and he and Claude began topping each other on the number of pancakes they could consume. I was surprised that Claude was so at ease with Hunter, though the fact that he was charming the child effortlessly was no surprise to me. Claude was a professional at charming.

"Do you live here in Bon Temps, Hunter?" Claude was asking.

"No," said Hunter, laughing at the absurdity of such an idea. "I live with my daddy."

Okay, that was enough sharing. I didn't want anyone supernatural knowing about Hunter, understanding what made him special.

"Claude, would you get out the syrup and the molasses?" I said. "It's in the pantry over there."

Claude located the pantry and brought out the Log Cabin and the Brer Rabbit. He even opened both bottles so Hunter could smell them and pick which one he wanted on his pancakes. I got the pancakes on the griddle and made some more coffee, pulling some plates out of the cabinets and showing Hunter where the forks and knives were so he could set the table.

We were a strange little family grouping: two telepaths and a fairy. During our breakfast conversation, I had to keep each male from knowing what the other was, and that was a real challenge. Hunter told me silently that Claude must be a vampire, because he couldn't hear Claude's thoughts, and I had to tell Hunter that there were some other people we couldn't hear, too. I pointed out that Claude couldn't be a vampire because it was daytime, and vampires couldn't come out in the daytime.

"There's a vampire in the closet," Hunter told Claude. "He can't come out in the daytime."

"Which closet would that be?" Claude asked Hunter.

"The one in my room. You want to come see?"

"Hunter," I said, "the last thing any vampire wants is to be disturbed in the daytime. I'd leave him alone."

"Your Eric?" Claude asked. He was excited by the idea of Eric being in the house. Damn.

"Yes," I said. "You know better than to go in there, right? I mean, I don't have to get tough with you, right?"

He smiled at me. "You, tough with me?" he said, mockingly. "Ha. I'm fae. I am stronger than any human."

I started to say, "So how come I survived

the war between the fae and so many fairies didn't?" Thank God I didn't. The minute after, I knew how good it was that I'd choked on those words, because I could see by Claude's face that he remembered who'd died all too well. I missed Claudine, too, and I told him so.

"You're sad," Hunter said accurately. And he was picking up on all this, which shouldn't be thought of in his hearing.

"Yes, we're remembering his sister," I said. "She died and we miss her."

"Like my mom," he said. "What's a fay?"

"Yes, like your mom." Sort of. Only in the sense that they were both dead. "And a fae is a special person, but we're not going to talk about that right now."

It didn't take a telepath to pick up on Claude's interest and curiosity, and when he sauntered back down the hall to use the bathroom, I followed him. Sure enough, Claude's steps slowed and stopped at the open door to the bedroom Hunter had used.

"Keep right on walking," I said.

"I can't take a peek? He'll never know. I've heard how handsome he is. Just a peek?"

"No," I said, knowing I'd better stay in sight of that door until Claude was out of the house. Just a peek, my round rosy ass.

"What about your ass, Aunt Sookie?"

"Oops! Sorry, Hunter. I said a bad word." Didn't want Claude to know I'd only thought it. I heard him laughing as he shut the bathroom door.

Claude stayed in the bathroom so long that I had to let Hunter brush his teeth in mine. After I heard the squeak of the stairs and the sound of the television overhead, I was able to relax. I helped Hunter get dressed, and then I got dressed myself and put on some makeup under Hunter's unwavering attention to the process. Evidently, Kristen had never let Hunter watch what he considered to be a fascinating procedure.

"You should come to live with us, Aunt Sookie," he said.

Thanks, Hunter, but I like to live here. I have a job.

You can get another one.

"It wouldn't be the same. This is my house, and I love it here. I don't want to leave."

There was a knock on the front door. Could Remy be arriving this early to collect Hunter?

But it was another surprise altogether, an unpleasant one. Special Agent Tom Lattesta stood on the front porch.

Hunter, naturally, had run to the door as

201

fast as he could. Don't all kids? He hadn't thought it was his dad, because he didn't know exactly when Remy was supposed to show up. He just liked to find out who was visiting.

"Hunter," I said, picking him up, "this is an FBI agent. His name is Tom Lattesta. Can you remember that?"

Hunter looked doubtful. He tried a couple of times to say the unfamiliar name and finally got it right.

"Good job, Hunter!" Lattesta said. He was trying to be friendly, but he wasn't good with kids and he sounded fake. "Ms. Stack-house, can I come in for a minute?" I looked behind him. No one else. I thought they always traveled in pairs.

"I guess so," I said, without enthusiasm. I didn't explain who Hunter was, because it was none of Lattesta's business, though I could tell he was curious. He'd also noticed there was another car parked outside.

"Claude," I called up the stairs. "The FBI is here." It's good to inform unexpected company that someone else is in the house with you.

The television fell silent, and Claude came gliding down the stairs. Now he was wear-ing a golden brown silk T-shirt and khakis, and he looked like a poster for a wet dream.

Even Lattesta's heterosexual orientation wasn't proof against a surge of startled admiration. "Agent Lattesta, my cousin Claude Crane," I said, trying not to smile.

Hunter and Claude and I sat on the couch while Lattesta took the La-Z-Boy. I didn't offer him anything to drink.

"How's Agent Weiss?" I asked. The New Orleans–based agent had brought Lattesta, based in Rhodes, out to my house last time, and in the course of many terrible events, she'd been shot.

"She's back at work," Lattesta said. "Still on a desk job. Mr. Crane, I don't believe I've met you before?"

No one forgot Claude. Of course, my cousin knew that very well. "You haven't had the pleasure," he told the FBI man.

Lattesta spent a moment trying to figure that out before he smiled. "Right," he said. "Listen, Ms. Stackhouse, I came up here today to tell you that you're no longer a subject for investigation."

I was stunned with the relief that swept over me. I exchanged glances with Claude. God bless my great-grandfather. I wondered how much he'd spent, how many strings he'd pulled, to make this come true.

"How come?" I asked. "Not that I'm going to miss it, you understand, but I have to wonder what's changed."

"You seem to know people who are powerful," Lattesta said, with an unexpected depth of bitterness. "Someone in our government doesn't want your name to come up in public."

"And you flew all the way to Louisiana to tell me that," I said, putting enough disbelief into my voice to let him know I thought that was bullshit.

"No, I flew all the way down here to go to a hearing about the shooting."

Okay. That made more sense. "And you didn't have my phone number? To call me? You had to come here to tell me you weren't going to investigate me, in person?"

"There's something wrong about you," he said, and the façade was gone. It was a relief. Now his outside matched his inside. "Sara Weiss has undergone some kind of . . . spiritual upheaval since she met you. She goes to séances. She's reading books about the paranormal. Her husband is worried about her. The bureau is worried about her. Her boss is having doubts about putting her back out in the field."

"I'm sorry to hear that. But I don't see that there's anything I can do about it." I thought for a minute, while Tom Lattesta stared at me with angry eyes. He was thinking angry thoughts, too. "Even if I went to her and told her that I can't do what she thinks I can do, it wouldn't help. She believes what she believes. I am what I am."

"So you admit it."

Even though I didn't want the FBI noticing me, that hurt, oddly enough. I wondered if Lattesta was taping our conversation.

"Admit *what?*" I asked. I was genuinely curious to hear what he'd say. The first time he'd been on my doorstep, he'd been a believer. He'd thought I was his key to a quick rise in the bureau.

"Admit you're not even a human being."

Aha. He really believed that. I disgusted and repelled him. I had more insight into what Sam was feeling.

"I've been watching you, Ms. Stackhouse. I've been called off, but if I can tie you in to any investigation that will lead back to you, I'll do it. You're *wrong*. I'm leaving now, and I hope you —" He didn't get a chance to finish.

"Don't think bad things about my aunt Sookie," Hunter said furiously. "You're a *bad man*."

I couldn't have put it better myself, but I wished for Hunter's own sake that he had kept his mouth shut. Lattesta turned white as a sheet.

Claude laughed. "He's scared of you," he told Hunter. Claude thought it was a great joke, and I had a feeling he'd known what Hunter was all along.

I thought Lattesta's grudge might constitute a real danger to me.

"Thanks for coming to give me the good news, Special Agent Lattesta," I said, in as mild a voice as I could manage. "You have a safe drive back to Baton Rouge, or New Orleans, or wherever you flew in."

Lattesta was on his feet and out the door before I could say another word, and I handed Hunter to Claude and followed him. Lattesta was down the steps and at his car, fumbling around in his pocket, before he realized I was behind him. He was turning off a pocket recording device. He wheeled around to give me an angry look.

"You'd use a kid," he said. "That's low."

I looked at him sharply for a minute. Then I said, "You're worried that your little boy, who's Hunter's age, has autism. You're scared this hearing you came to attend will go badly for you and maybe for Agent Weiss. You're scared because you reacted to Claude. You're thinking of asking to transfer into the BVA in Louisiana. You're mad that I know people who can make you back off."

If Lattesta could have pressed himself into

206

the metal of the car, he would've. I'd been a fool because I'd been proud. I should have let him go without a word.

"I wish I could tell you who it was who put me off-limits to the FBI," I said. "It would scare your pants off." In for a penny, in for a pound, right? I turned and went back up the front steps and into the house. A moment later, I heard his car tear down my driveway, probably scattering my beautiful gravel as it went.

Hunter and Claude were laughing in the kitchen, and I found them blowing with straws into the dishwashing water in the sink, which still had some soap bubbles. Hunter was standing on a stool I used to reach the top shelves of the cabinets. It was an unexpectedly happy picture.

"So, Cousin, he's gone?" Claude asked. "Good job, Hunter. I think there's a lake monster under that water!"

Hunter blew even harder, and water drops spattered the curtains. He laughed a little too wildly.

"Okay, kids, enough," I said. This was getting out of hand. Leave a fairy alone with a child for a few minutes, and this was what happened. I glanced at the clock. Thanks to Hunter's early wake-up call, it was only nine. I didn't expect Remy to come to collect Hunter until late afternoon.

"Let's go to the park, Hunter."

Claude looked disappointed that I'd stopped their fun, but Hunter was game to go somewhere. I grabbed my softball mitt and a ball and retied Hunter's sneakers.

"Am I invited, too?" Claude said, sounding a little miffed.

I was taken by surprise. "Sure, you can come," I said. "That would be great. Maybe you should take your own car, since I don't know what we'll be doing afterward." My self-absorbed cousin genuinely enjoyed being with Hunter. I would never have anticipated this reaction — and truthfully, I don't think he had anticipated it, either. Claude followed me in his Impala as I drove to the park.

I went to Magnolia Creek Park, which stretched on either side of the creek. It was prettier than the little park close to the elementary school. The park wasn't much, of course, since Bon Temps is not exactly a wealthy little town, but it had the standard playground equipment, a quarter-mile walking track, and plenty of open area, picnic tables, and trees. Hunter attacked the jungle gym as if he'd never seen one before, and maybe he hadn't. Red Ditch is smaller and poorer than Bon Temps.

I found that Hunter could climb like a monkey. Claude was ready to steady him at every move. Hunter would've found that annoying if I'd done it. I wasn't sure why that should be, but I knew it to be true.

A car pulled up as I enticed Hunter down from the jungle gym to play ball. Tara got out and came over to see what we were doing.

"Who's your friend, Sookie?" she called.

The tight top she was wearing made Tara look a little bigger than she had when she'd come into the bar to eat lunch. She was wearing some pre-pregnancy shorts scooted down under her belly. I knew extra money wasn't plentiful in the du Rone/Thornton household these days, but I hoped Tara could find money in the budget to get some real maternity clothes before too long. Unfortunately, her clothing store, Tara's Togs, didn't carry maternity stuff.

"This is my cousin Hunter," I said. "Hunter, this is my friend Tara." Claude, who had been swinging on the swing set, chose that moment to leap off and bound over to where we stood. "Tara, this is my cousin Claude."

Now, Tara had known me all her life, and she knew all the members of my family. I gave her high points for absorbing this introduction and giving Hunter a friendly smile, which she then extended to Claude. She must have recognized him — she'd seen him in action. But she never blinked an eye.

"How many months are you?" Claude asked.

"A little more than three months away from delivery," Tara said, and sighed. I guess Tara had gotten used to relative strangers asking her personal questions. She'd told me before that all conversational bars were removed when you were pregnant. "People will ask you anything," she'd said. "And the women'll tell you labor and delivery stories that make your hair curl."

"Do you want to know what you're having?" Claude asked.

That was way out of bounds. "Claude," I said reprovingly. "That's too personal." Fairies just didn't have the same concept of personal information *or* personal space that humans did.

"I apologize," my cousin said, very insincerely. "I thought you might enjoy knowing before you buy their clothes. You color-code babies, I believe."

"Sure," Tara said abruptly. "What sex is the baby?"

"Both," he said with a smile. "You're having twins, a boy and a girl."

"My doctor's heard only one heartbeat," she said, trying to be gentle about telling him he was wrong.

"Then your doctor is an idiot," Claude said cheerfully. "You have two babies, alive and well."

Tara obviously didn't know what to make of this. "I'll get him to look harder next time I go in," she said. "And I'll tell Sookie to let you know what he says."

Fortunately, Hunter had mostly ignored this conversation. He had just learned how to throw the softball up in the air and catch it, and he was distracted by the effort to put my mitt on his little hand. "Did you play baseball, Aunt Sookie?" he asked.

"Softball," I said. "You bet I did. I played right field. That means I stood way out in the field and waited to see if the girl batting would hit the ball out my way. Then I'd catch it, and I'd throw it in to the pitcher, or whichever player needed it most."

"Your aunt Sookie was the best right fielder in the history of the Lady Falcons," Tara said, squatting down to talk to Hunter eye to eye.

"Well, I had a good time," I said.

"Did you play softball?" Hunter asked Tara.

"No, I came and cheered for Sookie," Tara said, which was the absolute truth, God bless her.

"Here, Hunter," Claude said, and gave the softball an easy toss. "Go get it and throw it back to me."

The unlikely twosome wandered around the park, throwing the ball to each other with very little accuracy. They were having a great time.

"Well, well, well," Tara said. "You have a habit of picking up family in funny places. A cousin? Where'd you get a cousin? He's not a secret by-blow of Jason's, right?"

"He's Hadley's son."

"Oh . . . oh my God." Tara's eyes widened. She looked at Hunter, trying to pick out a likeness to Hadley in his features. "That's not the dad? Impossible."

"No," I said. "That's Claude Crane, and he's my cousin, too."

"He's sure not Hadley's kid," Tara said, laughing. "And Hadley's the only cousin you had that I ever heard of."

"Ah . . . sort of wrong-side-of-the-blanket stuff," I said. It was impossible to explain without casting Gran's integrity into question.

Tara saw how uncomfortable I was with the subject of Claude.

212

"How are you and the tall blond getting along?"

"We're getting along okay," I said cautiously. "I'm not looking elsewhere."

"I should say not! No woman in her right mind would go out with anyone else if she could have Eric. Beautiful *and* smart." Tara sounded a bit wistful. Well, at least JB was beautiful.

"Eric can be a pain when he wants to be. And talk about baggage!" I tried to picture stepping out on Eric. "If I tried to see someone else, he might . . ."

"Kill that someone else?"

"He sure wouldn't be happy," I said, in a massive understatement.

"So, you want to tell me what's wrong?" Tara put her hand on mine. She's not a toucher, so that meant a lot.

"Truth be told, Tara, I'm not sure." I had an overwhelming feeling that something was askew, something important. But I couldn't put my finger on what that might be.

"Supes?" she said.

I shrugged.

"Well, I got to go into the shop," she said. "McKenna opened for me today, but I can't ask her to do that for me all the time." We said good-bye, happier with each other than we'd been in a long time. I realized that I needed to throw Tara a baby shower, and I couldn't imagine why it hadn't occurred to me before now. I needed to get cracking on the planning. If I made it a surprise shower, and did all the food myself . . . Oh, and I'd have to tell people Tara and JB were expecting twins. I didn't doubt Claude's accuracy for a second.

I thought I would go out into the woods myself, maybe tomorrow. I'd be alone then. I knew that Heidi's nose and eyes — and Basim's, for that matter — were far more acute than mine, but I had an overwhelming impulse to see what I could see. Once again, something stirred in the back of my head, a memory that wasn't a memory. Something to do with the woods . . . with a hurt man in the woods. I shook my head to rid myself of the haziness, and I realized I couldn't hear any voices.

"Claude," I called.

"Here!"

I walked around a clump of bushes and saw the fairy and the little boy enjoying the whirligig. That's what I'd always called it, anyway. It's circular, several kids can stand on it, a few others run around the edges pushing, and then it whirls in a circle until the impetus is gone. Claude was pushing it way too fast, and though Hunter was enjoying it, his grin was looking a little tense, too. I could see the fear in his brain, seeping through the pleasure.

"Whoa, Claude," I said, keeping my voice level. "That's enough speed for a kid." Claude stopped pushing, though he was reluctant. He'd been having a great time himself.

Though Hunter pooh-poohed my warning, I could tell he was relieved. He hugged Claude when Claude told him he had to go to Monroe to open up his club. "What kind of club?" Hunter asked, and I had to give Claude a significant look and keep my head blank.

"See you later, sport," the fairy told the child, and hugged him back.

It was time for an early lunch, so I took Hunter to McDonald's as a big treat. His dad hadn't mentioned any ban on fast food, and I figured one trip was okay.

Hunter loved his Happy Meal, ran the toy car from the container over the tabletop until I was absolutely tired of it, and then wanted to go into the play area. I was sitting on a bench watching him, hoping the joys of the tunnels and the slide would hold him for at least ten more minutes, when another woman came out the door into the fenced area, with a boy about Hunter's age in tow. Though I practically heard the ominous thud of bass drums, I kept a smile pasted on my face and hoped for the best.

After a few seconds of regarding each other warily, the two boys began shouting and running around the small play area together, and I relaxed, but cautiously. I ventured a smile at Mom, but she was brooding off into the distance, and I didn't have to read her mind to see she'd had a bad morning. (I discovered that her dryer had broken down, and she couldn't afford another one for at least two months.)

"Is this your youngest?" I asked, trying to look cheerful and interested.

"Yes, youngest of four," she said, which explained her desperation about the dryer. "All the rest of 'em are at Little League baseball practice. It'll be summer vacation soon, and they'll be home for three months."

Oh. I was out of things to say.

My unwilling companion sank back into her own grim thoughts, and I did my best to stay out. It was a struggle, because she was like a black hole of unhappy thoughts, kind of sucking me in with her.

Hunter came to stand in front of her, regarding her with open-mouthed fascination.

"Hello," the woman said, making a great effort.

"Do you really want to run away?" he asked.

This was definitely an "oh shit" moment. "Hunter, we need to be going," I said quickly. "Come on, now. We're late, late!" And I picked Hunter up and carried him away, though he was squirming and wiggling in protest (and also much heavier than he looked). He actually landed a kick on my thigh, and I almost dropped him.

The mother in the play area was staring after us, her mouth agape, and her little boy had come to stand in front of her, puzzled at his playmate's abrupt departure.

"I was having a good time!" Hunter yelled. "Why do we have to go?"

I looked him straight in the eyes. "Hunter, you be quiet until we're in the car," I said, and I meant every word. Carrying him through the restaurant while he was yelling had focused every eye on us, and I hadn't enjoyed the attention. I'd noticed a couple of people I knew, and there would be questions to answer later. This wasn't Hunter's fault, but it didn't make me feel any kinder.

As I buckled his seat belt, I realized I'd let Hunter get too tired and overexcited, and I made a mental note not to do that again. I could feel his little brain practically jiggling up and down.

Hunter was looking at me as though his heart were broken. "I was having a good time," he said again. "That boy was my friend."

I turned sideways to look him in the face. "Hunter, you said something to his mom that let her know you're different."

He was realistic enough to admit the truth of what I was saying. "She was really mad," he muttered. "Moms leave their kids."

His own mother had left him.

I thought for a second about what I could say. I decided to ignore the darker theme here. Hadley had left Remy and Hunter, and now she was dead and would never return. Those were facts. There was nothing I could do to change them. What Remy wanted me to do was to help Hunter live the rest of his life.

"Hunter, this is hard. I know it. I went through the same thing. You could hear what that mom was thinking, and then you said it out loud."

"But she *was* saying it! In her head!"

"But not out loud."

"That was what she was *saying*."

"*In her head.*" He was just being stubborn now. "Hunter, you're a very young man. But to make your own life easier, you have to start thinking before you talk."

Hunter's eyes were wide and brimful with tears.

"You have to think, and you have to keep your mouth shut."

Two big tears coursed down his pink cheeks. Oh, geez Louise.

"You can't ask people questions about what you hear from their heads. Remember, we talked about privacy?"

He nodded once uncertainly, and then again with more energy. He remembered.

"People — grown-ups and children — are going to get real upset with you if they know you can read what's in their heads. Because the stuff in someone's head is private. You wouldn't want anyone telling you you're thinking about how bad you need to pee."

Hunter glared at me.

"See? Doesn't feel good, does it?"

"No," he said, grudgingly.

"I want you to grow up as normal as you can," I said. "Growing up with this condition is tough. Do you know any kids with problems everyone can see?"

After a minute, he nodded. "Jenny Vasco," he said. "She has a big mark on her face."

"It's the same thing, except you can hide your difference, and Jenny can't," I said. I was feeling mighty sorry for Jenny Vasco. It seemed wrong to be teaching a little kid that he should be stealthy and secretive, but the world wasn't ready for a mind-reading five-year-old, and probably never would be.

I felt like a mean old witch as I looked at his unhappy and tear-stained face. "We're going to go home and read a story," I said.

"Are you mad at me, Aunt Sookie?" he said, with a hint of a sob.

"No," I said, though I wasn't happy about being kicked. Since he'd know that, I'd better mention it. "I don't appreciate your kicking me, Hunter, but I'm not mad anymore. I'm really mad at the rest of the world, because this is hard on you."

He was silent all the way home. We went inside and sat on the couch after he paid a visit to the bathroom and picked a couple of books from the stash I'd kept. Hunter was asleep before I finished *The Poky Little Puppy.* I gently eased him down on the couch, pulled off his shoes, and got my own book. I read while he napped. I got up from time to time to get some small task done. Hunter slept for almost two hours. I found this an incredibly peaceful time, though if I hadn't had Hunter all day, it might simply have been boring.

After I'd started a load of laundry and

tiptoed back into the room, I stood by the sleeping boy and looked down. If I had a child, would my baby have the same problem Hunter had? I hoped not. Of course, if Eric and I continued in our relationship, I would never have a child unless I was artificially inseminated. I tried to picture myself asking Eric how he felt about me being impregnated by an unknown man, and I'm ashamed to say I had to smother a snigger.

Eric was very modern in some respects. He liked the convenience of his cell phone, he loved automatic garage-door openers, and he liked watching the news on television. But artificial insemination . . . I didn't think so. I'd heard his verdict on plastic surgery, and I had a strong feeling he'd consider this in the same category.

"What's funny, Aunt Sookie?" Hunter said.

"Nothing important," I said. "How about some apple slices and some milk?"

"No ice cream?"

"Well, you had a hamburger and French fries and a Coke at lunch. I think we'd better stick to the apple slices."

I put *The Lion King* on while I prepared Hunter's snack, and he sat on the floor in front of the television while he ate. Hunter got tired of the movie (which of course he'd seen before) about halfway through, and after that, I taught him how to play Candy Land. He won the first time.

As we were working our way through a second game, there was a knock. "Daddy!" Hunter shrieked, and pelted for the door. Before I could stop him, he'd pulled it open. I was glad he'd known who the caller was, because it gave me a bad moment. Remy was standing there in a dress shirt, suit pants, and polished lace-ups. He looked like a different man. He was grinning at Hunter as if he hadn't seen his child in days. In a second, the boy was up in his arms.

It was heartwarming. They hugged each other tight. I had a little lump in my throat.

In a second, Hunter was telling Remy about Candy Land, and about McDonald's, and about Claude, and Remy was listening with complete attention. He gave me a quick smile to say he'd greet me in a second, once the torrent of information had slowed down.

"Son, you want to go get all your stuff together? Don't leave anything," Remy cautioned his son. With a quick smile in my direction, Hunter dashed off to the back of the house.

"Did it go okay?" Remy asked, the minute

222

Hunter was out of earshot. Though in a sense Hunter was *never* out of hearing, it would have to do.

"Yes, I think so. He's been so good," I said, resolving to keep the kick to myself. "We had a little problem on the McDonald's playground, but I think it led to a good talk with him."

Remy looked as if a load had just dropped back onto his shoulders. "I'm sorry about that," he said, and I could have — well, kicked myself.

"No, it was only normal stuff, the kind of thing you brought him here so I could help with," I said. "Don't worry about it. My cousin Claude was here, and he played with Hunter at the park, though I was there all the time, of course." I didn't want Remy to think I'd farmed Hunter out to any old person. I tried to think of what else to tell the anxious father. "He ate real good, and he slept just fine. Not long enough," I said, and Remy laughed.

"I know all about that," he told me.

I started to tell Remy that Eric was asleep in the closet and that Hunter had seen him for a few minutes, but I had the confused feeling that Eric would be one man too many. I'd already introduced the idea of Claude, and Remy hadn't been totally delighted to hear about that. A typical dad reaction, I guessed.

"Did the funeral go okay? No last-minute hitches?" You never know what to ask about funerals.

"No one threw themselves into the grave or fainted," Remy said. "That's about all you can hope for. A few skirmishes over a dining room table that all the kids wanted to load into their trucks right then."

I nodded. I'd heard many brooding thoughts through the years about inheritances, and I'd had my own troubles with Jason when Gran died. "People don't always have their nicest face on when it comes to dividing up a household," I said.

I offered Remy a drink, but he smilingly turned me down. He was obviously ready to be alone with his son, and he peppered me with questions about Hunter's manners, which I was able to praise, and his eating habits, which I was able to admire, too. Hunter wasn't a picky kid, and that was a blessing.

Within a few minutes, Hunter had returned to the living room with all his stuff, though I did a quick patrol and found two Duplos that had escaped his notice. Since he'd liked *The Poky Little Puppy* so much, I stuck it in his backpack for him to enjoy at home. After a few more thank-yous, and an unexpected hug from Hunter, they were gone.

I watched Remy's old truck go down the driveway.

The house felt oddly empty.

Of course, Eric was asleep underneath it, but he was dead for a few more hours, and I knew I could rouse him only in the direst of circumstances. Some vampires couldn't wake in the daytime, even if they were set on fire. I pushed that memory away, since it made me shiver. I glanced at the clock. I had part of the sunny afternoon to myself, and it was my day off.

I was in my black-and-white bikini and lying out on the old chaise before you could say, "Sunbathing is bad for you."

CHAPTER 7

The minute the sun sank, Eric was out of the compartment below the guest-bedroom closet. He picked me up and kissed me thoroughly. I'd already warmed up some TrueBlood for him, and he made a face but gulped it down.

"Who is the child?" he asked.

"Hadley's son," I said. Eric had met Hadley when she'd been going with Sophie-Anne Leclerq, the now-finally-deceased Queen of Louisiana.

"She was married to a breather?"

"Yes, before she met Sophie-Anne," I said. "A very nice guy named Remy Savoy."

"Is that him I smell? Along with a big scent of fairy?"

Uh-oh. "Yes, Remy came to pick up Hunter this afternoon. I was keeping him because Remy had to go to a family funeral. He didn't think that would be a good place to take a kid." I didn't bring up Hunter's little problem. The fewer who knew about it, the better, and that included Eric.

"And?"

"I meant to tell you this the other night," I said. "My cousin Claude?"

Eric nodded.

"He asked if he could stay here for a while, because he's lonely in his house with both his sisters dead."

"You are letting a man live with you." Eric didn't sound angry — more like he was poised to be angry, if you know what I mean? There was just a little edge in his voice.

"Believe me, he's not interested in me as a woman," I said, though I had a guilty flash of him walking in on me in the bathroom. "He is all about the guys."

"I know you are fully aware of how to take care of a fairy who gives you trouble," Eric said, after an appreciable silence.

I'd killed fairies before. I hadn't particularly wanted to be reminded of that. "Yes," I said. "And if it'll make you feel better, I'll keep a squirt gun loaded with lemon juice on my bedside table." Lemon juice and iron — the fairy weaknesses.

"That would make me feel better," Eric said. "Is it this Claude that Heidi scented on your land? I felt you were very worried, and that's one reason I came over last night."

The blood bond was hard at work. "She says neither of the fairies she tracked was Claude," I said, "and that really worries me. But —"

"It worries me, too." Eric looked down at the empty bottle of TrueBlood, then said, "Sookie, there are things you should know."

"Oh." I'd been about to tell him about the fresh corpse. I was sure he would have led off the discussion with the body if Heidi had mentioned it, and it seemed pretty important to me. I may have sounded a little peeved at being interrupted. Eric gave me a sharp look.

Okay, I was at fault, *excuse me.* I should have been longing to be chockfull of information that Eric felt would help me negotiate the minefield of vampire politics. And there were nights I'd have been delighted to learn more about my boyfriend's life. But tonight, after the unusual stresses and strains of Hunter care, what I'd wanted was (again, *excuse me*) to tell him about the body-in-the-woods crisis and then have a good long screw.

Normally, Eric would be down with that program.

But not tonight, apparently.

We sat opposite each other at the kitchen table. I tried not to sigh out loud.

"You remember the summit at Rhodes, and how a sort of strip of states from south to north were invited," Eric began.

I nodded. This didn't sound too promising. My corpse was way more urgent. Not to mention the sex.

"Once we had ventured from one side of the New World to another, and the white breathing population migrated across, too — *we* were the first explorers — a large group of us met to divide things up, for better governing of our own population."

"Were there any Native American vampires here when you came? Hey, were you on the Leif Ericson expedition?"

"No, not my generation. Oddly enough, there were very few Native American vampires. And the ones that were here were different in several ways."

Now, that was pretty interesting, but I could tell Eric wasn't going to stop and fill in the blanks.

"At that first national meeting, about three hundred years ago, there were many disagreements." Eric looked very, very serious.

"No, really?" Vampires arguing? I could yawn.

And he didn't appreciate my sarcasm, either. He raised blond eyebrows, as if to say, "Can I go on and get to the point? Or are you going to give me grief?"

I spread my hands: "Keep on going."

"Instead of dividing the country the way humans would, we included some of the north and some of the south in every division. We thought it would keep the cross-representation going. So the easternmost division, which is mostly the coastal states, is called Moshup Clan, for the Native American mythical figure, and its symbol is a whale."

Okay, maybe I looked a little glazed at that point. "Look it up on the Internet," Eric said impatiently. "Our clan — the states that met in Rhodes compose this one — is Amun, a god from the Egyptian system, and our symbol is a feather, because Amun wore a feathered headdress. Do you remember that we all wore little feather pins there?"

Ah. No. I shook my head.

"Well, it was a busy summit," Eric conceded.

What with the bombs, and the explosions, and all.

"To our west is Zeus, from the Roman system, and a thunderbolt is their symbol, of course."

Sure. I nodded in profound agreement. Eric may have sensed that I was not exactly on board, by then. He gave me a stern look. "Sookie, this is important. As my wife, you must know this."

I wasn't even going to get into that tonight. "Okay, go ahead," I said.

"The fourth clan, the West Coast division, is called Narayana, from early Hinduism, and its symbol is an eye, because Narayana created the sun and moon from his eyes."

I thought of things I'd like to ask, like "Who the hell sat around and picked the stupid names?" But when I ran my questions through my inner censor, each one sounded snarkier than the last. I said, "But there were some vampires at the summit in Rhodes — the Amun Clan summit — that should be in Zeus, right?"

"Yes, good! There are visitors at the summits, if they have some vested interest in a topic under discussion. Or if they are engaged in a lawsuit against someone in that division. Or if they're going to marry someone in the division whose time it is to have a summit." His eyes crinkled at the corners with his smile of approval. *Narayana created the sun from his eyes,* I thought. I smiled back.

"I understand," I said. "So, how come Felipe conquered Louisiana, since we're Amun and he's . . . Ah, is Nevada in Narayana or Zeus?"

"Narayana. He took Louisiana because he wasn't as frightened of Sophie-Anne as everyone else. He planned, and executed quickly and with precision after the governing . . . board . . . of Narayana Clan approved his plan."

"He had to present a plan before he moved on us?"

"That's the way it's done. The kings and queens of Narayana wouldn't want their territory weakened if Felipe failed and Sophie-Anne managed to take Nevada. So he had to outline his plan."

"They didn't think we might want to say something about that plan?"

"Not their concern. If we're weak enough to be taken, then we are fair game. Sophie-Anne was a good leader, and much respected. With her incapacitation, Felipe judged we were weak enough to attack. Stan's lieutenant in Texas has struggled these past few months since Stan was injured in Rhodes, and it's been hard for him to hold on to Texas."

"How would they know how hurt Sophie-Anne was? How hurt Stan is?"

"Spies. We all spy on each other." Eric

shrugged. (Big deal. Spies.)

"What if one of the rulers in Narayana had owed some favor to Sophie-Anne and decided to tip her off to the takeover?"

"I'm sure some of them considered it. But with Sophie-Anne so severely wounded, I suppose they decided that the odds lay with Felipe."

This was appalling. "How do you trust anyone?"

"I don't. There are two exceptions. You, and Pam."

"Oh," I said. I tried to imagine feeling like that. "That's awful, Eric."

I thought he'd shrug that off. But instead, he regarded me soberly. "Yes. It's not good."

"Do you know who the spies in Area Five are?"

"Felicia, of course. She is weak, and it's not much of a secret that she must be in the pay of someone; probably Stan in Texas, or Freyda in Oklahoma."

"I don't know Freyda." I'd met Stan. "Is Texas in Zeus or Amun?"

Eric beamed at me. I was his star pupil. "Zeus," he said. "But Stan had to be at the summit because he was proposing to go in with Mississippi on a resort development."

"He sure paid for that," I said. "If they have spies, we have spies, too, right?"

"Of course."

"Who? I'm not missing anyone?"

"You met Rasul in New Orleans, I believe."

I nodded. Rasul had been of Middle Eastern stock, and he'd had quite a sense of humor. "He survived the takeover."

"Yes, because he agreed to become a spy for Victor, and therefore for Felipe. They sent him to Michigan."

"Michigan?"

"There is a very large Arab enclave there, and Rasul fits in well. He tells them he fled the takeover." Eric paused. "You know, his life will be ended if you tell anyone this."

"Oh, duh. I'm not telling anyone any of this. For one thing, the fact that you-all named your little slices of America after gods is just . . ." I shook my head. Really something. I wasn't sure what. Proud? Stupid? Bizarre? "For another thing, I like Rasul." And I thought it was pretty damn smart of him to take the chance to get out from under Victor's thumb, no matter what he'd agreed to do. "Why are you telling me all this, all of a sudden?"

"I think you need to know what's going on around you, my lover." Eric had never looked more serious. "Last night, while I was working, I found myself distracted by

234

the idea that you might suffer for your ignorance. Pam agreed. She's wanted to give you the background of our hierarchy for some weeks. But I thought the knowledge would burden you, and you had enough problems to handle. Pam reminded me that ignorance could get you killed. I value you too much to let yours continue."

My initial thought was that I'd really enjoyed that ignorance, and it would have been okay with me if I'd retained it. Then I had to hop all over myself. Eric was really trying to include me in his life and its ins and outs. And he was trying to help me acclimatize to his world because he considered me a part of it. I tried to feel warm and fuzzy about that.

Finally, I said, "Thanks." I tried to think of intelligent questions to ask. "Um, okay. So the kings and queens of each state in a particular division get together to make decisions and bond — what, every two years?"

Eric was eyeing me cautiously. He could tell not all was well in Sookieville. "Yes," he said. "Unless there's some crisis that calls for an extra meeting. Each state is not a separate kingdom. For instance, there's a ruler of New York City and a ruler of the rest of the state. Florida is also divided."

"Why?" That took me aback. Until I considered. "Oh, lots of tourists. Easy prey. High vampire population."

Eric nodded. "California is in thirds — California Sacramento, California San Jose, and California Los Angeles. On the other hand, North and South Dakota have become one kingdom, since the population is so thin."

I was getting the hang of looking at things through vampire eyes. There'd be more lions where the gazelles crowded around the watering hole. Fewer prey animals, fewer predators. "How does the business of — well, of Amun, say — get conducted between those biennial meetings?" There had to be stuff that came up.

"Message boards, mostly. If we have to have a face-to-face, committees of sheriffs meet, depending on the situation. If I had an argument with the vampire of another sheriff, I'd call that sheriff, and if he wasn't ready to give me satisfaction, his lieutenant would meet with my lieutenant."

"And if that didn't work?"

"We'd kick the dispute up the ladder, to the summit. In between meeting years, there's an informal gathering, with no ceremony or celebration."

I could think of a lot of questions, but they

were all of the "what if" variety, and there wasn't any immediate need for me to know the answers.

"Okeydokey," I said. "Well, that was real interesting."

"You don't sound interested. You sound irritated."

"This isn't what I expected when I found out you were sleeping in the house."

"What did you expect?"

"I expected you'd come over here because you couldn't wait an extra minute to have fabulous, mind-blowing sex with me." And to hell with the corpse, for the moment.

"I've told you things for your own good," Eric said soberly. "However, now that that's done, I am as ready as ever to have sex with you, and I can certainly make it mind-blowing."

"Then cut to the chase, honey."

With a movement too fast for me to follow, Eric's shirt was off, and while I was admiring the view, his other clothes followed.

"Do I actually get to chase you?" he asked, his fangs already out.

I made it halfway to the living room before he caught me. But he carried me back to the bedroom.

It was great. Even though I had a niggling

anxiety gnawing at me, that gnawing was successfully stifled for a very satisfying forty-five minutes.

Eric liked to lie propped on his elbow, his other hand stroking my stomach. When I protested that since my stomach wasn't completely flat, this made me feel fat, he laughed heartily. "Who wants a bag of bones?" he said, with absolute sincerity. "I don't want to hurt myself on the sharp edges of the woman I'm bedding."

That made me feel better than anything he'd said to me in a long time. "Did women . . . Were women curvier when you were human?" I asked.

"We didn't always have choices about how fat we were," Eric said dryly. "In bad years, we were all skin and bones. In good years, when we could eat, we did."

I felt abashed. "Oh, sorry."

"This is a wonderful century to live in," Eric said. "You can have food anytime you want."

"If you have the money to pay for it."

"Oh, you can steal it," he said. "The point is, the food is here to be had."

"Not in Africa."

"I know people still starve in many parts of the world. But sooner or later, this prosperity will extend everywhere. It just got here first."

I found his optimism amazing. "You really think so?"

"Yes," he said simply. "Braid my hair for me, would you, Sookie?"

I got my hairbrush and an elastic band. Color me silly, but I really enjoyed doing this. Eric sat on the stool in front of my vanity table, and I threw on a robe he'd given me, a beautiful peach-and-white-silk one. I began brushing Eric's long hair. After he said he didn't mind, I got some hair gel and slicked the blond strands back so there wouldn't be any loose hairs ruining the look. I took my time, making the neatest braid I could, and then I tied off the end. Without his hair floating around his face, Eric looked more severe, but just as handsome. I sighed.

"What is this sound coming from you?" he asked, turning from side to side to get several views of himself in the mirror. "Are you not happy with the result?"

"I think you look great," I said. Only the fact that he might accuse me of false modesty kept me from saying, "So what on earth are you doing with me?"

"Now I'll do your hair."

Something in me flinched. The night I'd had sex for the very first time, Bill had brushed my hair until the sensuality of the movement had turned into a very different kind of sensuality. "No, thanks," I said brightly.

I realized that I felt very odd, all of a sudden.

Eric swung around to look up at me. "What's making you so jumpy, Sookie?"

"Hey, what happened to Alaska and Hawaii?" I asked at random. I still had the brush in my hand, and without meaning to, I dropped it. It clattered on the wooden floor.

"What?" Eric looked down at the brush, then up at my face, in some confusion.

"What section are they in? They both in Nakamura?"

"Narayana. No. Alaska is lumped in with the Canadians. They have their own system. Hawaii is autonomous."

"That's just not right." I was genuinely indignant. Then I remembered there was something very important I had to tell Eric. "I guess Heidi reported back to you after she sniffed out my land? She told you about the body?" My hand jerked involuntarily.

Eric was watching my every move, his eyes narrowed. "We already talked about Debbie Pelt. If you really want me to, I'll move her."

I shivered all over. I wanted to tell him

240

that the body was fresh. I'd started out to do that, but somehow I was having trouble formulating my sentence. I felt so peculiar. Eric cocked his head, his eyes locked on my face. "You're behaving very strangely, Sookie."

"Do you think Alcide could tell from the smell that the corpse was Debbie?" I asked. What was wrong with me?

"Not from the scent," he said. "A body is a body. It doesn't retain the distinctive scent that identified it as a particular person, especially after this long. Are you so worried about what Alcide thinks?"

"Not as much as I used to be," I said, babbling on. "Hey, I heard on the radio today that one of the senators from Oklahoma came out as a Were. He said he'd register with some government bureau the day they pried his fangs from his cold, dead corpse."

"I think the backlash from this will benefit vampires," Eric said with some satisfaction. "Of course, we'd always realized the government would want to keep track of us somehow. Now it seems that if the Weres win their fight to be free of supervision, we may be able to do the same."

"You better get dressed," I said. Something bad was going to happen soon, and Eric needed clothes.

He turned and peered at himself in the mirror one last time. "All right," he said, a little surprised. He was still nude and magnificent. But at the moment, I wasn't feeling a bit lusty. I was feeling jangly, and nervous, and worried. I felt like spiders were crawling all over my skin. I didn't know what could be happening to me. I tried to speak but found I couldn't. I made my fingers move in a "hurry up" gesture.

Eric gave me a quick, worried glance and wordlessly began searching for his clothes. He found his pants, and he pulled them on.

I sank down to the floor, my hands on both sides of my head. I thought my skull might detach from my spine. I whimpered. Eric dropped his shirt.

"Can you tell me what's wrong?" he asked, sinking down to the floor beside me.

"Someone's coming," I said. "I feel so *strange*. Someone's coming. Almost here. Someone with your blood." I realized I'd felt a faint, faint trace of this same oddness before, when I'd confronted Bill's maker, Lorena. I hadn't had a blood bond with Bill, or at least not one anything like as binding as the one I had with Eric.

Eric rose to his feet in less than the blink of an eye, and I heard him make a sound deep in his chest. His hands were in white fists. I was huddled against my bed, and he was between me and the open window. In the blink of an eye, I realized there was someone right outside.

"Appius Livius Ocella," Eric said. "It's been a hundred years."

Geez Louise. Eric's maker.

CHAPTER 8

Between Eric's legs I could see a man, very scarred and very muscular, with dark eyes and hair. I knew he was short because I could only see his head and shoulders. He was wearing jeans and a Black Sabbath T-shirt. I couldn't help it. I giggled.

"Haven't you missed me, Eric?" The Roman's voice had an accent I really couldn't have broken down, it had so many layers.

"Ocella, your presence is always an honor," Eric said. I giggled harder. Eric was lying.

"What is wrong with my wife?" he asked.

"Her senses are confused," the older vampire said. "You have my blood. She's had your blood. And another child of mine is here. The bond between us all is scrambling her thoughts and feelings."

No shit.

"This is my new son, Alexei," Appius Liv-

244

ius Ocella told Eric.

I peered past Eric's legs. The new "son" was a boy of no more than thirteen or fourteen. In fact, I could hardly see his face. I froze, trying not to react.

"Brother," said Eric by way of greeting his new sibling. The words came out level and cold.

I was going to stand up now. I was not going to crouch here any longer. Eric had crowded me into a very small space between the bed and the nightstand, with the bathroom door to my right. He hadn't shifted from his defensive posture.

"Excuse me," I said, with a great effort, and Eric took a step forward to give me room, keeping himself between me and his maker and the boy. I rose to my feet, pushing on the bed to get upright. I still felt fried. I looked Eric's sire right in his dark and liquid eyes. For a fraction of a second, he looked surprised.

"Eric, you need to go to the front door and let them in," I said. "I'll bet they don't really need an invitation."

"Eric, she's rare," said Ocella in his oddly accented English. "Where did you find her?"

"I'm asking you in out of courtesy, because you're Eric's dad," I said. "I could just leave you outside." If I didn't sound as

245

strong as I wanted, at least I didn't sound frightened.

"But my child is in this house, and if he is welcome, so am I. Am I not?" Ocella's thick black brows rose. His nose . . . Well, you could tell why they coined the term "Roman nose." "I waited to come in out of courtesy. We could have appeared in your bedroom."

And the next moment they were inside.

I didn't dignify that with an answer. I spared a glance for the boy, whose face was absolutely blank. He was no ancient Roman. He hadn't been a vampire a full century, I estimated, and he seemed to come from Germanic stock. His hair was light and short and cut evenly, his eyes were blue, and when he met my own, he inclined his head.

"Your name is Alexei?" I asked.

"Yes," said his maker, while the boy stood mute. "This is Alexei Romanov."

Though the boy didn't react, and neither did Eric, I had a moment of sheer horror. "You *didn't*," I said to Eric's maker, who was about my height. "You *didn't*."

"I tried to save one of his sisters, too, but she was beyond my recall," Ocella said bleakly. His teeth were white and even, though he was missing the one next to his left canine. If you had lost teeth before you became a vampire, they didn't regenerate.

"Sookie, what is it?" Eric was not following, for once.

"The Romanovs," I said, trying to keep my voice hushed as though the boy couldn't hear me from twenty yards away. "The last Russian royal family."

To Eric, the executions of the Romanovs must seem like yesterday, and perhaps not very important in the tapestry of deaths he'd experienced in his thousand years. But he understood that his maker had done something extraordinary. I looked at Ocella without anger, without fear, for just a few seconds, and I saw a man who, finding himself an outcast and lonely, looked for the most outstanding "children" he could find.

"Was Eric the first vampire you made?" I asked Ocella.

He was bemused by what he saw as my brazen attitude. Eric had a stronger reaction. As I felt his fear roll through me, I understood that Eric had to physically perform whatever Ocella ordered him to do. Before, that had been an abstract concept. Now I realized that if Ocella ordered Eric to kill me, Eric would be compelled to do it.

The Roman decided to answer me. "Yes, he was the first one I brought over successfully. The others I tried to bring over — they died."

"Could we please leave my bedroom and go into the living room?" I said. "This is not the right place to receive visitors." See? I was trying to be polite.

"Yes, I suppose," said the older vampire. "Alexei? Where do you suppose the living room is?"

Alexei half turned and pointed in the right direction.

"Then that's where we'll go, dearest," Ocella said, and Alexei led the way.

I had a moment to look up at Eric, and I knew my face was asking, *"What the hell is going on here?"* But he looked stunned, and helpless. Eric. Helpless. My head was whirling.

When I had a second to think about it, I was pretty nauseated, because Alexei was a child and I was fairly sure that Ocella had a sexual relationship with the boy, as he'd had with Eric. But I wasn't foolish enough to think that I could stop it, or that any protest I made would make the slightest difference. In fact, I was far from sure Alexei himself would thank me for intervening, when I remembered Eric telling me about his desperate attachment to his maker during the first years of his new life as a vampire.

Alexei had been with Ocella for a long time now, at least in human terms. I couldn't remember exactly when the Romanov family had been executed, but I thought it was sometime around 1918, and apparently it had been Ocella who'd saved the boy from final death. So whatever constituted their relationship, it had been ongoing for more than eighty years.

All these thoughts flickered through my head, one after another, as we followed the two visitors. Ocella had said he could have entered without warning. It would have been nice if Eric had told me about that. I could see how he might have hoped that Ocella would never visit, so I was willing to give Eric a pass . . . but I couldn't help thinking that instead of his lecture on the ways vampires had sliced up my country according to their own convenience, it would have been more practical to let me know his maker could appear *in my bedroom.*

"Please, have a seat," I said, after Ocella and Alexei had settled on the couch.

"So much sarcasm," said Ocella. "Will you not offer us hospitality?" His gaze ran up and down me, and though the color of his eyes was rich and brown, they were utterly cold.

I had a second to realize how glad I was that I'd put a robe on. I would have rather eaten Alpo than been naked in front of these two. "I'm not happy with your popping up outside my bedroom window," I said. "You could have come to the door and knocked, like people with good manners do." I wasn't telling him anything he didn't already know; vampires are good at reading people, and the oldest vampires are usually better than humans at telling what humans are feeling.

"Yes, but then I wouldn't have seen such a charming sight." Ocella let his gaze brush Eric's shirtless body almost tangibly. Alexei, for the first time, showed an emotion. He looked scared. Was he afraid Ocella would reject him, throw him out onto the mercy of the world? Or was he afraid that Ocella would keep him?

I pitied Alexei from the bottom of my heart, and I feared him just as much.

He was as helpless as Eric.

Ocella had been looking at Alexei with an attention that was almost frightening. "He's already much better," Ocella murmured. "Eric, your presence is doing him so much good."

I'd kind of figured things couldn't get more awkward, but a peremptory knock at the back door followed by a "Sookie, you here?" told me that actually the night could get worse.

My brother, Jason, came in without waiting for me to answer. "Sookie, I saw your light on when I pulled up, so I figured you were awake," he said, and then he stopped abruptly when he realized how much company I had. And what they were.

"Sorry to interrupt, Sook," he said slowly. "Eric, how you doing?"

Eric said, "Jason, this is my . . . This is Appius Livius Ocella, my maker, and his other son Alexei." Eric said it properly, "AP-pi-us Li-WEE-us Oh-KEL-ah."

Jason nodded at both of the newcomers, but he avoided looking directly at the older vampire. Good instinct. "Good evening, O'Kelly. Hey, Alexei. So you're Eric's little brother, huh? Are you a Viking like Eric?"

"No," said the boy faintly. "I am Russian." Alexei's accent was much lighter than the Roman's. He looked at Jason with interest. I hoped he wasn't thinking about biting my brother. The thing about Jason, and what made him so attractive to people (particularly women), was that he practically radiated life. He just seemed to have an extra helping of vigor and vitality, and it was returning with a boom now that the misery of his wife's death was fading. This was his manifestation of the fairy blood in his veins.

"Well, good to meet you-all," Jason said. Then he quit paying attention to the visitors. "Sookie, I came to get that little side table from up in the attic. I came by here once before to pick it up, but you were gone and I didn't have my key with me." Jason kept a key to my house for emergencies, just as I kept a key to his.

I'd forgotten his asking me for the table when we'd had dinner together. At this point, he could have asked me for my bedroom set, and I would have agreed just to get him out of danger. I said, "Sure, I don't need it. Go on up. I don't think it's very far inside the door."

Jason excused himself, and everyone's eyes followed him as he bounded up the stairs. Eric was probably just trying to keep his eyes busy while he thought, but Ocella watched my brother with frank appraisal, and Alexei with a kind of yearning.

"Would you like some TrueBlood?" I asked the vampires, through clenched teeth.

"I suppose, if you won't offer yourself or your brother," the ancient Roman said.

"I won't."

I turned to go to the kitchen.

"I feel your anger," Ocella said.

"I don't care," I said, without turning to face him. I heard Jason coming downstairs, a little more slowly now that he was carrying the table. "Jason, you want to come with me?" I said over my shoulder.

He was more than glad to leave the room. Though he was civil to Eric because he knew I loved him, Jason was not happy in the company of vamps. He put the table down in a corner of the kitchen.

"Sook, what's going on here?"

"Come into my room for a second," I said after I'd gotten the bottles out of my refrigerator. I'd feel a lot better if I had more clothes on. Jason trailed after me. I shut the door once we were inside my bedroom.

"Watch the door. I don't trust that old one," I said, and Jason obligingly turned his back and watched the door while I pulled off the robe, getting into my clothes as fast as I've ever dressed in my life.

"Whoa," Jason said, and I jumped. I turned to see that Alexei had opened the door and would have entered if Jason hadn't been holding it.

"I'm sorry," Alexei said. His voice was a ghost of a voice, a voice that once had been.

"I apologize to you, Sookie, and you, Jason."

"Jason, you can let him in. What are you sorry for, Alexei?" I asked. "Come on, let's go to the kitchen and I'll warm up the True-Blood." We trailed into the kitchen. We were a little farther from the living room, and there was a chance Eric and Ocella wouldn't hear us.

"My master is not always like this. His age, it turns him."

"Turns him into what? A total jerk? A sadist? A child molester?"

A faint smile crossed the boy's face. "At times, all of those," he said succinctly. "But truthfully, I haven't been well myself. That's why we're here."

Jason began to look angry. He likes kids, always has. Even though Alexei could have killed Jason in a second, Jason thought of Alexei as a child. My brother was building up a big mad, actually thinking of charging into the living room to confront Appius Livius Ocella.

"Listen, Alexei, you don't have to stay with that dude if you don't want to," Jason said. "You can stay with me or Sookie, if Eric won't put you up. Nobody's gonna make you stay with someone you don't want to be with." Bless Jason's heart, he sure didn't know what he was talking about.

Alexei smiled, a faint smile that was simply heart-piercing. "Really, he is not so bad. He is a good man, I believe, but from a time you can't imagine. I think you are used to knowing vampires who are trying to . . . mainstream. Master, he is not trying to do this. He is much happier in the shadows. And I must stay with him. Please don't trouble yourselves, but I thank you for your concern. I'm feeling better already now that I'm with my brother. I don't feel as if I'll suddenly do something . . . regrettable."

Jason and I looked at each other. That was enough to make us both worried.

Alexei was looking around the kitchen as if he seldom saw one. I figured that was probably true.

I took the warm bottles out of the microwave and shook them. I put some napkins on the tray with the bottles. Jason got himself a Coke from the refrigerator.

I didn't know what to think about Alexei. He apologized for Ocella like the Roman was his grumpy grandpa, but it was apparent that he was in Ocella's sway. Of course he was; he was Ocella's child in a very real sense.

It was an awfully strange situation, having

a figure out of history sitting in your living room. I thought of the horrors he'd experienced, both before and after his death. I thought of his childhood as the tsarevitch, and I knew that despite his hemophilia, that childhood must have contained some glorious moments. I didn't know whether the boy often longed for the love, devotion, and luxury that had surrounded him from birth until the rebellion, or (considering he'd been executed along with his whole immediate family) whether it was possible he saw being a vampire as an improvement over being buried in a pit in the woods in Russia.

Though with the hemophilia, his life expectancy in those days would have been pretty damn short anyway.

Jason added ice to his glass and looked in the cookie jar. I didn't keep cookies anymore, because if I did, I'd eat 'em. He closed the jar sadly. Alexei was watching everything Jason did as if he were observing an animal he'd never seen before.

He noticed me looking at him. "Two men took care of me, two sailors," he said, as though he could read the questions in my mind. "They carried me around when the pain was bad. After the world turned upside down, one of them abused me when he had the chance. But the other died, simply because he was still kind to me. Your brother reminds me a little of that one."

"Sorry about your family," I said awkwardly, since I felt compelled to say something.

He shrugged. "I was glad when they found them and gave the burial," he said. But when I saw his eyes, I knew that his words were a thin layer of ice over a pit of pain.

"Who was that in your coffin?" I asked. Was I being tacky? What on earth else was there to talk about? Jason was looking from Alexei to me, mystified. Jason's idea of history was remembering Jimmy Carter's embarrassing brother.

"When the big grave was found, Master knew they would find my sister and me soon. We overestimated the searchers, perhaps. It took sixteen more years. But in the meantime, we revisited the place where I was buried."

I felt my eyes fill with tears. *The place where I was buried . . .*

He continued, "We had to provide some of my bones for it, because we had learned about DNA by then. Otherwise, of course, we could have found a boy about the right age. . . ."

I really couldn't think of anything remotely

normal to say. "So you cut out some of your own bones to put in the grave," I said, my voice clogged and shaky.

"In steps, over time. Everything grew back," he said reassuringly. "We had to burn my bones a little. They had burned Maria and me, and poured acid on us, too."

Finally, I managed, "Why was that necessary? To put your bones there?"

"Master wanted me to be at rest," he said. "He didn't want any sightings. He reasoned that if my bones were found, there would be no more controversy. Of course, by now no one would expect me to be alive anyway, much less looking like I did then. Perhaps we weren't thinking clearly. When you've been out of the world so long . . . And in the first five years after the revolution, I was seen by a couple of people who did recognize me. Master had to take care of them."

That, too, took a minute to sink in. Jason looked nauseated. I wasn't far behind him. But this little chitchat had already taken long enough. I didn't want "Master" to think we were plotting against him.

"Alexei," Appius Livius called in a sharp voice. "Is all well with you?"

"Yes, sir," Alexei said, and hurried back to the Roman.

"Jesus Christ, Shepherd of Judea," I said,

and turned to carry the tray of bottles into the living room. Jason was clearly unhappy, but he followed me.

Eric was fixed on Appius Livius Ocella like a 7-Eleven clerk watches a customer who may have a gun. But he seemed to have relaxed a smidgen, now that he'd had a little time to recover from the shock of his maker's appearance. Through the bond, I felt a wash of overwhelming relief from Eric. After I thought about that, I believed I understood. Eric was relieved beyond measure that the older vampire had brought a bedmate with him. Eric, who had given a pretty good impression of indifference about his many years as Ocella's sexual companion, had had a moment of crazed unwillingness when he actually saw his maker again. Eric was reassembling and rearming himself. He was returning to being Eric, the sheriff, from his abrupt reversion to Eric, the new vampire and love slave.

The way I perceived Eric would never be quite the same again. I knew now what he feared. What I was getting from Eric was that it wasn't so much the physical aspect as the mental; above all else, Eric did not want to be under the control of his maker.

I served each of the vampires a bottle, carefully placing it on a napkin. At least I didn't have to worry about serving an accompanying snack . . . unless Ocella decided all three of them would feed from me. In which case, I had no hope I would survive, and there wouldn't be a damn thing I could do about it. This should have made me the model of discretion. I should have determined to sit there with my ankles crossed and not let butter melt in my mouth.

But it just pissed me off.

Eric's hand twitched, and I knew he was reading my mood. He wanted to tell me to tone it down, to cool off, to come in under the radar. He might not want to be under Ocella's sway again, but he loved the vampire, too. I made myself back down. I hadn't given the Roman a chance. I didn't really know him. I only knew some things I didn't like about him, and there must be some other things I would like or admire. If he'd been Eric's for-real father, I'd have given him lots of chances to prove his worth.

I wondered how clearly Ocella could sense my emotions. He was still tuned in to Eric and always would be, and Eric and I were bonded. But it seemed my feelings didn't carry over; the Roman didn't so much as glance my way. I cast my eyes down. I would have to learn how to be stealthier, and in a hurry. Normally, I was good at hiding what I felt, but the nearness of the ancient vampire and his new protégé, their blood so like Eric's, had thrown me for a loop.

"I'm not sure what to call you," I said, meeting the Roman's eyes. I was trying to mimic my grandmother's best company voice.

"You may call me Appius Livius," he said, "since you are Eric's wife. It took Eric a hundred years to earn the right to call me Appius, rather than Master. Then centuries to be able to call me Ocella."

So only Eric got to call him Ocella. Fine with me. I noticed Alexei was still at the "Master" stage. Alexei was sitting as still as if he'd taken a huge tranquilizer, his synthetic blood sitting on the coffee table in front of him with only a sip missing.

"Thanks," I said, aware that I didn't sound very thankful. I glanced over at my brother. Jason was thinking he had a pretty good idea about what he wanted to call the Roman, but I gave my head a small but definite shake.

"Eric, tell me how you are doing these days," Appius Livius said. He sounded genuinely interested. His hand went over to Alexei, and I saw he was stroking the boy's back, as if Alexei were a puppy. But I couldn't deny there was affection in the gesture.

"I'm very well. Area Five is prosperous. I was the only Louisiana sheriff to survive the takeover by Felipe de Castro." Eric managed to sound matter-of-fact.

"How did that come about?"

Eric gave the older vampire a rundown on the political situation with Victor Madden. When he thought Appius Livius was up to speed on the Felipe de Castro/Victor Madden situation, Eric asked him, "How did you come to be on hand for the rescue of this young man?" Eric smiled at Alexei.

This would be a story worth listening to, now that I'd heard Alexei's horrifying tale about "salting" his grave. While Alexei Romanov sat by his side in remote silence, Appius told Eric about tracking down the Russian royal family in 1918.

"Though I had expected something of the sort, I had to move much faster than I had anticipated," Appius said. He finished his bottled blood. "The decision to execute them was made so swiftly, conducted at such speed. No one wanted the men to have time to think twice about it. For many of the soldiers, it was a terrible thing they were doing."

"Why did you want to save the Romanovs?" Eric asked, as if Alexei weren't there.

And Appius Livius laughed. He gave great laugh. "I hated the fucking Bolsheviks," he said. "And I had a tie to the boy. Rasputin had been giving him my blood for years. I happened to be in Russia already; you remember the St. Petersburg Massacre?"

Eric nodded. "I do indeed. I had not seen you in many years, and only caught a glimpse of you then." Eric had talked about the St. Petersburg Massacre before. A vampire named Gregory had had madness visited on him by a vengeful maenad, and it had taken twenty vampires to pin him down and then disguise the results.

"After that night, when so many of us worked together to tidy up the scene after Gregory was subdued, I developed a fondness for the Russian vampires — and the Russian people, too." He tacked the Russian people on with a gracious nod toward me and Jason, as representatives of the human race. "The fucking Bolsheviks killed so many of us. I was grieved. The deaths of Fedor and Velislava were particularly hard. They were both great vampires, and hundreds of years old."

"I knew them," Eric said.

"I sent them a message to get out before I

started to look for the royal family. I could track Alexei because he'd had my blood. Rasputin knew what we were. Whenever the empress would call him to heal the boy when the hemophilia was very bad, Rasputin would beg some of my blood and the boy would recover. I heard a rumor they were thinking of killing the royal family, and I began following the scent of my blood. When I set out to rescue them, you can imagine how like a crusader I felt!"

They both laughed, and I suddenly understood that the two vampires had actually seen crusaders, the original Christian knight crusaders. When I tried to comprehend how old they were, how much they'd witnessed, how many experiences they'd had that almost no one else walking the earth remembered, it made my head hurt.

"Sook, you got the most interesting company," Jason said.

"Listen, I know you want to go, but if you could stick around for a while, I'd appreciate it," I said. I wasn't happy with having Eric's maker and the poor child Alexei here, and since Alexei was clearly happy with Jason, his presence might help ease this uncomfortable situation.

"I'll just go put the table out in the truck and call Michele," he said. "Alexei, you want to come with me?"

Appius Livius didn't move, but he definitely grew tense. Alexei looked over at the ancient Roman. After a long pause, Appius Livius nodded at the boy. "Alexei, remember your company manners," Appius Livius said softly. Alexei bobbed his head.

Having been given permission, the tsarevitch of Russia went outside with the road-crew worker to stow a table in the back of a pickup.

When I was alone with Eric and his maker, I felt a stab of anxiety. Actually, it was flowing right through the bond I had with Eric. I wasn't the only one around here who was worried. And their conversation appeared to be at a standstill.

"Excuse me, Appius Livius," I said carefully. "Since you were in the right empire at the right time, I wonder if you ever saw Jesus?"

The Roman was staring at the hallway, willing Alexei to reappear. "The carpenter? No, I didn't see him," Appius said, and I could tell he was making an effort to be courteous. "The Jew died right around the time I was changed. As you will appreciate, I had many other things to think of. In fact, I didn't hear the whole myth until some time later when the world began to change as a result of his death."

That would really have been amazing, talking to a creature who'd seen the living God . . . even if he called him a "myth." And I went back to fearing the Roman — not for what he'd done to me, or what he'd done to Eric, or even what he was doing to Alexei, but for what he *might do* to all of us, if he took a mind to. I had always tried to find the good in people, but the best I could say of Appius was that he had good taste in those he picked to become vampires.

While I brooded, Appius was explaining to Eric how conveniently it had worked out in the cellar in Ekaterinburg. Alexei had almost bled out from his wounds, so he'd given the boy a big gulp of his blood — moving at superspeed, and therefore invisible to the execution squad. Then he'd watched from the shadows while the bodies were thrown down a well. The next day, the royal family was dug up again since the murderers feared the uproar that might follow the deaths of the Romanovs.

"I followed them the minute the sun set the next day," Appius said. "They'd stopped to rebury them. Alexei and one of his sisters . . ."

"Maria," Alexei said softly, and I jumped. He had reappeared silently in the living room, standing behind Appius's chair. "It was Maria."

There was a silence. Appius looked hugely relieved. "Yes, of course, dear boy," Appius said, and he did manage to sound as though he cared. "Your sister Maria was completely gone, but there was a tiny spark in you." Alexei put his hand on Appius Livius's shoulder, and Appius Livius reached up to pat him.

"They had shot him many times," he explained to Eric. "Twice in the head. I put my blood directly in the bullet holes." He turned his head to look at the boy behind him. "My blood worked well, since you had lost so much of yours." It was like he was recollecting happy times. Hoo, boy. The Roman turned back to look at Eric and me, and he smiled proudly. But I could see Alexei's face.

Appius Livius genuinely felt that he'd been a savior to Alexei. I wasn't so sure Alexei was totally convinced of that.

"Where's your brother?" Appius Livius suddenly asked, and I pushed to my feet to go find him. I had put two and two together, and I understood that Eric's maker wanted to be sure Alexei hadn't drained Jason and left him out in the yard.

Jason came into the living room just then,

slipping his cell phone into his pocket. He narrowed his eyes. Jason was not a nuance kind of guy, but he could tell when I was unhappy. "Sorry," he said. "Talkin' to Michele."

"Hmmm," I said. I made a mental note that Appius Livius was worried about Alexei being alone with humans, and I knew that should scare me quite a bit. The night was growing older, and I had things to find out. "I hate to change the subject, but there are a few things I need to know."

"What, Sookie?" Eric asked, looking directly at me for the first time since Old Master had popped up. He was pouring caution down the bond between us.

"I just have a couple of questions," I said, smiling as sweetly as I could. "Have you been in this area for any length of time?"

I met the ancient dark eyes again. It was hard to take Appius all in, somehow; I found I couldn't look at him as a cohesive individual. He scared the shit out of me.

"No," he said mildly. "We have not. We've come here from the southwest, from Oklahoma, and we have only just arrived in Louisiana."

"So you wouldn't know anything about the new body buried at the back of my land?"

268

"No, nothing. Would you like us to go dig it up? Unpleasant, but doable. You are wanting to see who it is?"

That was an unexpected offer. Eric was looking at me very oddly. "I'm sorry, honey," I told him. "I was trying to tell you when our unexpected guests showed up."

"Not Debbie," he said.

"No, Heidi says there's a new burial. But we do need to know who it is, and we need to find out who put it there."

"The Weres," Eric said instantly. "This is the thanks you get for letting them use your land. I'll call Alcide, and we'll have a meeting." Eric looked positively delighted to get the chance to do something bosslike. He whipped out his cell phone and dialed Alcide before I could say anything.

"Eric," he said into the phone by way of identification. "Alcide, we have to talk." I could hear the buzz on the other end of the line.

A moment later Eric said, "That's not good, Alcide, and I am sorry to hear you have troubles. But I have other concerns. What did you do on Sookie's land?"

Oh, crapanola.

"You should come here and see, then. I think some of your people have been bad. Very well, then. I'll see you in ten minutes. I am at her house."

He hung up, looking triumphant. "Alcide was in Bon Temps?" I asked.

"No, but he was on the interstate and nearly at our exit," Eric explained. "He's returning from some meeting in Monroe. The Louisiana packs are trying to present a united front to the government. Since they've never organized before, this is not going to work." Eric snorted, clearly scornful. "The Weres are always — what did you say the other day about FEMA, Sookie? 'A day late and a dollar short,' right? At least he's close, and when he gets here we'll get to the bottom of this."

I sighed, trying to make it discreet and silent. I hadn't realized things would go so far so fast. I asked Eric, Appius Livius, and Alexei if they wanted more TrueBlood, but they turned it down. Jason was looking bored. I glanced at the clock.

"I'm afraid I have only one spot that's suitable for a vampire. Where are you-all planning to sleep, come the dawn? I just want to know in case I need to call around and find a place."

"Sookie," said Eric gently, "I will take Ocella and his son back to my house. They can have the guest coffins there."

Eric ordinarily slept in his bed, because

his bedroom was windowless. There were a couple of other coffins in the guest bedroom, sleek fiberglass things that looked sort of like kayaks, which he kept stowed under the beds. The most wrong thing about Alexei and Appius Livius staying with Eric was that if they were there, I was definitely staying here.

"I think your darling would love to come in during the day and sink a stake into our chests," Appius Livius said, as if that were a big joke. "If you think you can do it, young woman, you are welcome to try."

"Oh, not at all," I said, absolutely insincerely. "I wouldn't dream of doing such a thing to Eric's dad." Not a bad idea, though.

Beside me, Eric twitched all over; it was a funny movement, like a dog running in its sleep. "Be polite," he told me, and there was no element of fun in his voice at all. He was giving me an order.

I took a deep breath. It was on the tip of my tongue to rescind Eric's invitation to my house. He'd have to leave, and presumably Appius Livius and Alexei would, too. It was that "presumably" that stopped me. The idea of being alone with Appius Livius even for a second trumped the pleasurable vision of the three vampires walking out backward.

It was probably lucky for all of us that the

doorbell rang then. I was out of my seat as if a rocket had fired me. It would be good to have more breathers around.

Alcide was wearing a suit. He was flanked by Annabelle, who was wearing a dark green sheath and heeled pumps, and Jannalynn, Sam's new interest. Jannalynn had a sense of style, though it was a style that left me stunned. She had on a shiny silver dress that barely covered her assets and silver high-heeled sandals that laced up the front. The silver eye shadow over her heavily outlined eyes completed the look. In a scary kind of way, she looked great. Sam certainly dated women who were extraordinary in some way, and he wasn't afraid of strong characters, which was a thought I'd have to save for later. Maybe it was a two-natured thing? Alcide was the same way.

I gave the packleader a hug, and I said hello to Annabelle and to Jannalynn, who gave me a curt nod.

"What is this problem Eric called me about?" Alcide was saying as I stood aside to let them enter. When the Weres realized they were in a room with three vampires, all of them tensed. They'd expected only Eric. When I glanced back at the vampires, I saw they were all standing, too, and even Alexei was on the alert.

Jason said, "Alcide, good to see you. Ladies, looking mighty fine tonight."

I went into high gear. "Hi, you-all!" I said brightly. "It was so nice of you to come at such short notice. Eric, you know Alcide. Alcide, this is Eric's longtime friend Appius Livius Ocella, who's in town visiting with his, ah, protégé, Alexei. Eric, I don't know if you've met Alcide's friend Annabelle, a new pack member, and Jannalynn, who's been in the Long Tooth pack for ages. Jannalynn, we've never had a chance to talk much, but of course Sam talks about you all the time. And I think you all know my brother, Jason."

Whew. I felt like I'd run an introduction marathon. Since vamps don't shake hands, that concluded the opening ceremonies. Then I had to get them all to sit down while I offered them drinks, which no one accepted.

Eric fired the opening volley. "Alcide, one of my trackers went over Sookie's land after Basim al Saud warned her about the strangers he smelled in her woods. Our tracker has found a new body buried there."

Alcide looked at Eric as though he had begun speaking in tongues.

"We didn't kill anyone that night," Alcide said. "Basim said he told Sookie we smelled

273

an old body, and a fairy or two, and a vampire. But he didn't mention a fresh body."

"Yet there's a new burial there now."

"Which we had nothing to do with." Alcide shrugged. "We were there three nights before your tracker smelled the scent of a fresh body."

"It seems quite a huge coincidence, doesn't it? A body on Sookie's land, right after your pack is there?" Eric was looking aggravatingly reasonable.

"Maybe it's more of a coincidence that there was already a body on Sookie's land."

Oh, boy, I *really* didn't want to go there.

Jannalynn was actually snarling at Eric. It was an interesting look, with the eye makeup and all. Annabelle was standing with her arms slightly away from her body, waiting to see which way she needed to jump.

Alexei was staring off into space, which seemed to be his fallback stance, and Appius Livius simply seemed bored.

"I say we should go see who it is," Jason said unexpectedly.

I looked at him with approval.

So out we went into the woods to dig up a corpse.

CHAPTER 9

Alcide changed to some boots he had in the truck, and he shed his tie and coat. Janna-lynn wisely took off her spike-heeled sandals and Annabelle her own more modest heels. I gave them both some sneakers of mine, and I offered Jannalynn an old T-shirt to cover her shiny silver dress so it wouldn't snag in the woods. She pulled it over her head. She even said, "Thanks," though she didn't sound actually grateful. I retrieved two shovels from the toolshed. Alcide took one shovel, Eric the other. Jason carried one of those great big flashlights called a lantern that he'd fished out of the toolbox on his truck. The lantern was for my benefit. The vampires could see perfectly well in the dark, and the Weres could see very well, too. Since Jason was a werepanther, he had excellent night vision. I was the blind one in the group.

"Do we know where we're going?" Annabelle said.

"Heidi said it was due east, close to the stream, in a clearing," I said, and we slogged eastward. I kept running into stuff, and after a while Eric handed off his shovel to Jason and crouched so I could cling to his back. I kept my head tucked behind his so branches wouldn't hit me in the face. Our progress was smoother after that.

"I smell it," Jannalynn said suddenly. She was out ahead of us all, as if her job in the pack were to make the way clear for the packleader. She was a different woman out in the woods. Though I couldn't see very well, I could see that. She was quick, sure-footed, and decisive. She darted ahead, and after a moment she called back, "Here it is!"

We got there to find her standing over a patch of dirt in a little clearing. It had been disturbed recently, though an attempt had been made to camouflage that disturbance.

Eric eased me down onto the ground, and Jason shone the lantern at the earth. "It's not . . . ?" I whispered, knowing everyone there could hear me.

"No," Eric said firmly. "Too recent." Not Debbie Pelt. She was elsewhere, in an older grave.

"Only one way to find out who it is," Alcide said. Jason and Alcide began to dig, and since they were both very strong, it went quickly. Alexei came over to stand by me, and it occurred to me that a grave in the woods had to be a bad flashback for him. I put an arm around him as if he were still human, though I noticed that Appius gave me a sardonic look. Alexei's eyes were on the gravediggers, especially Jason. I knew this child could dig the grave with his bare hands as fast as they were digging with shovels, but Alexei looked so frail it was hard to think of him being as strong as other vampires. I wondered how many people had made that mistake in the past few decades, and how many of those had died at Alexei's small hands.

Jason and Alcide could make the dirt fly. While they worked, Annabelle and Jannalynn prowled around the little clearing, probably trying to pick up what scents they could. Despite the rain of two nights ago, there might be something in the areas protected by the trees. Heidi hadn't been looking for a murderer; she'd been trying to make a list of who'd crossed the land. I was thinking that the only creatures who hadn't been tromping through my woods had been regular old humans. If the Weres were lying, a Were could be the killer. Or it could be one of the fae, who were a violent race, as I had observed. Or the killer could be Bill, since Heidi thought the vampire she'd scented was my neighbor.

I hadn't smelled the body while it was under the dirt as the others had, since my sense of smell was only a fraction of theirs. But as the dirt piles grew and the hole got deeper, I could tell it was there. Oh gosh, could I.

I put my hand across my nose, which didn't help at all. I couldn't imagine how the others were enduring it, since it would be so much sharper to their senses. Maybe they were also more practical, or simply more accustomed.

Then both the diggers stopped. "He's wrapped up," Jason said. Alcide bent over and fumbled with something at the bottom of the hole.

"I think I got it pulled apart," Alcide said after a moment.

"Pass me the lantern, Sookie," Jason said, and I tossed it to him. He shone it down. "I don't know this man," he said.

"I do," said Alcide in a strange voice. Annabelle and Jannalynn were at the edge of the grave instantly. I had to brace myself to step forward to look down into the pit.

I recognized him instantly. The three

Weres threw back their heads and howled.

"It's the Long Tooth enforcer," I told the vampires. I gagged and had to wait a minute before I could go on. "It's Basim al Saud." The passage of days had made a great difference, but I knew him instantly. Those corkscrew curls I'd envied, the muscled body.

"Shit," screamed Jannalynn, when the howling was done.

And that about summed it up.

When the Weres had calmed down, there was a lot to talk about.

"I only met him the once," I said. "Of course, he was fine when he got in the truck with Alcide and Annabelle."

"He told me what he'd smelled on the property, and I told him to tell Sookie," Alcide told Eric. "She had a right to know. We didn't talk about anything in particular on the way back to Shreveport, did we, Annabelle?"

"No," she said, and I could tell she was crying.

"I dropped him off at his apartment. When I called him the next day to go with me to a meeting with our representative, he said he had to pass because he had to work. He was a website designer, and he had a meeting with an important client. I wasn't too happy he couldn't go, but of course, the guy had to make a living." Alcide shrugged.

Annabelle said, "He didn't have to work that day."

There was a moment of silence.

"I was at his apartment when you called," she said, and I could tell the effort she was expending to keep her voice calm and level. "I had been there a few hours."

Wow. Unexpected revelation. Jason had hopped out of the grave, and he and I gave each other big eyes. This was like one of Gran's "stories," the soap operas she'd watched religiously.

Alcide growled. The ritual howling for the dead had brought out the wolf in him.

"I know," Annabelle said. "And we'll talk about it later. I'll take my punishment, which I deserve. But Basim's death is more important than my bad judgment. This is my duty, to tell you what happened. Basim got a phone call before yours, and he didn't want me to hear it. But I heard enough to understand his conversation was with someone who was paying him."

Alcide's growl intensified. Jannalynn was standing close to her pack sister, and the only way I can put it was that she was aimed at Annabelle. She was crouching slightly, her hands curved as if they were about to sprout claws.

Alexei had edged close to Jason, and when the tension kept ratcheting up, Jason's arm slung around the boy's shoulders. Jason was having the same problem separating illusion and reality that I was.

Annabelle flinched at the sound coming from Alcide, but she kept on going. "So Basim made up an excuse to get me out of the apartment, and he took off. I tried to follow him, but I lost him."

"You were suspicious," Jannalynn said. "But you didn't call the packmaster. You didn't call me. You didn't call anyone. We took you in and made you a member of our pack, and you betrayed us." Suddenly, she hit Annabelle in the head with her fist, actually leaping into the air to land the blow. Just like that, Annabelle was on the ground. I gasped, and I wasn't the only one.

But I was the only one who noticed that Jason was straining to hold Alexei back. Something about the violence in the air had sent the boy over the edge. If he'd been a little bigger, Jason would've been on the ground. I punched Eric in the arm, jerked my head in the direction of the struggle. Eric leaped over to help Jason restrain the boy, who fought and snarled in their arms.

For a moment there was silence in the

dark clearing as everyone watched Alexei struggle with his madness. Appius Livius looked profoundly sad. He worked his way into the knot of limbs and wrapped his own arms around his child. "Sshhhhh," he said. "My son, be still." And gradually Alexei grew quiet.

Alcide's voice was very close to a rumble when he said, "Jannalynn, you are my new second. Annabelle, get up. This is pack business now, and we'll settle it at a pack meeting." He turned his back on us and began moving.

The Weres were simply going to walk out of the woods and drive away. "Excuse me," I said sharply. "There's the little matter of the body being buried on my land. I think there's something pretty damn significant about that."

The Weres stopped walking.

Eric said, "Yes." The one word carried a lot of weight. "Alcide, I believe Sookie and I need to sit in on your pack meeting."

"Only pack members," Jannalynn snapped. "No oneys, no deaders." She was still as small as ever, but with her field promotion to second, she seemed harder and stronger in spirit. She was a ruthless little thing, no doubt about it. I thought Sam was mighty brave, or mighty foolish.

"Alcide?" Eric said quietly.

"Sookie can bring Jason, since he's two-natured," Alcide growled. "She's a oney, but she's a friend of the pack. No vamps."

Eric glanced at my brother. "Jason, will you accompany your sister?"

"Sure," Jason said.

So it was settled. Out of the corner of my eye, I saw Annabelle stagger to her feet and reorient herself. Jannalynn packed a wallop.

"What are you going to do with the body?" I called after Alcide, who was definitely moving out. "Do you want us to cover him back up or what?"

Annabelle took a hesitant step after Jannalynn and Alcide. That was going to be a happy ride back to Shreveport. "Someone will come get him tonight," Jannalynn called over her shoulder. "So there'll be activity in your woods. Don't be alarmed." When Annabelle glanced back, I noticed she was bleeding from one corner of her mouth. I felt the vampires come to attention. In fact, Alexei stepped away from Jason and would have followed her if Appius Livius hadn't kept his grip on the boy.

"Should we cover him back up?" Jason said.

"If they're sending a crew to get him, that seems like wasted effort," I said. "Eric, I'm so glad you sent Heidi. Otherwise . . ." I thought hard. "Listen, if he was buried on my land, it was so he could be found here, right? So there's no telling when someone's going to get a tip to come looking for him."

The only one who seemed to follow my reasoning was Jason, who said, "Okay, we got to get him out of here."

I was flapping my hands in the air, I was so anxious. "We've got to put him somewhere," I said. "We could just set him in the cemetery!"

"Naw, too close," Jason said.

"What about the pond behind your house?" I said.

"Naw, dammit! The fish! I couldn't ever eat those fish again."

"Aaargh," I said. Really!

"Is your time with her usually like this?" Appius Livius asked Eric, who was smart enough not to answer.

"Sookie," he said. "It won't be pleasant, but I think I can fly carrying him if you can suggest a good place to put him."

I felt like my brain was running through a maze and hitting all the dead ends. I actually smacked myself on the side of the head to jog an idea loose. It worked. "Sure, Eric. Put him in the woods right across the road from my driveway. There's a little bit of a driveway left there, but no house. The Weres can use the driveway as a marker when they come to retrieve him. Cause *someone's* coming to find him, and coming soon."

Without further discussion, Eric leaped into the hole and rewrapped Basim in the sheet or whatever the wrapping was. Though the lantern showed me his face was full of disgust, he scooped up the decomposing body and leaped into the air. He was out of view in a second.

"Damn," said Jason, impressed. "Cool."

"Let's fill in this grave," I said. We set to work, with Appius Livius watching. It obviously didn't occur to him that his help would make the job go much faster. Even Alexei shoved in piles of dirt, and he seemed to be having a pretty good time doing it. This was probably as close to a normal activity as the thirteen-year-old had come in some time. Gradually, the hole filled in. It still looked like a grave. The tsarevitch tore at the hard edges with his small hands. I almost protested, but then I saw what he was doing. He reconfigured the grave-shaped dent until it looked like an irregular dent, maybe created by rain or a collapsed mole tunnel. He beamed at us when he'd finished, and Jason clapped him on the back. Jason got a branch and swept it over the area, and then we tossed leaves and branches around. Alexei enjoyed that part, too.

Finally, we gave up. I couldn't think of one more thing to do.

Filthy and frightened, I shouldered one of the shovels and prepared to make my way through the woods. Jason took the other shovel in his right hand, and Alexei took Jason's left hand, as if he were even younger than the child he looked. My brother, though his face was a picture, kept hold of the vampire. Appius Livius at last made himself useful by leading us through the trees and undergrowth with some assurance.

Eric was at the house when we reached it. He'd already thrown his clothes into the garbage and gotten into the shower. Under other circumstances, I would have loved to join him, but it just wasn't possible to feel sexy at the moment. I was grimy and nasty, but I was still the hostess, so I heated up some more TrueBlood for the two visiting vampires and showed them the downstairs bathroom in case they wanted to wash up.

Jason came into the kitchen to tell me that he was going to shove off.

"Let me know when the meeting is," he said in a subdued way. "And I gotta report all this to Calvin, you know."

"I understand," I said, weary to death of politics of all kinds. I wondered if America knew what it was in for when it considered requiring the two-natured to register. America was really better off not having to go through this crap. Human politics were tedious enough.

Jason went out the back door. A second later, I heard his truck roaring away. Almost as soon as Appius Livius and Alexei had had their drinks, Eric came out of my bedroom in fresh clothes (he kept a change at my house) and smelling very much like my apricot body wash. With his maker around, Eric could hardly have a heart-to-heart with me, assuming he wanted to. He wasn't exactly acting like my honey now that his dad was in the house. There could be several reasons for this. I didn't like any of them.

Soon afterward, the three vampires left for Shreveport. Appius Livius thanked me for my hospitality in such an impassive way that I had no idea whether he was being sarcastic. Eric was as silent as a stone. Alexei, as calm and smiling as if he'd never gone mad, gave me a cold embrace. I had a hard time accepting it with equal calm.

Three seconds after they were out the

door, I was on the phone.

"Fangtasia, where all your bloody dreams come true," said a bored female voice.

"Pam. Listen."

"The phone is pressed to my ear. Speak."

"Appius Livius Ocella just dropped in."

"Fuck a zombie!"

I wasn't sure that I'd heard that correctly. "Yes, he's been here. I guess he's your granddad? Anyway, he's got a new protégé with him, and they're heading for Eric's to spend the day."

"What does he want?"

"He hasn't said yet."

"How is Eric?"

"Very tightly wound. Plus, a lot of stuff happened that he'll tell you about."

"Thanks for the warning. I'll go to the house now. You're my favorite breather."

"Oh. Well . . . great."

She hung up. I wondered what preparations she would make. Would the vamps and humans who worked at the Shreveport nightclub go into a cleaning frenzy at Eric's? I'd only seen Pam and Bobby Burnham there, though I assumed some of the crew came in from time to time. Would Pam rush some willing humans over to act as bedtime snacks?

I was too tense to think about going to

bed. Whatever Eric's maker was doing here, it wasn't something I was going to like. And I already knew Appius Livius's presence was bad for our relationship. While I was in the shower — and before I picked up the wet towels Eric had left on the floor — I did some serious thinking.

Vampire plotting can be pretty convoluted. But I tried to imagine the significance of the Roman's surprise visit. Surely he hadn't shown up in America, in Louisiana, in Shreveport, just to catch up on the geezer gossip.

Maybe he needed a loan. That wouldn't be too bad. Eric could always make more money. Though I had no idea how Eric stood financially, I had a little nest egg in the bank since Sophie-Anne's estate had paid up the money she'd owed me. And whatever Claudine had had in her checking account would be coming to join it. If Eric needed it, he could have it.

But what if money wasn't the issue? Maybe Appius Livius needed to hole up because he'd gotten in trouble somewhere else. Maybe some Bolshevik vampires were after Alexei! That would be interesting. I could always hope they'd catch up with Appius Livius . . . as long as it wasn't at Eric's house.

Or perhaps Eric's maker had been courted by Felipe de Castro or Victor Madden because they wanted something from Eric that he hadn't given up yet, and they planned on using Eric's maker to pull his strings.

But here was my most likely scenario: Appius Livius Ocella had dropped by with his "new" boy toy just to mess with Eric's head. That was the guess I was putting my money on. Appius Livius was hard to read. At moments he seemed okay. He seemed to care about Eric, and he seemed to care about Alexei. As for Eric's maker's relationship with Alexei — the boy would have died if Appius Livius hadn't intervened. Given the circumstances — Alexei's witnessing the murders of his entire family and their servants and friends — letting the tsarevitch die might have been a blessing.

I was sure Appius Livius was having sex with Alexei, but it was impossible to tell whether Alexei's passive demeanor came from the fact that he was in an unwanted sexual relationship or from his being permanently traumatized from seeing his family shot multiple times. I shuddered. I dried off and brushed my teeth, hoping I could sleep.

I realized there was another phone call I should make. With great reluctance, I called

Bobby Burnham, Eric's daytime guy. Bobby and I had never liked each other. Bobby was weirdly jealous of me, though he didn't have the hots for Eric sexually at all. In Bobby's opinion, I diverted Eric's attention and energy away from its proper focus, which was Bobby and the business affairs he handled for Eric while Eric slept the day away. I was down on Bobby because instead of silently disliking me, he actively tried to make my life more difficult, which was a whole different kettle of fish. But still, we were both in the Eric business.

"Bobby, it's Sookie."

"I got caller ID."

Mr. Sullen. "Bobby, I think you ought to know that Eric's maker is in town. When you go over to get your instructions, be careful." Bobby normally got briefed right before Eric went to ground for the day, unless Eric stayed over at my place.

Bobby took his time with his reply — probably trying to figure out if I was playing some elaborate practical joke on him. "Is he likely to want to bite me?" he asked. "The maker?"

"I don't know what he's going to want, Bobby. I just felt like I ought to give you a heads-up."

"Eric won't let him hurt me," Bobby said

confidently.

"Just as general information — if this guy says jump, Eric has to ask how high."

"No way," Bobby said. To Bobby, Eric was the most powerful creature under the moon.

"Way. They gotta mind their maker. This is no lie."

Bobby had to have heard that news item before. I know there's some kind of website or message board for vampires' human assistants. I'm sure they swap all kinds of handy hints about dealing with their employers. Whatever the reason, Bobby didn't argue or accuse me of trying to deceive him, which was a nice change.

"Okay," he said, "I'm ready for 'em. Was . . . What kind of person is Eric's maker?"

"He's not much like a person at all anymore," I said. "And he's got a thirteen-year-old boyfriend who used to be Russian royalty."

After a long silence, Bobby said, "Thanks. It's good to be prepared."

That was the nicest thing he'd ever said to me.

"You're welcome. Good night, Bobby," I said, and we hung up. We'd managed to have an entire civil conversation. Vampires, bringing America together!

I changed into a nightshirt and crawled into bed. I had to try to get some sleep, but it took its own sweet time coming. I kept seeing the light from the lantern dance across the clearing in the woods as the dirt mounded up around the edges of Basim's grave. And I saw the dead Were's face. But eventually, finally, the edges of that face blurred and darkness slid over me.

I slept late and heavily the next day. The minute I woke, I knew someone was in the kitchen cooking. I let my extra sense check it out, and I found that Claude was frying bacon and eggs. There was coffee in the pot, and I didn't need telepathy to know that. I could smell it. The perfume of morning.

After a trip to the bathroom, I stumbled into the hall and made my way into the kitchen. Claude was sitting at the table eating, and I could see there was enough coffee in the pot for me.

"There's food," he said, pointing to the stove.

I got a plate and a mug, and settled in for a good start to my day. I glanced over at the clock. It was Sunday, and Merlotte's wouldn't be open until the afternoon. Sam was trying Sundays again in a limited way, though the whole staff half hoped it wouldn't be profitable. As Claude and I ate in a companionable silence, I realized I felt wonderfully peaceful because Eric was in his day sleep. That meant I didn't have to feel him walking around with me. His problematic sire and his new "brother" were out of it, too. I sighed with relief.

"I saw Dermot last night," Claude said.

Crap! Well, so much for peace. "Where?" I asked.

"He was at the club. Staring at me with longing," Claude said.

"Dermot's gay?"

"No, I don't think so. It wasn't my dick he was thinking of. He wanted to be around another fairy."

"I sure hoped he was gone. Niall told Jason and me that Dermot helped kill my parents. I wish he'd gone into the fae land when it was closing up."

"He would have been killed on sight." Claude took the time to sip some coffee before he added, "No one in the fae world understands Dermot's actions. He should have sided with Niall from the beginning, because he's kin and because he's half-human and Niall wanted to spare humans. But his own self-loathing — or at least that's all I can imagine — led him to take the side of the fairies who really couldn't stand him, and that side lost." Claude looked happy.

"So Dermot has cut off his own nose to spite his face. I love that saying. Sometimes humans put things very well."

"Do you think he still means to hurt my brother and me?"

"I don't think he ever intended to hurt you," Claude said, after thinking it over. "I think Dermot is crazy, though he used to be an agreeable guy a few score years ago. I don't know if it's his human side that's gone batshit, or his fae side that's soaked up too many toxins from the human world. I can't even explain his part in killing your parents. The Dermot I used to know would never have done such a thing."

I considered pointing out that truly crazy people can hurt others around them without meaning to, or without even realizing they're doing it. But I didn't. Dermot was my great-uncle, and according to everyone who'd met him, he was nearly a dead ringer for my brother. I admitted to myself I was curious about him. And I wondered about what Niall had said about Dermot having been the one who'd opened the truck doors so my parents could be pulled out and drowned by Neave and Lochlan. Dermot's behavior, the bit that I'd observed, didn't gibe with the horror of that incident. Would Dermot think of me as kin? Were Jason and

I fae enough to attract him? I had doubted Bill's assertion that he felt better from my nearness because of my fairy blood.

"Claude, can *you* tell I'm not entirely human? How do I register on the fairy meter?" Fae-dar.

"If you were in a crowd of humans, I could pick you out blindfolded and say you are my kin," Claude said without hesitation. "But if you were in the middle of the fae, I would call you human. It's an elusive scent. Most vamps would think, 'She smells good,' and they'd enjoy being close to you. That would be the extent of it. Once they know you have fairy blood, they can attribute that enjoyment to it."

So Bill really could be comforted by my little streak of fae, at least now that he knew how to identify it. I got up to rinse off my plate and pour another mugful of coffee, and in passing I grabbed Claude's empty plate, too. He didn't thank me.

"I appreciate your cooking," I said. "We haven't talked about how we'll handle grocery expenses or household items."

Claude looked surprised. "I hadn't thought about it," he said.

Well, at least that was honest. "I'll tell you how Amelia and I did it," I said, and in a few sentences I laid out the guidelines.

Looking a little stunned, Claude agreed.

I opened the refrigerator. "These two shelves are yours," I said, "and the rest are mine."

"I get it," he said.

Somehow I doubted that. Claude sounded like he was simply trying to give the impression that he understood and agreed. There was a good chance we'd have to have this conversation again. When he'd left to go upstairs, I took care of the dishes — after all, he'd cooked — and after I got dressed, I thought I'd read for a while. But I was too restless to concentrate on my book.

I heard cars coming down the driveway through the woods. I looked out the front window. Two police cars.

I'd been sure this was coming. But my heart sank down to my toes. Sometimes I hated being right. Whoever had killed Basim had planted his body on my land to implicate me in his death. "Claude," I called up the stairs. "Get decent, if you're not. The police are here."

Claude, curious as ever, came down the stairs at a trot. He was wearing jeans and a T-shirt, like me. We went out on the front porch. Bud Dearborn, the sheriff (the regular human sheriff), was in the first car, and Andy Bellefleur and Alcee Beck were in the second. The sheriff and two detectives — I must be a dangerous criminal.

Bud got out of his car slowly, the way he did most things these days. I knew from his thoughts that Bud was increasingly a victim to arthritis, and he had some doubts about his prostate, too. Bud's mashed-in face didn't give any hint about his physical discomfort as he came up to the porch, his heavy belt creaking with the weight of all the things hanging from it.

"Bud, what's up?" I asked. "Not that I'm not glad to see you-all."

"Sookie, we got an anonymous phone call," Bud said. "As you know, law enforcement couldn't solve much without anonymous tips, but I personally don't respect a person who won't tell you who they are."

I nodded.

"Who's your friend?" Andy asked. He looked worn. I'd heard his grandmother, who'd raised him, was on her deathbed. Poor Andy. He'd much rather be there than here. Alcee Beck, the other detective, really didn't like me. He never had, and his dislike had found a good foundation to settle on — his wife had been attacked by a Were who was trying to get to me. Even though I'd taken the guy out, Alcee was down on me. Maybe he was one of the rare people repulsed by my trace of fairy blood, but more likely, he just didn't care for me. There was no point in trying to win him over. I gave him a nod, which he did not return.

"This here is my cousin Claude Crane from Monroe," I said.

"How's he related?" Andy asked. All three of these men knew the skein of blood ties that bound together practically the whole parish.

"It's kind of embarrassing," Claude said. (Nothing would embarrass Claude, but he gave a good imitation.) "I'm from what you call the wrong side of the blanket."

For once, I was grateful to Claude for taking that weight. I cast my eyes down as though I couldn't bear to talk about the shame of it. "Claude and I are trying to get acquainted since we found out we were related," I said.

I could see that fact go into their mental files. "Why y'all here?" I asked. "What did the anonymous caller say?"

"That you had a body buried in your woods." Bud looked away as if he were a little ashamed to say something so outrageous, but I knew different. After years in law enforcement, Bud knew exactly what human beings could do, even the most normal-looking human beings. Even young blondes with big boobs. Maybe especially them.

"You didn't bring any tracking dogs," Claude observed. I was kind of hoping that Claude would keep his mouth shut, but I saw I wasn't going to get my wish.

"I think a physical search will do it," Bud said. "The location was real specific." (And the tracking dogs were expensive to hire, he thought.)

"Oh my gosh," I said, genuinely startled. "How could this person claim not to be involved if they knew where the body was exactly? I don't get it." I'd hoped Bud would tell me more, but he didn't bite.

Andy shrugged. "We got to go look."

"Look away," I said, with absolute confidence. If they'd brought the dogs, I'd have been sweating bullets that they'd scent Debbie Pelt or the former resting site of Basim. "You'll excuse me if I just stay here in the house while you-all tramp through the woods. I hope you don't pick up too many ticks." Ticks lurked on bushes and weeds, sensing your chemicals and body heat as you passed, then making a leap of faith. I watched Andy tuck his pants into his boots, and Bud and Alcee sprayed themselves.

After the men had disappeared into the

woods, Claude said, "You'd better tell me why you're not scared."

"We moved the body last night," I said, and turned to sit down at the desk where I'd installed the computer I'd gotten from Hadley's apartment. Let Claude put that in his pipe and smoke it! After a few seconds, I heard him stomp back up the stairs.

Since I had to wait for the men to come out of the woods, I might as well check my e-mail. A lot of forwarded messages, most of them inspirational or patriotic, from Maxine Fortenberry, Hoyt's mother. I deleted those without reading them. I read an e-mail from Andy Bellefleur's pregnant wife, Halleigh. It was a strange coincidence, hearing from her while her husband was out in back of my house on a wild-goose chase.

Halleigh told me she was feeling great. Just great! But Grandmama Caroline was failing fast, and Halleigh feared Miss Caroline wouldn't live to see her great-grandchild born.

Caroline Bellefleur was very old. Andy and Portia had been brought up in Miss Caroline's house after their parents had died. Miss Caroline had been a widow for longer than she'd been married. I had no memory of Mr. Bellefleur at all, and I was pretty sure Portia and Andy hadn't known him that long. Andy was older than Portia, and Portia was a year older than me, so I estimated that Miss Caroline, who'd once been Renard Parish's finest cook and had made the best chocolate cake in the world, was at least in her nineties.

"Anyway," Halleigh went on, "she wants to find the family Bible more than anything else on this earth. You know she's always got a bee in her bonnet, and now it's finding that Bible, which has been missing for umpty-ump years. I had a wild thought. She thinks way back our family was connected to some branch of the Comptons. Would you ask your neighbor, Mr. Compton, if he would mind very much looking for that old Bible? It seems like a long shot, but she hasn't lost any of her personality though she's physically weak."

That was a nice way of saying that Miss Caroline was bringing up that Bible real often.

I was in a quandary. I knew that Bible was over at the Compton house. And I knew after she studied it, Miss Caroline would find out that she was a direct descendant of Bill Compton. How she'd feel about that was anybody's guess. Did I want to screw with her worldview when the woman was on her deathbed?

On the other hand, did . . . Oh, hell, I was tired of trying to balance everything out, and I had enough on my plate to worry about. In a reckless moment, I forwarded Halleigh's e-mail to Bill. I had come late to e-mail, and I still didn't entirely trust it. But at least I felt I'd put the ball into Bill's court. If he chose to lob it back, well, okay.

After I'd messed around a little on eBay, marveling at the things people were trying to sell, I heard voices in the front yard. I looked out to see Bud, Alcee, and Andy brushing dust and twigs off their clothes. Andy was rubbing at a bite on his neck.

I went outside. "Did you find a body?" I asked them.

"No, we did not," Alcee Beck said. "We did see that people had been back there."

"Well, sure," I said. "But no body?"

"We won't trouble you any further," Bud said shortly.

They left in a cloud of dust. I watched them go, and shivered. I felt like the guillotine had been descending on my neck and had been prevented from cutting off my head only because the rope was too short.

I went back to the computer and sent Alcide an e-mail. It said only, "The police were just here." I figured that would be enough. I knew I wouldn't hear from him until he was ready for me to come to Shreveport.

I was surprised that it took three days to receive a reply from Bill. Those days had been remarkable only for the number of people I hadn't heard from. I hadn't heard from Remy, which wasn't too extraordinary. None of the members of the Long Tooth pack called, so I could only assume they'd retrieved the body of Basim from its new resting place and that they would let me know when the meeting would be held. If someone came into my woods and tried to find out why Basim's body had vanished, I didn't know about it. And I didn't hear from Pam or Bobby Burnham, which was a little worrisome, but still . . . no big.

What did gripe me in a major way was not hearing from Eric. Okay, his (maker, sire, dad) mentor Appius Livius Ocella was in town . . . but geez Louise.

In between sessions of worrying, I looked up Roman names and found that "Appius" was his praenomen, his common name. Livius was his nomen, his family name, handed down from father to son, indicating that he was a member of the Livii family or clan. Ocella was his cognomen, so it was meant to indicate what particular branch of the

Livii had borne him; or it could have been given as an honorific for his service in a war. (I had no idea what war that could have been.) As a third possibility, if he'd been adopted into another family, the cognomen would reflect his birth family.

Your name said a lot about you in the Roman world.

I wasted a lot of time finding out all about Appius Livius Ocella's name. I still had no idea what he wanted or what he intended to do to my boyfriend. And those were the things I needed to know the most. I have to say, I was feeling pretty sulky, pugnacious, and sullen (I looked up a few words while I was online). Not a pretty posy of emotions, but I couldn't seem to upgrade to dull unhappiness.

Cousin Claude was making himself scarce, too. I glimpsed him only once in those three days, and that was when I heard him go through the kitchen and out the back door and got up in time to see him getting into his car.

This goes to explain why I was delighted to see Bill at my back door when the sun had set on the third day after I'd sent him Halleigh's e-mail. He was not looking appreciably better than he had the last time I'd seen him, but he was dressed in a suit and tie and his hair was carefully combed. The Bible was under his arm.

I understood why he was groomed, what he meant to do. "Good," I said.

"Come with me," he said. "It will help if you're there."

"But they'll think . . ." And then I made my mouth shut. It was unworthy to be worrying about the Bellefleurs' assuming Bill and I were a couple again when Caroline Bellefleur was about to meet her maker.

"Would that be so terrible?" he asked with simple dignity.

"No, of course not. I was proud to be your girlfriend," I said, and turned to go back to my room. "Please come in while I change clothes." I'd finished the lunch-and-afternoon shift, and I'd changed to shorts and a T-shirt.

Since I was in a hurry, I changed to an above-the-knee black skirt and a white cap-sleeve fitted blouse I'd gotten on sale at Stage. I slid a red leather belt through the belt loops and got some red sandals from the back of my closet. I fluffed my hair, and I was ready.

I drove us over in my car, which was beginning to need an alignment.

It wasn't a long ride to the Bellefleur mansion; it didn't take long to get anywhere in

Bon Temps. We parked in the driveway at the front door, but as we'd driven up I'd glimpsed several cars in the back parking area. I'd seen Andy's car there, and Portia's, too. There was an ancient gray Chevy Chevette parked sort of unobtrusively at the rear, and I wondered if Miss Caroline had a round-the-clock caregiver.

We walked up to the double front doors. Bill didn't think it was appropriate ("seemly" was the word he used) to go to the back, and under the circumstances, I had to agree. Bill walked slowly and with effort. More than once I wanted to offer to carry the heavy Bible but I knew he wouldn't let me, so I saved my breath.

Halleigh answered the door, thank God. She was startled when she saw Bill, but she recovered her poise very quickly and greeted us.

"Halleigh, Mr. Compton has brought the family Bible that Andy's grandmother wants to see," I said, in case Halleigh had gone temporarily blind and hadn't noticed the huge volume. Halleigh was looking a little rough around the edges. Her brown hair was a mess, and her green flowered dress looked almost as tired as her eyes. Presumably, she'd come over to Miss Caroline's after she'd worked all day teaching school.

Halleigh was obviously pregnant, something Bill hadn't known, I could tell by the fleeting expression on his face.

"Oh," Halleigh said, her face visibly relaxing with relief. "Mr. Compton, please come in. You have no idea how Miss Caroline's fretted about this." I think Halleigh's reaction was a pretty good indicator of just how much Miss Caroline had fretted.

We stepped into the entrance hall together. The wide flight of stairs was ahead of us and to our left. It curved gracefully up to the second floor. Lots of local brides had had their pictures made on this staircase. I had come down it in heels and a long dress when I'd been a stand-in for a sick bridesmaid at Halleigh and Andy's wedding.

"I think it would be real nice if Bill could give the Bible to Miss Caroline," I said, before the pause could become awkward. "There's a family connection."

Even Halleigh's excellent manners faltered. "Oh . . . how interesting." Her back stiffened, and I saw Bill appreciating the curve of her pregnancy. A faint smile curved his lips for a second. "I'm sure that would be just fine," Halleigh said, rallying. "Let's just go upstairs."

We went up the stairs after her, and I had to struggle with the impulse to put a hand under Bill's elbow to help him a little. I would have to do something to help Bill. He obviously wasn't getting any better. A little fear crept into my heart.

We walked a little farther along the gallery to the door to the largest bedroom, which was open a discreet few inches. Halleigh stepped in ahead of us.

"Sookie and Mr. Compton have brought the family Bible," she said. "Miss Caroline, can he bring it in?"

"Yes, of course, have him bring it," said a weak voice, and Bill and I walked in.

Miss Caroline was the queen of the room, no doubt about it. Andy and Portia were standing to the right of the bed, and they looked both worried and uneasy as Bill ushered me in. I noticed the absence of Portia's husband, Glen. A middle-aged African-American woman was sitting in a chair to the left of the bed. She was wearing the bright, loose pants and cheerful tunic that nurses favored now. The pattern made her look as though she worked on a pediatric ward. However, in a room decorated in subdued peach and cream, the splash of color was welcome. The nurse was thin and tall, and wore an incredible wig that reminded me of a movie Cleopatra. She nodded to us as we came closer to the bed.

Caroline Bellefleur, who looked like the steel magnolia she was, lay propped up on a dozen pillows in the four-poster bed. There were shadows of exhaustion under her old eyes, and her hands curled in wrinkled claws on the bedspread. But there was still a flicker of interest in her eyes as she looked at us.

"Miss Stackhouse, Mr. Compton, I haven't seen you since the big wedding," she said with an obvious effort. Her voice was thin as paper.

"That was a beautiful occasion, Mrs. Bellefleur," Bill said with an almost equal effort. I only nodded. This was not my conversation to have.

"Please take a seat," the old woman said, and Bill pulled a chair up closer to her bed. I sat a couple of feet back.

"Looks like that Bible is too big for me to handle now," the ancient lady said, with a smile. "It was so nice of you to bring it over. I have sure been wanting to see it. Has it been in your attic? I know we don't have much connection with the Comptons, but I sure wanted to find that old book. Halleigh was nice enough to do some checking for me."

"As a matter of fact, this book was on my coffee table," Bill said gently. "Mrs. Bellefleur — Caroline — my second child was a daughter, Sarah Isabelle."

"Oh my goodness," said Miss Caroline, to indicate she was listening. She didn't seem to know where this was headed, but she was definitely attentive.

"Though I didn't learn this until I read the family page in this Bible after I returned to Bon Temps, my daughter Sarah had four children, though one baby was born dead."

"That happened so often back then," she said.

I glanced over at the Bellefleur grandchildren. Portia and Andy weren't happy that Bill was here, not at all, but they were listening, too. They hadn't spared a glance for me, which was actually just fine. Though they were puzzled by Bill's presence, the focus of their thoughts was the woman who had raised them and the visible fact that she was fading away.

Bill said, "My Sarah's daughter was named Caroline, for her grandmother . . . my wife."

"My name?" Miss Caroline sounded pleased, though her voice was a little weaker.

"Yes, your name. My granddaughter Caroline married a cousin, Matthew Phillips Holliday."

"Why, those are my mother and father."

She smiled, which did drastic things to her scores of wrinkles. "So you are . . . Really?" To my amazement, Caroline Bellefleur laughed.

"Your great-grandfather. Yes, I am."

Portia made a sound as though she were choking on a stinkbug. Miss Caroline disregarded her granddaughter entirely, and she didn't look over at Andy — which was lucky, because he was turkey-wattle red.

"Well, if this isn't funny," she said. "I'm as wrinkled as unironed linen, and you're as smooth as a fresh peach." She was genuinely amused. "Great-granddaddy!"

Then a thought seemed to occur to the dying lady. "Was it you arranged for that timely windfall we got?"

"The money couldn't have been put to better use," Bill said gallantly. "The house looks beautiful. Who will live in it after you die?"

Portia gasped, and Andy looked a little taken aback. But I glanced at the nurse. She gave me a brief nod. Miss Caroline's time was very near, and the lady was fully aware of it.

"Well, I think Portia and Glen will stay here," Miss Caroline said slowly. It was evident she was tiring fast. "Halleigh and Andy want to have their baby in their own home, and I don't blame them one bit. You're not saying you're interested in the house?"

"Oh, no, I have my own," Bill reassured her. "And I was glad to give my own family the wherewithal to repair this place. I want my descendants to keep on living here through the years and have many happy times in this place."

"Thank you," Miss Caroline said, and now her voice was barely a whisper.

"Sookie and I must go," Bill said. "You rest easy, now."

"I will," she said, and smiled, though her eyes were closing.

I rose as quietly as I could and slipped out of the room ahead of Bill. I thought Portia and Andy might want to say a few things to Bill. Sure enough, they didn't want to disturb their grandmother, so they followed Bill out onto the gallery.

"Thought you were dating another vampire now?" Andy asked me. He didn't sound as snarky as he usually did.

"I am," I said. "But Bill is still my friend."

Portia had briefly dated Bill, though not because she thought he was cute or anything. I was sure that added to her embarrassment as she stuck out her hand to Bill. Portia needed to brush up on her vampire etiquette. Though Bill looked a little taken aback, he accepted the handshake. "Portia," he said. "Andy. I hope you don't find this too awkward."

I was busting-at-the-seams proud of Bill. It was easy to see where Caroline Bellefleur had gotten her graciousness.

Andy said, "I wouldn't have taken the money if I'd known it came from you." He'd evidently come straight from work, because he was wearing all his gear: a badge and handcuffs clipped to his belt, a holstered gun. He looked pretty formidable, but he was no match for Bill, even as sick as Bill was.

"Andy, I know you're not a fan of the fang. But you're part of my family, and I know you were raised to respect your elders."

Andy looked completely taken aback.

"That money was to make Caroline happy, and I think it did," Bill continued. "So it served its purpose. I've gotten to see her and to tell her about our relationship, and she has the Bible. I won't burden you with my presence any longer. I would ask that you have the funeral at night so I can attend."

"Who ever heard of a funeral at night?" Andy said.

"Yes, we'll do that." Portia didn't sound warm and welcoming, but she did sound absolutely resolved. "The money made her last few years very happy. She loved restoring the house to its best state, and she loved giving us the wedding here. The Bible is the frosting on the cake. Thank you."

Bill nodded to both of them, and without further ado we left Belle Rive.

Caroline Bellefleur, Bill's great-granddaughter, died in the early hours of the morning.

Bill sat with the family during the funeral, which took place the next night, to the profound amazement of the town.

I sat at the back with Sam.

It wasn't an occasion for tears; without a doubt, Caroline Bellefleur had had a long life — a life not devoid of sorrow, but at least full of moments of compensatory happiness. She had very few remaining contemporaries, and those who were still alive were almost all too tottery to come to her funeral.

The service seemed quite normal until we drove out to the cemetery, which didn't have night lighting — of course — and I saw that temporary lights had been set up around the perimeter of the grave in the Bellefleur plot. That was a strange sight. The minister had a hard time reading the service

315

until a member of the congregation held his own flashlight to the page.

The bright lights in the dark night were an unpleasant reminder of the recovery of Basim al Saud's body. It was hard to think properly about Miss Caroline's life and legacy with all the conjecture rattling around in my head. And why hadn't anything already happened? I felt as though I were living waiting for the other shoe to drop. I wasn't aware my hand had tightened on Sam's arm until he turned to look at me with some alarm. I forced my fingers to relax and bowed my head for the prayer.

The family, I heard, was going to Belle Rive for a buffet meal after the service. I wondered if they'd gotten Bill his favorite blood. Bill looked awful. He was using a cane at the grave site. Something had to be done about finding his sibling, since he wasn't taking action himself. If there was a chance his sibling's blood might cure him, the effort had to be made.

I'd driven to the funeral with Sam, and since my house was so close, I told Sam I'd walk back from the grave site. I'd stuck a little flashlight in my purse, and I reminded Sam I knew the cemetery like the back of my hand. So when all the other attendees

316

took off, including Bill, to go to Belle Rive for the buffet meal, I waited in the shadows until the cemetery employees started filling in the hole, and then I walked through the trees to Bill's house.

I still had a key.

Yes, I knew I was being a terrible busybody. And maybe I was doing the wrong thing. But Bill was wasting away, and I just couldn't sit by and let him do it.

I unlocked the front door and went to Bill's office, which had been the Compton formal dining room. Bill had all his computer gear set up on a huge table, and he had a rolling chair he'd gotten at Office Depot. A smaller table served as a mailing station, where Bill prepared copies of his vampire database to send to purchasers. He advertised heavily in vampire magazines — *Fang,* of course, and *Dead Life,* which appeared in so many languages. Bill's newest marketing effort involved hiring vampires who spoke many different languages to translate all the information so he could sell foreign-language editions of his worldwide vampire listing service. As I remembered from a previous visit, there were a dozen CD copies of his database in cases by his mailing station. I double-checked to make sure I had one that was in English. Wouldn't do me much good to get one in Russian.

Of course, Russian reminded me of Alexei, and thinking of Alexei reminded me all over of how worried/angry/frightened I was about Eric's silence.

I could feel my mouth pinching together in a really unpleasant expression as I thought about that silence. But I had to pay attention to my own little problem right now, and I scooted out of the house, relocked the door, and hoped Bill wouldn't pick up on my scent in the air.

I went through the cemetery as quickly as if it had been daytime. When I was in my own kitchen, I looked around for a good hiding place. I finally fixed on the linen closet in the hall bathroom as a good spot, and I put the CD under the stack of clean towels. I didn't think even Claude could use five towels before I got up the next day.

I checked my answering machine; I checked my cell phone, which I hadn't taken to the service. No messages. I undressed slowly, trying to imagine what could have happened to Eric. I'd decided I wouldn't call him, no matter what. He knew where I was and how to reach me. I hung my black dress in the closet, put my black heels on the shoe rack, and then pulled on my Tweety Bird nightshirt, an old favorite.

Then I went to bed, mad as a wet hen. And scared.

CHAPTER 10

Claude hadn't come home the night before. His car wasn't by the back door. I was glad someone had gotten lucky. Then I told myself not to be so pitiful.

"You're doing okay," I said, looking in the mirror so I'd believe it. "Look at you! Great tan, Sook!" I had to be in for the lunch shift, so I got dressed right after I'd eaten breakfast. I retrieved the purloined CD from under the towels. I'd either pay Bill for it or return it, I told myself virtuously. I hadn't really stolen it if I planned to pay for it. Someday. I looked at the clear plastic case in my hands. I wondered how much the FBI would pay for it. Despite all Bill's attempts to make sure only vampires bought the CD, it would be truly amazing if no one else had it.

So I opened it and popped it into my computer. After a preliminary whir, the screen popped up. "The Vampire Directory," it said in Gothic lettering, red on a black screen. Stereotype, anyone?

"Enter your code number," prompted the screen.

Uh-oh.

Then I remembered there'd been a little Post-it on top of the case, and I dug it out of the wastebasket. Yep, this was surely a code. Bill would never have attached the code to the box if he hadn't believed his house was secure, and I felt a pang of guilt. I didn't know what procedure he'd established, but I assumed he put the code in a directory when he mailed out the disc to a happy customer. Or maybe he'd put a "destruct" code on the paper for fools like me, and the whole thing would blow up in my face. I was glad no one else was in the house after I typed in the code and hit Enter, because I dropped to my knees under the desk.

Nothing happened, except some more whirring, and I figured I was safe. I scrambled back into my chair.

The screen was showing me my options. I could search by country of residence, country of origin, name, or last sighting. I clicked on "Residence," and I was prompted: "Which country?" I could pick from a list. After I clicked on "USA," I got another prompt: "What state?" And another list. I clicked on "Louisiana" and then on "Compton." There he was, in a modern picture taken at his house. I recognized the paint color. Bill was smiling stiffly, and he didn't look like a party animal, that's for sure. I wondered how he'd fare with a dating service. I began to read his biography. And sure enough, there at the bottom, I read, "Sired by Lorena Ball of Louisiana, 1870."

But there was no listing for "brothers" or "sisters."

Okay, it wasn't going to be that easy. I clicked on the boldfaced name of Bill's sire, the late, unlamented Lorena. I was curious as to what her entry would say, since Lorena had met the ultimate death, at least until they learned how to resuscitate ashes.

"Lorena Ball," her entry read, with only a drawing. It was a pretty good likeness, I thought, cocking my head as I looked it over. Turned in 1788 in New Orleans . . . lived all across the South but returned to Louisiana after the Civil War . . . had "met the sun," murder by person or persons "unknown." Huh. Bill knew perfectly well who'd killed Lorena, and I could only be glad he hadn't put my name in the directory. I wondered what would have happened

322

to me if he had. See, you think you have enough to worry about, but then you think of a possibility you'd never imagined and you realize you have even *more* problems.

Okay, here we go. . . . "Sired Bill Compton (1870) and Judith Vardamon (1902)."

Judith. So this was Bill's "sister."

After some more clicking and reading, I discovered that Judith Vardamon was still "alive," or at least she had been when Bill had been compiling his database. She lived in Little Rock.

I further discovered I could send her an e-mail. Naturally, she wasn't obliged to answer it.

I stared down at my hands, and I thought hard. I thought about how awful Bill looked. I thought about his pride, and the fact that he hadn't yet contacted this Judith, though he suspected her blood would cure him. Bill wasn't a fool, so there was some good reason he hadn't called this other child of Lorena. I just didn't know that reason. But if Bill had decided she shouldn't be contacted, he knew what he was doing, right? Oh, to hell with it.

I typed in her e-mail address. And moved the cursor down to the topic. Typed "Bill's ill." Thought that looked almost funny. Almost changed it, but didn't. Moved the cursor down to the body of the e-mail, clicked again. Hesitated. Then I typed, "I'm Bill Compton's neighbor. I don't know how long it's been since you heard from him, but he lives at his old home place in Bon Temps, Louisiana, now. Bill's got silver poisoning. He can't heal without your blood. He doesn't know I'm sending this. We used to date, and we're still friends. I want him to get better." I signed it, because anonymous is not my style.

I clenched my teeth really hard together. I clicked on Send.

As much as I wanted to keep the CD and browse through it, my little code of honor told me I had to return it without enjoying it, because I hadn't paid. So I got Bill's key and put the disc back in its plastic case and started across the cemetery.

I slowed as I drew near to the Bellefleur plot. The flowers were still piled on Miss Caroline's grave. Andy was standing there, staring at a cross made out of red carnations. I thought it was pretty awful, but this was definitely an occasion for the thought to count more than the deed. I didn't think Andy was registering what was right in front of him anyway.

I felt as though "Thief" were burned onto my forehead. I knew Andy wouldn't care if

I backed up a truck to Bill's house and loaded up all the furniture and drove off with it. It was my own sense of guilt that was plaguing me.

"Sookie," Andy said. I hadn't realized he'd noticed me.

"Andy," I said cautiously. I wasn't sure where this conversation would go, and I had to leave for work soon. "You still have relatives in town? Or have they left?"

"They're leaving after lunch," he said. "Halleigh had to work on some class preparations this morning, and Glen had to run into his office to catch up on paperwork. This has been hardest on Portia."

"I guess she'll be glad when things get back to normal." That seemed safe enough.

"Yeah. She's got a law practice to run."

"Did the lady who was taking care of Miss Caroline have another job to go to?" Reliable caregivers were as scarce as hens' teeth and far more valuable.

"Doreen? Yeah, she moved right across the garden to Mr. DeWitt's." After an uncomfortable pause, he said, "She kind of got on to me that night, after you-all left. I know I wasn't polite to . . . Bill."

"It's been a hard time for you-all."

"I just . . . It makes me mad that we were getting charity."

"You weren't, Andy. Bill is your family. I know it must feel weird, and I know you don't think much of vampires in general, but he's your great-great-great-grandfather, and he wanted to help out his people. It wouldn't make you feel funny if he'd left you money and he was out here with Miss Caroline under the ground, would it? It's just that Bill's still walking around."

Andy shook his head, as if flies were buzzing around it. His hair was thinning, I noticed. "You know what my grandmother's last request was?"

I couldn't imagine. "No," I said.

"She left her chocolate cake recipe to the town," he said, and he smiled. "A damn recipe. And you know what, they were as excited at the newspaper when I took that recipe in as if it were Christmas and I'd brought them a map to Jimmy Hoffa's body."

"It's going to be in the paper?" I sounded as thrilled as I felt. I bet there would be at least a hundred chocolate cakes in the oven the day the paper came out.

"See, you're all excited, too," Andy said, sounding five years younger.

"Andy, that's big news," I assured him. "Now, if you'll excuse me, I have to go return something." And I hurried through the rest of the cemetery to Bill's house. I put the CD, complete with its little sticky note, on top of the pile from which I'd taken it, and I skedaddled.

I second-guessed myself, and third-, fourth-, and fifth-guessed, too. At Merlotte's I worked in a kind of haze, concentrating fiercely on getting lunch orders right, being quick, and responding instantly to any request. My other sense told me that despite my efficiency, people weren't glad to see me coming, and really I couldn't blame them.

Tips were low. People were ready to forgive inefficiency, as long as you smiled while you were sloppy. They didn't like the unsmiling, quick-handed me.

I could tell (simply because he thought it so often) that Sam was assuming I'd had a fight with Eric. Holly thought that I was having my period.

And Antoine was an informant.

Our cook had been lost in his own broody mood. I realized how resistant he normally was to my telepathy only when he forgot to be. I was waiting on an order to be up at the hatch, and I was looking at Antoine while he flipped a burger, and I heard directly from him, *Not getting off work to meet that asshole again, he can just stuff it up his butt. I'm not telling him nothing else.* Then

Antoine, whom I'd come to respect and admire, flipped the burger onto its waiting bun and turned to the hatch with the plate in his hand. He met my eyes squarely.

Oh shit, he thought.

"Let me talk to you before you do anything," he said, and I knew for sure that he was a traitor.

"No," I said, and turned away, going right to Sam, who was behind the bar washing glasses. "Sam, Antoine is some kind of agent for the government," I said, very quietly.

Sam didn't ask me how I knew, and he didn't question my statement. His mouth pressed into a hard line. "We'll talk to him later," he said. "Thanks, Sook." I regretted now that I hadn't told Sam about the Were buried on my land. I was always sorry when I didn't tell Sam something, it seemed.

I got the plate and took it to the right table without meeting Antoine's eyes.

Some days I hated my ability more than others. Today was one of those days. I had been much happier (though in retrospect, it had been a foolish happiness) when I'd assumed Antoine was a new friend. I wondered if any of the stories he'd told about going through Katrina in the Superdome had been true, or if those had been lies, too. I'd felt such sympathy for him. And I'd never had a hint until now that his persona was false. How could that be?

First, I don't monitor every single thought of every person. I block a lot of it out, in general, and I try especially hard to stay out of the heads of my co-workers. Second, people don't always think about critical stuff in explicit terms. A guy might not think, *I believe I'll get the pistol from under the seat of my truck and shoot Jerry in the head for screwing my wife.* I was much more likely to get an impression of sullen anger, with overtones of violence. Or even a projection of how it might feel to shoot Jerry. But the shooting of Jerry might not have reached the specific planning stage at the moment the shooter was in the bar, when I was privy to his thoughts.

And mostly people *didn't* act on their violent impulses, something I didn't learn until after some very painful incidents as I grew up.

If I spent my life trying to figure out the background of every single thought I heard, I wouldn't have my own life.

At least I had something to think about besides wondering what the hell was happening with Eric and the Long Tooth pack. At the end of my shift, I found myself in Sam's office with Sam and Antoine.

Sam shut the door behind me. He was furious. I didn't blame him. Antoine was mad at himself, mad at me, and defensive with Sam. The atmosphere in the room was choking with anger and frustration and fear.

"Listen, man," Antoine said. He was standing facing Sam. He made Sam look small. "Just listen, okay? After Katrina, I didn't have no place to live and nothing to do. I was trying to find work and keep myself going. I couldn't even get a damn FEMA trailer. Things were going *bad*. So I . . . I borrowed a car, to get to Texas to some relatives. I was gonna dump it where the cops could find it, get it back to the owner. I know it was stupid. I know I shouldn'ta done it. But I was desperate, and I did something dumb."

"Yet you're not in jail," Sam observed. His words were like a whip that barely flicked Antoine, drew a little bit of blood.

Antoine breathed out heavily. "No, I'm not, and I'll tell you why. My uncle is a werewolf, in one of the New Orleans packs. So I knew something about 'em. An FBI agent named Sara Weiss came to talk to me in jail. She was okay. But after she spoke with me once, she brought this guy Lattesta, Tom Lattesta. He said he was based in Rhodes, and I couldn't figure out what he was doing in New Orleans. But he told me that he knew all about my uncle, and he figured that you-all were coming out sooner or later since the vamps did. He knew what you were, that there were other things besides wolves. He knew there'd be a lot of people didn't like hearing that people who were part animal lived in with the rest of us. He described Sookie to me. He said she was something strange, too, and he didn't know what. He sent me here to watch, to see what happened."

Sam and I exchanged glances. I don't know what Sam had anticipated, but this was way more serious than I'd imagined. I figured back. "Tom Lattesta has known all along?" I said. "When did he start thinking there was something wrong with me?" Had it been before he saw the footage from the hotel explosion in Rhodes, which he'd used as the reason for approaching me a few months ago?

"Half the time he's sure you're a fraud. Half the time he thinks you're the real deal."

I turned to my boss. "Sam, he came to my house the other day. Lattesta. He told me that someone close to me, one of the *great* relatives" — I didn't want to get more specific in front of Antoine — "had fixed it so he had to back off."

"That explains why he was so mad," Antoine said, and his face hardened. "That explains a lot."

"What did he tell you to do?" Sam asked.

"Lattesta said the car theft thing was forgotten as long as I kept an eye on Sam and any other people who weren't all the way human who came into the bar. He said he couldn't touch Sookie now, and he was mighty pissed."

Sam looked at me, a question on his face.

"He's sincere," I said.

"Thank you, Sookie," Antoine said. He looked abjectly miserable.

"Okay," Sam said, after looking at Antoine for a few more seconds. "You still have a job."

"No . . . conditions?" Antoine was looking at Sam unbelievingly. "He expects me to keep watching you."

"Not a condition, but a warning. If you tell him one thing more besides the fact that I'm here and running this business, you're outta here, and if I can think of something else to do to you, I will."

Antoine seemed weak with relief. "I'll do my best for you, Sam," he said. "Tell the truth, I'm glad it all came out. It's been sitting heavy on my conscience."

"There'll be a backlash," I said when Sam

and I were alone.

"I know. Lattesta will come down on him hard, and Antoine will be tempted to make something up to tell him."

"I think Antoine is a good guy. I hope I'm not wrong." I'd been wrong about people before. In major ways.

"Yeah, I hope he lives up to our expectations." Sam smiled at me suddenly. He has a great smile, and I couldn't help but smile back. "It's good to have faith in people sometimes, give them another chance. And we'll both keep our eyes on him."

I nodded. "Okay. Well, I better get home." I wanted to check my cell phone for messages and my landline, too. And my computer. I was dying for someone to reach out and touch me.

"Is something the matter?" Sam asked. He reached out to give me a tentative pat on the shoulder. "Anything I can do?"

"You're the greatest," I said. "But I'm just trying to get through a bad situation."

"Eric's out of touch?" he said, proving that Sam is one shrewd guesser.

"Yeah," I admitted. "And he's got . . . relatives in town. I don't know what the hell's going on." The word "relatives" jogged my brain. "How are things going in your family, Sam?"

"The divorce is no-fault, and it's going through," he said. "My mom is pretty miserable, but she'll be better as time goes on, I hope. Some of the people in Wright are giving her the cold shoulder. She let Mindy and Craig watch her change."

"What form did she pick?" I'd rather be a shapeshifter than a wereanimal, so I'd have a choice.

"A Scottie, I think. My sister took it real well. Mindy's always been more flexible than Craig."

I thought women were almost always more flexible than men, but I didn't think I needed to say that out loud. Generalizations like that can come back to bite you in the ass. "Deidra's family settled down?"

"It looks like the wedding's back on, as of two nights ago," Sam said. "Her mom and dad finally got that the 'contamination' couldn't spread to Deidra and Craig and their kids, if they have any."

"So you think the wedding will take place?"

"Yeah, I do. You still going to go to Wright with me?"

I started to say, "You still want me to?" but that would have been unduly coy, since he'd just asked me. "When the date is set, you'll have to ask my boss if I can get off work," I told him. "Sam, it may be tacky of me to persist in asking, but why aren't you taking Jannalynn?"

I wasn't imagining the discomfort that emanated from Sam. "She's . . . Well, ah . . . She's . . . I can just tell that she and my mom wouldn't get along. If I do introduce her to my family, I think I better wait until the tension of the wedding isn't part of the picture. My mom's still jangled from the shooting and the divorce, and Jannalynn is . . . not a calm person." In my opinion, if you were dating someone you were clearly embarrassed to introduce to your family, you were probably dating the wrong person. But Sam hadn't asked me for my opinion.

"No, she certainly isn't a calm individual," I said. "And now that she's got those new responsibilities, she's got to be pretty focused on the pack, I guess."

"What? What new responsibilities?"

Uh-oh. "I'm sure she'll tell you all about it," I said. "I guess you haven't seen her in a couple of days, huh?"

"Nope. So we're both down in the dumps," he said.

I was willing to concede I'd been pretty grim, and I smiled at him. "Yeah, that's a big part of it," I said. "With Eric's maker being in town, and him being scarier than

Freddy Krueger, I'm pretty much on my own, I guess."

"If we don't hear from our significant others, let's go out tomorrow night. We can hit Crawdad Diner again," Sam said. "Or I can grill us some steaks."

"Sounds good," I told him. And I appreciated his offer. I'd been feeling kind of cast adrift. Jason was apparently busy with Michele (and after all, he'd stayed the other night when I'd half expected him to scoot out of the house), Eric was busy (apparently), Claude was almost never at the house and awake when I was awake, Tara was busy being pregnant, and Amelia had time to send me only the occasional e-mail. Though I didn't mind being by myself from time to time — in fact, I enjoyed it — I'd had a little too much of it lately. And being alone is a lot more fun if it's optional.

Relieved that the conversation with Antoine was over, and wondering what trouble Tom Lattesta might cause in the future, I grabbed my purse from the drawer in Sam's desk and headed for home.

It was a beautiful late afternoon when I pulled up in back of the house. I thought of working out to an exercise DVD before I fixed supper. Claude's car was gone. I hadn't noticed Jason's truck, so I was surprised to see him sitting on my back steps.

"Hey, Brother!" I called as I got out of the car. "Listen, let me ask you . . ." And then, getting his mental signature, I realized the man sitting on the steps wasn't Jason. I froze. All I could do was stare at my half-fae great-uncle Dermot and wonder if he had come to kill me.

CHAPTER 11

He could have slain me about sixty times in the seconds I stood there. Despite the fact that he didn't, I still didn't want to take my eyes off him.

"Don't be afraid," Dermot said, rising with a grace that Jason could never have matched. He moved like his joints were machine made and well oiled.

I said through numb lips, "Can't help it."

"I want to explain," he said as he drew nearer.

"Explain?"

"I wanted to get closer to both of you," he said. He was well into my personal space by then. His eyes were blue like Jason's, candid like Jason's, and really, seriously, crazy. *Not* like Jason's. "I was confused."

"About what?" I wanted to keep the conversation going, I surely did, because I didn't know what would happen when it came to a halt.

"About where my loyalties lay," he said, bowing his head as gracefully as a swan.

"Sure. Tell me about that." Oh, if only I had my squirt gun, loaded with lemon juice, in my purse! But I'd promised Eric I'd put it on my nightstand when Claude had come to live with me, so that was where it lay. And the iron trowel was where it was supposed to be, in the toolshed.

"I will," he said, standing close enough that I could smell him. He smelled great. Fairies always do. "I know you met my father, Niall."

I nodded, a very small movement. "Yes," I said, to make sure.

"Did you love him?"

"Yes," I said without hesitation. "I did. I do."

"He's easy to love; he's charming," Dermot said. "My mother, Einin, was beautiful, too. Not a fairy kind of beautiful, like Niall, but she was human-beautiful."

"That's what Niall told me," I said. I was picking my way through a conversational minefield.

"Did he tell you the water fairies murdered my twin?"

"Did Niall tell me your brother was murdered? No, but I heard."

"I saw parts of Fintan's body. Neave and

339

Lochlan had torn him limb from limb."

"They helped drown my parents, too," I said, holding my breath. What would he say?

"I . . ." He struggled to speak, his face desperate. "But I *wasn't there*. I . . . Niall . . ." It was terrible to watch Dermot struggle to speak. I shouldn't have had any mercy for him, since Niall had told me about Dermot's part in my parents' deaths. But I really couldn't endure his pain.

"So how come you ended up siding with Breandan's forces in the war?"

"He told me my father had killed my brother," Dermot said bleakly. "And I believed him. I mistrusted my love for Niall. When I remembered my mother's misery after Niall stopped coming to visit her, I thought Breandan must be right and we weren't meant to mingle with humans. It never seems to turn out well for them. And I hated what I was, half-human. I was never at home anywhere."

"So, are you feeling better now? About being a little bit human?"

"I've come to terms with it. I know my former actions were wrong, and I'm grieved that my father won't let me into Faery." The big blue eyes looked sad. I was too busy trying not to shake to get the full impact.

In a breath, out a breath. Calm, calm. "So

340

now you're thinking Jason and I are okay? You don't want to hurt us anymore?"

He put his arms around me. This was "hug Sookie" season, and no one had told me ahead of time. Fairies were very touchy-feely, and personal space didn't mean anything to them. I would have liked to tell my great-uncle to back off. But I didn't dare. I didn't need to read Dermot's mind to understand that almost anything could set him off, so delicate was his mental balance. I had to stiffen all my resolution to maintain my even breathing so I wouldn't shiver and shake. His nearness and the tension of being in his presence, the huge strength that hummed through his arms, took me back to a dark ruined shack and two psycho fairies who really had deserved their deaths. My shoulders jerked, and I saw a flash of panic in Dermot's eyes. *Calm. Be calm.*

I smiled at him. I have a pretty smile, people tell me, though I know it's a little too bright, a little nuts. However, that suited the conversation perfectly. "The last time you saw Jason," I said, and then couldn't think how to finish.

"I attacked his companion. The beast who'd hurt Jason's wife."

I swallowed hard and smiled some more.

"Probably would've been better if you'd explained to Jason why you were going after Mel. And it wasn't Mel who killed her, you know."

"No, it was my own kind that finished her off. But she would have died anyway. He wasn't taking her to get help, you know."

Wasn't much I could say, because his account of what had happened to Crystal was accurate. I noticed I hadn't gotten a coherent response from Dermot on why he'd left Jason in ignorance of Mel's crime. "But you didn't explain to Jason," I said, breathing in and out — in a very soothing way. I hoped. It seemed to me that the longer I touched Dermot, the calmer we both got. And Dermot was markedly more coherent.

"I was very conflicted," he said seriously, unexpectedly borrowing from modern jargon.

Maybe that was as good an answer as I was going to get. I decided to take another tack. "Did you want to see Claude?" I said hopefully. "He's living with me now, just temporarily. He should be back later tonight."

"I'm not the only one, you know," Dermot told me. I looked up and met his mad eyes. I understood that my great-uncle was trying to tell me something. I wished to God

I could make him rational. Just for five minutes. I stepped back from him and tried to figure out what he needed.

"You're not the only fairy left out in the human world. I know Claude's here. Someone else is, too?" I would've enjoyed my telepathy for a couple of minutes.

"Yes. *Yes*." His eyes were pleading with me to understand.

I'd risk a direct question. "Who else is on this side of Faery?"

"You don't want to meet him," Dermot assured me. "You have to be careful. He can't decide right now. He's ambivalent."

"Right." Whoever "he" was, he wasn't the only one who had mixed feelings. I wished I knew the right nutcracker that would open up Dermot's head.

"Sometimes he's in your woods." Dermot put his hands on my shoulders and squeezed gently. It was like he was trying to transmit things he couldn't say directly into my flesh.

"I heard about that," I said sourly.

"Don't trust other fairies," Dermot told me. "I shouldn't have."

I felt like a lightbulb had popped on above my head. "Dermot, have you had magic put on you? Like a spell?"

The relief in his eyes was almost palpable. He nodded frantically. "Unless they're at war, fairies don't like to kill other fairies. Except for Neave and Lochlan. They liked to kill everything. But I'm not dead. So there's hope."

Fairies might be reluctant to kill their own kind, but they didn't mind making them insane, apparently. "Is there anything I can do to reverse this spell? Can Claude help?"

"Claude has little magic, I think," Dermot said. "He's been living like a human too long. My dearest niece, I love you. How is your brother?"

We were back in nutty land. God bless poor Dermot. I hugged him, following an impulse. "My brother is happy, Uncle Dermot. He's dating a woman who suits him, and she won't take any shit off him, either. Her name is Michele — like my mom's, but with one *l* instead of two."

Dermot smiled down at me. Hard to say how much of this he was absorbing.

"Dead things love you," Dermot told me, and I made myself keep smiling.

"Eric the vampire? He says he does."

"Other dead things, too. They're pulling on you."

That was a not-so-welcome revelation. Dermot was right. I'd been feeling Eric through our bond, as usual, but there were two other gray presences with me every moment after dark: Alexei and Appius Livius. It was a drain on me, and I hadn't realized it until this moment.

"Tonight," Dermot said, "you'll receive visitors."

So now he was a prophet. "Good ones?"

He shrugged. "That's a matter of taste and expedience."

"Hey, Uncle Dermot? Do you walk around this land very often?"

"Too scared of the other one," he said. "But I try to watch you a little."

I was figuring out if that was a good thing or a bad thing when he vanished. Poof! I saw a kind of blur and then nothing. His hands were on my shoulders, and then they weren't. I assumed the tension of conversing with another person had gotten to Dermot.

Boy. That had been really, really weird.

I glanced around me, thinking I might see some other trace of his passage. He might even decide to return. But nothing happened. There wasn't a sound except the prosaic growl of my stomach, reminding me that I hadn't eaten lunch and that it was now suppertime. I went into the house on shaking legs and collapsed at the table. Conversation with a spy. Interview with an insane fairy. Oh, yes, phone Jason and tell him to be back on fairy watch. That was something I could do sitting down.

After that conversation, I remembered to carry in the newspapers when I got my legs to working again. While I baked a Marie Callender's pot pie, I read the past two days' papers.

Unfortunately, there was a lot of interest on the front page. There had been a gruesome murder in Shreveport, probably gang-related. The victim had been a young black man wearing gang colors, which was like a blinking arrow to the police, but he hadn't been shot. He'd been stabbed multiple times, and then his throat had been slashed. Yuck. Sounded more personal than a gang killing to me. Then the next night the same thing had happened again, this time to a kid of nineteen who wore different gang colors. He'd died the same awful way. I shook my head over the stupidity of young men dying over what I considered nothing, and moved on to a story that I found electrifying and very worrisome.

The tension over the werewolf registration issue was rising. According to the newspapers, the Weres were the big controversy. The stories hardly mentioned the other two-natured, yet I knew at least one werefox, one werebat, two weretigers, a score of werepanthers, and a shapeshifter. Were-wolves, the most numerous of the two-natured, were catching the brunt of the backlash. And they were sounding off about it, as they should have.

"Why should I register, as if I were an illegal alien or a dead citizen?" Scott Wacker, an army general, was quoted as saying. "My family has been American for six generations, all of us army people. My daughter's in Iraq. What more do you want?"

The governor of one of the northwestern states said, "We need to know who's a werewolf and who's not. In the event of an accident, officers need to know, to avoid blood contamination and to aid in identification."

I plunged my spoon into the crust to release some of the heat from the pot pie. I thought that over. *Bullshit,* I concluded.

"That's bushwah," General Wacker responded in the next paragraph. So Wacker and I had something in common. "For one thing, we change back to human form when we're dead. Officers already glove up when they're handling bodies. Identification is not going to be any more of a problem than with the one-natured. Why should it be?"

You go, Wacker.

According to the newspaper, the debate raged from the people in the streets (including some who weren't simply people) to members of Congress, from military personnel to firefighters, from law experts to constitutional scholars.

Instead of thinking globally or nationally, I tried to evaluate the crowd at Merlotte's since the announcement. Had revenue fallen off? Yes, there'd been a slight decrease at first, right after the bar patrons had watched Sam change into a dog and Tray become a wolf, but then people had started drinking as much as they had formerly.

So was this a created crisis, a nothing issue?

Not as much as I would have liked, I decided, having read a few more articles.

Some people really hated the idea that individuals they'd known all their lives had another side, a mysterious life unbeknownst (isn't that a great word? It had been on my Word of the Day calendar the week before) to the general public. That was the impression I'd gotten before, and it seemed that still held true. No one was budging on that position; the Weres got angrier, and the public got more frightened. At least a very vocal part of the public.

There had been demonstrations and riots in Redding, California, and Lansing, Michigan. I wondered if there were going to be riots here or in Shreveport. I found that hard to believe and painful to picture. I looked through the kitchen window at the gathering dusk, as if I expected to see a crowd of villagers with torches marching to Merlotte's.

It was a curiously empty evening. There wasn't much to clean up after I'd eaten, my laundry was up to date, and there was nothing on television I wanted to watch. I checked my e-mail; no message from Judith Vardamon.

There was a message from Alcide. "Sookie, we've set the pack meeting for Monday night at eight at my house. We've been trying to find a shaman for the judging. I'll see you and Jason then." It had been nearly a week since we'd found Basim's body in the woods, and this was the first I'd heard. The pack's "day or two" had stretched into six. And that meant it had been a very long time since I'd heard from Eric.

I called Jason again and left voice mail on his cell phone. I tried not to worry about the pack meeting, but every time I'd been with the whole pack, something violent had happened.

I thought again about the dead man in the grave in the clearing. Who had put him there? Presumably, the killer had wanted Basim's silence, but the body hadn't been planted on my land by mistake.

I read for thirty minutes or so, and then it was full dark and I felt Eric's presence, and then the lesser though undeniable company of the other two vampires. As soon as they woke, I felt tired. This made me so twitchy I broke my own resolution.

I knew that Eric realized I was unhappy and worried. It was impossible for him not to know that. Maybe he thought by keeping me away he was protecting me. Maybe he didn't know that his maker and Alexei were both in my consciousness. I took a deep breath and called him. The phone rang, and I pressed it to my ear as though I were holding Eric himself. But I thought, and I wouldn't have believed this possible a week ago, *What if he doesn't pick up?*

The phone rang, and I held my breath. After the second ring, Eric answered. "The pack meeting has been set," I blurted.

"Sookie," he said. "Can you come here?"

On my drive to Shreveport, I wondered at least four times if I was doing the right thing. But I concluded that whether I was right or wrong (in running to see Eric when he asked me to) was simply a dead issue. We were both on the ends of the line stretched between us, a line spun from blood. It trumped how we felt about each other at any given moment. I knew he was tired and desperate. He knew I was angry, uneasy, hurt. I wondered, though. If I'd called him and said the same thing, would he have hopped into his car (or into the sky) and arrived on my doorstep?

They were all at Fangtasia, he'd said.

I was shocked to see how few cars were parked in front of the only vampire bar in Shreveport. Fangtasia was a huge tourist draw in a town that was boasting a tourist increase, and I'd expected it to be packed. There were almost as many cars parked in the employee parking at the back as there were at the main door. That had never happened before.

Maxwell Lee, an African-American businessman who also happened to be a vampire, was on duty at the rear entrance, and that was a first, too. The rear door had never been specially guarded, because the vampires were so sure they could take care of themselves. Yet here he was, wearing his usual three-piece suit but doing a task he normally would have considered beneath him. He didn't look resentful; he looked worried.

I said, "Where are they?"

He jerked his head toward the main room of the bar. "I'm glad you're here," he said, and I knew Eric's maker's visit wasn't going well.

So often having out-of-town visitors is awkward, huh? You take them to see the local sights, you try to feed them and keep them entertained, but then you're really wishing they would leave. It wasn't hard to see that Eric was on his last nerve. He was sitting in a booth with Appius Livius Ocella and Alexei. Of course, Alexei looked too young to be in a bar, and that added to the absurdity of the moment.

"Good evening," I said stiffly. "Eric, you wanted to see me?"

Eric scooted over closer to the wall so I'd have plenty of room, and I sat by him. Appius Livius and Alexei both greeted me, Appius with a strained smile and Alexei with more ease. When we were all together, I discovered that being close to them relaxed the tense thread inside me, the thread that bound us all together.

"I've missed you," Eric said so quietly that at first I thought I'd imagined it.

I wouldn't refer to the fact that he'd been completely out of touch for days. He knew that.

It took all my self-control to bite back a

few choice words. "As I was trying to tell you over the phone, the pack meeting about Basim has been set for Monday night."

"Where and when?" he said, and there was a note in his voice that let me know he was not a happy camper. Well, he could pitch his tent right alongside mine.

"At Alcide's house. The one that used to be his dad's. At eight o'clock."

"And Jason's going with you? Without a doubt?"

"I haven't talked to him yet, but I left him a message."

"You've been angry with me."

"I've been worried about you." I couldn't tell him anything about how I'd felt that he didn't already know.

"Yes," Eric said. His voice was empty.

"Eric is an excellent host," the tsarevitch said, as if I expected a report.

I scratched up a smile to offer the boy. "That's good to hear, Alexei. What have you two been doing? I don't think you've ever been to Shreveport before."

"No," Appius Livius said in his curious accent. "We hadn't been here to visit. It's a nice little city. My older son has been doing his best to keep us busy and out of trouble."

Okay, that had been a tad on the sarcastic side. I could tell from Eric's tension that he hadn't entirely succeeded in the "keeping them out of trouble" part of his agenda.

"The World Market is fun. You can get stuff from all over the world there. And Shreveport was the capitol of the Confederacy for a while." Geez Louise, I needed to do better than that. "If you go to the Municipal Auditorium, you can see Elvis's dressing room," I said brightly. I wondered if Bubba ever visited there to see his old stomping grounds.

"I had a very good teenager last night," Alexei said, matching my cheerful tone. As though he'd said he'd run a red light.

I opened my mouth and nothing came out. If I said the wrong thing, I might be dead right then and there. "Alexei," I said, sounding much calmer than I felt, "you have to watch it. That's against the law here. Your maker and Eric could both suffer for it."

"When I was with my human family, I could do anything I wanted," Alexei said. I really couldn't read his voice at all. "I was so sick, they indulged me."

Eric twitched.

"I can sure understand that," I said. "Any family would be tempted to do that with a sick child. But since you're well now, and you've had lots of years to mature, I know you understand that doing exactly what you want to do is not a good plan." I thought of at least twenty other things I could have said, but I stopped right there. And that was a good thing. Appius Livius looked directly into my eyes and nodded almost imperceptibly.

"I don't look grown up," Alexei said.

Again, too many options on what I could say. The boy — the old, old, boy — definitely expected me to answer. "No, and it's an awful pity what happened to you and your family. But —"

And Alexei reached over, took my hand, and *showed me* what had happened to him and his family. I saw the cellar, the royal family, the doctor, the maid, facing the men who had come to kill them, and I heard the guns fire, and the bullets found their marks; or in the case of the women, they didn't, since the royal women had sewn jewels into their clothes for the escape that never came about. The jewels saved their lives for all of a few seconds, until the soldiers killed each groaning and bleeding and screaming individual. His mother, his father, his sisters, his doctor, his mother's maid, the cook, his father's valet . . . and his dog. And after the shooting, the soldiers went around with bayonets.

I thought I was going to throw up. I

swayed where I sat, and Eric's cold arm went around me. Alexei had let go, and I was never gladder of anything in my life. I would not have touched the child again for anything.

"You see," Alexei said triumphantly. "You see! I should be free to go my own way."

"No," I said. And I was proud that my voice was firm. "No matter how we suffer, we have an obligation to others. We have to be unselfish enough to try to live in the right way, so others can get through their own lives without us fouling them up."

Alexei looked rebellious. "That's what Master says, too," he muttered. "More or less."

"Master is right," I said, though the words tasted bad in my mouth.

"Master" waved for the bartender to come over. Felicia slunk up to the table. She was tall and pretty and as gentle as a vampire can be. She had some fresh scars on her neck. "What can I get you-all?" she said. "Sookie, can I bring you a beer or . . . ?"

"Some iced tea would be great, Felicia," I said.

"And some TrueBlood for all of you?" she asked the vampires. "Or, we do have a bottle of Royalty."

Eric's eyes closed, and Felicia realized her

blunder. "Okay," she said briskly. "True-Blood for Eric, tea for Sookie."

"Thank you!" I said, smiling up at the bartender.

Pam strode up to the table. She was trailing the gauzy black costume she wore at Fangtasia, and she was as close to panic as I'd ever seen her. "Excuse me," she said, bowing in the direction of the guests. "Eric, Katherine Boudreaux is visiting Fangtasia tonight. She's with Sallie and a small party."

Eric looked as if he were going to explode. "Tonight," he said, and one word spoke volumes. "With much regret, Ocella, I must ask you and Alexei to go back to my office."

Appius Livius got up without asking for further explanation, and Alexei, to my surprise, followed him without any questions. If Eric had been in the habit of breathing, I would say that he exhaled with relief when his visitors had left his sight. He said a few things in an ancient tongue, but I didn't know which one.

Then a stout, attractive blonde in her forties was standing by the table, another woman right behind her.

"You must be Katherine Boudreaux," I said pleasantly. "I'm Sookie Stackhouse; I'm Eric's girlfriend."

"Hi, honey. I'm Katherine," she said.

"This is my partner, Sallie. We're here with some friends who were curious about my job. I try to visit all the vampire workplaces during the year, and we hadn't been to Fangtasia in months. Since I'm based right here in Shreveport, I ought to make it in more often."

"We're so glad you're here," Eric said smoothly. He sounded like his normal self. "Sallie, always good to see you. How's the tax business?"

Sallie, a slim brunette whose hair was just beginning to gray, laughed. "Taxes are booming, as always," she said. "You ought to know, Eric, you pay enough of them."

"It's good to see our vampire citizens getting along with our human citizens," Katherine said heartily, looking around the bar, which was so thinly populated it almost wasn't open. Her blond eyebrows contracted slightly for a moment, but that was the only sign Ms. Boudreaux gave that she noticed Eric's business was down.

Pam said, "Your table is ready!" She swept her hand toward two tables that had been put together for the party, and the state BVA agent said, "Excuse me, Eric. I've gotta go pay attention to my company."

After a shower of pleasantries and pleased-to-meet-yous, we were finally by ourselves, if sitting in a booth in the middle of a bar can be counted as being by ourselves. Pam started over, but Eric checked her with a raised finger. He took my hand with one of his and rested his forehead on his other hand.

"Can you tell me what's up with you?" I said bluntly. "This is awful. It's very hard to have faith in us when I don't know what's happening."

"Ocella has had some business to discuss with me," Eric said. "Some unwelcome business. And as you saw, my half brother is ailing."

"Yes, he shared that with me," I said. It was still hard to believe what I'd seen and suffered with the child, through his memory of the deaths of everyone he'd loved. The tsarevitch of Russia, sole survivor of a mass murder, could use some counseling. Maybe he and Dermot could be in the same therapy group. "You don't go through something like that and come out Mr. Mental Health, but I've never experienced anything like that. I know it must have been hell for him, but I've got to say . . ."

"You don't want to go through it, too," Eric said. "You're not alone in that. It's clearest for us: Ocella, me, you. But he can share that with other people, too. It's not as detailed for them, they tell me. No one wants that memory. We all carry plenty of our own bad memories. I'm afraid that he may not be able to survive as a vampire." He paused, turning the bottle of TrueBlood around and around on the table. "Apparently, it's a nightly grind to get Alexei to do the simplest things. And not to do others. You heard his remark about the teenager. I don't want to go into the details. However . . . have you read the papers lately, the Shreveport papers?"

"You mean *Alexei* might be responsible for those two murders?" I could only sit there staring at Eric. "The stab wounds, the throats? But he's so small and young."

"He's insane," Eric said. "Ocella finally told me that Alexei had had episodes like this before — not as severe. It has led him to consider, very reluctantly, giving Alexei the final death."

"You mean putting him to sleep?" I said, not sure I'd heard him right. "Like a dog?"

Eric looked me straight in the eyes. "Ocella loves the boy, but he cannot be allowed to kill people or other vampires when these fits take him. Such incidents will get into the paper. What if he were caught? What if some Russian recognized him as a result of the notoriety? What would that do to our relationship with the Russian vampires? Most important, Ocella cannot keep track of him every moment. Two times, the boy has gotten out on his own. And two deaths resulted. In my area! He'll subvert all we're trying to do here in the United States. Not that my maker cares about my position in this country," Eric added, a little bitterly.

I gave Eric a sort of heavy pat on the cheek. Not a slap. A heavy pat. "Yeah, let's not forget the *two dead men*," I said. "That Alexei murdered, in a painful and horrible way. I mean, I realize that this is all about him and your maker and your personal cred, but let's spare a tip of the hat to those guys he killed."

Eric shrugged. He was worried and he was at his wit's end, and he didn't care at all about the deaths of two humans. He was probably thankful that Alexei had picked victims who wouldn't attract much sympathy and whose deaths were easily explained. Gang members killed one another all the time, after all. I gave up on making my point. At least partly because I'd had a thought — if Alexei was capable of turning against his own kind, maybe we could steer him onto Victor?

I shuddered. I was creeping myself out.

"So your maker brought Alexei to you hoping that you'd have some bright ideas about keeping your half brother alive, teaching him some self-control?"

"Yes. That's one of the reasons he's here."

"Appius Livius having sex with the kid can't be helping Alexei's mental health," I said, since I simply couldn't *not* say it.

"Please understand. In Ocella's time, that was not a consideration," Eric said. "Alexei would be old enough, in those times. And men of a certain station were free to indulge themselves with very little guilt or question. Ocella doesn't think in the modern way about such things. As it happens, Alexei has become so . . . Well, they are not having sex now. Ocella is an honorable man." Eric sounded very intent, very serious, as if he had to persuade me of his maker's integrity. And all this concern was about the man who'd murdered him. But if Eric admired Ocella, respected him, didn't I have to do the same?

And — it popped into my head that Eric wasn't doing anything for his brother that I wouldn't do for mine.

Then I had another unwelcome thought, and my mouth went dry. "If Appius Livius isn't having sex with Alexei, who *is* he having sex with?" I asked in a small voice.

"I know this is your business, since we're married — something I've insisted on and you've belittled," Eric said, and the bitterness was back in his voice. "I can only tell you that I'm not having sex with my maker. But I would if he told me that was what he wanted. I would have no choice."

I tried to think of a way to round this conversation off, escape with some dignity. "Eric, you're busy with your visitors." Busy in a way I'd never imagined. "I'm going to that meeting at Alcide's Monday night. I'll tell you what happens, when and if you call me. There are a couple of things I need to bring you up to speed on, if you ever have a chance to come to my place to talk." Like Dermot appearing on my doorstep. That was a story Eric would be interested to hear, and God knows I wanted to tell him about it. But now was not the right time.

"If they stay until Tuesday, I'm going to see you no matter what they're doing," Eric told me. He sounded a little more like himself. "We'll make love. I feel like buying you a present."

"That sounds like a great night to me," I said, feeling a surge of hope. "I don't need a present, just you. So I'll see you Tuesday, no matter what. That's what you said, right?"

"That's what I said."

"Okay then, until Tuesday."

"I love you," Eric said in a drained voice. "And you are my wife, in the only way that matters to me."

"Love you, too," I said, passing on the last half of his closing statement because I didn't know what it meant. I got up to go, and Pam appeared by my side to walk me to my car. Out of the corner of my eye, I saw Eric get up and walk over to the Boudreaux table to make sure his important visitors were happy.

Pam said, "He'll ruin Eric if he stays."

"How so?"

"The boy will kill again, and we won't be able to cover it up. He can escape if you so much as blink. He has to be watched constantly. Yet Ocella argues with himself about putting the boy down."

"Pam, let Ocella decide," I warned her. I thought since we were by ourselves I could take the huge liberty of calling Eric's maker by his personal name. "I'm serious. Eric'll have to let him kill you if you take Alexei out."

"You care, don't you?" Pam was unexpectedly touched.

"You're my bud," I said. "Of course I care."

"We are friends," Pam said.

"You know it."

"This isn't going to end well," Pam said, as I got in my car.

I couldn't think of a single thing to say. She was right.

I ate a Little Debbie cinnamon roll when I got home, just because I thought I deserved one. I was so worried I couldn't even think of going to bed just yet. Alexei had given me his own personal nightmare. I'd never heard of a vampire (or any other being, human or not) being able to transmit a memory like that. It struck me as peculiarly horrible that it should be Alexei who was so "gifted," when he had such a ghastly memory to share. I went though the royal family's excruciating ordeal again. I could understand why the boy was the way he was. But I could also understand why he might have to be — put to sleep. I pushed up from the table, feeling thoroughly exhausted. I was ready for bed. But my plan got altered when the doorbell rang.

You'd think, living out in the country at the end of a long driveway through the woods, that I would have plenty of warning of guests. But that wasn't always the case, especially with supes. I didn't recognize the woman I saw through the peephole, but I knew she was a vampire. That meant she couldn't come in without being invited, so it was safe to find out why she was there. I opened the door, feeling mostly curious.

"Hi, can I help you?" I asked.

She looked me up and down. "Are you Sookie Stackhouse?"

"I am."

"You e-mailed me."

Alexei had blown out my brain cells. I was slow tonight. "Judith Vardamon?"

"The same."

"So Lorena was your sire? Your maker?"

"She was."

"Please come in," I said, and stepped aside. I might have been making a big mistake, but I'd almost given up hope that Judith would respond to my message. Since she'd come all the way here from Little Rock, I thought I owed her that much trust.

Judith raised her eyebrows and stepped over my threshold. "You must love Bill, or else you're a fool," she said.

"Neither, I hope. You want some True-Blood?"

"Not now, thank you."

"Please, have a seat."

I sat on the edge of the recliner while Judith took the couch. I thought it was incredible that Lorena had "made" both Bill and

Judith. I wanted to ask a lot of questions, but I didn't want to offend or irritate this vampire, who'd already done me a huge favor.

"Do you know Bill?" I said, to kick off the talk we had to have.

"Yes, I know him." She seemed cautious, which was odd when I considered how much stronger she was than I.

"You're the younger sister?" She looked to be about thirty, or at least that had been her death age. She had dark brown hair and blue eyes, and she was short and pleasantly round. She was one of the most nonthreatening vampires I'd ever met, at least superficially. And she looked oddly familiar.

"I beg your pardon?"

"Lorena turned you after she turned Bill? Why'd she pick you?"

"You were Bill's lover for some months, I gather? Reading between the lines of your message?" she asked in turn.

"Yes, I was. I'm with someone else now."

"How is it that he never told you how he came to meet Lorena?"

"I don't know. His choice."

"Very strange." She looked openly distrustful.

"You can think it's strange till the cows come home," I said. "I don't know why Bill didn't tell me, but he didn't. If you want to tell me, fine. Tell me. But that's not really important. The important thing is that Bill's not getting well. He got bitten by a fairy with silver-tipped teeth. If he has your blood, he might get over it."

"Did Bill perhaps hint to you that you should ask me?"

"No, ma'am, he didn't. But I hate to see him hurting."

"Has he mentioned my name?"

"Ah. No. I found out by myself so I could get in touch with you. It seems to me that if you're Lorena's get, too, you must have known he was suffering. I find myself wondering why you haven't shown up before."

"I'll tell you why." Judith's voice was ominous.

Oh, great, another tale of pain and suffering. I knew I wasn't going to like this story.

I was right.

CHAPTER 12

Judith began her story by asking me a question. "Have you ever met Lorena?"

"Yes," I said, and left it at that. Evidently, Judith didn't know exactly how I'd met Lorena, which had been a few seconds before I drove a stake through her heart and ended her long, nasty life.

"Then you know she's ruthless."

I nodded.

"You need to know why I've stayed away from Bill all these years, when I'm very fond of him," Judith said. "Lorena has had a hard life. I wouldn't necessarily believe everything she's told me, but I've heard confirmation of a few parts of it from others." Judith wasn't seeing me anymore; she was looking past me, down the years, I guess.

"How old was she?" I said, just to keep the story rolling.

"By the time Lorena met Bill she had been a vampire for many decades. She had been turned in 1788 by a man named Solomon Brunswick. He met her in a brothel in New Orleans."

"He met her in the obvious way?"

"Not exactly. He was there to take blood from another whore, one who specialized in the odder desires of men. Compared to some of her other customers, a little bite wasn't anything too remarkable."

"Had Solomon been a vampire a long time?" I was curious despite myself. Vampires as living history . . . Well, since they'd come out of the coffin, they'd added a lot to college courses. Bring a vampire to class to tell his or her story, and you got great attendance.

"Solomon had been a vampire for twenty years by then. He became a vampire by accident. He was a sort of tinker. He sold pots and pans, and he mended broken ones. He had other goods that were hard to find in New England then: needles, thread, odds and ends like that. He took his horse and cart from town to town and farm to farm, all by himself. Solomon encountered one of us while he camped in the woods one night. He told me that he survived the first encounter, but the vampire followed him during the night to his next camp and attacked him again. This second attack was a critical one. Solomon was one of the unfortunates who get turned accidentally. Since the vampire who drank from him left him for dead, unaware of the change — or at least, I like to think so — Solomon was untrained and had to learn all by himself."

"Sounds really awful," I said, and I meant that.

She nodded. "It must have been. He worked his way down to New Orleans to avoid people who wondered why he hadn't aged. Where he came upon Lorena. After he'd had his meal, he was leaving out the back when he spotted her in the dark courtyard. She was with a man. The customer tried to leave without paying, and in the blink of an eye Lorena seized him and cut his throat."

That sounded like the Lorena I'd known.

"Solomon was impressed with her savagery and excited by the fresh blood. He grabbed the dying man and drained him, and when he threw the body into the yard of the next house, Lorena was impressed and fascinated. She wanted to be like he was."

"That sounds about right."

Judith smiled faintly. "She was illiterate but tenacious and a tremendous survivor. He was far more intelligent, but he had poor killing skills. By then, he had figured some things out, and so he was able to bring her over. They took blood from each other sometimes, and that gave them the courage to find others like us, to learn what they needed to learn to live well instead of merely surviving. The two of them practiced how to be successful vampires, tested the limits of their new natures, and made an excellent team."

"So Solomon was your grandfather, since he begat Lorena," I said biblically. "What happened after that?"

"Eventually, the bloom went off the rose," Judith said. "Makers and their children stay together longer than a merely sexual couple but not forever. Lorena betrayed Solomon. She was caught with the half-drained body of a dead child, but she was able to play a human woman pretty convincingly. She told the men who grabbed her that Solomon was the one who'd killed the child, that he'd made her carry the body, so the blood was all over her. Solomon barely got out of the town alive — they were in Natchez, Mississippi. He never saw Lorena again. He's never met Bill, either. Lorena found him after the War between the States.

"As Bill later told me, one night Lorena was wandering through this area. It was much harder then to stay concealed, especially in rural areas. There weren't as many people to hunt you down, true, and there was little or no communication. But strangers were conspicuous and with the thinner population, the choices of prey were less. An individual death was noticed more. A body had to be hidden very carefully, or the death meticulously staged. At least there wasn't much organized law enforcement."

I reminded myself not to look disgusted. This knowledge was nothing new. That was how vampires had lived until a few years ago.

"Lorena saw Bill and his family through the windows of their house." Judith looked away. "She fell in love. For several nights, she listened to the family. During the day she would dig a hole in the woods and bury herself. At night, she'd watch.

"Finally, she decided to act. She realized — even Lorena realized — Bill would never forgive her if she killed his children, so she waited until he came out in the middle of the night to find out why the dog wouldn't stop barking. When Bill came out with his rifle, she crept up behind him and took him."

I thought of Lorena, so close to my own family, right through the woods. . . . She could have come to my great-great-grandparents' place just as easily, and my whole family history would have been different.

"She turned him that night, buried him, and helped him resurrect three nights later."

I couldn't imagine how shattered Bill must have been. Everything gone in the blink of an eye: his whole life taken and altered and given back to him in a terrible form.

"I guess she took him away from here," I said.

"Yes, that was essential. She had arranged a death for him. She'd smeared a clearing with his blood and left his gun there and rags from his clothing. He told me it looked as though a panther had gotten him. So they traveled together, and while he was bound to her, he hated her, too. He was miserable with her, but she remained obsessed with him. After thirty years, she tried to make him happier by killing a woman who looked very much like his wife."

"Oh, gosh," I said, trying not to feel sick. "You, huh?" That was why her face had been vaguely familiar. I'd seen Bill's old family pictures.

Judith nodded. "Evidently, Bill saw me entering a neighbor's house, going to a

374

party with my family. He followed me home and watched me, because the resemblance caught his fancy. When Lorena discovered this new interest, she thought Bill would stay with her if she provided him with a companion."

"I'm sorry," I said. "I'm really, really sorry."

Judith shrugged. "It wasn't Bill's fault, but you'll understand why I had to think about it before I came in answer to your message. Solomon is in Europe now, or I would have asked him to come with me. I dread seeing Lorena again, and I was afraid . . . afraid she would be here, afraid you would have asked her to help Bill, too. Or she might have made up this story to bring me here, for all I knew. Is she . . . Is she around?"

"She's dead. Didn't you know?"

Judith's round blue eyes went wide. She couldn't be any more pale, but her eyes closed for a long moment. "I felt a strong wrench around eighteen months ago. . . . That was Lorena's death?"

I nodded.

"That's why she hasn't summoned me. Oh, this is wonderful, wonderful!"

Judith looked like a different woman.

"I guess I'm a little surprised that Bill

didn't get in touch with you to tell you."

"Maybe he thought I would know it. Children and makers are bound. But I wasn't sure. It seemed too good to be true." Judith smiled, and she looked suddenly pretty, even with the fangs. "Where is Bill?"

"He's through the woods." I pointed in the right direction. "In his old home."

"I'll be able to track him once I'm outside," she said happily. "Oh, to be with him without Lorena near!"

Ah. What?

Before, it had been okay for Judith to sit and talk my ear off, but now all of a sudden, she was ready to take off like a scalded cat. I was sitting there with my eyes narrowed, wondering what I'd done.

"I'll heal him, and I'm sure he'll thank you after," she said, and I felt like I'd been dismissed. "Was Bill there when Lorena died?"

"Yeah," I said.

"Did he suffer much punishment for killing her?"

"He didn't kill her," I said. "I did."

She froze, staring at me as if I'd suddenly announced I was King Kong. She said, "I owe you my freedom. Bill must think very highly of you."

"I believe he does," I said. To my embarrassment, she bent to kiss my hand. Her lips were cold.

"Bill and I can be together now," she said. "Finally! I'll see you another night to tell you how grateful I am, but now I have to go to him." And she was out of the house and zipping through the woods to the south before I could say Jack Robinson.

I kind of felt like a very large fist had hit me upside the head.

I would be a total sleaze to feel anything but happy for Bill. Now he could hang around with Judith for centuries, if he wanted to. With the never-aging duplicate of his wife. I made myself smile with gladness.

When looking happy didn't make me happy, I did twenty jumping jacks, then twenty push-ups. *Okay, that's better,* I thought, as I lay on my stomach on the living room floor. Now I was ashamed that my arm muscles were trembling. I remembered the workouts the Lady Falcons softball coach had put us through, and I knew Coach Peterson would kick my butt if she could see me now. On the other hand, I wasn't seventeen anymore.

As I rolled over to lie on my back, I considered that fact soberly. It wasn't the first occasion I'd felt the passage of time, but it was the first occasion that I'd noticed my body had changed into something a little less efficient. I had to contrast that with the lot of the vampires I knew. At least 99 percent of them had become vamps at the peak of their lives. There were a few who had been younger, like Alexei, and a few who had been older, like the Ancient Pythoness, but most of them had ranged in age from sixteen to thirty-five at the time of their first death. They'd never have to apply for Social Security or Medicare. They'd never need to worry about hip replacements or lung cancer or arthritis.

By the time I reached middle age (if I was so lucky, since my life was what you would call "high risk"), I would be slowing down in perceptible ways. After that, the wrinkles would only grow and deepen, my skin would look looser on my bones and sport a spot or two, and my hair would thin out. My chin would sag a little, and my boobs would, too. My joints would ache when I sat too long in one position. I'd have to get reading glasses.

I might develop high blood pressure. I might have a blocked artery. My heart might beat irregularly. When I got the flu, I would be *very* sick. I'd fear Parkinson's, Alzheimer's, a stroke, pneumonia . . . the boogie-bears that hid under the beds of the aging.

What if I told Eric I wanted to be with him forever? Assuming he didn't scream and run as fast as he could in the other direction, assuming he actually changed me, I tried to imagine what being a vampire would be like. I would watch all my friends grow old and die. I would sleep in the hidey-hole in the closet floor myself. If Jason married Michele, she might not like me holding their babies. I would feel the urge to attack people, to bite them; they'd all be walking McBloodburgers to me. I'd think of people as food. I stared up at the ceiling fan and tried to imagine wanting to bite Andy Bellefleur or Holly. Ick.

On the other hand, I'd never be sick again unless someone shot me or bit me with silver, or staked me, or put me out in the sun. I could protect frail humans from danger. I could be with Eric forever . . . except for that bit where vampire couples usually didn't stay together all that long.

Okay, I could still be with Eric for a few years.

How would I make my living? I could only take the later shift at Merlotte's, and that after dark had fallen, if Sam let me keep my job. And Sam, too, would grow old and die.

A new owner might not like having a permanent barmaid who could only work one shift. I could go back to college and take night classes and computer classes until I got some kind of degree. In what?

I'd reached the limit of my imagination. I rolled to my knees and rose from the floor, wondering if I was imagining a slight stiffness in my joints.

Sleep was long in coming that night, despite my very long and very scary day. The silence of the house pressed in around me. Claude came home in the wee hours, whistling.

When I got up the next morning, not bright but way too early, I felt sluggish and dispirited. I found two envelopes shoved under my front door on my way to the porch with my coffee. The first note was from Mr. Cataliades, and it had been hand-delivered by his niece Diantha at three a.m., she'd noted on the envelope. I was sorry to miss a chance to talk to Diantha, though I was grateful she hadn't woken me. I opened that envelope first out of sheer curiosity. "Dear Miss Stackhouse," Mr. Cataliades wrote. "Here is a check for the amount in Claudine Crane's account when she passed away. She wanted you to have it."

Short and to the point, which was more

than most people I'd talked to recently. I flipped the check over and found that it was for a hundred and fifty thousand dollars.

"Oh my God," I said out loud. "Oh my God." I dropped it because my fingers suddenly lost their power, and the check drifted down to the porch. I scrambled to retrieve it and read it again to make sure I hadn't been mistaken.

"Oh," I said. I was sticking with the classics, because saying anything else seemed to be beyond me. I couldn't even imagine what I would do with so much money. That was beyond me, too. I had to give myself a little space until I could think about this unexpected legacy with any rational plan.

I carried the amazing check into the house and put it in a drawer, terrified something would happen to it before I got it to the bank. Only when I was sure it was safe did I even think of opening my other note, which was from Bill.

I carried it back out to the porch chair and took a gulp of my cooling coffee. I tore open the envelope.

"Dearest Sookie — I didn't want to frighten you by knocking on your door at two in the morning, so I'm leaving this for you to read in the daylight. I wondered why you had been in my house last week. I knew you'd come in, and I knew that sooner or later your motive would become apparent. Your generous heart has given me the cure I needed.

"I never thought I would see Judith after the last time we parted. There were reasons I didn't call her over the years. I understand she told you why Lorena picked her to turn vampire. Lorena didn't ask me before she attacked Judith. Please believe this. I would never condemn someone to our life unless she wanted it and told me so."

Okay, Bill was giving me credit for some complicated thinking. I'd never dreamed of suspecting that Bill had asked Lorena to find him a mate resembling his late wife.

"I would never have been brave enough to contact Judith myself for fear she hated me. I am so glad to see her again. And her blood, freely given, has already worked a great healing in me."

All right! That had been the whole point.

"Judith has agreed to stay for a week so we can 'catch up' with each other. Maybe you will join us some evening? Judith was most impressed with your kindness. Love, Bill."

I forced myself to smile down at the folded piece of paper. I'd just write him right back and tell him how pleased I was that he was better and that he'd renewed his old relationship with Judith. Of course, I hadn't been happy when he was dating Selah Pumphrey, a human real estate dealer, because we had only recently broken up, and I knew he didn't really care about her. Now I was determined to be happy for Bill. I was not going to be one of those awful people who gets all bent out of shape when the ex acquires a replacement. That was hypocritical and selfish to the extreme, and I hoped I was a better person than that. At least I was determined to provide a good imitation of such a person.

"Okay," I said to my coffee mug. "That turned out great."

"Would you rather talk to me than to your coffee?" Claude asked.

I'd heard feet on the creaky stairs through the open window, and I'd registered that another brain was up and working, but I hadn't foreseen that he'd join me on the porch.

"You got in late," I said. "You want me to get you a cup of coffee? I made plenty."

"No, thank you. I'll have some pineapple juice in a minute. It's a beautiful day." Claude was shirtless. At least he was wearing drawstring pants with the Dallas Cowboys all over them. Ha! He wished!

"Yeah," I said, with a marked lack of enthusiasm. Claude raised one perfectly shaped black eyebrow.

"Who's down in the dumps?" he asked.

"No, I'm very happy."

"Yes, I can see the joy written all over your face. What's the matter, Cousin?"

"I did get the check from Claudine's estate. God bless her. That was so generous." I looked up at Claude, putting all my sincerity into my face. "Claude, I hope you're not mad at me. That's just . . . so much money. I haven't got a clue what I want to do with it."

Claude shrugged. "That was what Claudine wished. Now, tell me what's wrong."

"Claude, you'll have to excuse me being surprised that you care. I would've said you didn't give a flying eff how I felt. Now you're being all sweet with Hunter, and you're offering to help me clean out the attic."

"Maybe I'm developing a cousinly concern for you." He raised one eyebrow.

"Maybe pigs will fly."

He laughed. "I'm trying to be more human," he confessed. "Since I'll live out my long existence among humans, apparently, I'm trying to be more . . ."

"Likable?" I supplied.

"Ouch," he said, but he wasn't really hurt. Being hurt would presuppose that he cared about my opinion. And that was something you couldn't be taught, right?

"Where's the boyfriend been?" he asked. "I do so love the smell of vampire around the house."

"Last night was the first time I've seen him in a week. And we didn't have any alone time."

"You two have a fight?" Claude settled one hip on the porch railing, and I could tell he was determined to show me he could be interested in someone else's life.

I felt a certain amount of exasperation. "Claude, I'm drinking my very first cup of coffee, I didn't get a lot of sleep, and I've had a bad few days. Could you just scoot away and take a shower or something?"

He sighed as if I'd broken his heart. "All right, I can take a hint," he said.

"That really wasn't so much a hint as an outright statement."

"Oh, I'll go."

But as he straightened up and took a step toward the door, I realized I did have something else to say. "I take that back. There *is* something we have to talk about," I said. "I haven't had a chance to tell you that Dermot was here."

Claude stood up straight, almost as if he were prepared to bolt. "What did he say? What did he want?"

"I'm not sure what he wanted. I think, like you, he wanted to be close to someone else with a bit of fairy blood. And he wanted to tell me that he was under a spell."

Claude paled. "From whose magic? Has Grandfather come back through the gate?"

"No," I said. "But could a fairy have cast a spell on him before the gate closed? And I think you must know there's another full-blooded fairy on this side of the portal, or gate, whatever you call it." As I understood fairy morals, it was not possible to answer me with a direct lie.

"Dermot is crazy," Claude said. "I have no idea what he'll do next. If he approached you directly, he must be under extreme pressure. You know how ambivalent he is about humans."

"You didn't answer my question."

"No," Claude said. "I didn't. And there's a reason for that." He turned his back to me and looked out over the yard. "I like my head on my shoulders."

"So there *is* someone else around, and you know who it is. Or you know more about putting spells on than you're admitting?"

"I'm not going to talk about it." And

Claude went inside. Within minutes, I heard him going out the back of the house, and his car passed by on its way down the drive to Hummingbird Road.

So I had gained a valuable piece of knowledge that was completely useless. I couldn't summon up the fairy, ask the fairy why he or she was still on this side, what his or her intentions were. But if I had to guess, I would have to say I was pretty sure that Claude wouldn't be this frightened of a sweet fairy who wanted to spread goodness and light. And a really nice fairy wouldn't have put some spell on poor Dermot that made him so discombobulated.

I said a prayer or two, hoping that would restore my normal good mood, but it didn't work today. Possibly I wasn't approaching prayer in the right spirit. Communicating with God isn't the same as taking a happy pill — far from it.

I pulled on a dress and sandals and went to Gran's grave. Having a conversation with her usually reminded me of how levelheaded and wise she'd been. Today all I thought about was her wildly out-of-character indiscretion with a half fairy that had resulted in my dad and his sister, Linda. My grandmother had (maybe) had sex with a half fairy because my grandfather couldn't make babies. So she'd gotten to carry and birth her children, two of them, and she'd raised them with love.

And she'd buried both of them.

As I crouched by the headstone looking down at the grass that was getting thicker on her grave, I wondered if I should draw some meaning from that. You could make a case that Gran had done something she shouldn't have . . . to get something she wasn't supposed to get . . . and after she'd gotten it, she'd lost it in the most painful way imaginable. What could be worse than losing a child? Losing two children.

Or you could decide that everything that had happened was completely at random, that Gran had done the best she could at the moment she'd had to make a decision, and that her decision simply hadn't worked out for reasons equally beyond her control. Constant blame, or constant blamelessness.

There had to be better choices.

I did the best possible thing for me to do. I put in some earrings and went to church. Easter was over, but the flowers on the Methodist altar were still beautiful. The windows were open because the temperature was pleasant. A few clouds were gathering in the west, but nothing to worry about for the next few hours. I listened to every word of the sermon and I sang along with the hymns, though I kept that down to a whisper because I have a terrible voice. It was good for me; it reminded me of Gran and my childhood and faith and clean dresses and Sunday lunch, usually a roast surrounded by potatoes and carrots that Gran put it in the oven before we left the house. She would have made a pie or a cake, too.

Church isn't always easy when you can read the minds around you, and I worked very hard on blocking them out and thinking my own thoughts in an attempt to connect to the part of my upbringing, the part of myself, that was good and kind and intent on trying to become better.

When the service was over, I talked to Maxine Fortenberry, who was in seventh heaven over Hoyt and Holly's wedding plans, and I saw Charlsie Tooten toting her grandbaby, and I talked to my insurance agent, Greg Aubert, who had his whole family with him. His daughter turned red when I looked at her, because I knew a few things about her that made her conscience twinge. But I wasn't judging the girl. We all misbehave from time to time. Some of us get caught, and some of us don't.

Sam was in church, too, to my surprise.

I'd never seen him there before. As far as I knew, he'd never been to any church in Bon Temps.

"I'm glad to see you," I said, trying not to sound too startled. "You been going somewhere else, or is this a new venture?"

"I just felt it was time," he said. "For one thing, I like church. For another thing, a bad time is coming for us two-natured folks, and I want to make sure everyone in Bon Temps knows I'm an okay guy."

"They'd have to be fools not to know that already," I said quietly. "Good to see you, Sam." I moved off because a couple of people were waiting to talk to my boss, and I understood that he was trying to anchor his position in the community.

I tried not to worry about Eric or anything else the rest of the day. I'd had a text message inviting me to have lunch with Tara and JB, and I was glad to have their company. Tara had gotten Dr. Dinwiddie to check very carefully, and sure enough, he'd found another heartbeat. She and JB were stunned, in a happy way. Tara had fixed creamed chicken to spoon over biscuits, and she'd made a spinach casserole and a fruit salad. I had a great time at their little house, and JB checked my wrists and said they were almost back to normal. Tara was all excited about the baby shower JB's aunt was planning on giving them in Clarice, and she assured me I'd get an invitation. We picked a date for her shower in Bon Temps, and she promised she'd register online.

By the time I got home, I figured I'd better put a load of wash in, and I washed my bath mat, too, and hung it out on the line to dry. While I was outside, I made sure I had my little plastic squirt gun, full of lemon juice, tucked in my pocket. I didn't want to get caught by surprise again. I just couldn't figure out what I'd done to deserve having an apparently (judging by Claude's reaction) hostile fairy tromping around my property.

My cell phone rang as I trailed gloomily back to the house. "Hey, Sis," Jason said. He was cooking on the grill. I could hear the sizzle. "Michele and me are cooking out. You want to come? I got plenty of steak."

"Thanks, but I ate at JB and Tara's. Give me a rain check on that."

"Sure thing. I got your message. Tomorrow at eight, right?"

"Yeah. Let's ride over to Shreveport together."

"Sure. I'll pick you up at seven at your place."

"See you then."

"Gotta go!"

Jason did not like long phone conversations. He'd broken up with girls who wanted to chat while they shaved their legs and painted their nails.

It was not a great commentary on my life that the prospect of meeting with a bunch of unhappy Weres seemed like a good time — or at least an interesting time.

Kennedy was bartending when I got to work the next day. She told me that Sam had a final, take-the-checkbook appointment with his accountant, who'd gotten an extension since Sam had been so late turning all the paperwork over.

Kennedy looked as pretty as she always did. She refused to wear the shorts most of the rest of us wore in warm weather, instead opting for tailored khakis and a fancy belt with her Merlotte's T-shirt. Kennedy's makeup and hair were pageant quality. I glanced automatically at Danny Prideaux's usual barstool. Empty.

"Where's Danny?" I asked when I went to the bar to get a beer for Catfish Hennessy. He was Jason's boss, and I half expected to see Jason come in to join him, but Hoyt and a couple of the other roadwork guys sat at Catfish's table.

"He had to work at his other job today," Kennedy said, trying to sound offhand. "I appreciate Sam making sure I've got protection while I'm working, Sookie, but I really don't think there's going to be any trouble."

The bar door slammed. "I'm here to protest!" yelled a woman who looked like anyone's grandmother. She had a sign, and she hoisted it up. NO COHABITATION WITH ANIMALS, it read, and you could see that she'd written "cohabitation" while she looked at a dictionary; each letter was written with such care.

"Call the police first," I told Kennedy. "And then Sam. Tell him to get back here no matter *what* he's talking about." Kennedy nodded and turned to the wall phone.

Our protester was wearing a blue and white blouse and red pants she'd probably gotten at Bealls or Stage. She had short permed hair dyed a reasonable brown and wore wire-rimmed glasses and a modest wedding ring on her arthritic fingers. Despite this completely average exterior, I could feel her thoughts burning with the fire of a zealot.

"Ma'am, you need to take yourself outside. This building is privately owned," I said, having no idea if this was a good line to take or not. We'd never had anyone protesting before.

"But it's a public business. Anyone can come inside," she said, as if she were the authority.

Not any more than I was. "No, not if Sam doesn't want them in here, and as his representative, I'm telling you to leave."

"You're not Sam Merlotte, or his wife. You're that girl who dates a vampire," she said venomously.

"I am Sam's right-hand person at this bar," I lied, "and I'm telling you to get out, or I'll put you out."

"You lay one finger on me, and I'll call the law on you," she said, jerking her head.

Rage flared up in me. I really, really don't like threats.

"Kennedy," I said, and in a second she was standing by me. "I'd say between us we're strong enough to pick up this lady and take her out of the bar. What do you say?"

"I'm all for it." Kennedy stared down at the woman as if she were only waiting for the starting gun to go off. "And you're that girl who shot her boyfriend," the woman said, beginning to look properly frightened.

"I am. I was really mad at him, and at the moment I'm pretty pissed off at you," Kennedy said. "You get your butt out of here and take your little sign with you, and you do it right now."

The older woman's courage broke, and she scuttled out, remembering at the last moment to keep her head up and her back straight since she was one of God's soldiers. I got that direct from her head.

Catfish clapped for Kennedy, and a few others joined in, but mostly the bar patrons sat in stunned silence. Then we heard the chanting from the parking lot, and we all surged to the windows.

"Jesus Christ, Shepherd of Judea," I breathed. There were at least thirty protesters in the parking lot. Most of them were middle-aged, but I spotted a few teenagers who should have been in school, and I recognized a couple of guys who I knew to be in their early twenties. I sort of recognized most of the crowd. They attended a "charismatic" church in Clarice, a church that was growing by leaps and bounds (if construction was any indicator). The last time I'd driven by when I was going to have physical therapy with JB, a new activities building had been going up.

I wished they were being active *there,* where they belonged, rather than here. Just as I was about to do something idiotic (like going out in the parking lot), two Bon

Temps police cars pulled up, lights flashing. Kevin and Kenya got out. Kevin was skinny and white, and Kenya was round and black. They were both good police officers, and they loved each other dearly . . . but unofficially.

Kevin approached the chanting group with apparent confidence. I couldn't hear what he said, but they all turned to face him and began talking all at once. He held up his hands to pat the air in a "back off and get quiet" gesture, and Kenya circled around to come up behind the group.

"Maybe we should go out there?" Kennedy said.

Kennedy, I noted, was not in the habit of sitting back and letting things take their course. Nothing wrong with being proactive, but this was not the time to escalate the confrontation in the parking lot, and that was what our presence would do. "No, I think we need to stay right here," I said. "There's no point in throwing fuel on the fire." I looked around. None of the patrons were eating or drinking. They were all looking out the windows. I thought of requesting that they sit down at their tables, but there was no point in asking them to do something they clearly weren't going to do, with so much drama going on outside.

Antoine came out of the kitchen and stood by me. He looked at the scene for a long moment. "I didn't have nothing to do with it," he said.

"I never thought you did," I said, surprised. Antoine relaxed, even inside his head. "This is some crazy church action," I said. "They're picketing Merlotte's because Sam is two-natured. But the woman who came in here, she was pretty aware of me and she knew Kennedy's history, too. I hope this is a one-shot. I'd hate to have to deal with protesters all the time."

"Sam'll go broke if this keeps up," Kennedy said in a low voice. "Maybe I should just quit. It's not going to help Sam that I work here."

"Kennedy, don't set yourself up to be a martyr," I said. "They don't like me, either. Everyone who doesn't think I'm crazy thinks there's something supernatural about me. We'd all have to quit, from Sam on down."

She looked at me sharply to make sure I was sincere. She gave me a quick nod. Then she looked out the window again and said, "Uh-oh." Danny Prideaux had pulled up in his 1991 Chrysler LeBaron, a machine he found only slightly less fascinating than he found Kennedy Keyes.

Danny had parked right at the edge of the crowd, and he hopped out and began to hurry toward the bar. I just knew he was coming to check on Kennedy. Either they'd had a police band radio on at the home builders' supply place or Danny had heard the news from a customer. The jungle drums beat fast and furious in Bon Temps. Danny was wearing a gray tank top and jeans and boots, and his broad olive shoulders were gleaming with sweat.

As he strode toward the door, I said, "I think my mouth is watering." Kennedy put her hand over her mouth to stifle a yip of laughter.

"Yeah, he looks pretty good," she said, trying to sound offhand. We both laughed.

But then disaster struck. One of the protesters, angry at being shooed away from Merlotte's, brought his sign down on the hood of the LeBaron. At the sound Danny turned around. He froze for a second, and then he was heading at top speed toward the sinner who'd marred the paint job on his car.

"Oh, no," Kennedy said and hurtled out of the bar as if she'd been fired from a slingshot. "Danny!" she yelled. "Danny! You stop!"

Danny hesitated, turning his head just a

fraction to see who was calling him. With a leap that would have done a kangaroo proud, Kennedy was beside him and wrapping her arms around him. He made an impatient movement, as if to shake her off, and then it seemed to dawn on him that Kennedy, whom he'd spent hours admiring, was embracing him. He stood stiffly, his arms at his side, apparently afraid to move.

I couldn't tell what Kennedy was saying to him, but Danny looked down at her face, completely focused on her. One of the demonstrators had forgotten herself enough to get an "Awww" expression on her face, but she snapped out of her lapse into humanity and brandished her sign again.

"Animals go! People stay! We want Congress to show the way!" one of the older demonstrators, a man with a lot of white hair, shouted as I opened the door and stepped out.

"Kevin, get them out of here!" I called. Kevin, whose thin, pale face was creased into unhappy lines, was trying to shepherd the little crowd out of the parking lot.

"Mr. Barlowe," Kevin said to the white-haired man, "what you're doing is illegal, and I could put you in jail. I really don't want to have to do that."

"We're willing to be arrested for our beliefs," the man said. "Isn't that so, you-all?"

Some of the church members didn't look entirely certain of that.

"Maybe you are," Kenya said, "but we got Jane Bodehouse in one of the cells now. She's coming off a bender, and she's throwing up about every five minutes. Believe me, people, you do *not* want to be in there with Jane."

The woman who'd originally come into Merlotte's turned a little green.

"This is private property," Kevin said. "You cannot demonstrate here. If you don't clear this parking lot in three minutes, all of you are under arrest."

It was more like five minutes, but the parking lot was clear of demonstrators when Sam joined us in the parking lot to thank Kevin and Kenya. Since I hadn't seen his truck drive up, his appearance was quite a surprise.

"When did you get back?" I asked.

"Less than ten minutes ago," he said. "I knew if I showed myself, they'd just get pumped up again, so I parked on School Street and walked through the back way."

"Smart," I said. The lunch crowd was leaving Merlotte's, and the incident was already on the track to becoming a local legend. Only one or two of the patrons seemed upset; the rest regarded the demonstration as good entertainment. Catfish Hennessy clapped Sam on the shoulder as he went by, and he wasn't the only one who made an extra effort to show support. I wondered how long the tolerant attitude would last. If the picketers kept it up, a lot of people might decide that coming here simply wasn't worth the trouble.

I didn't need to say any of this out loud. It was written on Sam's face. "Hey," I said, slinging an arm around his shoulders. "They'll go away. You know what you should do? You should call the pastor of that church. They're all from Holy Word Tabernacle in Clarice. You should tell him that you want to come talk to the church. Show them you're a person just like everyone else. I bet that would work."

Then I realized how stiff his shoulders were. Sam was rigid with anger. "I should not have to tell anyone anything," he said. "I'm a citizen of this country. My father was in the army. I was in the army. I pay my share of taxes. And I'm *not* a person like everyone else. I'm a shifter. And they need to just put that on their plates and eat it." He whirled to go back into his bar.

I flinched, though I knew his anger wasn't directed at me. As I watched Sam stalk away, I reminded myself that none of this was about me. But I couldn't help but feel I had a stake in the outcome of this new development. Not only did I work at Merlotte's, but the woman who'd come in initially had named me as part of the problem.

Furthermore, I still thought approaching the church in person was a good idea. It was reasonable and civil.

Sam wasn't in a reasonable and civil mood, and I could understand that. I just didn't know where he was going to put his anger.

A newspaper reporter came in an hour later and interviewed all of us about "the incident," as he called it. Errol Clayton was a guy in his forties who wrote about half the stories in the little Bon Temps paper. He didn't own it, but he managed it on a shoestring budget. I had no issue with the paper, but of course lots of folks made fun of it. The *Bon Temps Bugle* was frequently called the *Bon Temps Bungle.*

While Errol was waiting for Sam to finish a phone call, I said, "You want a drink, Mr. Clayton?"

"I'd sure appreciate some iced tea,

Sookie," he said. "How's that brother of yours?"

"He's doing well."

"Getting over the death of his wife?"

"I think he's come to terms with it," I said, which covered all sorts of ground. "That was a terrible thing."

"Yes, very bad. And it was right here in this parking lot," Errol Clayton said, as if I might have forgotten. "And right here, in this parking lot, was where the body of Lafayette Reynold was found."

"That's true, too. But of course, none of that was Sam's fault, or had anything to do with him."

"Never arrested anyone for Crystal's death that I recall."

I reared back to give Errol Clayton a hard stare. "Mr. Clayton, if you've come here to make trouble, you can just leave now. We need things to be better, not worse. Sam is a good man. He goes to the Rotary, he puts an ad in the high school yearbook, he sponsors a baseball team at the Boys and Girls Club every spring, and he helps with the Fourth of July fireworks. Plus, he's a great boss, a veteran, and a tax-paying citizen."

"Merlotte, you got you a fan club," Errol Clayton said to Sam, who'd come to stand right behind me.

"I've got a friend," Sam said quietly. "I'm lucky enough to have a lot of friends and a good business. I sure would hate to see that ruined." I heard an apology in his voice, and I felt his hand pat my shoulder. Feeling much better, I slipped away to do my job, leaving Sam to talk to the newspaperman.

I didn't get a chance to talk to my boss again before I left to go home. I had to stop at the store because I needed a couple of things — Claude had made inroads into my potato chip stash and my cereal, too — and I wasn't just imagining that the store was full of people who were busy talking about what had happened at lunchtime at Merlotte's. There was silence every time I came around a corner, but of course that didn't make any difference to me. I could tell what people were thinking.

Most of them didn't share the beliefs of the demonstrators. But the mere fact of the incident had set some of the previously indifferent townspeople to thinking about the issue of the two-natured, and about the legislation that proposed to take away some of their rights.

And some of them were all for it.

CHAPTER 13

Jason was on time, and I climbed up into his truck. I'd changed into blue jeans and a pale blue thin T-shirt I'd bought at Old Navy. It said PEACE in golden Gothic letters. I hoped I didn't look like I was hinting. Jason, in an ever-appropriate New Orleans Saints T-shirt, looked ready for anything.

"Hey, Sook!" He was buzzing with happy anticipation. He'd never been to a Were meeting, of course, and he wasn't aware of how dangerous they could be. Or maybe he was, and that was why he was so excited.

"Jason, I got to tell you a few things about Were gatherings," I said.

"Okay," he said, a bit more soberly.

Aware that I sounded more like his know-it-all older sister instead of his younger sister, I gave him a little lecture. I told Jason that the Weres were touchy, proud, and protocol minded; explained how the Weres

405

could abjure a pack member; emphasized the fact that Basim was a newer pack member who'd been trusted with a position of great responsibility. That he'd betrayed that trust would make the pack even touchier, and they might question Alcide's judgment in picking Basim as enforcer. He might even be challenged. The pack judgment on Annabelle was impossible to predict. "Something pretty awful may happen to her," I warned Jason. "We got to suck it up and accept it."

"You're saying they might physically punish a woman because she cheated on the packleader with another pack officer?" Jason said. "Sookie, you're talking to me like I'm not two-natured, too. You think I don't know all that?"

He was right. That was exactly how I'd been treating him.

I took a deep breath. "I apologize, Jason. I still think about you as my human brother. I don't always remember that you're a lot more. In all honesty, I'm scared. I've seen them kill people before, like I've seen your panthers kill and maim people when they thought that was justice. What scares me is not that you do it, which is bad enough, but that I've come to accept it as just . . . the way you do things if you're two-natured. When those demonstrators were at the bar today, I was so mad at them for hating Weres and shifters without really knowing anything about them. But now I'm wondering how they'd feel if they actually knew more about how packs work; how Gran would feel if she knew I was willing to watch a woman, or anyone, be beaten and maybe killed for an infraction of some rules I don't live by."

Jason was silent for what seemed like a long time. "I think the fact that a few days have passed is a good thing. It's given Alcide time to cool off. I hope the other pack members have had time to think, too," he said finally. And I knew that was all we could say about this, and maybe more than I should have said. We fell silent for a short time.

"Can't you listen in to what they're thinking?" Jason asked.

"Full Weres are pretty hard to read. Some are harder than others. Of course, I'll see what I can get. I can block a lot when I make myself, but if I let my guard down . . ." I shrugged. "This is a case where I want to know everything I can as soon as I can."

"Who do you think killed that dude in the grave?"

"I've given it some thought," I said gently. "I see three main possibilities. But the key to me suspecting all three is that he was buried on my land, and I have to assume that wasn't by chance."

Jason nodded.

"Okay, here goes. Maybe Victor, the new vamp leader of Louisiana, killed Basim. Victor wants to knock Eric out of his position, since Eric's a sheriff. That's a pretty important position."

Jason looked at me like I was an idiot. "I may not know all their fancy titles and all their little secret handshakes," he said, "but I know someone in charge when I see him. If you say this Victor outranks Eric and wants him gone, I believe you."

I had to stop underestimating my brother's shrewdness. "Maybe Victor thought that if I got arrested for murder — since someone tipped off the law that there was a body on my land — Eric would go down with me. Maybe Victor thought that would be enough for their mutual boss to take Eric out of his position."

"Wouldn't it have been better to put the body in Eric's house and call the police?"

"That's a good point. But finding a body in Eric's house would mean bad press for all vampires. Another idea I had, maybe the killer was Annabelle, who was screwing both Basim and Alcide. Maybe she got jealous, or maybe Basim said he was going to tell. So she killed him, and since they'd just been on my land, she thought of it as a good place to bury a body."

"That's a long way to drive with a body in the trunk," Jason said. He was clearly going to play devil's advocate.

"Sure, it's easy to punch holes in all my ideas," I said, sounding exactly like his little sister. "Once I go to all the work of coming up with them! But you're right. That'd be a risk I wouldn't want to take," I added, on a more mature level.

"Alcide could've done it," Jason said.

"Yeah. He could've. But you were there. Did it seem to you — remotely — like he knew it was going to be Basim?"

"No," he said. "I thought he got a huge shock. But I wasn't looking at Annabelle."

"I wasn't, either. So I don't know how she reacted."

"So you got any other ideas?"

"Yeah," I said. "And this is my least favorite. You know I told you that Heidi the vampire scented fairies in the woods?"

"I did, too," Jason said.

"Maybe I should get you to check out the woods on a regular basis," I said. "Anyway, Claude said it wasn't him, and Heidi confirmed that. But what if Basim saw Claude meeting with another fairy? In the area around the house, where Claude's scent would be natural?"

"When would this have happened?"

"The night the pack was on the property. Claude hadn't moved in then, but he'd come around to see me."

I could see Jason trying to figure out the sequence. "So Basim warned you about the fairies he tracked, but he didn't tell you he'd seen some? I don't think that holds together, Sook."

"You're right," I admitted. "And we still don't know who the other fairy would be. If there are two, and one of them isn't Claude, and the other one is Dermot . . ."

"That leaves one fairy we don't know about."

"Dermot's seriously messed up, Jason."

Jason said, "I'm worried about *all* of 'em."

"Even Claude?"

"Look, how come he showed up now? When you have other fairies in the woods? And does that sound crazy when you say it out loud, or what?"

I laughed. Just a little. "Yeah, it sounds nuts. And I get your point. I don't entirely trust Claude, even if he is a little bit family. I wish I hadn't said yes to him moving in. On the other hand, I don't believe he means to hurt me or you. And he's not *quite* as much of an asshole as I thought he was."

We tried to put together a few more theories about Basim's death, but we could punch too many holes in all of our theories. It passed the time until we arrived.

The house Alcide had moved into when his dad died was a large two-story brick home on large grounds, enhanced with impressive landscaping. The — estate? manor house? — was in a very nice area of Shreveport, of course. In fact, it wasn't too far from Eric's neighborhood. That gnawed at me, thinking of Eric so close to me but in so much trouble.

The confusion of what I was feeling through our blood bond was making me more jittery with every passing night. There were so many people sharing in that bond now, so much feeling going back and forth. It wore me out emotionally. Alexei was the worst. He was a very dead little boy, that was the only way I could put it: a child locked in a permanent grayness, a child who experienced only occasional flashes of pleasure and color in his new "life." After days of experiencing what amounted to an echo of him living in my head, I'd decided the boy was like a tick sucking on the life of Appius Livius, Eric, and now me. He siphoned off a little every day.

Apparently, Appius Livius was so used to Alexei's draining him that he accepted it as part of his existence. Maybe — possibly — the Roman felt responsible for the trouble Alexei caused, since he'd brought him over. If that was Appius Livius's conviction, I thought he was absolutely correct. I was sure that bringing Alexei to Eric, thinking the presence of another "child" would soothe Alexei's psychosis, was a last-ditch effort to cure the boy. And Eric, my lover, was caught in the middle of all this along with all the problems he was staving off involving Victor.

I felt less and less like a good person every day. As we walked from the driveway to Alcide's front door, I admitted to myself that since my visit to Fangtasia, I found myself wishing that all of them would die — Appius Livius, Alexei, Victor.

I had to shove all that into a mental corner, because I had to be on my game to enter a house full of Weres. Jason put his arm around my shoulders and gave me a half hug. "Sometime you'll have to explain to me how come we're doing this," he said. "Because I think I kind of forgot."

I laughed, which was what he'd wanted. I put up a hand to ring the bell, but the door swung open before my fingertip made contact. Jannalynn was standing there in a sports bra and running shorts. (She always came up with wardrobe choices that startled me.) The running shorts showed concave dips by her hipbones, and I sighed. "Concave" was not a word I'd ever used in relation to my body.

"Getting into the new job?" Jason asked her, stepping forward. Jannalynn had to either back up or block his way, and she chose to back up.

"I was born for this job," the young Were said.

I had to agree. Jannalynn seemed to love doling out violence. At the same time, I wondered what job she could hold in the real world. She'd been bartending at a Were-owned bar in Shreveport when I'd first seen her, and I knew the owner of that bar had died in the struggle between the packs. "Where are you working now, Jannalynn?" I asked, since there shouldn't be any need to keep that secret that I could see.

"I manage the Hair of the Dog. The ownership passed to Alcide, and he felt I could handle the job. I have some help," she said, which was a confession that surprised me.

Ham, his arm around a pretty brunette in

413

a sundress, was waiting across the foyer by the opened doors to the living room. He patted my shoulder and introduced his companion as Patricia Crimmins. I recognized her as one of the women who'd joined the Long Tooth pack in surrender after the Were war, and I tried to focus on her. But my attention kept straying. Patricia laughed and said, "It's quite a place, isn't it?"

I nodded in silent agreement. I'd never been in the house before, and my eyes were drawn to the French doors on the other side of the big room. There were lights out in the large backyard, which not only was enclosed by a fence that had to be seven feet tall, but was also lined outside with those quick-growing cypresses that shoot up like spears. In the middle of the patio was a fountain, which would make getting a drink easy if you'd turned into a wolf. There was a lot of wrought iron furniture set around on the flagstones, too. Wow. I'd known the Herveauxes were well-to-do, but this was impressive.

The living room itself was very "men's club," all glossy dark leather and paneling, and the fireplace was as big as fireplaces got in this day and age. There were animal heads mounted on the walls, which I thought was kind of amusing. Everyone seemed to have a drink in hand, and I located the bar at the center of the thickest cluster of Weres. I didn't spot Alcide, who because of his height and his presence was usually a standout in any crowd.

I spotted Annabelle. She was in the center of the room on her knees, though she was not constrained in any way. There was an empty space all around her.

"Don't approach," Ham said quietly as I took a step forward. I stopped in my tracks.

"You can talk to her later, probably," Patricia whispered. It was the "probably" that bothered me. But this was pack business, and I was on pack land.

"I'm getting me a beer," Jason said after he'd had a good look at Annabelle's situation. "What do you want, Sook?"

"You need to go upstairs," Jannalynn said very quietly. "Don't drink anything else. Alcide's got a drink for you." She jerked her head toward the stairs to my left. I puckered my brows together, and Jason looked as though he were going to protest, but she jerked her head again.

I found Alcide in a study at the head of the stairs. He was looking out the window. There was a glass of cloudy yellow liquid sitting on the desk blotter.

"What?" I said. I was getting an even

worse feeling about this evening than I'd already had.

He turned to face me. His black hair was still in a tumble, and he could have used a shave, but grooming had nothing to do with the charisma that surrounded him like a cocoon. I didn't know if the role had enhanced the man, or if the man had grown into the role, but Alcide had come far from the charming, friendly guy I'd met two winters ago.

"We don't have a shaman anymore," he said with no preamble. "We haven't had one for four years. It's hard to find a Were who's willing to take the position, and you have to have the talent for it to even consider it anyway."

"Okay," I said, waiting to see where he was going.

"You're the closest we've got."

If there'd been drums in the background, they would've started an ominous roll. "I'm not a shaman," I said. "In fact, I don't know what a shaman is. And you don't have me."

"That's a term we use for a medicine man or woman," Alcide said. "One with a gift for interpreting and applying magic. It sounded better to us than 'witch.' And this way, we know who we're talking about. If we had a pack shaman, that shaman would drink the stuff in this glass and be able to help us determine the truth of what happened to Basim, and the degree of guilt of everyone involved. Then the pack would decide on proportionate justice."

"What is it?" I asked, pointing at the liquid.

"It's what was left over in the last shaman's stash."

"What is it?"

"It's a drug," he said. "But before you walk out, let me tell you that the last shaman took it several times without any lasting ill effect."

"Lasting."

"Well, he had stomach cramps the next day. But he was able to go back to work the day after that."

"Of course, he was a Were, and he'd be able to eat things I can't eat anyway. What does it do to you? Or rather, what would it do to me?"

"It gives you a different perception of reality. That's what the guy told me. And since I clearly wasn't shaman material, that's *all* he told me."

"Why would I take an unknown drug?" I asked, genuinely curious.

"Because otherwise we'll never get to the bottom of this," Alcide said. "Right now, the only guilty person I can see is Anna-belle. She may only be guilty of being unfaithful to me. I hate that, but she doesn't deserve to die for it. But if I can't find out who killed Basim and planted him in your ground, I think the pack will condemn her, since she's the only one who was involved with him. I guess I'd be a good suspect for killing Basim out of jealousy. But I could have done it legally, and I wouldn't have blamed you."

I knew that was true.

"They'll put her to death," he said, harp-ing on the point that would have the most effect on me.

I was almost tough enough to shrug. Al-most.

"Can't I try to do this my way?" I said. "Laying my hands on them?"

"You've told me yourself it's hard to get a clear thought from Weres." Alcide said it almost sadly. "Sookie, I'd hoped we'd be a couple one day. Now that I'm packmaster and you're in love with that cold ass Eric, I guess that'll never happen. I thought we might have a chance because you couldn't read my thoughts that clearly. Since I know that, I don't think I can rely on you laying on your hands and getting an accurate read-ing."

He was right.

"A year ago," I said, "you wouldn't have asked this of me."

"A year ago," he answered, "you wouldn't have hesitated to drink."

I crossed to the desk and tossed it down.

CHAPTER 14

I went down the stairs on Alcide's arm. I was already feeling a little swimmy in the head, having taken an illegal drug for the first time in my life.

I was an idiot.

However, I was an increasingly warm and comfortable idiot. A delightful side effect of the shaman's drink was that I couldn't feel Eric and Alexei and Appius Livius with nearly as much immediacy, and the relief was incredible.

A less pleasant side effect was that my legs didn't feel quite real underneath me. Maybe that was why Alcide was keeping such a tight grip on my arm. I remembered what he'd said about his former hope that we'd be a couple one day, and I thought it might be nice to kiss him and remind myself what it felt like. Then I realized I'd better channel those warm and fuzzy feelings into finding out the answers to the puzzles facing

Alcide. I directed my feelings, which was an excellent decision. I was so proud of my excellence I could have rolled in it.

The shaman had probably known a few tricks for keeping all this dreaminess focused on the matter at hand. I made a huge effort to sharpen up. In my absence, the group in the living room had swollen in numbers; the whole pack was here. I could feel the totality of it, the completeness.

Eyes turned to look at us as we descended the stairs. Jason looked alarmed, but I gave him a reassuring smile. Something must have been off about it, because his face didn't smooth out.

Alcide's second went to stand by the kneeling Annabelle. Jannalynn threw back her head and gave a series of yips. Now I was standing by my brother, and he was holding on to me. Somehow, Alcide had passed me over to Jason's keeping.

"Geez," Jason muttered. "What's wrong with waving your hand in the air or ringing a triangle?" I could assume yipping was not a summons in the panther pride. That was okay. I smiled at Jason. I felt a lot like Alice in Wonderland after she took a bite of the mushroom.

I was on one side of the empty space around Annabelle, Alcide on the other. He looked around to collect the pack's attention. "We're here tonight with two visitors to decide what to do about Annabelle," he said without a preamble. "We're here to judge whether she had anything to do with the death of Basim, or if that death can be laid at the door of anyone else."

"Why are there visitors?" asked a woman's voice. I tried to find her face, but she was standing so far in the back I couldn't see her. I estimated there were perhaps as many as forty people in the room, ranging in age from sixteen (the change began after puberty) to seventy. Ham and Patricia were to my left, about a quarter of the circle away. Jannalynn had stayed by Annabelle. The few other pack members I knew by name were scattered through the crowd.

"Listen hard," Alcide said, looking directly at me. *Okay, Alcide, message received.* I closed my eyes, and I listened. Well, this was abso-fucking-lutely amazing. I found I knew when his gaze swept the assembled pack members by the ripple of fear that followed. I could *see* the fear. It was dark yellow. "Basim's body was found on Sookie's land," Alcide said. "It was planted there in an attempt to blame her for his death. The police came to search for it right after we removed it."

There was a general surge of surprise . . . from almost everyone.

"You moved the body?" Patricia said. My eyes flew open. Why had Alcide elected to keep that a secret? Because it had been a total shock to Patricia, and to a few others, that Basim's body was *not* still in the clearing. Jason moved up behind me and put his beer down. He knew he needed his hands free. My brother might not be a mental giant, but he had good instincts.

I was amazed at Alcide's cleverness in setting up the scene. I might not get Were thoughts that clearly, but Were emotions . . . That was what he was after. Now that I was concentrating, focusing on the creatures in the room, almost out of my body with the intensity of it, I saw Alcide as a ball of red energy, pulsing and attractive, and all the other Weres were circling around him. I understood for the first time that the packleader was the planet around which all others orbited in the Were universe. The pack members were various shades of red and violet and pink, the colors of their devotion to him. Jannalynn was a blazing streak of intense crimson, her adoration making her almost as bright as Alcide himself. Even Annabelle was a watery cerise, despite her infidelity.

But there were a few spots of green. I held my hand out in front of me as if I were telling the rest of the world to stop while I considered this new interpretation of perception.

"Tonight Sookie is our shaman," Alcide's voice boomed from a distance. I could safely ignore that. I could follow the colors, because they betrayed the person.

Green, look for the green. Though my head remained still and my eyes closed, I turned them somehow to look at the green people. Ham was green. Patricia was green. I looked the other way. There was one more green one, but he fluctuated between pale yellow and faint green. Ha! *Ambivalent,* I told myself wisely. *Not a traitor yet, but doubtful about Alcide's leadership.* The wavering image belonged to a young male, and I dismissed him as insignificant. I looked at Annabelle again. Cerise still, but flickering with amber as her intense fear broke through her loyalty.

I opened my eyes. What was I supposed to say — "They're green, get them!"? I found myself moving, drifting through the pack like a balloon through the trees. Finally, I was right in front of Ham and Patricia. This was where the hands would come in handy. Ha! That was funny! I laughed a little.

"Sookie?" Ham said. Patricia shrank back, letting go of him.

"Don't go anywhere, Patricia," I said, smiling at her. She flinched, ready to run, but a dozen hands grabbed her and held her firmly. I looked up at Ham and put my fingers on his cheeks. If I'd had some finger paint, he'd have looked like a movie Indian on the warpath. "So jealous," I said. "Ham, you told Alcide there were people camping on the stream and that was why the pack needed to run in my woods. You invited those men, didn't you?"

"They — no."

"Oh, I see," I said, touching the tip of his nose. "I see." I could hear his thoughts as clearly as if I were inside his head now. "So they *were* from the government. They were trying to gather information on the Were packs in Louisiana and anything bad the packs might have done. They asked you to bribe an enforcer, a second. To describe all the bad stuff he'd done. So they could push through that bill, the one that'll require you-all to register like aliens. Hamilton Bond — shame on you! You told them to force Basim to tell them stuff, the stuff that had gotten him kicked out of the Houston pack."

"None of this is true, Alcide," Ham said. He was trying to sound all Big Serious Man, but to me he sounded like a squeaky little mouse. "Alcide, I've known you my whole life."

"And you thought that Alcide would make you his second," I said. "Instead, he picked Basim, who already had a track record as an enforcer."

"He got thrown out of Houston," Ham said. "That's how bad he was." The anger broke through, pulsing in gold and black.

"I'd ask him, and I'd know the truth, but I can't now, right? Because you killed him and put him in the cold, cold ground." Actually, it hadn't been all that cold, but I felt I was due a little artistic license. My mind soared and swooped, way above everything. I could see so much! I felt like God. This was fun.

"I didn't kill Basim! Well, maybe I did, but it was because he was screwing our packleader's girlfriend! I couldn't stomach such disloyalty!"

"Beep! Try again!" I fanned my fingers over his cheeks. We needed to know something else, didn't we? Some other question had to be answered.

"He met with a creature in your woods on our moon night," Ham blurted. "He, I don't know what he talked about."

"What kind of creature?"

"I don't know. Some guy. Some . . . I've never seen anything like him. He was really handsome. Like a movie star or something. He had long hair, really pale long hair, and he was there one minute and gone the next. He talked to Basim while Basim was in his wolf form. Basim was by himself. After we ate the deer, I'd fallen asleep on the other side of some laurel bushes. When I woke up, I heard them talking. The other guy was trying to frame you for something because you'd done something to him. I don't know what. Basim was going to kill someone and bury him on your land, and then call the cops. That would take care of you, and then the fair . . ." Ham's voice died away.

"You knew it was a fairy," I said, smiling at Ham. "You knew. So you decided to do the job first."

"It wasn't something Alcide would have wanted Basim to do, right, Alcide?"

Alcide didn't answer, but he was pulsating like a skyrocket on the periphery of my vision.

"And you told Patricia. And she helped," I said, stroking his face. He wanted to make me stop, but he didn't dare.

"Her sister died in the war! She couldn't accept her new pack. I was the only one who was nice to her, she said."

"Aw, you're so generous to be nice to the pretty Were woman," I said mockingly. "Good Ham! Instead of Basim killing someone and burying them, you killed Basim and buried him. Instead of Basim getting a reward from the fairy, you thought you would get a reward from the fairy. Because fairies are rich, right?" I let my nails dig into his cheek. "Basim wanted the money to get out from under the government guys. You wanted the money just because you wanted the money."

"Basim owed a blood debt in Houston," Ham said. "Basim wouldn't have talked to the anti-Were people for any reason. I can't go to my death with that lie on my soul. Basim wanted to pay off the debt he owed for killing a human who was a friend of the pack. It was an accident, while Basim was in wolf form. The human poked him with a hoe, and Basim killed him."

"I knew about that," Alcide said. He hadn't spoken until now. "I told Basim I would loan him the money."

"I guess he wanted to earn it himself," Ham said miserably. (Misery, I learned, was deep purple.) "He thought he'd meet with the fairy again, find out exactly what the fairy wanted him to do, get a body from a mortuary or a drunk's body from some alley, and plant it on Sookie's land. That would fulfill the letter of what the fairy wanted. No harm would have been done. But instead, I decided . . ." He began sobbing, and his color turned all washed-out gray, the color of faded faith.

"Where were you going to meet him?" I asked. "To get your money? Which you had earned, I'm not saying you didn't." I was proud of how fair I was being. Fairness was blue, of course.

"I was going to meet him at the same spot in your woods," he said. "On the south side by the cemetery. Later tonight."

"Very good," I murmured. "Don't you feel better now?"

"Yes," he said, without a trace of irony in his voice. "I do feel better, and I'm ready to accept the judgment of the pack."

"I'm not," Patricia cried. "I escaped death in the pack war by surrendering. Let me surrender again!" She fell to her knees, like Annabelle. "I beg forgiveness. I'm only guilty of loving the wrong man." Like Annabelle. Patricia bowed her head, and her dark braid fell over one shoulder. She put her clasped hands to her face. Pretty as a picture.

"You didn't love me," Ham said, genuinely shocked. "We *screwed.* You were upset with

Alcide because he didn't pick you to bed. I was upset with Alcide because he didn't pick me as his second. That was the sum total of what we had in common!"

"Their colors are certainly getting brighter *now*," I observed. The passion of their mutual accusation was perking up their auras to something combustible. I tried to summarize to myself what I'd learned, but it all came out a jumble. Maybe Jason could help me sort it out later. This shaman stuff was kind of taxing. I felt that soon I would be depleted, as if the end of a race were in sight. "Time to decide," I said, looking at Alcide, whose brilliant red glow was still steady.

"I think Annabelle should be disciplined but not cast out of the pack," Alcide said, and there was a chorus of protest.

"Kill her!" said Jannalynn, her fierce little face determined. She was so ready to do the killing. I wondered if Sam really understood what he'd bitten off in going out with such a ferocious thing. He seemed so far away now.

"This is my reasoning," Alcide said calmly. The room quieted as the pack listened. "According to them," and he pointed at Ham and Patricia, "Annabelle's only guilt is a moral one, in sleeping with two men at the

430

same time while telling one of them she was faithful. We don't know what she told Basim."

Alcide spoke the truth . . . at least, the truth as he saw it. I looked at Annabelle and saw her all: the disciplined woman who was in the Air Force, the practical woman who balanced her pack life with the rest of her life, the woman who lost all her practicality and restraint when it came to sex. Annabelle was a rainbow of colors right now, none of them happy except the vibrating white line of relief that Alcide did not plan to kill her.

"As for Ham and Patricia. Ham is the murderer of a pack member. Instead of an open challenge, he took the path of stealth. That would call for severe punishment, maybe death. We should consider that Basim was a traitor — not only a pack member, but a second, who was willing to deal with someone outside the pack, to plot against the pack interests and against the good name of a friend of the pack," Alcide continued.

"Oh," I murmured to Jason. "That's me."

"And Patricia, who promised to be loyal to this pack, broke her vow," Alcide said. "So she should be cast out forever."

"Packmaster, you're too merciful," Jannalynn said vehemently. "Ham clearly deserves death for his disloyalty. Ham, at least."

There was a long silence, broken by a growing buzz of discussion. I looked around the room, seeing the color of thoughtfulness (brown, of course) turning into all kinds of shades as passions rose. Jason put his arms around me from behind. "You need to back out of this," he whispered, and I could see his words turn pink and curly. He loved me. I put a hand over my mouth so I wouldn't laugh out loud. We stepped backward; one step, two, three, four, five. Then we were standing in the foyer.

"We need to leave," Jason said. "If they're going to kill two good-looking gals like Annabelle and Patricia, I don't want to be around to see it. If we don't see anything, we won't have to testify in court, if it comes to that."

"They won't debate long. I think Annabelle will see tomorrow. Alcide will let Jannalynn persuade him to kill Ham and Patricia," I said. "His colors tell me so."

Jason gaped at me. "I don't know what you took or smoked or inhaled upstairs," he said, "but you need to get out of here now."

"Okay," I said, and suddenly I realized I felt pretty damn bad. I made it outside to Alcide's shrubbery before I threw up. I waited for the second wave to roll over me before I risked getting into Jason's truck.

"What would Gran say about me leaving before I saw the results of what I'd done?" I asked him sadly. "I left after the Were war when Alcide was celebrating his victory. I don't know how you panthers celebrate, but believe me, I didn't want to be around when he fucked one of the Weres. It was bad enough seeing Jannalynn execute the wounded. On the other hand . . ." I lost my train of thought in another wave of sickness, though this one wasn't as violent.

"Gran would say you're not obliged to watch people kill each other, and you didn't cause it, they did," Jason said briskly. I could tell that my brother, though sympathetic, wasn't thrilled about driving me all the way home with my stomach so jittery.

"Listen, can I just drop you by Eric's?" he said. "I know he's gotta have a bathroom or two, and that way my truck can stay clean."

Under any other circumstances I would have refused, since Eric was in such a charged situation. But I felt shaky, and I was still seeing colors. I chewed two antacids from the glove compartment and rinsed my mouth out repeatedly with some Sprite Jason had in the truck. I had to agree that it would be better if I could spend the night in Shreveport.

"I can come back and get you in the morning," Jason offered. "Or maybe his day guy can give you a ride to Bon Temps."

Bobby Burnham would rather transport a flock of turkeys.

While I hesitated, I discovered that now that I wasn't surrounded by Weres, I felt the misery rolling through the blood bond. It was the strongest, most active emotion I'd felt from Eric in days. The misery began to swell as unhappiness and physical pain overwhelmed him.

Jason opened his mouth to ask questions about what I'd taken before the pack meeting. "Get me to Eric's," I said. "Quick, Jason. Something's wrong."

"There, too?" he said plaintively, but we roared out of Alcide's driveway.

I was practically shaking with anxiety when we stopped at the gate so Dan the security guard could give me a look. He hadn't recognized Jason's truck.

"I'm here to see Eric, and this is my brother," I said, trying to act normal.

"Go on through," Dan said, smiling. "It's been a while."

When we pulled into Eric's driveway, I saw that his garage door was open, though the garage light was off. In fact, the house was in total darkness. Maybe everyone was over at Fangtasia. Nope. I knew Eric was there. I simply knew it.

"I don't like this," I said, and sat up a little straighter. I struggled against the effects of the drug. Though I was a little closer to normal since I'd been sick, I still felt as though I were experiencing the world through gauze.

"He don't leave it open?" Jason peered out over his steering wheel.

"No, he *never* leaves it open. And look! The kitchen door is open, too." I got out of the truck, and I heard Jason get out on his side. His truck lights stayed on automatically for a few seconds, so I got to the kitchen door easily enough. I always knocked at Eric's door if he didn't expect me, because I never knew who would be there or what they'd be talking about, but this time I simply pushed the door even wider. I could see a short distance into the kitchen because of the truck lights. The wrongness rolled out in a cloud, that feeling a mixture of the sense I'd been born with and the extra layer of senses the drug had imparted. I was glad Jason was right behind me. I could hear his breathing, way too fast and noisy.

"Eric," I said, very quietly.

No one answered. There was no sound of any kind.

I stepped into the kitchen just as Jason's truck lights went off. There were streetlights out on the street, and they supplied a dim glow. "Eric?" I called. "Where are you?" Tension made my voice crack. Something was awfully wrong.

"In here," he said from farther in the house, and my heart clenched.

"Thank you, God," I said, and my hand went out to the wall switch. I flicked it down, flooding the room with light. I looked around. The kitchen was pristine, as always.

So the awful things hadn't happened here.

I crept from the kitchen into Eric's big living room. I knew immediately that someone had died here. There were bloodstains everywhere. Some of them were still wet. Some of them dripped. I heard Jason's breath catch in his throat.

Eric was sitting on the couch, his head in his hands. There was no one else alive in the room.

Though the smell of blood was almost choking me, I was by him in a second. "Honey?" I said. "Look at me."

When he raised his head, I could see a terrible gash across his forehead. He'd bled copiously from the head wound. There was

436

dried blood all over his face. When he straightened, I could see the blood on his white shirt. The head wound was healing, but the other one . . . "What's under the shirt?" I said.

"My ribs are broken and they've come through," he said. "They'll heal, but it'll take time. You'll have to push them back into place."

"Tell me what's happened," I said, trying very hard to sound calm. Of course, he knew I wasn't.

"Dead guy over here," Jason called. "Human."

"Who is it, Eric?" I eased his bare feet up onto the sofa so he could lie down.

"It's Bobby," he said. "I tried to get him out of here in time, but he was so sure there was something he could do to help me." Eric sounded incredibly tired.

"Who killed him?" I hadn't even scanned for other beings in this house, and I almost gasped at my own carelessness.

"Alexei snapped," Eric said. "Tonight he left his room when Ocella came in here to talk to me. I knew Bobby was still in the house, but I simply didn't think about his being in danger. Felicia was here, too, and Pam."

"Why was Felicia here?" I asked, because

Eric didn't ask his staff to his house, as a rule. Felicia, the Fangtasia bartender, had been lowest on the vampire totem pole.

"She was dating Bobby. He had some papers I needed to sign, and she'd just come over with him."

"So Felicia . . . ?"

"Part of a vampire left over here," Jason called. "Looks like the rest has flaked away."

"She's gone to her final death," Eric told me.

"Oh, I'm so sorry!" I put my arms around him, and after a second, his shoulders relaxed. I had never seen Eric so defeated. Even the awful night we'd been surrounded by the vampires of Las Vegas and forced to surrender to Victor, the night he'd thought we might all die, he'd had that spark of determination and vigor. But at the moment he was literally overwhelmed with depression and anger and helplessness. Thanks to his damn *maker,* whose ego had required he bring back a traumatized boy from the dead.

"Where's Alexei now?" I asked, making my voice as brisk as I could manage. "Where's Appius? Is he still alive?" To hell with the two-name requirement. I thought it would be great if Alexei had been helpful enough to kill the old vampire, save me the trouble.

"I don't know." Eric sounded completely defeated.

"Why not?" I was genuinely shocked. "He's your maker, buddy! You'd know if he died. If I've been feeling you three for a week, I know you've been feeling him even stronger." Judith had said she'd felt a tug the day of Lorena's death, though she hadn't understood what it meant. Eric had been alive for so long, maybe it would actually cause him physical harm if Appius died. In a snap, I completely reversed my thinking. Appius should live until Eric recovered from his wounds. "You need to get out of here and go find him!"

"He asked me not to follow when he went after Alexei. He doesn't want us all to die."

"So you're just going to sit home because he said so? When you don't know where they are or what they're doing, or who they're doing it to?" I didn't know what I wanted Eric to actually do. The drug was still coasting through my system, though it was slightly weaker — I was only seeing colors where they shouldn't be every now and then. But I had very little control over my thoughts and my speech. I was simply trying to get Eric to act like Eric. And I wanted him to stop bleeding. And I wanted Jason to come push Eric's bones back in because I could see them sticking out.

"Ocella asked this of me," Eric said, and he glared at me.

"So, he *asked?* That doesn't sound like a direct order to me. It sounds like a request. Correct me if I'm wrong," I said, as snarkily as I could.

"No," Eric said through clenched teeth. I could feel his anger rising. "It was *not* a direct order."

"Jason!" I yelled. My brother appeared, looking very grim. "Please push Eric's ribs back in," I said, which is another sentence I never thought I'd hear myself saying. Without a word, but with a hard-set mouth, Jason put his hands on each side of the gaping wound. He looked at Eric's nose, and said, "Ready?" Without waiting for an answer, he pushed in.

Eric made an awful noise, but I noticed the bleeding stopped and the healing began. Jason looked down at his reddened hands and went to find a bathroom.

"Well, then?" I said, handing Eric an open bottle of TrueBlood that had been left on the coffee table. He made a face, but gulped it down. "What are you gonna do?"

"Later on we'll have words about this," he said. He gave me a look.

"Fine with me!" I glared right back and

went off on an irrational tangent. "And while you're listing the things you should be doing, where's the cleaning crew?"

"Bobby . . ." he began, and then stopped short.

Bobby would have called the cleaning crew for Eric.

"Okay, how's about I do that part," I said, and wondered where to find a phone book.

"He kept a list of important numbers in the right-hand desk drawer in my office," Eric said, very quietly.

I found the name of the vampire cleaning service based midway between Shreveport and Baton Rouge, Fangster Cleanup. Since it was vampire run, they'd be open. A male answered the phone immediately, and I described the problem. "We'll be there in three hours, if the homeowner can guarantee us a safe sleeping place in case the job runs over," he said.

"No problem." There was no telling where the other two resident vampires were or if they'd survive to return before the dawn. If they did, they could all sleep in Eric's big bed or in the other light-tight bedroom, if the coffins were required. I thought there were a couple of the fiberglass pods stashed in the laundry room, too.

Now the carpets and the furniture would

be cleaned. We just had to make sure no one else died tonight. After I hung up I felt super efficient but strangely empty, which I attributed to having lost everything that had been in my stomach. Since I was so light, I floated when I walked. Okay, maybe I still had more drug in me than I'd thought.

Then it suddenly hit me — Eric had said that Pam was in the house, too. Where was she? "Jason," I yelled, "please, please — find Pam."

I returned to the foul-smelling living room, marched over to the windows, and opened them. I swung around to face my boyfriend, who before this night had been many things: Arrogant, quick thinking, strong willed, secretive, and tricky were only the short list. But he'd never been indecisive, and he'd never been hopeless.

"What's the plan?" I asked him.

He was looking a little better now that Jason had done his thing. I couldn't see any bones anymore. "There isn't one," Eric said, but at least he looked guilty about it.

"What's the *plan?*" I asked again.

"I told you. I haven't made a plan. I don't know what to do. Ocella may be dead by now, if Alexei was clever enough to waylay him." Eric's bloody tears ran down his cheeks.

"Bzzzzzt!" I made the noise of a buzzer going off. "You'd know if Appius Livius was dead. He's your maker. *What's the plan?*"

Eric shot to his feet, with only a slight wince. Good. I'd goaded him upright. "I haven't got one!" he roared. "No matter what I do, someone will die!"

"With *no* plan, someone's going to die. And you know it. Someone's probably dying right this second! Alexei is crazy! Let's *have a plan.*" I threw my hands up in the air.

"Why do you smell strange?" He'd finally taken in the PEACE T-shirt. "You smell of Were and of drugs. And you've been sick."

"I've already been through hell tonight," I said, maybe overstating a little bit. "And now I get to go through it twice, because *someone's* got to get your Viking butt on the road."

"What am I supposed to do?" he said, in a strangely reasonable voice.

"So you're okay with Alexei killing Appius? I mean, I sure am, but I would've thought you would've objected. Guess I was wrong."

Jason staggered in. "I found Pam," he said. He sat down very suddenly on an armchair. "She needed blood."

"But she's moving?"

"Only barely. She's cut, her ribs are kicked in, and her left arm and her right leg are broken."

"Oh God," I said, and dashed back to find her. I definitely hadn't been thinking straight because of the drugs, or she would've been my first priority once I found Eric alive. She'd begun crawling to the living room from the bathroom, where Alexei had evidently trapped her. The knife slashes were the most obvious injury, but Jason had been right about the broken bones. And this was after she'd had Jason's blood.

"Don't say anything," she grunted. "He caught me unawares. I am . . . so . . . stupid. How is Eric?"

"He's going to be okay. Can I help you up?"

"No," she said bitterly. "I prefer to drag myself along the hardwood floor."

"Bitch," I said, squatting to help her up. It was hard work, but since Jason had donated so much blood to Pam, I hated to ask him for help. We staggered into the living room.

"Who would have thought Alexei could do so much damage? He's so puny, and you're a great fighter."

"Flattery," she said, her voice ragged, "is not effective at this point. It was my fault. The little shit was following Bobby around, and I saw he'd gotten a knife from the kitchen. I tried to corner him while Bobby got out of the house. To give Ocella a chance to cool the boy down. But he went for me. He's fast as a snake."

I was beginning to doubt I could get Pam to the couch.

Eric rose unsteadily and put his arm around her. Between us, we maneuvered her over to the couch he'd vacated.

"Do you need my blood?" he asked her. "I thank you for doing your best to stop him."

"He's my kin, too," Pam said, settling back on a pillow with relief. "Through you, I'm related to that little murderer." Eric made a gesture with his wrist. "No, you need all your blood if you're going after him. I'm healing."

"Since you got a few pints of mine," Jason said weakly, with a ghost of his usual swagger.

"It was good. Thank you, panther," she said, and I thought my brother smirked a little; but just then, his cell phone rang. I knew the ring tone; it was from a song he loved, Queen's "We Are the Champions." Jason extricated the phone from his pocket and opened it. "Hey," he said, and then he listened.

"You okay?" he asked.

He listened some more.

"Okay. Thanks, honey. You stay inside, lock the doors, and don't answer them until you hear my voice. Wait, wait! Until you hear my cell phone! Okay?"

Jason flipped the phone shut. "That was Michele," he said. "Alexei was just at my house looking for me. She went to the door, but when she saw he was a deader, she didn't ask him in. He told her he wants to warm himself in my life, whatever that means. He'd tracked me there from your house by my smell." Jason looked self-conscious, as if he were afraid he'd forgotten to put on deodorant.

"Did the older one come after him?" I asked. I leaned against a handy wall. I was beginning to feel really ragged.

"Yeah, within a minute."

"What did Michele tell them?"

"She told 'em to go back to your house. She figured if they were vamps, they were some problem of yours." That was Michele, all right.

My cell was out in Jason's truck. I used his to call my house. Claude answered. "What are you doing there?" I said.

"We're closed on Monday," he said.

"Why'd you call if you didn't want me to answer?"

"Claude, there is a very bad vamp headed to the house. And he can come in, he's been there before," I said. "You gotta get out. *Get in your car and get out.*"

Alexei's psychotic break plus Claude's fairy allure to vampires: This was a deadly combination. The night, apparently, was still not over. I wondered if it ever would be. For an awful moment, I looked into an endless nightmare of wandering from crisis to crisis, always one step behind.

"Give me your keys, Jason," I said. "You're in no shape to drive after your blood donation, and Eric's still healing. I don't want to drive his car." My brother fished his keys from his pocket and tossed them to me, and I was grateful for someone who didn't argue.

"I'm coming," Eric said, and pushed to his feet once more. Pam had shut her eyes, but they flew open as she realized we were leaving.

"All right," I said, since I would take any help I could get. Even a weak Eric was stronger than almost anything. I told Jason about the cleanup crew that was coming, and then we were out the door and into the truck with Pam still protesting that if we loaded her in she would heal along the way.

I drove, and I drove fast. There was no point in asking if Eric could fly so he could get there faster, because I knew he couldn't. Eric and I didn't talk along the way. We had either too much to say, or not enough. When we were about four minutes away from the house, Eric doubled over with pain. It wasn't his. I got a backwash of it from him. Something big had happened. We were rocketing down the driveway to my house less than forty-five minutes after we'd left Shreveport, which was pretty damn good.

The security light in my front yard illuminated a strange scene. A pale-haired fairy I'd never seen before was standing back-to-back with Claude. The one I didn't know had a long, thin sword. Claude had two of my longest kitchen knives, one in each hand. Alexei, who appeared to be unarmed, was circling them like a small white killing machine. He was naked and covered in splotches, which were all shades of red. Ocella was lying sprawled on the gravel. His head was covered in dark blood. That seemed to be the theme of the night.

We skidded to a stop and scrambled out of Jason's truck. Alexei smiled, so he knew we were there, but he didn't stop his circling. "You didn't bring Jason," he called. "I wanted to see him."

"He had to give Pam a lot of blood to keep her from dying," I said. "He was too weak."

"He should have let her pass away," Alexei called, and darted under the sword to give the unknown fairy a hard fist to the stomach. Though Alexei had a knife, he seemed to be feeling playful. The fairy swung the sword faster than I could follow with my eyes, and it nicked Alexei, adding another rivulet to the blood already coursing down his chest.

"Can you please stop?" I asked. I staggered, because I seemed to have run out of steam. Eric put his arm around me.

"No," Alexei said in his high boy's voice. "Eric's love for you is pouring through our bond, Sookie, but I can't stop. This is the best I've felt in decades." He did feel wonderful; I could feel that coming through the bond. Though the drugs had temporarily deadened it, now I was feeling nuances, and there was such a contradictory bundle of them that it was like standing in a wind that kept changing directions.

Eric was trying to ease us over to where his maker lay. "Ocella," he said, "do you live?"

Ocella opened one black eye behind a

mask of blood. He said, "For the first time in centuries, I think I wish I didn't."

I think I wish you didn't, too, I thought, and I felt him glance at me.

"She'll kill me with no compunction, that one," the Roman said, almost sounding amused. In the same voice he said, "Alexei has severed my spinal column, and until it heals, I will not be able to move."

"Alexei, please don't kill the fairies," I said. "That's my cousin Claude, and I don't have much family left."

"Who's the other one?" the boy asked, making an incredible leap to pull at Claude's hair and vault the other fairy, whose sword was not quick enough this time.

"I have no idea," I said. I started to add that he was no friend of mine and was probably an enemy, since I figured he was the one who'd been colluding with Basim, but I didn't want to see anyone else die . . . except possibly Appius Livius.

"I am Colman," the fairy bellowed. "I am of the sky fae, and my child is dead because of you, woman!"

Oh.

This was the father of Claudine's baby.

When Eric's arms left me, I had to struggle to stay on my feet. Alexei did one of his darting runs into the circle of blades, punching Colman's leg so hard that the fairy almost went down. I wondered if Colman's leg had broken. But while Alexei was close, Claude managed to stab backward and wound Alexei in the spot right below his shoulder. It would have killed the boy if he'd been human. As it was, Alexei nearly slipped on the gravel but managed to scrabble to his feet and keep on going. Vampire or not, the boy was tiring. I didn't dare look away to see what Eric was doing, where he was.

I had an idea. Under its impetus, I ran into the house, though I couldn't run in a straight line and I had to stop and breathe on my way up the porch steps.

In a drawer in my night table was the silver chain I'd gotten so long ago when the drainers had kidnapped Bill for his blood. I grabbed the chain, staggered back out of the house with it concealed in my hand behind my back, and edged near to the three combatants — but closest of all to the dancing, whirling Alexei. Even in that short time I'd been gone, he seemed to have gotten a little slower — but Colman was down on one knee.

I hated my plan, but this had to stop.

The next time the boy came by I was

ready, with plenty of slack in the chain I was gripping with both hands. I swung my arms up, then down, the slack of the chain landing around Alexei's neck. I crossed my hands and pulled. Then Alexei was on the ground and screaming, and a shaved moment after that, Eric was there with a tree branch he'd broken off. He raised both arms and brought them down. The second after that, Alexei, tsarevitch of Russia, had gone to his final death.

I panted, because I was too exhausted to cry, and I sank to the ground. The two fairies gradually dropped their battle stances. Claude helped Colman stand, and they put their hands on each others' shoulders.

Eric stood between the fairies and me, keeping a watchful eye on them. Colman was my enemy, no doubt about that, and Eric was being cautious. I took advantage of the fact that he wasn't looking at me to pull the stake from Alexei and crawl over to the helpless Appius. He watched me coming with a smile.

"I want to kill you right now," I said, very quietly. "I want you dead so bad."

"Since you've stopped to speak to me, I know you're not going to do it." He said that with the utmost confidence. "You won't keep Eric, either."

I wanted to prove him wrong on both counts. But there'd been so much death and blood already that night. I hesitated. Then I raised the broken bit of branch. For the first time, Appius looked a little worried — or maybe he was simply resigned.

"Don't," Eric said.

I might still have done it if there hadn't been pleading in his voice.

"You know what you could do that would actually be some help, Appius Livius?" I said. There was a shout from Eric. Appius Livius's eyes flickered past me, and I *felt* him tell me to move. I thrust myself off to the side with every ounce of strength left in my body. The sword intended for me went right into Appius Livius, and it was a fairy blade. The Roman went into convulsions instantly, as the area around the wound blackened with shocking rapidity. Colman, who had been looking down at his accidental murder victim with shocked eyes, stiffened, and his shoulders went back. He began to topple, and I saw that there was a dagger between them. Eric shoved the quivering Colman away.

"Ocella!" Eric screamed, terror in his voice. Suddenly, Appius Livius went still.

"Well, all right," I said wearily, and turned my heavy head to see who had thrown the knife. Claude was looking down at the two blades still in his hands as if he expected to see one of them vanish.

Color us puzzled.

Eric seized the wounded Colman and latched on to his neck. Fairies are incredibly attractive to vampires — their blood, that is — and Eric had a great reason to kill this fairy. He wasn't holding back at all, and it was pretty gross. The gulping, the blood running down Colman's neck, his glazed eyes . . . Both of them had glazed eyes, I realized. Eric's were full of bloodlust, and Colman's were becoming full of death. Colman had been too weakened by his many wounds to fight Eric off. Eric was looking rosier by the second.

Claude limped over to sit on the grass beside me. He put my knives carefully on the ground by me, as if I'd been badgering him for their return. "I was trying to persuade him to go home," my cousin said. "I saw him only once or twice. He had an elaborate scheme to put you in a human jail. He planned to kill you until he saw you with the child Hunter in the park. He thought of taking the child, but even in a rage he couldn't do it."

"You moved in to protect me," I said. That was amazing, from someone as selfish as Claude.

"My sister loved you," Claude said. "Colman was fond of Claudine, and very proud she chose him to father her child."

"I guess he was one of Niall's followers." He'd said he was one of the sky fairies.

"Yes, 'Colman' means 'dove.' "

It didn't make any difference now. I was sorry for him. "He had to know nothing I said would have stopped Claudine from doing what she thought was right," I said.

"He knew," Claude admitted. "That was why he couldn't bring himself to kill you, even before he saw the child. That's why he talked to the werewolf, concocted such an indirect scheme." He sighed. "If Colman had really been convinced you caused Claudine's death, nothing would have stopped him."

"I would have stopped him," said a new voice, and Jason stepped out of the woods. No, it was Dermot.

"Okay, *you* threw the knife," I said. "Thanks, Dermot. Are you okay?"

"I hope. . . ." Dermot looked at us pleadingly.

"Colman had a spell on him," Claude observed. "At least, I think so."

"He said you didn't have a lot of magic," I said to Claude. "He told me about the spell, as close as he could say it. I thought it must be the other fairy, Colman, who put it on him. But since Colman is dead, I would have thought that would break the spell."

Claude frowned. "Dermot, so it wasn't Colman who laid the spell?"

Dermot sank to the ground in front of us. "So much longer," he said elliptically. I puzzled over that for a moment.

"He was spelled much longer ago," I said, finally feeling a little throb of excitement. "Are you saying that you were spelled months ago?"

Dermot seized my hand in his left and took Claude's hand in his right.

Claude said, "I think he means that he's been spelled for much longer. For years." Tears rolled down Dermot's cheeks.

"I bet you money that Niall did it," I said. "He probably had it all worked out in his head. Dermot deserved it for, I don't know, having qualms about his fairy legacy or something."

"My grandfather is very loving but not very . . . tolerant," Claude said.

"You know how they undo spells in fairy tales?" I said.

"Yes, I have heard that humans tell fairy tales," Claude said. "So, tell me how they say to break spells."

"In the fairy tales, a kiss does it."

"Easily done," Claude said, and as if we had practiced synchronized kissing, we leaned forward and kissed Dermot.

And it worked. He shuddered all over, then looked at us both, intelligence flooding his eyes. He began to weep in earnest, and after a moment Claude got to his knees and helped Dermot up. "I'll see you in a while," he said. Then he guided Dermot into the house.

Eric and I were alone. Eric had sunk onto his haunches a little distance from the three bodies in my front yard.

"This is positively Shakespearean," I said, looking around at the remains and the blood soaking into the ground. Alexei's corpse was already flaking away, but much more slowly than that of his ancient maker. Now that Alexei had met his final death, the pathetic bones in his grave in Russia would vanish, too. Eric had cast the body of the fairy onto the gravel, where it began to turn to dust, in the way fairies did. It was quite different from vampire disintegration, but just as handy. I realized I wouldn't have three corpses to hide. I was so tired from the sum total of a truly horrific day that I found it the happy moment of the past few hours. Eric looked and smelled like something out of a horror movie. Our eyes met. He looked away first.

"Ocella taught me everything about being a vampire," Eric said very quietly. "He taught me how to feed, how to hide, when it was safe to mingle with humans. He taught me how to make love with men, and later he freed me to make love with women. He protected me and loved me. He caused me pain for decades. He gave me life. My maker is dead." He spoke as if he could scarcely believe it, didn't know how to feel. His eyes lingered on the crumbling mass of flakes that had been Appius Livius Ocella.

"Yes," I said, trying not to sound happy. "He is. And I didn't do it."

"But you would have," Eric said.

"I was thinking about it," I said. There was no point in denying it.

"What were you going to ask him?"

"Before Colman stabbed him?" Though "stabbed" was hardly the right word. "Transfixed" was more accurate. Yes, "transfixed." My brain was moving like a turtle.

"Well," I said. "I was going to tell him I'd be glad to let him live if he'd kill Victor Madden for you."

I'd startled Eric, as much as anyone as wiped out as he was could be startled. "That would have been good," he said slowly.

"That was a good idea, Sookie."

"Yeah, well. Not gonna happen."

"You were right," Eric said, still in that very slow voice. "This is just like the end of one of Shakespeare's plays."

"We're the people left standing. Yay for us."

"I'm free," Eric said. He closed his eyes. Thanks to the last traces of the drug, I could practically watch the fairy blood zinging through his system. I could see his energy level picking up. Everything physically wrong with him had healed, and now with the rush of Colman's blood he was forgetting his grief for his maker and his brother, and feeling only the relief of being free of them. "I feel so good." He actually drew a breath of the night air, still tainted with the odors of blood and death. He seemed to savor the smell. "You are my dearest," he said, his eyes manic blue.

"I'm glad to hear that," I said, utterly unable to smile.

"I have to return to Shreveport to see about Pam, to arrange for the things I must do now that Ocella is dead," Eric said. "But as soon as I can, we'll be together again, and we'll make up for our lost time."

"Sounds good to me," I said. We were alone in our bond once more, though it

459

wasn't as strong as it had been because we hadn't renewed it. But I wasn't about to suggest that to Eric, not tonight. He looked up, inhaled again, and launched himself into the night sky.

When all the bodies had completely disintegrated, I got to my feet and went into the house, the very flesh on my bones feeling as if it could fall off from weariness. I told myself that I should feel a certain measure of triumph. I wasn't dead; my enemies were. But in the void left by the drug, I felt only a certain grim satisfaction. I could hear my great-uncle and my cousin talking in the hall bathroom, and the water running, before I shut my own bathroom door. After I'd showered and was ready for bed, I opened the door to my room to find them waiting for me.

"We want to climb in with you," Dermot said. "We'll all sleep better."

That seemed incredibly weird and creepy to me — or maybe I only thought it should have. I was simply too tired to argue. I climbed in the bed. Claude got in on one side of me, Dermot on the other. Just when I was thinking I would never be able to sleep, that this situation was too odd and too wrong, I felt a kind of blissful relaxation roll through my body, a kind of unfamiliar

460

comfort. I was with family. I was with blood. And I slept.

ABOUT THE AUTHOR

New York Times bestselling author **Charlaine Harris** writes both fantasies and mysteries. She lives in a small town in southern Arkansas with her family.